Grey Stones

GRAVE SECRETS

By

Gideon Jones

Copyright © Gideon Jones 2024
A CIP catalogue record for this title is available from the British Library.
All rights reserved. No part of this book may be reproduced or translated by any form or by any means, electronic or mechanical, including photocopying, recording or by any information storage and retrieval system without written permission from the author.
Book cover designed by Thomas Bannon (@thomasbannondraws)

This is a work of fiction. Names, characters, businesses, organisations, places, events and incidents either are the product of the author's imagination or are used fictitiously. Any resemblance to actual persons, living or dead, events, or locales is entirely coincidental.

For Ian and Alan

Cast thy bread upon the waters:
for thou shalt find it after many days.

Ecclesiastes 11.1

CONTENTS

PROLOGUE 1
CHAPTER 1 *A Foreign Field* 3
CHAPTER 2 *The Image of His Father* 10
CHAPTER 3 *New Friends* 17
CHAPTER 4 *A Vicar Calls* 28
CHAPTER 5 *Margaret* 37
CHAPTER 6 *The Enemy Within* 45
CHAPTER 7 *The Archive* 52
CHAPTER 8 *Running Scared* 62
CHAPTER 9 *Ambush* 66
CHAPTER 10 *Deep Breaths* 72
CHAPTER 11 *Private Rimmer* 85
CHAPTER 12 *Engaging the Enemy* 91
CHAPTER 13 *No Surrender* 98
CHAPTER 14 *Making Plans* 105
CHAPTER 15 *Camera Shy* 110
CHAPTER 16 *Burying the Dead* 121
CHAPTER 17 *Contradictions* 124
CHAPTER 18 *An Inside Job* 132
CHAPTER 19 *A Port in a Storm* 139
CHAPTER 20 *Restoration* 146
CHAPTER 21 *A Letter Home* 154
CHAPTER 22 *Decision Time* 156
CHAPTER 23 *Moving On* 159
CHAPTER 24 *Pressing On* 167
CHAPTER 25 *An Inspector Calls* 180
CHAPTER 26 *Finding Tristan* 185
CHAPTER 27 *An Invitation* 190
CHAPTER 28 *The Eavesdropper* 199
CHAPTER 29 *Trailblazers* 203
CHAPTER 30 *Four Against One* 208
CHAPTER 31 *Visiting Time* 215
CHAPTER 32 *The Room* 227
CHAPTER 33 *Snow Fights* 236

CHAPTER 34 *The Christmas Chase* *244*
CHAPTER 35 *Stage Fright* *252*
CHAPTER 36 *Second Thoughts* *266*
CHAPTER 37 *First Impressions* *270*
CHAPTER 38 *Resurrection* *279*
CHAPTER 39 *Recollections* *288*
CHAPTER 40 *A Logical Deduction* *297*
CHAPTER 41 *Re-wind* *305*
CHAPTER 42 *Grave Mistakes* *309*
CHAPTER 43 *Farewells* *313*
EPILOGUE 316

PROLOGUE

Standing in the bright spring sunshine, the Reverend John Grundy ushered the departed on her way in the time-honoured fashion.

"We now commit her body to the ground; earth to earth, ashes to ashes, dust to dust; in the sure and certain hope of the resurrection to eternal life."

Behind the vicar, a young lady stooped to the ground, picked up a handful of earth and dropped it onto the coffin. Head bowed, she closed her eyes and prayed for a moment before turning to thank the cleric and shake his hand. From a respectful distance, an elderly man and woman looked on. As the pallbearers returned to the church, the couple advanced. Dressed in black, her face hidden behind a veil, the woman reached out and took the young lady's hand, gently pressed it and conveyed her condolences. The collar of his overcoat turned up to his face, the man said nothing. Seconds later, they departed, leaving the young lady alone with her loss.

Resting on their spades, two gravediggers waited patiently. Conscious that she was keeping the men from their work, the young lady cast them a brief smile before turning to read the inscription on the headstone resting by the graveside:

Jane Connolly
26 February 1919 – 18 May 1966
Wife of Tristan
Much Loved Mother of Grace
Rest in Peace Mum

Lifting the fingers of her right hand to her lips, the young lady lowered herself to one knee and transferred a gentle kiss onto the prone headstone. Moments later, her farewell complete, she rose to her feet and left the graveyard.

CHAPTER ONE

A Foreign Field

"Smile for the camera," encouraged the photographer crouching behind the tripod.

Tom Cole did his best to comply, but his heart wasn't in it.

"Hold the smile … nearly there … got you," confirmed the photographer quietly.

The whirring of the camera shutter signalled the end of Tom's ordeal.

"Thank God for that," he said as he strolled across the drawing room towards his parents. "Can I take this off now?"

Having removed the Victoria Cross from the breast of his tunic, Tom weighed it briefly in the palm of his hand.

"If it were me, I'd wear it all the time," said Edward, who, aged sixteen, thought the war a terrific adventure.

"Here then," said Tom, tossing the medal to his brother. "Look after it until I get back."

Edward pouched the catch and smiled.

It was January 1917, and Tom was about to return to his regiment. His ten days' leave at Blackberry Hill, the Cole family home located on the outskirts of Keswick, had flown like hope from catastrophe. A battle-hardened veteran at just twenty-two, the recently promoted captain was impatient to return to the carnage. Far better, he thought, to confront his fate head-on than cower before it. Staring out of the drawing room's large bay window, he lingered to bid farewell to some old friends: the peaks of Skiddaw and Latrigg to the east, Catbells and High Spy to the west and, stretching south below him, its surface gently rippling in the pale winter sunshine, Derwentwater.

Before the war, Tom Cole had harboured two ambitions: to teach history and to play cricket. The call to arms in 1914 changed all that. The enthusiasm of those rushing to enlist was infectious. Encouraged by his father and eager to do his duty, Tom completed his degree at Durham University before accepting a commission with the 5th Battalion, King's Own Border Regiment. In April 1915, Second Lieutenant Cole saw his first action at the Second Battle of Ypres and was forever changed. By the end of the year, now promoted to full lieutenant, Tom's only ambition was to survive.

It was on the 28th of September 1916, during the Battle of Thiepval Ridge, that Tom won his Victoria Cross. On the third day of the battle, Captain Percival, intent on gaining higher ground, led his men across the ridge. Almost immediately, an enemy machine gun opened fire. Within a minute, nearly a third of the advancing line lay dead or wounded. His body pressed into the cratered terrain, Sergeant Holmes grimaced as enemy bullets roiled the earth around him. Raising his head slightly, he saw Captain Percival running across the eighty yards of killing ground in a desperate attempt to silence the gun. From his position further along the line, a terror-stricken Tom Cole observed the heroic charge and awaited the inevitable outcome. When the German gunners found their target, Captain Percival, bullets tearing through his tunic, descended slowly, gracefully almost, to the ground. Distracted by the captain's suicidal advance, the German gun crew belatedly noticed the young officer now bearing down on them from the other side of the line. Deaf to the encouragement that chased him, impervious to the fear that only seconds before had paralysed him, Tom Cole was just thirty yards from his objective when the nozzle of the machine gun jerked in his direction. Throwing himself to the ground, he pulled the pin from a Mills bomb and bowled it overarm towards the gun. The grenade exploded immediately upon reaching its target. Tom never heard it.

Scrambling forward, he delivered a second grenade and again hit the ground. Seconds later, he was inside the trench. Confronted by the only surviving member of the gun crew, Tom did for him with a single shot from his revolver. Oblivious to the commotion of war, Tom calmly travelled the trench, slaughtering those in his way. The sound of shouting, English shouting, suddenly assaulted his senses. The fear came shrieking back. The spell was broken. The company was on the charge.

"I repeat. Will you please accept our surrender?"

The desperate pleading of the German officer, his arms raised aloft, finally registered. Slightly touched by the politeness of the request, Tom hesitated for a couple of seconds before answering.

"Accepted. Order your men to ground their weapons and raise their hands."

The officer barked out the order. Ignoring the risk, Tom mounted the lip of the trench.

"Cease fire!" he bellowed. "Cease fire!"

Tom watched with envy as the German officer led his men into captivity. For them, the carnage was over; they would survive, they had a future. Within an hour, Tom was in the large tent that facilitated the field hospital. Bloodied, bandaged and dying, Captain Percival lay motionless on a wooden cot.

"You took it then," gasped the captain, his ruddy cheeks smeared with mud, "you took the trench."

This was not a question but a statement of fact.

"We couldn't have done it without you, sir," said Tom.

"Heard you took them on single-handed. Was that wise?"

Tom forced a weak smile.

"Can't think who gave me that idea."

His life rapidly evaporating, the captain beckoned Tom closer.

"A favour."

"Anything," whispered Tom.

"Write to my parents ... Make something up about how this mess of a war is worth fighting ... Try to convince them that my going wasn't in vain ... Soften the blow if you can ... I'm afraid this will hit them very hard."

The captain fell silent before rallying to impart one final instruction.

"And Tom ... tell them I was thinking about them at the last. Tell them that. Tell them I love them ... you must tell them that."

"I'm sure they don't need telling," said Tom quietly.

"Promise me you will tell them."

"I promise," whispered Tom.

"Good. I know you are a man of your word."

Seemingly content, Captain Percival's head fell slightly to one side, and he was gone. Tom wished he could muster a tear or at least register some sense of grief, but he could not. Numbness enveloped him like armour. So familiar had he become with death that he no longer railed against its intrusion even if he did fear its approach. He left the tent to the wounded and dying, their groans and screams ushering him on his way. Had the captain's death been in vain? Tom hoped not, but he couldn't be sure. But he was sure of one thing: there was nothing glorious about war.

Once outside, Tom reached into his pocket for his cigarettes and placed one between his lips. He was immediately joined by Sergeant Holmes.

"Allow me, sir," said the sergeant, striking a match and offering the flame to Tom.

Pitching his head towards the sergeant's cupped hands, Tom lit his cigarette, inhaled deeply and watched the wisps of smoke float away on the wind. Holmes extinguished the match before snapping it in half and discarding it.

"Just an old fishing superstition," explained the sergeant in response to the quizzical look on the young officer's face.

Tom's face brightened.

"Didn't know you were a fisherman, Bernard. Ever fished Derwentwater?" he asked expectantly.

"Many times, sir. Derwentwater is a favourite haunt of mine."

"I was brought up on that lake, caught my first fish there ..."

Stopping mid-sentence, Tom took another long pull on his cigarette. Derwentwater was another life away.

"Are you alright, sir?" asked the sergeant.

Tom stared at him for a few seconds.

"I'm fine," he replied.

"The men asked me to thank you, sir. They all know that if it hadn't been for you and the captain, most of us would never have got off that ridge."

Making a conscious effort to pull himself together, Tom dropped his cigarette to the floor and crushed it under his boot.

"Captain Percival was a good man," he said. "We shall all miss him."

For Tom and the men of the reinforced company, there was little relief from the fighting. By mid-November 1916, the battlefields of the Somme had turned into quagmires as the worst winter of the war took hold. The fighting slackened after that. Both physically and mentally, Tom was exhausted. In late December, his promotion to captain having been confirmed, he took the leave he was due. Returning to England, he went to Southampton where, making good on his promise, he called upon Captain Percival's parents and conveyed to them their son's final message. When they offered to put him up for the night, Tom politely refused. Mr and Mrs Percival's grief, though dignified, was overwhelming and he needed to escape: grief was not an emotion he could afford to indulge.

The following day, Tom met his family in London before attending the palace where he was presented with the Victoria Cross by a grateful monarch. It was a subdued Tom who accompanied his parents and Edward back to Keswick. Throughout Christmas, friends and relatives visited Blackberry Hill, intent on pressing the hand of the returning hero who, single-handedly, had captured a German trench. When asked to recount his heroic deed, Tom repeatedly gave all credit to Captain Percival only to be chastised for his modesty. But Tom was not being modest. For reasons he refused to acknowledge or contemplate, he felt a sense of guilt for having survived, a guilt which was only partly assuaged by his belief that it was only a matter of time before he, too, joined the ranks of the 'glorious dead'.

Strangely, the calm of the Borrowdale Valley played on Tom's nerves. Sleep offered no respite sheltering as it did the ghosts of fallen comrades, their decaying and mutilated forms tearing at his being in an attempt to gather him into their ranks. His parents, afraid for him, hid their concerns behind ready smiles and assured him that he would soon be home for good. Brigit Cole was a good actress. How she wanted to wrap her boy in her arms. How she wanted to tell him he did not have to go back. How she wanted to throw away his uniform and shut the door on the world and its troubles. How she wanted to chase away the demons and tell her boy that it had all been a bad dream. But she could not. All she could offer was a brave face. Richard Cole, for his part, suffered with his conscience. He had, after all, been the one who had encouraged Tom to take a commission. How proud he had been of his son's willingness to fight for 'King and Country'. How sure he had been that Tom had done the right thing. How convinced he had been that the might of the British would secure victory within months. How ashamed he now was for having led his son to the altar of war. How he wished he could take his place.

*

Collecting his equipment, the photographer thanked one and all and promised to fulfil his commission within a week.

"And the best of British to you, sir," he said to Tom on his way out. "Give the Bosch hell. We'll all be rooting for you."

"Thank you. Do my best," replied Tom quietly.

By eleven o'clock, the family car was waiting to take Tom to the station.

"Surely you could stay for lunch, Tom?" protested Brigit.

"Sorry, Mother, no time. The army doesn't wait for lunch, I'm afraid."

"Now, Brigit, let the lad get off," said Richard in a game effort to effect an air of normality. "Come on, Tom, I'll get your bag."

"I'll take good care of it, Tom, promise," said Edward, holding up the Victoria Cross.

"Make sure you do," smiled Tom. "Right, time I was off."

Once outside, Tom took his bag from his father and shook his and Edward's hand. Having kissed his mother goodbye, he made his way down the steps to the waiting car where the driver took his bag and placed it in the vehicle. As he was about to get into the car, Tom hesitated. Remembering his conversation with the dying Captain Percival, he turned towards his family.

"You know I love you, don't you? I love you all," he said in a very matter-of-fact way.

Brigit Cole, her bright eyes brimming, moved instinctively towards her son but was restrained by the gentle hand of her husband.

"Of course we do," replied Richard, who, try as he might, could do nothing to repel the tremor invading his voice. "We have always known."

"Good," said Tom, who, without further comment, got into the car and returned to the war.

CHAPTER TWO

The Image of His Father

It was September 1966 and Grey Stones was preparing for the new academic year. From the open window of his first-floor study, Mr G.A. Snyder looked out upon the gravelled drive along which a procession of cars cautiously approached the school. Immediately below him, a throng of pupils, parents, staff and porters manhandled suitcases and trunks through the Victorian entrance hall en route to the dormitories enclosing the quad. Lifting his eyes from the drive, his expressionless stare morphed into a smile as his gaze settled on the Cumbrian countryside. Overlooked by the fells of the Borrowdale Valley, flanked by the Great Wood to the south, Keswick to the north, rolling farmland to the east and the shores of Derwentwater to the west, the school's glorious location offered much to smile about.

Tall with a slight stoop, elongated chin, prominent nose and bald dome, Mr Snyder looked the clichéd epitome of the public school headmaster, especially when wearing his gown. A testament to his vanity, Mr Snyder always wore his gown, even when meeting parents. He liked to impress, and his gown, he thought, made him look very impressive.

From the wall behind his desk, an oil painting of Mr Snyder, resplendent in his gown, dominated the study. Posing in front of the enormous oak doors of the Great Hall, the head exuded authority and poise: a lord on the steps of his manor. Etched into the weathered stone arch above the ancient doors, the motto *Fronti Nulla Fides* hung above Snyder's head like a halo. The joke was not lost on those who knew their Latin: the portrait, commissioned only two years before, captured him with a full head of hair.

Turning from the window, Mr Snyder approached the large gilt-framed mirror above the fireplace on the opposite wall. Still smiling, he admired his reflection, straightened his tie, caressed the ever-shrinking crescent of hair that guarded his dome and readied himself for the charm offensive he was about to unleash upon Mr and Mrs Johnston. As headmaster, it was not his custom to greet new boarders in person unless their parents were particularly wealthy. When informed that the Johnstons were prominent in the oil business, Mr Snyder immediately singled them out for special attention. As he continued to stare into the mirror, he had every confidence that a healthy donation would soon be winging its way into the school's coffers.

At precisely ten o'clock, Miss Cropper, Mr Snyder's secretary, knocked on his door.

"Enter."

There was a distinct lilt in Mr Snyder's voice.

A portly lady in her mid-fifties, Miss Cropper crept into the room.

"Mr and Mrs Johnston and their son, James," she announced, her tone utterly subservient.

"Yes, of course," acknowledged Mr Snyder as he allowed himself one last peek in the mirror. "Show them in."

Miss Cropper held open the door and ushered the Johnstons into the room.

"Mr Johnston, what a pleasure," sang Mr Snyder as he advanced from the fireplace. "Welcome to Grey Stones."

"Hello, pleased to meet you," responded a cautious Mr Johnston as he clasped the head's hand and shook it firmly.

Tall and well-built, Mr Johnston had the look and sound of a self-made man. Momentarily taken aback by Mr Johnston's Liverpool accent, Mr Snyder paused before turning to Mrs Johnston.

"My dear lady, at last, we meet."

Mrs Johnston returned a confident smile before accepting the head's outstretched hand.

"Hello. What a lovely office," she said with an accent which confirmed that she, too, hailed from the banks of the Mersey.

The smile on Mr Snyder's face wavered as he motioned the Johnstons to the three chairs in front of his desk.

"Please, do sit down," he said, the lilt in his voice having disappeared.

A period of silence ensued as Mr Snyder fixed his gaze on James, who, seated between his parents, stared back and smiled. Mr Snyder emitted a quiet cough and took a few seconds to weigh up the new boarder. Fourteen years old, of average height and medium build, with black hair and blue eyes, the boy looked normal enough.

"So, this is James," said Mr Snyder brightly.

"Jimmy, we call him Jimmy," corrected Mrs Johnston.

"Jimmy?" repeated Mr Snyder quizzically.

"Yes, Jimmy," confirmed Mrs Johnston firmly. "He isn't called James, he's called Jimmy."

Silence again intervened as Mr Snyder struggled to accept the vulgar transition that had turned a James into a Jimmy. When he next spoke, it was as if he was talking to himself.

"I don't think we have ever had a *Jimmy* at Grey Stones."

Mrs Johnston changed the conversation.

"That's an impressive portrait," she said, looking at the painting on the wall. "Your father? There's a definite likeness."

Mr Snyder's eyes narrowed.

"My father?" he replied, his bafflement all too apparent.

"Well, he does look like you," said Mrs Johnston, completely unaware of the harm she was inflicting upon the head's ego.

The look of pained disbelief on the head's face encouraged Mr Johnston to interject.

"Now, come on, love, let's not forget the school motto."

"I'm sorry?" replied Mrs Johnston.

"The school motto," repeated Mr Johnston, forcing a smile. "*Fronti Nulla Fides* … 'don't judge a book by its cover' and all that."

"Yes, I know what the school motto is," confirmed Mrs Johnston a touch impatiently.

"Let's move on, shall we?" encouraged Mr Johnston. "I hope you don't mind, but we can't stay long as we have business to attend to."

Although this was true, it was also the case that Mr Johnston, for whom parting with his son was something of a wrench, did not like long goodbyes.

"Business?" queried Mr Snyder, his spirit soaring as he remembered the oil. "Yes, of course, you are in the oil business, I believe."

Mr Snyder's tone again exuded warmth.

"Yes, that's right," smiled Mrs Johnston. "We're expecting a tanker."

"A tanker," repeated Mr Snyder, his mind's eye picturing the heavily-laden ship en route from the Gulf.

"Yes, a tanker," confirmed Mr Johnston, "and we've got to get back to take delivery."

"I understand completely," sympathised Mr Snyder. "The life of an oil tycoon must be a very busy one."

"Well, I wouldn't say *tycoon* exactly," protested Mr Johnston mildly.

Convinced that a sizable donation to the school was in the bag, Mr Snyder beamed.

"And where is she bound?" he asked, embracing the terminology of the seafarer.

"She?" queried Mr Johnston with a glance towards his wife. "She's coming with me."

"No, no, my dear fellow," chuckled Mr Snyder. "I mean the tanker. For which port is it bound?"

"Southport," replied Mrs Johnston. "It's arriving at our petrol station in Southport at about four o'clock, and Frank has to be there to pay the driver."

"Petrol station?" repeated Mr Snyder, the colour flooding from his dome.

"That's right, a petrol station," confirmed Mr Johnston.

"Petrol station as in where motorists buy petrol?" asked Mr Snyder, with a hint of contempt that was not lost on Mrs Johnston.

"And other things," she replied sternly.

Mr Johnston rose to his feet and looked Mr Snyder in the eye.

"We've been in the business ten years now, started from nothing. We have five stations on the go and another in the pipeline. I hope you approve."

Mr Snyder, his eyes once again fixed on Jimmy, had stopped listening. He felt utterly deflated, cheated even. The Johnstons were 'trade'; they ran a petrol station. They didn't own an oil business. They were not wealthy. They wouldn't be pouring huge donations of cash into the school coffers. They were nothing more than gate-crashers, social climbers intent on rising above their station, their petrol station. But Mr Snyder's hands were tied. The first year's fees had been paid in full and the school was contractually bound to accept young Johnston into the fold. When he next addressed Mr and Mrs Johnston, his tone was flat.

"Well, I'm sure I need not keep you from attending to your business interests any longer," he said. "Suffice to say that you leave your son in very capable hands and I am sure he will settle in quickly. Do you have any questions?"

"I don't think so," said Mr Johnston.

"No, we're sure you will take very good care of our boy," said Mrs Johnston, whose eyes visibly softened.

"And what about James, I mean Jimmy?" asked Mr Snyder, who was now going through the motions. "Do you have any questions?"

"Yes," said Jimmy, who then paused for a moment. "What's your detention policy?"

"Jimmy," exclaimed Mrs Johnston as she elbowed her son in the ribs.

"Boys, eh!" chuckled Mr Johnston. "Don't worry about him; he's a good lad, he won't give you any trouble."

"Of that, I have no doubt," replied Mr Snyder dryly.

"You will be alright, won't you, Jimmy?" asked Mrs Johnston, her stare fixed fondly on the boy.

Jimmy smiled at her.

"I'll be fine, Mum."

"Well, if that's it, we'll be off," said Mr Johnston. "Now remember, son, if you need me for anything, anything at all, just give me a ring and I'll be here before you can say 'fill her up'."

Mr Snyder stifled a groan.

"Thanks, Dad," replied Jimmy.

Mr Snyder pressed a button on his desk and spoke into an intercom, his manner now brisk and commanding.

"Miss Cropper, Mr and Mrs Johnston are just leaving. Please show them out and send for a porter."

As the Johnstons made their way out of the room, Jimmy suddenly felt rather alone. When they reached the door, Mrs Johnston turned to face him.

"Come here, you," she ordered softly, her arms outstretched.

Crossing the floor, Jimmy walked into his mum's tight embrace. Unsure of what to say, Mr Johnston placed a gentle hand on his son's head.

"Be good; we're all very proud of you," whispered Mrs Johnston.

And with that, they were gone. As the study door closed, Jimmy turned to face Mr Snyder.

"Sit down, boy," ordered the head. "You are now a pupil of Grey Stones and you will act in the appropriate manner."

"Yes, sir," replied Jimmy, taking his seat.

"For as long as you are at this school, I shall be watching your every step," warned the head. "Do your best to fit in and stay out of trouble."

Before Jimmy could respond, there was a knock on the door and a porter entered the study. Tall, thick-set, aged about forty, Stanley Rimmer took off his black bowler hat and silently awaited his instructions.

"Ah, Rimmer," said Mr Snyder. "Allow me to introduce James Johnston, a new fourth-year boarder. Please escort him to his accommodation. Miss Cropper will tell you where."

"Certainly, sir," replied Rimmer gruffly. "Come with me, please."

Jimmy stood up from his chair and paused for a moment, thinking that he was to be lectured further, but Mr Snyder simply rose to his feet and turned his back on the boy. Realising that release was at hand, Jimmy followed Rimmer out of the study. As the door closed, the head looked up at his portrait, his hands once more caressing his bald dome, his injured pride illuminated by the grimace on his face.

"My father?" he muttered.

Mr Snyder pulled his gown around his shoulders, straightened his tie and returned to the window. His day could only get better.

CHAPTER THREE

New Friends

Having collected his suitcase from the main entrance, Jimmy followed Rimmer to the room that was to be his home for the academic year. Upon reaching their destination, Rimmer spoke for the first time since leaving Mr Snyder's office.

"Here we are, sir, this is you."

Jimmy, somewhat bemused at being addressed as 'sir', waited in silence as Rimmer rapped the door three times with his fist. Within seconds, the door was opened by a gangly youth wearing spectacles and sporting a recently inflicted 'short back and sides'. Upon seeing Rimmer, the boy smiled a polite smile that expressed a desire to please.

"Morning, sir," grunted Rimmer.

Jimmy was having trouble taking this 'sir' business in.

"Got a new roommate for you, you're expecting him, I believe," said Rimmer.

"Oh right, yes," replied the boy transferring his smile to Jimmy. "Come in."

Rimmer stepped aside and Jimmy manoeuvred his suitcase across the threshold.

"I'll be off then," said Rimmer.

As soon as Rimmer had gone, the boy closed the door and stared at Jimmy for a few seconds before thrusting out his right hand.

"Anthony Letts-Hyde, welcome to Grey Stones," grinned

Anthony as he enthusiastically shook Jimmy's hand.

Jimmy, who was not at all accustomed to such formal introductions, especially from boys his own age with double-barrelled surnames, responded in kind.

"Jimmy Johnston, pleased to meet you."

"You're from Liverpool, aren't you? I can tell from your accent," said Anthony.

Jimmy, who had no idea where Anthony came from on account that he had no accent at all, managed to retrieve his hand from his roommate's vice-like grip.

"That's right," he replied. "I'm from Aintree."

Situated on the ground floor of the northern dormitory, the room, like most of the student accommodation at Grey Stones, catered for three pupils. To Jimmy's left, wall cupboards overlooked a table and four chairs, beyond which was a bathroom. Directly ahead of him, a large window looked out onto the quad. Through an arch to his right, three beds, separated by single wardrobes and chests of draws, hugged the furthermost wall. Placing his suitcase on the unclaimed bed by the window, Jimmy thought about unpacking.

"Who else bunks here then?" he asked. "I thought there were supposed to be three of us?"

"Mark, Mark Peck," replied Anthony. "You'll like him. He's just nipped to the school shop. He'll be back any minute."

At that very instant, the door opened and a boy, his head bowed, entered the room. Dark-skinned, of average build and height, the boy briefly looked up at Jimmy before turning to close the door. There, he paused for some seconds, raising his hand to his face in an attempt to hide his closing right eye and bloodied nose. Taking a deep breath, he raised his head, attempted a smile and turned to welcome his new roommate.

"Hi, I'm Mark ... Mark Peck."

Jimmy, distracted by the boy's injuries, did not respond.

"Not again ... not already," complained Anthony moving towards his friend.

"Afraid so," replied Mark trying to muster a laugh. "Thought he might have forgotten about me over the summer."

"Not him," declared Anthony angrily. "Not Lunt. First day back and he's up to his old tricks. Sit down, and I'll get something for your face."

As Mark sat at the table, Anthony disappeared into the bathroom to fetch a damp towel.

"This is Jimmy, Jimmy Johnston," shouted Anthony from the bathroom.

"Hi," said Jimmy, who was still taking the situation in.

"Sorry about this, it being your first morning and all," replied Mark.

"Sorry!" exclaimed Anthony returning with the towel. "What have you got to be sorry about? It's that ignorant oversized oaf who should be sorry. Where did it happen this time?"

"Behind the science lab on the way to the shop. He saw me coming, him and his two friends."

"Who? Reilly and Woosey?" asked Anthony knowingly.

"Who else?" winced Mark as he applied the wet towel to his eye. "They said they were extremely pleased to see me, bundled me behind the lab, searched my pockets and took my money, a ten-bob note. Next thing, Lunt started punching me in the face."

"Didn't you hit him back?" asked Jimmy, who, given the silence that followed, was immediately sorry he had asked the question.

"Not my style, I'm afraid."

Mark's tone was almost apologetic.

"You don't take on the likes of Lunt, Reilly and Woosey," explained Anthony in defence of his friend. "They're animals. We're fourth-formers; they're fifth-formers. They're older and bigger than us ... two of them anyway ... they do what they like and nobody seems to care."

"But why you, Mark?" asked Jimmy. "Why do they pick on you?"

Anthony jumped in before his friend could answer.

"Because his parents work abroad."

"Come off it," protested Mark, "you know that's not the real reason."

Anthony hesitated for a moment.

"Not that it would do any good telling parents."

"Why wouldn't it?" asked Jimmy.

"Simple," replied Anthony. "The Snide absolutely adores Lunt because his father donates masses of money to the school."

"The Snide?" queried Jimmy.

"Mr Snyder, the head," explained Mark.

"Oh, him," said Jimmy.

"So, if you do tell, nothing happens, and you get called a 'snitch', and when the time is right, Lunt and his friends take their revenge. Take my advice," warned Anthony, "stay out of Lunt's way."

Following lunch, Jimmy's roommates showed him around the school. Although there was every prospect that Mark might run into Lunt again, he would not be put off. Those they met who were curious about how Mark had sustained his injuries were told that he had fallen off his bike. Jimmy toed the party line.

"Anything you want to know about the school's history, just ask," said Anthony as the boys entered the magnificent library in Baird House.

Jimmy said nothing.

"Anything you want to know, anything at all, just ask," repeated Anthony.

"Right, okay," replied Jimmy looking about the library.

"Is there nothing you want to know?" asked Anthony a touch impatiently.

"I don't think so," replied Jimmy politely.

"Humour him," advised Mark, "and ask him something before he starts quoting Compton Hobbs."

Anthony's face visibly brightened at the mention of the name.

"Compton who?" asked Jimmy.

"Compton Hobbs. He wrote a book called *Mysteries of the Borrowdale Valley*," beamed Anthony. "There's a chapter in it about the lost treasure of Grey Stones."

"Lost treasure?" repeated Jimmy expectantly.

"Here we go," muttered Mark.

Before taking Jimmy into his confidence, Anthony looked around to ensure nobody was within earshot.

"According to Compton Hobbs, the school was built on the site of Derwent Abbey, a Cistercian monastery founded in the twelfth century. In 1537, during the Reformation, Henry VIII looted the abbey and burned most of it to the ground."

"Really?" said Jimmy diplomatically.

"Oh yes, that's a matter of record," confirmed Anthony with authority. "But Compton Hobbs reckons that the monks saved most of the abbey's treasure by smuggling it out through secret passages. When Henry's men found that virtually everything of value had disappeared, they tortured the monks for days on end."

"Then what happened?" asked Jimmy, his interest momentarily stirred.

"The monks refused to talk and were put to the sword," replied an animated Anthony. "It's said that their ghosts have roamed the grounds ever since in their blood-stained habits."

"Well, I've never seen them," said Mark stifling a yawn.

Ignoring Mark's apparent lack of interest, Anthony ploughed on.

"By 1539, according to Compton Hobbs, what was left of the abbey and its lands had been sold to Nicholas Farringdon, the fourth Earl of Borrowdale. He built a country mansion from the grey stone that gives the school its name."

"You sound like a tourist guide," complained Mark shaking his head.

"No, no, that's really interesting," assured Jimmy, determined to keep the peace.

"Compton Hobbs says that by the1860s, most of the estate had been sold to pay off gambling debts. What was left was bought by Sir Malcolm Baird, who opened the school in 1870."

"And here we are," said Jimmy, thankful that Anthony's history lesson had ended. "Where to next?"

"Why don't we show Jimmy around Cole House before doing the rest of our unpacking?" suggested Anthony.

"If you like," replied a subdued Mark.

"Cole House it is then," beamed Anthony.

Leaving Baird House by its main entrance, the boys turned right along the gravelled drive and entered Cole House through the large foyer that graced the front of the building. Once inside, Jimmy stopped in front of a statue of a middle-aged man. An inscription cut into the plinth read:

Richard Cole

1862-1942

Filius est pars patris

"Who's he?" asked Jimmy.

"Richard Cole?" replied Mark, intent on stealing Anthony's thunder. "He was the father of Captain Thomas Howard Cole VC, who was killed in the Great War of 1914-18."

"Richard Cole built this place as a memorial to his son," said Anthony, keen to reassert his standing as guide-in-chief. "There's a photograph of the captain inside."

Passing through the foyer into the hall, Jimmy was struck by the cathedral-like hush that enveloped him. Two large chandeliers, identical in every detail, bathed the hall's oak-panelled walls in a warm, golden glow. All around him, hundreds of photographs, chronologically displayed, served to introduce the incumbents of Grey Stones to the pupils and staff who had gone before them. Cricket teams, rugby teams, boxers, athletes and tennis players peered at Jimmy from every angle, their arms folded, their expressions aloof, all competing for the attention that might, if only for a moment, recognise their previous existence. As the pictorial history reached into the first decade of the twentieth century, Jimmy was struck by just how serious the subjects looked.

"Unhappy looking bunch, aren't they?" he commented. "Not a smile among them."

"Maybe they knew what was coming," said Anthony.

Shifting his gaze in the direction of Anthony's outstretched arm, Jimmy saw two large mahogany boards looking down at him from the far end of the hall. Like a team sheet posted before a cricket match, the names engraved upon the wooden tablets confirmed the identity of those selected to play and die for their country in two world wars.

"There must be seventy or eighty who died in the First World War alone," said Jimmy quietly.

By the 1920s, the former pupils of Grey Stones were staring confidently into the camera. By the 1930s, the black-and-white images exuded nonchalance, but by 1940 the younger masters had again taken their leave. By the 1950s, those captured on camera retaliated with smiles which, by the 1960s, were preserved in glorious colour. By then, everybody was smiling: girls had been allowed across the threshold, their presence liberating the hall from its masculine straightjacket.

Sandwiched between the mahogany tablets at the far end of the hall, a photograph of Captain Thomas Howard Cole, his Victoria Cross pinned to his chest, hung unaccompanied. Below the photograph, a bronze plate bore the following inscription:

Captain T. H. Cole of the King's Own Border Regiment
Born 28th May 1894
Died 21st March 1918
Filius est pars patris

Jimmy's face lit up for a moment.

"Hey, look! Me and the captain have the same birthday!"

"He's related to Robert Cole, you know," said Anthony, ignoring Jimmy's revelation.

"Robert who?" asked Jimmy.

"Robert Cole, our history master," replied Mark. "Captain Cole was his uncle."

"And Captain Edward Cole was his father," said Anthony, pointing to the mahogany board that commemorated the fallen of the Second World War.

"Captain Edward Robert Cole MC, Royal Engineers, died 18th March 1945 aged forty-four," recited Mark. "Two brothers, both killed in different wars."

"What's this?" asked Jimmy peering into the display cabinet beneath the captain's photograph.

Inside the cabinet, several pages of typed correspondence lay next to a creased brown envelope.

"That's a typed copy of the captain's last letter home," explained Anthony. "It's dated 20th March 1918. I suppose the family has the original."

"Can we go now?" asked Mark.

"Yes, come on," said Anthony. "We'd better finish unpacking."

"You two go," said Jimmy. "I'll be along in a minute."

Slightly taken aback by Jimmy's interest in the captain, Mark and Anthony exchanged looks before leaving the hall. Left alone, Jimmy read the letter carefully, fascinated that it had been written in the trenches the day before the captain's death. Before leaving the hall, he paused and looked again at the photograph, aware that he had made some connection with the soldier who had died forty-eight years before.

That evening, sitting around the table in their room, Mark and Anthony warned Jimmy about the teachers he would encounter at Grey Stones, especially those they deemed exceptionally strict, exceptionally weird and exceptionally stupid. That their favourite subject was history was perhaps explained by the fact that it was taught by their favourite teacher, Robert Cole.

"So where do you come from, Anthony?" asked Jimmy as the evening wore on.

"I'm from Oxford," replied Anthony.

"What do your mum and dad do?" Jimmy asked.

"They're dentists," replied Anthony baring his teeth in a wide grin. "Can't you tell?"

"Anthony prides himself on his teeth; they glow in the dark," said Mark.

"Best set of choppers in Grey Stones," bragged Anthony.

"Grey Stones is a long way from Oxford; couldn't you find a school closer to home?" asked Jimmy.

"I wanted to come here," explained Anthony. "My father was raised in Keswick and my grandmother, Granny Hyde, still lives here. We go and see her sometimes, don't we, Mark? You can come with us next time if you like."

"And what about you, Mark?" asked Jimmy moving the conversation on. "Where are you from?"

"Me? I'm from Lancaster," replied Mark.

"And what do your parents do?"

The question drew a subdued response.

"Oh, they work abroad," Mark replied quietly. "My mum and dad are teachers. My dad, well, my dad is also a vicar; he and mum teach in a missionary in Kenya."

"Sounds great," said Jimmy, immediately aware that he had touched a nerve.

"Not that great," muttered Mark. "Haven't seen them for nearly a year."

"I've got lemonade and chocolate in the cupboard," enthused Anthony in a noble attempt to distract his friend. "Who wants some?"

"I'll have some," said Jimmy brightly.

"Not for me, thanks," said Mark. "I'm supposed to be in training."

"Training? Training for what?" asked Jimmy.

"The 'Christmas Chase', that's what," replied Anthony. "The school holds a cross-country run on the last Wednesday before the Christmas break. Never, not in the school's entire history, has the race ever been won by a fourth former. Not until this year, that is."

"What? Do you mean that …?"

Anthony never gave Jimmy a chance to finish his question.

"Mark is the best runner the fourth form has ever produced, and this is going to be his year."

"Take no notice of Anthony; he tends to exaggerate," advised Mark shaking his head.

"Do you think you have a chance?" asked Jimmy.

Mark hesitated before answering.

"If I train hard between now and Christmas, I might have a chance, but only a small one. I'll be up against a strong field."

It was becoming clear to Jimmy that Mark took the race very seriously.

"He's going to walk it, believe me," said Anthony.

Appreciative of Anthony's somewhat obvious attempt to restore his good humour, Mark looked up and smiled.

That night, as he lay in bed, Jimmy contemplated the day's events, confident that he had formed a bond with his roommates. During the early hours of the morning, he was awoken by the sound of gentle sobbing coming from Mark's bed. Aware that any intrusion would only embarrass his new friend, Jimmy turned on his side and waited for the sobbing to subside. Only then did he drift back off to sleep.

CHAPTER FOUR

A Vicar Calls

Peering expectantly from her dining room window, Grace Connolly took a sip of red wine before glancing at her watch: it was just after eight o'clock in the evening. Moving to the dining room table, she gently ran her fingers across the small leather case she had recovered earlier that day when rooting through the attic. The contents of the case, items of family memorabilia, lay strewn across the table. A small photograph album, its black and white exhibits exposed for the first time in years, lay next to a yellowish newspaper cutting from an edition of the *Liverpool Echo* dated 22nd December 1940. A headline, underlined in pencil, declared:

Great Loss of Life as Shelter Takes Direct Hit

Casually turning the pages of the album, the ringing of the front doorbell brought Grace back to the present. The Reverend Grundy had arrived. A small, grey-haired man in his late sixties, he had been appointed vicar of St John's Church in Keswick just three years before.

"Good evening, Grace," beamed the clergyman when she opened the door. "My apologies for being a little late, but I'm afraid this evening's service overran. My sermons must be getting longer."

"Come in, Vicar," responded Grace warmly. "It's good of you to call."

"Well, I was beginning to think we would never meet again," he said as Grace led him into the dining room. "When was it we buried your mother? Last May? I fully intended to visit you shortly after the funeral."

"My fault entirely," confessed Grace. "I'm afraid my spare time has been pretty limited with moving from London and preparing for life at Grey Stones."

"No need to apologise; I understand completely, though I have to say, you hardly look old enough to be standing in front of a class of children."

"I'm twenty-five," laughed Grace. "I was teaching for three years before I left London."

"Twenty-five and a schoolmistress at Grey Stones," marvelled the vicar shaking his head. "Well, it pleases me greatly that you have decided to return home for good, though I wish it hadn't taken the sad death of your mother to persuade you."

"Oh, it wasn't just Mum's passing that made me want to stay," explained Grace. "Coming back to Borrowdale, to Derwent Cottage … I don't know … I suddenly realised just how much I missed the place."

"And what a stroke of luck that was! I mean, walking straight into the job at Grey Stones."

"Luck? Luck didn't come into it," joked Grace. "I spent at least ten minutes of my interview praising the magnificence of the head's portrait."

"Yes, well, I can see how that particular tactic might work," replied the vicar knowingly.

"It's my first day tomorrow; perhaps you should say a prayer for me."

"Consider it done."

"Please, sit down. Can I offer you a glass of wine?"

"Why not," smiled the vicar.

Left alone when Grace went to fetch a glass, the Reverend Grundy sat at the table and turned the pages of the photograph album.

"I hope you don't mind," he said when Grace reappeared.

"Not at all; I found all this stuff in the attic today," she explained.

"Well, it's good to look back now and again and remember our loved ones," said the vicar sagely. "It keeps them alive in our hearts."

Grace smiled and handed the clergyman a glass of wine before sitting beside him at the table.

"The truth is, I've never seen any of this stuff before. Look at this," she said, turning the pages of the album, "a photograph of mum when she was a child. The people with her are probably her sisters and parents."

"Probably?"

"Well, believe it or not, I've never seen photographs of my mother's family before." explained Grace.

"Never?" queried the vicar. "Where was this photograph taken?"

"It must have been taken in Liverpool, probably in the house where she was brought up."

"So how was it that she came to live in Keswick?"

"Now, *there's* a story," sighed Grace running her hand through her brown hair. "The war brought her here. My mother joined the Women's Land Army in the summer of 1939 when she was just twenty. Following her training, she was billeted at a hostel in Keswick. From there, she was sent to work on the local farms in place of the men who had been called up to fight in the war. Not long after arriving here, she met my father, fell in love and married him within months. I suppose that sort of thing was common during the war."

"And your father?" asked the vicar, taking a sip of wine. "What happened to him?"

"Tristan Connolly? Unfortunately, I never knew him. He was a pilot in the RAF. He was shot down in June 1940 over the English Channel. His body was never recovered. My mother never got over his death and found it difficult to talk much about him, even to me. All I know is that he came from Carlisle and married Mum in the spring of 1940. By the time I was born, he was dead. But I never knew until today that he was awarded a medal during the war; it's here in the case."

Delving into the case, Grace retrieved the medal and handed it to her guest.

"*For Valour*," recited the vicar reading the words embossed on the bronze cross.

A short silence followed.

"My dear child, do you know what this is?"

"Other than it is a medal, I'm afraid not. Military history was never my subject."

"But Grace, this is a Victoria Cross, the highest military decoration awarded for bravery in the face of the enemy. You have heard of the Victoria Cross, haven't you?"

"Of course I have," replied Grace, "but until now, I would never have recognised one."

Taking the medal back from Reverend Grundy, Grace caressed it gently in the palm of her hand and wondered how it had been earned.

"Your father must have been a very brave man," observed the vicar. "But tell me, how on earth did your poor mother cope after he died?"

"Truth be told, not very well. She had a very tragic war. You see, after my father died, my mother decided to return to her family in Liverpool to have me."

"So, you were born in Liverpool?"

"No. My mother's family lived quite close to the docks, which were heavily bombed during the Blitz. Mum arrived home in Liverpool only to discover that her family had been killed in an air raid the night before. They had taken shelter under nearby railway arches."

Grace paused momentarily, her blue eyes looking back in time.

"The arches took a direct hit."

The Reverend Grundy looked appalled, but before he could speak, Grace had returned to the present.

"Look, it's reported here," she said, directing him to the newspaper cutting on the table.

"And what of your father's family?" asked the vicar after briefly studying the cutting. "Did they not take your mother in?"

"Unfortunately, my father had no surviving family when he died. He was some years older than my mother. There was just him and Mum, and after that, Mum and me."

"There was nobody?" asked the vicar.

"Well, not according to Mum, though I have to say, she very rarely talked about the past. The shock of losing my father and her family affected her deeply for the rest of her life. I know very little about my father."

"So where did your mother go to have you?" asked the vicar as Grace topped his glass up with wine.

"She returned to Keswick, here to Derwent Cottage, where I was born on Christmas Day 1940. My father had obviously left her well provided for because she never had to work, and shortly after I was born, she hired a housekeeper who was also my nanny for a while, a lady called Doris Crisp. She left when I was eleven."

The Reverend Grundy shook his head sympathetically.

"It could not have been easy for you or your mother."

"We managed," smiled Grace.

"You must have been very close."

"Strangely not," replied Grace. "In fact, there was always something of a barrier between us, a distance if you like. It was not that she didn't love me, I'm sure she did, it was just that she always seemed so preoccupied, like she was caught in the past. As I said, Mum never really got over her loss."

"Can I take it that the album contains a photograph of your father?" asked the vicar expectantly as he thumbed through the pages. "A wedding photograph, perhaps?"

"No, I've checked," said Grace. "According to Mum, the marriage was a very hurried affair, what with the war and everything. My parents were married in a registry office, with very little fuss, when my father returned to Keswick on leave. According to Mum, they were so much in love and in such a rush that the last thing they thought about was taking photographs."

"Surely, you must have a photograph of your father?" remarked the vicar.

"You may find this difficult to believe, but I grew up having no idea what my father looked like."

"My dear, how sad."

"You have to remember that my parents did not know each other for very long: they spent more time apart than they did together. I always assumed that the few photographs that might have been taken had simply been lost. I remember as a schoolgirl writing to the RAF asking if they could provide a photograph of my father, but nobody could help."

"How unfortunate," consoled the vicar.

"No, it's fine," assured Grace rising from the table and making her way to the sideboard behind her.

The Reverend Grundy looked on as Grace opened a drawer and retrieved a small silver case before returning to the table.

"Here you are," she smiled, "a photograph of my father."

"Why, it's beautiful," said the vicar taking the case from Grace. "What is it, a cigarette case?"

"I think so."

"I see it has an inscription. *T.H.C. Fillius est pars patris.*"

"A son is part of the father," translated Grace, eager to show off her Latin.

Reverend Grundy smiled at her.

"The phrase rings a bell," said Grace, "but I can't remember why. Open it."

Acting upon Grace's instruction, the vicar placed the cigarette case on the table and opened it as he would a book.

"There, you see?" smiled Grace.

Pressed into the concave sides of the case, protected by a transparent veneer, were two photographs.

"There they are, my parents," said Grace proudly.

Wearing the uniform of the Woman's Land Army, her hair caught by the wind and her face radiating a joyous smile, Jane Connolly looked up with confidence from the table.

"What a happy face … what a *beautiful* face," observed the vicar.

"She was not much more than a girl when that was taken," said Grace.

"And so, *this* is your father," said the vicar, diverting his gaze slightly.

Like the head on a stamp, the second photograph captured the subject's left profile, creating the impression that his gaze was forever fixed on Jane.

"I think it must have been taken when they were walking the fells," said Grace. "There appears to be a cairn in the background."

"Have you any idea where it was taken?"

"No, but I like to think that he is looking across Derwentwater from the top of Catbells or High Spy, searching out Derwent Cottage to keep an eye on me."

"That's a lovely thought," smiled the vicar, "but wasn't your mother able to tell you where the photograph was taken?"

"No. Like the rest of this stuff, I only discovered the cigarette case after mum died. I found it in the bottom of a drawer in her bedroom."

"But why did she never show it to you?"

"As I say, the tragic events of the war affected Mum for the rest of her life. I don't think she wanted to share my father's memory with me or anybody else. Perhaps it was because she had so little to remember him by that she wanted to keep what she had for herself."

Silence descended as the Reverend Grundy respectfully allowed his hostess a few moments to ponder the past. The doorbell rang.

"I've no idea who that could be," said Grace as she made her way to the front door.

Left alone for a second time, the vicar picked up the silver case and closed it before placing it back on the table.

"Reverend Grundy, may I introduce Robert Cole," smiled Grace upon her return. "Robert teaches history at Grey Stones. He's been showing me the ropes and helping me to settle in."

"Oh, no need for introductions, my dear," said the vicar as he warmly shook Robert by the hand. "Robert and I already know each other. I have been known to visit the school now and again, you know."

"Hello, Vicar, how are you? Just thought I'd pay the school's new girl a quick visit and wish her luck for tomorrow."

"Very noble, I must say. Well, don't mind me. I must be on my way. Mine was only a quick visit to welcome Grace back to the parish. Thank you very much for the wine, my dear, and for telling me about your family."

Amid mutual farewells and good wishes, Grace showed Reverend Grundy to the front door from where she imparted one last wave as he disappeared from view. Returning to the dining room, she found Robert standing over the table, casually inspecting the photograph album.

"Well, I am honoured," said Grace, placing her arms around Robert's neck.

"And so you should be," replied Robert playfully.

"No, I mean it, I'm so glad you came."

Placing his arms around her waist, Robert gently drew her towards him.

"So am I," he said, his eyes locked into hers.

Half an hour later, following some gentle encouragement, Robert Cole drained his second cup of coffee before reluctantly taking his leave. With her heart set on a bath and an early night, Grace approached the dining room table to tidy away her recently discovered memorabilia. Drawn once more to the cutting taken from the *Liverpool Echo*, she sat at the table and read it again. A few seconds later, her mind racing, Grace raised a hand to her open mouth.

CHAPTER FIVE

Margaret

Each school year comprised four forms, each representing one of four school houses: Blencathra, Catbells, Helvellyn and Skiddaw. The pupils of Form 4C, as indicated by the letter 'C', belonged to Catbells House. At nine o'clock on the first day of term, Form 4C met for registration.

Dressed in their smart grey uniforms, the classmates talked quietly among themselves as they awaited the arrival of Mr Cheatham, their new form master and Mr Snyder's deputy. A strict disciplinarian of military bearing and background, The Cheat revelled in his reputation as Mr Snyder's executioner-in-chief. An enthusiastic advocate of corporal punishment, an assortment of rattan canes hung from the walls of his office, a menacing reminder to the pupils who entered of his licence to inflict pain. A devotee of the Machiavellian philosophy that it was better to be feared than loved, he wielded the rod often and with relish. As soon as he entered the room, the class fell silent. Having placed the register on his desk, Mr Cheatham gazed upon his charges, his look of puzzlement quickly turning to one of anger.

"On your feet!" he shouted. "You do not remain seated when I enter the room."

Twenty-five chairs screeched across the floor as the pupils shot to their feet. Mr Cheatham paused for a few moments before barking his next order.

"Now sit down and answer 'present' when your name is called."

At the back of the classroom, where she invariably sat, a stressed

Margaret Arbuckle slipped her hand into her blazer pocket, extracted a large piece of chocolate and furtively placed it into her mouth. Tall for her age and overweight, her cumbersome deportment and shy demeanour exposed her to the cruel wit of those who rejoiced in the attention bought at her expense. A quietly determined girl, Margaret pretended to ignore the hurtful jokes and jibes, knowing that to do otherwise would only encourage repetition. As soon as the chocolate entered her mouth, Margaret realised she was in trouble: her surname being Arbuckle, it was the first on the register.

"Arbuckle," shouted Mr Cheatham, anticipating an instant reply.

Margaret's jaws froze.

"Arbuckle," repeated The Cheat before looking up from the register.

Bowing her head, Margaret raised a hand to her mouth in a desperate attempt to conceal the obvious.

"Arbuckle, I know you are here: I can see you."

With the eyes of the class upon her and her mouth still struggling to process her illegal treat, Margaret failed to respond.

"Are you eating?" asked Mr Cheatham, advancing from his desk. "You *are* eating!"

"Letts-Hyde, sir," shouted Anthony, jumping to his feet and standing to attention.

"What?" snapped the distracted master as he spun around to face the boy.

"Letts-Hyde, sir," repeated Anthony, pushing out his chest as if awaiting inspection.

A bemused Mr Cheatham, all thought of Margaret having momentarily fled his brain, approached the boy directly.

"Let's hide where, boy?" he asked, concerned for Anthony's mental well-being.

Muffled laughter trickled forth from the class as Margaret, taking advantage of the valuable time Anthony's intervention had bought, finally cleared her mouth.

"Letts-Hyde, sir," repeated Anthony quietly. "Letts-Hyde, that's my name, sir. Just letting you know I'm present and correct, sir."

To the sound of nervous laughter, Mr Cheatham returned to the register and ran his finger down the list of names. Sure enough, about halfway down, the name 'Letts-Hyde A.' confirmed the boy's identity. Suddenly aware of the laughter, Mr Cheatham threw the class a threatening glance. Silence returned to the room. His authority restored, Mr Cheatham once again addressed Anthony who was still standing to attention.

"Very good, very good, at ease … I mean, sit down. Now, I like the cut of your cloth, Letts-Hyde, but please, in future, wait your turn before answering the register. Let's start again."

Mr Cheatham sat down and read from the top of the register.

"Arbuckle," he called.

"Present, sir," replied Margaret, her high-pitched voice as clear as a bell.

Looking up from the register, Mr Cheatham fixed Margaret with an icy stare before deciding to move on.

"Burton."

"Present, sir."

"Davis."

"Present, sir."

"Drummond."

"Present, sir."

Minutes later, registration over, the pupils of Form 4C were sent to their first class of the morning. Laughter filled the corridor as the class recounted Margaret's lucky escape. Unaccustomed to receiving help from anybody, Margaret bustled her way towards Mark, Anthony and Jimmy.

"Hey," she shouted, causing the boys to turn around.

Unsure of what to say next, Margaret stared at them.

"Well?" said Anthony, his impatient demeanour putting Margaret on the back foot.

"Just wanted to say thanks, you know, for ..."

Fearing a withering put-down, Margaret faltered.

"No need to thank me," said Anthony, forcing a smile. "Just don't get caught next time."

"Thanks anyway," said Margaret quietly.

As the three boys turned away, Margaret, much to her surprise, made an awkward attempt to continue the conversation.

"So, who's the new boy then?" she blurted.

"This is Jimmy," said Mark. "Jimmy Johnston. He's rooming with us."

"Hi, I'm Margaret ... nice to meet you."

Before Jimmy could respond, Margaret, her discomfort now manifest, pushed past the boys and hurried along the corridor.

"Who's she?" asked Jimmy with a grin.

"Margaret Arbuckle, the class freak," replied Anthony.

"Not a friend of yours then?" asked Jimmy.

"Certainly not," replied Anthony defensively. "She's a day pupil. I don't think she has any friends."

"You could have fooled me," said Jimmy.

"What do you mean?" asked Anthony.

"Well, you don't go sticking your neck out for someone like you just did if they're not a friend," reasoned Jimmy.

Anthony looked uneasy.

"Come on," said Mark, "we're going to be late for history."

Still finding his bearings, Jimmy followed the class across the quad, through the Great Hall and under the covered walkway into Cole House. The History Department was located on the first floor.

"Morning, everybody," shouted a smiling Robert Cole as he entered the raucous classroom.

It was 9:20 am precisely.

"Morning, sir," boomed the class.

Jimmy, being the new boy, kept quiet but he could see that the teacher was very popular with his pupils. A former opening batsman for Lancashire, Robert Cole's affable manner and generosity of spirit invited the trust of those he taught.

"Right, settle down, you lot," ordered Mr Cole, his voice raised above the din. "Did we all have a good summer?"

"Yes, sir," cried the class, with the exception of Jimmy.

"Are we all glad to be back?" shouted Mr Cole.

"No, sir," shouted the class in unison.

"Hands up those who want to go home," shouted Mr Cole, raising his hand into the air.

Except for Jimmy, who was still finding his feet, the cheering pupils raised their hands.

"Ah ha!" exclaimed Mr Cole, his eyes fixed on the new boy. "I see the motion has not been carried unanimously. Stand up, young man, and identify yourself."

As Jimmy rose to his feet, the class fell silent.

"I'm Jimmy Johnston, sir."

"Well, Jimmy Johnston," teased Mr Cole as he wandered between the desks, "history has always looked kindly on those courageous enough to defy the mob."

Uncomfortable at being singled out, the ensuing ripple of laughter encouraged Jimmy to relax a little.

"So, why don't you want to go home?"

"I've only just got here, sir," replied Jimmy defensively.

"Well, that's a disappointing answer," said Mr Cole. "I was hoping you were going to say you wanted to stay because you liked history."

"I do, sir," said Jimmy.

"Creep."

Laughter once again filled the classroom, causing Jimmy to turn in search of his heckler.

"Emily Burton."

Mr Cole had recognised her voice immediately.

"It's not like you to launch a sneak attack. On your feet and show yourself."

Tall, slender and dark of hair, Emily, a self-conscious smile hovering on her face, rose from her seat amid a chorus of cheers.

"I was only joking, sir," said Emily, her tone floating between apology and protest.

"Well, I know that, and the class knows that," confirmed Mr Cole, "but does Jimmy know that?"

Unsure of what she would say next, Jimmy offered Emily a weak smile.

"Well, I'm sorry if he doesn't," replied Emily, who was not one to remain on the back foot indefinitely, "but judging by the smile on his face, he isn't easily offended."

More laughter.

"I'm not offended," assured Jimmy, who just wanted to sit down.

"Well, that's a relief," retorted Emily before taking her seat.

Jimmy followed suit and the laughter died down.

"End of round one, I think. Welcome to Grey Stones, Jimmy," grinned Mr Cole before bringing the class to order.

"Okay, as you all know, this term marks the beginning of the 'O' level syllabus, and that means that every effort you make from this moment on will impact your grade."

As Mr Cole walked the aisles distributing handouts, the class groaned in recognition that it was time to get down to business. Having lectured the class on the study skills required to shine at history, he spent the remainder of the lesson reviewing the curriculum, the first topic of which was the First World War.

"Over the forthcoming weeks," enthused Mr Cole, "we'll be looking at the Great Powers of Europe in 1900: Britain, France, Russia, Austria-Hungary and, of course, Germany. The alliance system: 'The Dual Alliance', 'Triple Alliance', 'Franco-Russian Alliance', the 'Entente Cordiale' and the 'Triple Entente'. How did they work? What were their aims?"

Jimmy's head was spinning as Anthony, in his customary position at the front of the class, scribbled furiously in an attempt to record Mr Cole's every word.

"Next, we will consider the Road to War," continued an animated Mr Cole. "The arms race between Britain and Germany, the Moroccan crisis of 1905-06, the Agadir crisis of 1911, the Balkans crisis, and ask to what extent these events triggered the conflict. Was war really inevitable following the assassination of Archduke Franz Ferdinand of Austria, or was his murder simply used as an excuse to settle old scores?"

And so the lesson continued with Mr Cole guiding the class through the issues to be covered in future lessons.

"Now, before you go," said Mr Cole as the lesson drew to a close, "those of you with a particular interest in this topic might want to visit Cole Hall and look at the photographs of some of the pupils who attended the school in the years leading up to 1914. Look at the names on the photographs and see how many you can find on the memorial citing those who died in the conflict. You might find the exercise quite moving. Not only will you learn that the history of the First World War is also part of the history of this school, you will also, I hope, come to realise that this tragedy was a human event as opposed to something you simply read about in a history book. Now remember, next lesson we'll be concentrating on the great powers of Europe in 1900 and the Road to War. Do the reading. I expect you all to contribute to the discussion, so make sure you turn up armed with an opinion. Right, off you go."

As if waiting for Mr Cole to finish, the school bell signalled the end of the lesson. As the class was filing out of the room, Mr Cole approached Mark and placed his hand on the boy's shoulder.

"Mark, have you got a minute?"

Once the class had moved into the corridor, Mr Cole quietly closed the door before returning to his desk where Mark was waiting.

"Been in the wars, have we?" he asked, his question an obvious reference to the bruising around Mark's right eye.

"Fell off my bike, sir."

"Must have been some fall."

"Was, sir. Wasn't looking where I was going."

"You know what, Mark?" sighed Mr Cole. "I don't think I believe you."

"I'm telling the truth, sir, honestly," replied Mark, his head bowed to avoid Mr Cole's penetrating stare.

Mr Cole looked at the boy for a few seconds.

"Okay," he said, his tone tinged with resignation. "On your way."

As Mark reached the door, Mr Cole addressed him once again.

"Mark, you do know that I'm here if you need to talk to me about anything, anything at all."

"Of course, sir," he replied brightly.

And with that, Mark made his way to his next class.

CHAPTER SIX

The Enemy Within

Five minutes into the last lesson of the morning, Jimmy was losing the will to live. Maths had never been his strong point. His hatred of the subject was so intense that, inevitably, every maths lesson seemed to last for hours. The monotone delivery of the maths master did little to stir his interest: Mr Sloane did not *teach* maths, he *recited* maths in a manner bereft of flair, pace or enthusiasm.

"An integer is any whole number, whether positive, negative or zero," droned Mr Sloane.

Jimmy felt the knot in his stomach tighten.

"Five is a factor of thirty because thirty can be written as five times an integer. Thirty equals five times six. Five is not a factor of thirty-three because thirty-three cannot be written as five times an integer. The factors of twenty are two, four, five and ten and also one and twenty itself," continued the robotic Mr Sloane.

Jimmy switched off. Multiples and prime numbers passed him by as he sought distraction through the classroom window. When none was to be found, his mind wandered back to Cole Hall and the photograph of the charismatic captain. For what valiant deed had Captain Cole been decorated with the highest award for bravery his country could bestow? What sort of person was he? How had he met his end in France in 1918? By the time the bell rang for lunch, Jimmy was in a world of his own.

"Come on then," said Anthony, who, being Anthony, had hung on Mr Sloane's every word. "I'm famished."

"Oh, right," said Jimmy, suddenly aware that the class was on the move.

"Get a move on," encouraged Mark, "or we'll be last in the queue."

Last out of the classroom, the boys followed the throng to the refectory situated at the rear of Baird House. Margaret Arbuckle, who considered lunchtime a sacred event, hurried through the crowd. By the time Mark, Anthony and Jimmy arrived, Margaret was near the front of the queue, clutching her tray, her mind already contemplating seconds.

The autumn sunshine flooding through the glass construction of its outer wall, the refectory hummed with conversation. As they advanced along the queue, Jimmy was earnestly explaining his hatred of maths when he noticed the approach of three older boys, each of whom carried an empty tray. One of the boys pushed into Mark, causing him to stumble.

"Well, if it isn't our friend Pecky," sneered Lunt.

Tall, heavily built and broad of shoulder, Eric Lunt, his short, cropped hair accentuating his large head, stepped towards Mark.

"I take it you don't have a problem with us joining the queue in front of you," said Lunt.

Mark stared defiantly at his tormentor.

"Of course, he doesn't," said Reilly, his tall frame pitched forward in an attempt to convey menace.

"Step aside," said Woosey, who, being the smallest of the three, always felt the need to sound the toughest.

"Leave us alone," said Anthony. "We don't want any trouble."

"Shut up, four-eyes," snapped Lunt. "Speak when you're spoken to."

By now, those in the immediate vicinity had fallen silent, their attention fixed on the developing confrontation.

"Look at him," mocked Lunt, his hulking head stooping to within two inches of Mark's face. "Looks like a scared little rat."

"Scared little rat," echoed Reilly.

"Scared, ugly little rat," said Woosey.

Jimmy had heard enough.

"You must be Lunt," he said calmly.

"Mr Lunt to you," snarled Lunt.

"I've heard of you," replied Jimmy.

"What have you heard?" asked Lunt, who continued to stand over Mark.

"I've heard you're a coward," replied Jimmy in a raised voice.

Drawing himself to his full height, Lunt turned his head towards Jimmy.

"What did you say?" he asked.

"I've heard you're a coward," repeated Jimmy. "I've heard that you and your friends gang up on people smaller than you and take their money."

Anthony momentarily closed his eyes as Lunt stared at Jimmy in stunned silence.

"What's the matter? You deaf as well as yellow?" goaded Jimmy.

"Oh my God," groaned Anthony, anticipating an immediate assault.

"Here, hold this," ordered Lunt, who passed his tray to Woosey before lurching towards Jimmy.

Jimmy did not flinch.

"Leave him alone, Lunt. Don't you touch him."

Lunt turned around and saw Mark Peck staring at him, his fists clenched.

"Fight him and you fight both of us," warned Mark with unquestionable resolve.

By now, the confrontation had captured a wider audience. Pupils were looking up from their tables, aware that something was happening. Even Mr Snyder and Mr Cheatham, who were taking coffee in the staff area of the refectory, were looking up from their table.

"Don't worry, Mark," assured Jimmy, "he won't try anything here. Too many witnesses, aren't there, Lunt?"

"Yeah, why don't you just push off, Lunt?" said Anthony, emboldened by the fact that he had not yet been knocked off his feet.

Lunt, his blood up, moved towards Jimmy but was stopped by the restraining grip of Reilly.

"Not here," said Reilly. "Later. We can deal with them later."

Lunt hesitated.

"Later," echoed Woosey. "We can deal with them later, Eric."

Composing himself, Lunt abruptly removed Reilly's hand from his arm.

"I don't know your name," he said quietly in an attempt to impart menace, "but you're dead. You are all dead."

"My name is Jimmy Johnston: you owe my friend ten shillings."

It was Lunt who broke the ensuing silence.

"There won't always be witnesses."

Grabbing his tray from Woosey, Lunt, his cronies in tow, barged his way to the front of the queue.

"I'll tell you one thing," said Anthony, "if Lunt has his way, you will never have to sit through another maths lesson again. None of us will."

"I wish," replied Jimmy with feeling.

But Jimmy's carefree demeanour only disguised his concern at having made an enemy on his first day at school. Although the immediate danger posed by Lunt and his friends had passed, Jimmy knew that the situation was far from resolved. He had met bullies like Lunt before and knew that he and his roommates would need to be constantly on their guard.

News of the confrontation travelled fast. Throughout the rest of the afternoon, Mark, Anthony and Jimmy were constantly approached by those who wanted to know every detail of the skirmish. By the end of the afternoon, rumour had it that Lunt and his friends were planning to ambush the boys before they returned to their room. Leaving their French lesson at the end of the day, it occurred to Jimmy that a detour might be prudent.

"Do you remember what Mr Cole said about the First World War being part of the school's history?" he asked as the boys left class. "Let's pay a visit to Cole Hall and see if we can find some of the photographs he was talking about."

"What, photographs of former pupils killed in the war?" asked Mark. "That sounds jolly."

"It's a great idea," enthused Anthony, who, conscious of the ambush rumours, was more than happy to plot a course away from their room.

"Okay," said Mark, "but I can't stay too long; I'm off for a run later."

Upon entering Cole Hall, Jimmy immediately looked to the far end of the hall where he saw a young woman standing directly below the photograph of Captain Cole. As the boys looked for photographs of the 'lost generation', the young lady remained at her station.

"Who's she?" whispered Jimmy, not wanting his voice to carry across the hall.

"She's a new teacher, I think," replied Mark.

Leaving his friends to their browsing, Jimmy made his way across the hall, his eyes again fixed on the captain. Not wanting to distract the young woman, Jimmy stopped behind her and again read the inscription on the bronze plate below the photograph.

"Excuse me, miss, what does *Filius est pars patris* mean?" he asked.

The young woman turned around too quickly to hide the tears that welled in her eyes or the silver cigarette case that she clasped in her hand.

"Sorry, miss," said Jimmy instinctively.

Recovering her poise, the young woman attempted a smile.

"No, that's perfectly alright," she replied. "*Filius est pars patris?* It means 'a son is part of the father'."

"Related to Mr Cole, you know," chipped in Anthony, who, with Mark, had followed Jimmy across the hall.

"Mr Cole, the history master?" queried the young woman. "I was wondering if there was a connection."

"There is, miss," said Anthony. "Mr Cole is Captain Cole's nephew."

"He must have been very brave, miss," said Mark looking up at the photograph.

"Yes, he must," she replied. "Funny, but my father was also awarded the Victoria Cross."

"Really, miss?" asked an impressed Anthony.

"Oh yes," replied the young woman, her tone now flippant, irreverent almost.

"Tristan Herbert Connolly; he was a pilot in the RAF. He was shot down and killed in June 1940, quite the hero. Funny then, don't you think, that his old squadron has no record of him? Perhaps he never really existed, perhaps …"

Checking herself, the young lady suddenly fell silent, turned her head away from the boys and wrested back her self-control.

"I do apologise, boys," she said after a few moments. "You must think me terribly silly getting so emotional about a photograph."

Casting one final lingering glance at the captain, the woman raised a tissue to her face and quickly dabbed away her tears.

"Anyway, I must be off," she said, her voice tinged with embarrassment. "Bye."

"Bye, miss," chorused the boys.

From the balcony at the other end of the hall, Stanley Rimmer, the porter, looked on unnoticed as the young lady took her leave.

"What do you make of that then?" asked Anthony of nobody in particular when she was out of earshot.

"Beats me," said Mark.

"She looked sort of sad and angry at the same time," said Jimmy.

"Why would a photograph make her cry?" asked Mark.

"Who knows?" replied Jimmy.

"Do you think it's safe to go back to our room now?" asked Anthony.

"Well, we can't hang around here forever," said Jimmy.

"Come on then," said Mark, "enough of this hiding. Let's go."

CHAPTER SEVEN

The Archive

It was Friday morning and Form 4 C had assembled for their final lesson of the day, physical geography. The week had passed quietly causing Jimmy to hope that Lunt and his friends had forgotten about the confrontation in the refectory. When the teacher entered the room, Jimmy immediately recognised her as the woman he had seen crying in front of Captain Cole's photograph.

"Morning, everybody; my name is Miss Connolly."

Looking around the class, her eyes fell on Mark, Anthony and Jimmy.

"I see I have met some of you before," she said cheerily.

Jimmy returned her smile and warmed to her immediately.

"Now, as I am sure you all know, I am new to the school, so I hope I can rely on you all to help me settle in. In return, I promise to do my best to make my subject as interesting as possible."

The class laughed politely, if not a little nervously.

"And that should not be too difficult because, as everybody knows, physical geography can be an earth-moving experience."

This time, the polite laughter was accompanied by a few groans.

"You're right," confessed Miss Connolly, "it's not a great joke. But physical geography is a great subject and can be fun to study, especially when we escape to the hills on our field trips."

Having put the class at ease, Miss Connolly outlined the course to be tackled in the immediate weeks ahead. When the bell sounded for lunch, it was clear that Form 4C had been won over.

Leaving the classroom at the end of the lesson, Jimmy was in no hurry to get to the refectory. Friday afternoons were given over to sport and a cross-country run had been timetabled for after lunch: the last thing he wanted to do was to weigh himself down by eating. After the class had dispersed, Miss Connolly made her way to the staff room in Baird House, where she hoped she might find Robert Cole. Spotting Robert in a corner reading a newspaper, she approached him directly.

"What are you up to?" asked Grace.

"Not much," replied Robert looking up with a smile. "How's it going?"

Grace smiled back, sat down and opened her lunch box.

"Oh, I think I'll survive. Sandwich?"

"What have you got?" asked Robert peering into the box.

"Cheese and pickle made by my own fair hand."

"Sounds good to me, thanks," said Robert helping himself.

Taking a bite of her sandwich, Grace gazed out the window.

"Tell me," she said after a few moments, "what's this I hear about you being related to the people who built Cole House?"

"Nothing much to tell, really. My grandfather, Richard Cole, commissioned the building following the death of his son, my uncle, in the First World War."

"The son being Captain Thomas Howard Cole VC, whose photograph hangs in Cole Hall?"

"That's right," confirmed Robert. "Richard's youngest son, Edward, my father, was killed at the end of the Second World War. By then, Richard was no longer alive: he and my grandmother died within months of each other in 1944. Why the interest in my family history?"

"Well, no interest, really," fibbed Grace. "It's just that I also have a connection with the school. A friend of the family taught here. His name was Michael Edwards. Ever heard of him?"

"Michael Edwards? I'm afraid not. Before my time, I think."

"*Well* before your time. He was headmaster here."

"When was this?"

"I think he was head here in 1937 though I couldn't tell you when he was appointed. He and my mother were friends and I thought it would be interesting to learn a bit more about him."

"You should have been a historian," said Robert smiling.

"I take it there are school records? I mean, where would I look? Where would I start?"

"Well, if he was headmaster of the school, his name and term of office would be on the board hanging in the Great Hall. You could also look in the archives …"

"Archives? The school has archives?" interrupted Grace.

"I'll say. They go back to the opening of the school in 1870."

"Where are they?"

"Hidden in a cellar below the library," whispered Robert in mock secrecy. "Show you if you like."

"What, now?"

"Why not? Classes have finished for the day. Come on, bring your sandwiches."

"Okay, but can we stop off at the Great Hall first? I'm interested to know when he became head and when he retired."

"If you like," agreed Robert. "There will also be a portrait of him in the hall."

"A portrait?" queried Grace.

"Yes, it's customary for all new heads to sit and have their portrait painted. The portrait then hangs in their office until they retire or move on before being exhibited in the Great Hall for posterity."

"Hence the portrait in Mr Snyder's office," said Grace, suddenly enlightened. "Come on then, you've got to show me."

Before Robert could reply, Grace was making her way out of the staff room.

On entering the Great Hall, Robert led Grace towards a huge rectangular stained-glass window under which hung the roll of past headmasters. Casting her eyes upon yet another mahogany commemoration, Grace soon found what she was looking for.

"There he is," she said, her tone triumphant. "Michael Edwards: 1937 to 1941."

"Strange," murmured Robert.

"What is?" asked Grace.

"Well, he wasn't head for very long and it would appear he was getting on a bit when appointed. I mean, assuming that he retired in 1941 aged 65 or thereabouts, he must have been into his sixties when he got the job."

"No, he wasn't that old," asserted Grace.

"How do you know?"

"Oh … I can't remember," lied Grace. "I think my mother mentioned something about him being relatively young when he was appointed."

"Well, it would be interesting to know why he stood down after only four years in the job," mused Robert.

"He might have gone off to fight in the war," suggested Grace.

"It's possible, I suppose," replied Robert, "but why would he wait until 1941 to enlist?"

"Perhaps the archives will tell us. Where's his portrait then?" asked Grace.

"Well, according to this, it should be hanging between his predecessor Gilbert Roach and his successor Martin Giles," replied Robert, his eyes fixed on the mahogany board.

"Show me," urged Grace.

Retracing their steps, Robert led Grace to the south wall from where a series of portraits stared across the hall.

"Here we are," said Robert looking up at the portraits. "Donald Ames, the first head of Grey Stones, 1870 to 1881. What a formidable looking bloke."

But Grace was not listening; she was already advancing along the wall in search of Michael Edwards.

"Well, here is Gilbert Roach, 1931 to 1937, and here is Martin Giles, 1941 to 1955. So where is Michael Edwards?" asked Grace impatiently.

"Are you sure he's not there?" queried Robert as he approached her.

"Positive."

"Well, that's odd," said Robert scratching his head. "Looks like we have a mystery on our hands."

"And the mystery deepens because I'll tell you something else. I have examined virtually every photograph in Cole Hall and he's not there either. There isn't a photograph of him to be found."

"What are you on about?" asked Robert.

"Almost every pupil who attended this school, along with every teacher who ever taught here, has found their way onto a photograph in Cole Hall," explained Grace. "Everybody, that is, except our Mr Edwards."

"You mean *your* Mr Edwards. For a person you never knew, friend of the family or not, you seem to be taking an excessive interest in this fellow. Is there something you're not telling me?"

"Of course not."

Grace hesitated.

"I'm just curious, that's all. What about the archives?"

"What about them?" asked Robert looking at his wristwatch.

"You said you would show me the archives under the library.

Remember?"

"Okay. But on one condition."

"What?"

"That you come out with me this evening."

Caught off guard, Grace paused before replying.

"You mean a date?" she asked quietly.

"Yes, a date," replied Robert smiling, "and take that serious look off your face; we've been on dates before, you know."

An embarrassing silence followed as Grace, her face a picture of uncertainty, looked Robert in the eye.

"Well, yes, okay then," she said.

"Right then," said Robert noting her reluctance. "Follow me."

Situated on the ground floor of the south wing of Baird House, the library basked in quiet academic splendour. Beyond the map room at the far end, a stone stairway spiralled down to an ancient door. Having activated the light switches at the top of the stairway, Robert led Grace down the steps, turned the large key that sat in the door's lock and opened it. Bathed in a dim yellow light, the low vaulted ceiling of the cavernous cellar travelled the entire length of the library and beyond. Rows of metal shelving formed bays of various sizes, creating a maze-like effect. Alcoves containing chests, wooden crates and yet more shelving penetrated the walls at regular intervals. The further into the cellar they went, the more worn its treasures appeared as box files and document wallets sought to hide their age behind increasing quantities of dust.

"Sorry about the mess," said Robert coming to a halt. "I don't think the cleaners usually come this far; they think the place is haunted."

"Haunted?" repeated Grace.

"Cistercian monks," laughed Robert. "They're supposed to turn up every now and then looking for their lost treasure."

"Cistercians?" queried Grace, who was suddenly feeling the cold.

"Didn't you know? This place was built on the site of an ancient abbey," explained Robert.

"No, I didn't," replied Grace.

"I'll have to introduce you to my friend, Compton Hobbs," said Robert airily.

"Compton who?" asked Grace.

"Compton Hobbs, he's a local historian. He knows all about this place. Legend has it that before the abbey was ransacked on the orders of Henry VIII, most of its treasures were concealed in secret tunnels. Many monks were slaughtered for refusing to cooperate with Henry's men and the treasure was never recovered. There are those, especially amongst our cleaners, it would seem, who think the monks are still here."

The prospect of being left alone in the cellar was not one that Grace relished.

"Anyway, here we are," continued Robert. "As you can see, it's pretty disorganised down here. Most of the shelving units have a date on them. Look at this one here: 1946. Anything relevant to that year will be on these shelves. But we need to look at the records for 1941."

"Why?" asked Grace.

"Follow me," said Robert, who wandered deeper into the cellar before coming to a halt.

"So, what have we got here?" asked Grace as Robert confronted the materials before him.

"Well, these are the school registers for 1941, and here we have exam papers and copies of school reports next to them."

"What are these?" asked Grace, delving into a large cardboard box.

"Those are old editions of the monthly school magazine, *The Scholar*, which is still going strong today."

"Bit of a pompous title, isn't it?"

"Try telling that to Mr Snyder," replied Robert.

"What's this?" asked Grace, opening another box file.

"That's the yearbook," replied Robert. "In there, you will find the name of every pupil, member of staff and employee who attended or worked at the school during the academic year of 1941."

Drawing herself closer to Robert, Grace thumbed through the pages of the dusty leather-backed yearbook as he continued to search the contents of the shelving in front of him.

"Found them!" he said triumphantly.

"Found what?"

"The minutes of the Governors' Meetings."

"And what will they tell us?"

"Well, I'm hoping they might shed some light on why Michael Edwards stood down as head. I'm assuming that the governors would usually meet once a term and that the departure of a headmaster would merit a mention somewhere in the minutes."

After studying the record for a minute or so, Robert suddenly looked up.

"Brace yourself for a shock," he said.

"What have you found?"

"Listen to this," said Robert, who proceeded to read from the minutes.

"Prior to the meeting being called to order, a minute's silence was observed in memory of the former headmaster, Michael Edwards, whose murder last August shocked the school. Special thanks were extended to the Reverend Herbert Knox of St John's Church, Keswick, for his assistance in arranging and conducting the funeral."

"Murdered?" queried Grace.

"I'm afraid so," confirmed Robert.

"How? Who by? Why?"

"I'm afraid I can't help you there. Bit of a turn up, though, isn't it?" said Robert blithely as he looked at his watch.

"Do you have to go somewhere?" asked Grace.

"Yes," replied Robert. "Off for a spot of rowing."

"Marvellous," said Grace, whose mind was clearly elsewhere.

"Are you okay?" asked Robert.

"I'm fine, I'm fine," insisted Grace. "Just a bit shocked, that's all. All I wanted to do was to find out a bit more about him. I wasn't expecting to discover that he had been murdered. I don't know what to do now."

"Tell you what," said Robert, who really did want to help. "There are a couple of boys in the Fourth Form who would love to research a murder victim. I'm sure they would jump at the chance to spend some time down here researching the records. They could probably confirm when it was that he came to the school. Who knows what else they may find out?"

"Sounds too good to be true," said Grace, surveying the ranks of shelving in an attempt to avoid eye contact.

"Are you sure you're okay?" asked Robert as he gently took hold of Grace by the shoulders and turned her towards him.

"I'm fine," said Grace, her eyes moistening.

"But you're crying! What's the matter?"

"Just a bit shocked, that's all. It's not every day you discover a family friend has been murdered," said Grace unconvincingly.

Robert was sure that she was keeping something from him.

"You would tell me, wouldn't you?"

"Tell you what?" asked Grace, recovering her composure.

"Tell me if anything was wrong."

"There's nothing wrong, honestly."

As Robert leaned forward to kiss her, Grace turned her cheek, causing him to hesitate.

"Well, as I said, I'm off for a spot of rowing," said Robert, trying his best to hide his embarrassment.

"Right," replied Grace quietly, "then we'd better be off."

CHAPTER EIGHT

Running Scared

Following lunch, Mark, Anthony and Jimmy returned to their room, changed into their PE kit and made their way to the gym. By the time Mr Dudley and Miss Saunders arrived, approximately one hundred runners had assembled in readiness for the cross-country run. A small, balding, chubby individual in his mid-forties, Mr Dudley's best days as an athlete were clearly behind him. As for Miss Saunders, although younger and taller than Mr Dudley, her well-developed second chin suggested that she too had long given up rigorous physical exercise. Accompanied by Miss Saunders, Mr Dudley ascended the steps of the gym, imparted three sharp blasts of his whistle and called the group to order.

"Quiet please," shouted Mr Dudley, the wind playing havoc with his comb-over. "Please organise yourselves into your houses, starting with Blencathra on the left, Catbells next, Helvellyn in front of me and Skiddaw to the right."

Moans of discontent multiplied as the runners took up their positions.

"Now then," shouted Mr Dudley. "This afternoon, you will be running the Christmas Chase course. For the benefit of the uninitiated, the route is as follows: take the path beyond the playing field and run through the woods towards the lake. Turn left and pick up the path that runs alongside the Borrowdale Road. After a couple of miles, you will come to a signpost for Falcon Crag. Take the path to the immediate left of the signpost, keeping the Great Wood to your left."

Far from impressed, Margaret Arbuckle ruefully anticipated the inevitable taunts and ridicule that would overtake her around the course. But Mr Dudley had not finished.

"Continue along the path until you reach the signpost for Walla Crag and take the track that leads directly into the Great Wood. Follow the track through the wood until you come to the signpost for Winter Farm. Turn left along the footpath until you re-join the lakeside path. Turn right onto the path and head back towards the boathouse and the school. Run one lap of the running track and you will have completed the course."

Noting the darkening sky and rising wind, Mr Dudley paused briefly before continuing.

"Now, the course is just over six miles long and Miss Saunders and I have agreed to allow you a generous two hours to complete it."

"Please be advised," shouted Miss Saunders, "that some of our fifth-formers have kindly volunteered to supervise the run to ensure nobody gets lost. They will take up positions at certain points on the course and guide you around. Will the volunteers come forward please?"

As the fifth-formers ascended the steps of the gym, Mark, Anthony and Jimmy looked on in silence. Amid the volunteers, their menacing stares fixed firmly on the three boys, stood Lunt, Reilly and Woosey.

"Right, any questions?"

Mr Dudley paused briefly before answering his own question.

"No. Then let's get on with it."

Getting to her feet, Margaret looked on miserably as the volunteers ran off to their positions on the course. A couple of minutes later, Mr Dudley sent Blencathera on its way.

"We'd better stay together," warned Jimmy as Catbells prepared for the off.

"What good will that do?" asked Anthony gloomily.

"We could try and outrun them," suggested Mark. "Lunt is hardly built for speed."

"That's why we won't see them coming," said Jimmy. "Be ready for an ambush."

"Ambush? Where?" asked a horrified Anthony.

"They'll probably come at us somewhere around the Great Wood," said Mark, who knew the course well. "By the time we get there, the field will be stretched and there will be plenty of places for them to hide."

"God, I hate cross-country," moaned Anthony.

"Catbells, are we ready?" shouted Mr Dudley when Blencathra had disappeared beyond the playing field. "Then off you go."

"Stick together," said Jimmy, "and stay at the back of the pack."

By the time they had crossed the playing field and reached the path, Margaret, the rank outsider, had already fallen forty yards behind. By the time Mr Dudley sent Helvellyn on its way, Margaret had slowed to a barely noticeable walk.

As the boys descended the path towards the lake, the school boathouse came into sight. A flurry of activity, crews of varying numbers manoeuvred their craft across the concrete slipway that sloped from the boathouse to the water's edge. Beyond the slipway, various boats, their oars striking the water in synchronised accord, cut their way through the choppy waters into the ever-stiffening wind. Before reaching the boathouse, the runners, urged on by two of Mr Dudley's volunteers, veered left and picked up the lakeside path.

"Now what?" asked Anthony when the boathouse was behind them.

"Keep going for a bit and let the others get away," replied Jimmy. "See that bend in the distance? We'll leave the path somewhere there."

It was not long before the rest of their classmates were out of sight.

"Right, let's get off here," ordered Jimmy as the bend came into play, concealing them from those behind.

Veering off to their immediate left, the boys dived into a thicket of undulating woodland and took cover in a small hollow some thirty yards from the path. From their position face down amongst the trees and ferns, they peered over the lip of the hollow and waited for the rest of the Fourth Form to pass.

"This should do us," said Jimmy. "Everybody has to come back this way. If we sit tight, we can join the front runners on their way back to school and Lunt won't have a clue where we've been."

"The boy's a genius," observed a much-relieved Anthony.

"Could be a bit of a wait though," said Mark as he slipped below the lip of the hollow to escape the strengthening wind.

"And it looks like rain," said Jimmy peering through the branches above his head.

"Great," said Anthony, "that's all we need."

*

"You were right," shouted Woosey as he approached Lunt and Reilly. "They're hiding in the trees about half a mile back."

"Are you sure?" asked Lunt.

"Positive," replied his minion.

"Right, lead the way," ordered Lunt.

At the head of the pack for once, Woosey allowed himself a smile as he re-traced his steps along the path.

CHAPTER NINE

Ambush

Fifteen minutes had passed and the weather was deteriorating quickly. Black swollen storm clouds swept in from the south, the ever-strengthening wind whipping the lake's surface into frothy peaks. Heavy globules of rain smacked into the tormented canopy, heralding a downpour of such intensity that the boys, their white singlets clinging to their bodies, were drenched within seconds. As darkness repelled the light, the trees, begging the wind's mercy, stooped and bowed in frantic subservience.

"Time to go, I think," said Jimmy as droplets of rain cascaded from the tip of his nose.

"Too right," agreed Anthony, wiping the rain from his glasses. "Nobody could expect us to stay out in this."

Returning to the path, Mark looked to his left and froze.

"Hello, Pecky," shouted Lunt from a distance of forty yards.

Flanked by Reilly and Woosey, his fists clenched, Lunt strode through the wind and rain in smirking anticipation of the beatings he and his friends were about to administer.

"Get here, the three of you!" yelled Lunt as he continued to advance.

Momentarily caught in the headlights of Lunt's intimidating stare, Jimmy was the first to react.

"Leg it!" he shouted.

Turning on their heels, the boys left the path, crossed the Borrowdale Road and sprinted towards the boathouse.

"After them!" yelled Lunt.

Belting along the shore of the lake, Jimmy and Mark made light of the uneven terrain.

"Come on!" encouraged Mark. "Push it!"

Spurred on, the boys increased their lead, but Anthony, the poorest runner of the three, was struggling to maintain the pace.

"Sorry … can't keep this up," he gasped.

"Keep going! You can do it!" shouted Mark, grabbing his friend by the arm.

Jimmy lifted his head for a second and caught sight of the armada of boats now steering a hasty course across the churning water towards the boathouse. By now, Woosey, the frontrunner of the chasing pack, was gaining and it was clear that Anthony was not going to outrun anybody. There was nothing else for it; they would have to stop.

"It's Mark they want," wheezed Anthony to Jimmy. "You two keep going."

"Behave yourself," replied Mark. "If one stops, we all stop."

"Sorry, boys," said Anthony, his desperate sprint degenerating into a walk.

"Nothing to apologise for," replied Jimmy, breathing heavily.

The three friends turned to face their pursuers, who were now walking towards them. Woosey, as keen as ever to impress, still led the way.

"This isn't good," shouted a voice from the lake's edge.

Looking to their right, Mark, Anthony and Jimmy saw the unmistakable figure of Margaret Arbuckle, a half-eaten chocolate bar in her hand, peering across the water.

"What are you doing here?" asked Anthony as he and his friends sidled towards her, their gaze concentrated upon the advancing threat.

"She's heeling badly. It's the wind, she needs to lose some sail," shouted Margaret ignoring Anthony's question.

"Heeling? What are you talking about?" asked Jimmy as he looked across the lake.

"Listing," shouted Margaret. "She's listing badly. Her rudder is out of the water."

"Two hundred yards from the shore, shrouded in the low-lying cloud, a lone yachtsman struggled to right his vessel in an attempt to repel the invading waves. As Jimmy tried to take in what was happening on the lake, Woosey, his arms outstretched, beckoned the boys to step forward and fight.

"Come on then, who's first?"

"If he doesn't lose some sail quickly, he's going to broach," warned Margaret.

"Meaning?" asked Anthony.

"Meaning he could turtle … capsize," replied an increasingly anxious Margaret.

Unhappy that he was being ignored, an agitated Woosey stepped forward.

"You! Fatso! Get lost, now!" he shouted before knocking the remnants of Margaret's chocolate bar from her hand.

Staring at the chocolate on the rain-soaked ground, its wrapper carried away by the wind, Margaret's face darkened. Slowly raising her head, she looked the smirking Woosey in the eye before landing a hefty right-hand jab flush on his nose. Sitting on his backside, blood gushing from his nostrils, Woosey's fight was over. Lunt and Reilly stepped forward, but Jimmy ignored them: the person in the boat was definitely in trouble. Buffeted by the wailing wind, the yachtsman was struggling to remain upright aboard the pitching vessel.

"What's he doing?" asked Anthony.

"He's trying to get rid of his headsail," shouted Margaret above the wind. "If he can reduce canvas, he can regain control of the boat."

"Mark, you're the fastest," shouted Jimmy. "Run to the boathouse and bring help."

"He's going nowhere!" yelled Lunt as he walked past the moaning Woosey.

"Lunt!" shouted Anthony. "For God's sake, whoever is out there needs our help."

Ignoring Anthony completely, Lunt walked up to Mark and punched him hard in the face, splitting his lip and knocking him to the ground. Stepping back, Lunt made ready to kick his fallen quarry but was knocked sideways by the onrushing Jimmy.

"Leave him alone," snarled Jimmy after placing himself between his friend and his attacker.

Enraged, Lunt advanced once again.

"Lunt!" cried Anthony. "Stop this lunacy and help."

Lunt turned to Reilly.

"Shut that four-eyed weakling up."

But Reilly was already backing away, his desire for confrontation dulled by what was happening on the lake.

"If you're not going to help, just leave," ordered Jimmy.

"Look!" shouted Anthony, peering across the lake.

Knocked off his feet by the swinging boom, his head crashing into the gunwale, the yachtsman disappeared from view. Still over-canvassed, the boat lurched onto its side and capsized.

"Help him!" pleaded Jimmy.

Lunt, his face devoid of expression, backed away from the lakeside, slowly shaking his head.

"You help him."

Within seconds, Lunt, Reilly and a dazed Woosey were running from the scene. Back on his feet, Mark pressed his arm to his mouth to stem the flow of blood. There was no sign of the yachtsman. Neither was there any sign of Margaret.

"Where's Margaret?" yelled Jimmy.

"There!" shouted Anthony, pointing into the lake. "There she is."

Forty yards from shore, the wind and rain against her, her hefty forearms clawing through the resisting waves, Margaret Arbuckle was striking out towards the stricken vessel. Jimmy kicked off his pumps.

"Come on," he shouted.

"I can't swim," responded Anthony.

Jimmy, who had already launched himself into the freezing water in pursuit of Margaret, did not hear him. Holding his glasses to his face, Anthony waded into the lake and looked on helplessly as Margaret and Jimmy slowly advanced towards the pitching hull.

His eyes fixed on the boathouse, Mark wiped the blood from his lips and ran. Concerned that he may have set off too quickly, he reduced his pace slightly and tried to relax. Tension, he knew, was the enemy of the sprinter. After one hundred yards, the ground felt light beneath his feet and his technique remained sound. His bottom lip throbbing, he breezed through one hundred and fifty yards, his rhythm still intact. Through two hundred yards and he was beginning to blow. 'Control the breathing. Shoulders back,' commanded an inner voice as Mark sprinted into unknown territory. Through two hundred and fifty yards, the cracks began to appear as his head rolled sideways and his speed diminished. 'Push it! Push it!" commanded the inner voice. Lifting his head, angling his torso forward, Mark sought to steady the ship. Through three hundred yards, he could feel his calf muscles tightening: through three hundred and fifty, he was decelerating quickly. It was then that technique gave way to sheer bloody-mindedness. His lungs bursting, Mark attempted to lengthen his stride. 'Keep going, keep going,' pleaded the faltering inner voice through four hundred, four hundred and fifty and five hundred yards. Ahead of him, the open doors of the boathouse exposed the sheltering throng. Why hadn't they seen what was happening on the lake? Why were they standing there, drying themselves and laughing? His sprint reduced to little more than a weaving jog, Mark made one last adrenalin fuelled effort to cover the remaining distance.

Travelling across the uneven terrain, he stumbled and fell: he could hardly breathe. Still some eighty yards short of his destination, Mark got to his feet and staggered on. Upon reaching the boathouse, he threw himself across the threshold and pierced the crowded entrance. Robert Cole spotted him immediately.

"Mark!" he shouted, rushing towards the boy. "Are you alright? What happened to your lip?"

"Boat, sir … yachtsman in trouble," gasped Mark pointing across the lake.

Reaching for the binoculars hanging on the wall, Robert hurried passed Mark and turned them on the lake.

"To the right," directed Mark as he fought to regain his breath.

Scanning through the gloom, Robert spotted the boat. There was someone in the water, no, two people in the water. And they were swimming towards the boat, not away from it.

"Peters!" boomed Mr Cole. "Two, possibly three people in the water. Phone for help. Now!"

"What's going on?" responded Peters.

Robert Cole did not reply. He was already running.

CHAPTER TEN

Deep Breaths

Clinging to the upturned boat, Margaret paused for breath and considered her options. Positioning herself halfway along the eighteen-foot hull, she took three deep breaths before feeling for the gunwale and levering herself underwater. Carefully avoiding the mainsail and rigging, she emerged inside the hull. Consumed by darkness, her outstretched arm instantly confirmed the presence of a body buoyed by a life jacket. Propelling herself upwards, Margaret, her lungs replenished by the cavity of trapped air she now occupied, manoeuvred herself towards the head of the motionless body. Lightly placing her hand over the stubbled face of the yachtsman, she tried in vain to establish evidence of breathing. Confronted with this failure, Margaret's first impulse was to force him down into the lake, shove him into clear water and allow the life jacket to carry him to the surface. But second thoughts prevailed: even if she could manage such a feat alone, the risk of entangling her charge in the rigging was far too great. It was then that she heard three loud thumps on the hull and the sound of muffled shouting.

"Margaret! Margaret!"

It was Jimmy.

"Margaret! Margaret!" he yelled again, thumping the hull with the side of his fist.

Exposed to the ripping wind and driving rain, Jimmy was desperately considering his next move when Margaret appeared beside him, popping out of the water like a piece of escaping debris.

Jimmy could see that she was close to exhaustion.

"He's in the boat," spluttered Margaret, in between taking gulps of air.

"Is he …?"

Afraid of the answer he might receive, Jimmy could not complete the question.

"Dunno," replied Margaret, "but his head is above water."

Jimmy looked back to the shore, desperately hoping that help, and a solution, was at hand. He could see Anthony standing in the water and a lone figure hurtling along the shoreside from the direction of the boathouse.

"Listen, his legs are about here," shouted Margaret indicating the position inside the hull with her outstretched arm. "Follow me in. Use his legs to pull yourself up into the air pocket. Between us, we should be able to force him down and out into the lake. His life jacket should do the rest."

"Right," replied Jimmy.

"Look out for the sail and loose rigging."

Back inside the hull, Margaret again propelled herself to the roof of the capsized vessel. Wedging herself between the yachtsman's limp form and the mast, she clamped her left arm under his chin, forced his mouth firmly shut and waited. Seconds later, she felt Jimmy's presence beside her. Using the thumb and forefinger of her right hand, Margaret pinched closed the yachtsman's nostrils.

"Okay? Take a deep breath and let's go," she ordered.

Moments later, free from the capsized vessel and assisted by the now collaborating life jacket, they broke the lake's surface.

"Who is he?" shouted Jimmy over the wind. "Do you know him?"

"It's Dominic Price, the head boy," replied Margaret.

"Is he breathing?"

"Dunno, can't tell," grimaced Margaret, who was now clearly

struggling.

"Come on," shouted Jimmy. "You take one arm I'll take the other."

Linking their arms under Dominic's armpits, the pair kicked towards the shore.

*

It was the constant twisting and turning between the wickets when piling on the runs for Lancashire that had done for Robert Cole's right knee. On the straight, as his dash along the lakeside path demonstrated, he was still an able athlete. Within minutes of leaving the boathouse, his rowing shoes and tracksuit abandoned on the shore, Robert Cole was wading into the lake.

"Who's out there?" he shouted as he approached Anthony.

"Jimmy Johnston, Margaret Arbuckle and whoever was in the boat," replied Anthony, who had not moved from his post.

"Get back to the shore, you can do no good standing here," ordered Robert before executing a standing dive into the heaving lake.

Wiping his glasses on his saturated vest, Anthony remained where he was.

*

"Keep it going," shouted Jimmy.

Margaret did not respond. Although the wind was now behind them, their progress was slow. Unable to fully extend her right arm and losing the strength to kick, Margaret was in trouble. With over a hundred yards still to swim, Jimmy was not confident.

"Come on, Margaret, we can do it," he cried.

"Sorry … I'm going to have to stop," panted Margaret.

"We can't stop, Margaret," insisted Jimmy. "We've got to keep going."

But Margaret could go no farther. Tired and numb with cold, she simply could not swim and tow Dominic at the same time.

"Give him to me!" bellowed Robert Cole, who, seemingly from nowhere, rose from the lake like a titan.

"You two okay?"

"Think so, sir," replied Jimmy.

"Margaret? Can you make it back to the shore?" shouted Robert.

"I'm alright," replied Margaret, for whom the relief of off-loading her burden was immediate. "Get him back. I'm okay."

Hooking an arm under Dominic's chin, Robert made for the shore. By the time he and Anthony had dragged the motionless boy out of the lake, Margaret and Jimmy were still some sixty yards from the bank. As he neared the shore, Jimmy could see people running along the path from the boathouse.

"You alright?" asked Anthony as he re-entered the water to help his friend.

"Just about," replied an out-of-breath and shivering Jimmy.

Taking Anthony's arm, Jimmy stumbled to the shore.

"How is he doing?"

"Don't know," replied Anthony, "but it's not looking good."

A few yards away, Robert Cole was kneeling next to Dominic, the heels of his hands repeatedly pressing down into the boy's chest. Over six feet tall with carrot-red hair and an athletic frame, Dominic remained motionless.

"Come on, Dominic, come on," implored Robert as he continued to apply downward pressure.

There was no response. Tilting the boy's head back and pinching his nose, Robert took a deep breath and administered the kiss of life. A crowd had gathered. Returning cross-country runners had stopped to see what was going on, and others had arrived from the boathouse with blankets. With Robert Cole continuing to press down on Dominic's chest, Jimmy turned away and found Mark standing behind him.

"Think he's had it," whispered Jimmy.

Unable to watch any longer, Jimmy looked out onto the lake at the upturned boat. Moments later, a spluttering cough, followed by a roar of hope and encouragement from the onlooking crowd, caused him to spin around.

"Get me a blanket!" barked Robert as he furiously rubbed the boy's ice-cold limbs.

"Keep back. Give him space," shouted Mr Peters, his approach blocked by the encroaching crowd.

"Come on, Dominic, steady breaths. Come on now, breathe," commanded Robert.

But the boy's breathing was erratic and he was shivering violently.

"Ambulance is on its way," advised Mr Peters, having pushed through the crowd. "How's he doing?"

"He's hypothermic," replied Robert. "Work his legs and arms, we've got to warm him up. Where's that ambulance?"

As Daniel Peters frantically massaged Dominic's legs, Robert sat him up and continued to talk to him. The sound of two approaching ambulances could be heard, their klaxons growing louder with each advancing yard. A car carrying Mr Snyder and Mr Cheatham arrived.

"You're doing fine, Dominic," assured Robert as he maintained his abrasive grip. "You're doing fine. Can you hear me, Dominic? Can you hear me?"

"Y–yes, sir."

"What day is it, Dominic? Do you know what day it is?"

"It's ... it's Friday, sir."

"Good lad, Dominic, good lad," replied Robert, his relief all too evident. "We'll soon have you away from here."

"Stand back, stand back," ordered Mr Cheatham, holding an umbrella over Mr Snyder's dome. "Stand back and make way for the head."

The ambulances had arrived and two stretcher-bearing medics were making their way to the lakeside. Within no time, an oxygen mask covering his face and his body wrapped in blankets, Dominic was on his way to Keswick.

As if to signify the end of the drama, the rain stopped as suddenly as it had started and the passing storm gave way to resurgent sunlight. By this time, other staff members, including an out-of-breath Mr Dudley and Miss Saunders, had arrived at the scene and were directing pupils back to the school. Grace Connolly, satisfied that the situation was under control, made her way towards Robert Cole, who, a blanket draped around his shoulders, was in conversation with Daniel Peters.

"Is he going to be alright?" asked a concerned Grace.

"I think so," replied Robert, "but it was touch and go."

"What about the others?" enquired Daniel. "You said there were two or three people in the water. Are they okay?"

Robert winced. *The others!* He had been so preoccupied with Dominic, they had completely slipped his mind. Urgently looking about him, he was relieved to see Mark and Anthony standing over Jimmy, who was putting his pumps back on near the edge of the lake. The three boys looked drained: Jimmy and Anthony were visibly shivering and Mark, with his split lip and bloodstained singlet, looked a mess.

"Are you three alright?" asked Robert as he advanced towards them.

"Get these around you," ordered Grace, passing out the blankets Dominic had left behind.

"Where's Margaret?" asked Robert.

This time, it was Jimmy who winced. The last time he had seen her, she was still in the lake.

"Margaret!" he yelled as he scanned the immediate vicinity.

There was no sign of her.

"Maybe she has gone back to school," suggested Daniel.

"I didn't see her on the path," said Grace.

"She couldn't have gone back," insisted Jimmy, "she was completely done in."

"Margaret!" boomed Robert, advancing towards the lakeside. "Where did you last see her, Jimmy?"

"When we were in the lake … I thought she had come out behind me."

"Margaret!" shouted Grace, frantically looking about her.

And then Jimmy saw her. Partially concealed by an inlet, sitting cross-legged on the shale, her ample bulk pitching forward in a gentle rocking motion, Margaret Arbuckle stared across the water as if in a trance.

"Margaret!" shouted Jimmy, who was the first to reach her.

"Hello, new boy," said Margaret quietly, her speech slurred and her body shivering. "Is the head boy okay? I've got some chocolate if he wants some."

"He's going to be fine, love," assured Grace as she placed her coat around Margaret's frozen shoulders. "We can give him the chocolate later, lass."

Daniel Peters was already running to fetch the remaining ambulance crew when Robert dropped on his haunches next to Margaret.

"That was one of the bravest things I have ever seen, Margaret," he said as he and Grace massaged the girl's arms and legs.

"You don't know the half of it," declared Jimmy almost angrily. "But for her, he would still be in the boat."

"Just want to have a sleep," said Margaret drowsily.

"Can't sleep yet, Margaret," chastised Grace gently. "We've got to get that boy his chocolate, remember?"

The ambulance crew arrived.

"Looks like mild hypothermia," said one of the medics. "We'll have to get her out of these wet clothes."

"We can do that in the ambulance," said Grace. "I'll come with you."

As the stretcher-bearers struggled to carry Margaret across the uneven terrain, their stumbling progress was watched by Max Bradley, one of the volunteers appointed by Mr Dudley. Standing next to him, his friends, Lunt, Woosey and Reilly, adopted the pose of innocent bystanders. As Mark, Anthony and Jimmy followed the stretcher, Lunt established eye contact with them. Raising the forefinger of his right hand to his pursed lips, he paused for a moment before drawing the same finger across his throat. The message was clear: 'talk, and you're dead'.

"Didn't know whales swam in the lake," said Bradley to nobody in particular as the stretcher-bearers passed by.

Jimmy reacted immediately.

"What did you say?"

"Sorry?" queried Bradley innocently.

"She happens to be a friend of mine," said Jimmy stepping towards the bigger boy.

"So?" replied the cocksure Bradley.

"So, this," said Jimmy, lashing out with his fist.

Bradley stepped back and avoided the punch with ease, at which point Jimmy was restrained by Robert Cole.

"Enough of that," said Robert, lifting Jimmy off his feet and away from the smiling Bradley.

Jimmy glared at Bradley before following the stretcher to the ambulance.

"I'll deal with you later, Bradley," said Robert before walking after Jimmy.

"How's your lip, Pecky?"

Robert Cole spun around immediately but was unable to identify the source of the taunt. Nevertheless, he was sure the person responsible was one of the boys standing beside Bradley. With the crowd dispersing, Robert approached the ambulance as Grace climbed into the back of the vehicle.

"Grace," he called. "How is she?"

"Improving by the minute," replied Grace. "I'll give you a progress report as soon as I get back."

As the medic closed the door behind her, he issued a final instruction to Robert.

"Get yourself and those lads to a fire, get out of your wet clothes, drink something hot and get warmed up."

When the ambulance had pulled away, Robert escorted Mark, Anthony and Jimmy back to the boathouse, where they were provided with dry clothes, blankets and hot coffee which they drank huddled around an electric fire. When asked to explain what had happened, the boys gave a full account, omitting, of course, any reference to Lunt, Reilly or Woosey. When asked to explain his cut lip, Mark told Robert that he had fallen on the lakeside path. Not for the first time, Robert Cole did not believe him but let the matter pass. Once recovered, the boys were taken to the school infirmary for a check-up before being allowed back to their room. Later that day, they received a visit from Robert Cole and Grace Connolly.

"The school has been in touch with your parents to tell them what happened and to reassure them that you are all okay," said Robert.

"Unfortunately, Mark," advised Grace, "the school could not contact your parents, so we spoke with your Aunt Laura instead."

"Thanks," said Mark, his tone tinged with resignation.

"Now then," said a smiling Robert. "You will be pleased to know that the hospital has been in touch to inform us that both patients have made a rapid recovery and will be discharged tomorrow."

"They're being kept in overnight, but only as a precaution," added Grace.

"That's great news, miss," said Anthony.

"As a matter of fact, we're on our way to the hospital now to pay them a visit and wondered whether you three might want to come along," said Robert.

Half an hour later, in the reception area of the Mary Heweston Hospital, the boys waited quietly while Mr Cole and Miss Connolly enquired about the patients' whereabouts. Minutes later, they were ushered into a private room where a smiling Dominic Price, flanked by his parents, greeted them warmly.

"Hi, come in. I'm Dominic. I've been told what you did for me."

He paused for a moment.

"To tell you the truth, I'm a bit lost for words. How am I ever going to repay you?"

"It's Jimmy and Mark you should thank, and Mr Cole, of course," said Anthony modestly.

"Not forgetting Margaret Arbuckle," added Jimmy quickly. "It was thanks to her that we were able to get you out of the boat."

"Don't worry yourself on that score," said Dominic's father as he shook each boy's hand. "We know all about Margaret's part in the rescue."

"I'll be in to see her as soon as they let me," promised Dominic.

"We will never be able to repay you for what you did," said Mrs Price, who was reluctant to leave her son's side.

"I'm sure Dominic would have been the first to help if the boot had been on the other foot," said Robert.

"Nevertheless, we are forever in your debt," replied Mr Price.

"Well, we'll leave you with your parents," said Grace smiling. "I know the boys are anxious to see Margaret before they leave."

"Tell her we will be in to see her shortly," said Mr Price, "and thank you all again."

"Listen," said Dominic firmly, "if there is anything I can ever do for you three or Margaret, you only have to ask."

Looking into Dominic's eyes, Jimmy knew he meant what he said.

Having said their farewells, the boys, led by Robert Cole and Grace Connolly, made their way along the corridor where, in another private room, they found Margaret Arbuckle sitting up in bed talking to her parents.

"Hello," said a surprised Margaret as her visitors entered the room.

An awkward silence followed.

"Er … nice flowers," said Mark upon seeing the huge bouquet on the bedside cabinet.

"They're from the head boy's parents," explained Margaret. "How is he?"

"He's fine, thanks to you," said Jimmy.

"And you," replied Margaret.

"He'll be in to see you when they let him," said Anthony.

"Your parents must be very proud of you," said a smiling Robert.

"We certainly are," replied Mrs Arbuckle from the chair beside her daughter's bed.

"And so happy to see that her friends have taken the trouble to visit her," added a beaming Mr Arbuckle.

Margaret's face reddened.

"Why don't we leave you with your friends for a minute while we talk to Mr Cole and Miss Connolly outside?" suggested Mr Arbuckle.

"No. No need to …"

Unable to finish her sentence, Margaret's eyes widened in trepidation as the adults left the room.

"Sorry about that," she said when alone with the boys. "The *friends* thing, I mean."

Embarrassment quickly gave way to irritation.

"You didn't have to come, you know!" blurted Margaret.

"We wanted to, honestly," insisted Jimmy before looking to his roommates. "Didn't we?"

Mark and Anthony mumbled their agreement.

"Well, I don't know what all the fuss is about, I'll be out tomorrow," said Margaret.

"We know that," said Anthony, "we just wanted to ... we just ..."

"We just wanted you to know that what you did today ... we thought ... well, we thought you were fantastic," said Mark.

Margaret eyed the boys suspiciously for a few moments before responding.

"How's your lip? It looks very sore."

"Oh, I've had worse," shrugged Mark with a smile.

"Anyway," said Jimmy, "how do you know so much about boats?"

"What do you mean?" asked Margaret.

"You know, all that 'heeling', 'broaching' and 'reducing canvas' stuff you were going on about at the lake," said Anthony. "You sounded like a proper old sea dog."

Margaret hesitated for a moment before deciding that Anthony was trying to be nice.

"Been a member of Derwentwater Sailing Club for as long as I can remember ... just know a lot about boats, that's all."

"Right, you three," said Grace Connolly as the adults re-entered the room. "Time to let Margaret get some rest."

After further thanks from Mr and Mrs Arbuckle and much shaking of hands, the boys followed Robert and Grace out of the hospital.

"Who's for a fish and chip supper before returning to school?" asked Robert.

"I think we are all up for that," replied a cheerful Grace.

As they ate their fish and chips in the centre of Keswick, Robert brought up the subject of Michael Edwards and asked the boys if they would be interested in searching the school archive for any reference to the former headmaster. Much to Grace's delight, Mark, Anthony and Jimmy enthusiastically agreed to take on the task.

"Not exactly what I had in mind when I asked you out," said Robert after they had returned to school and the boys had made their way to their room.

"Perhaps it's for the best," replied Grace with a rueful smile.

Before he could muster a reply, Grace leaned forward and kissed Robert gently on the cheek.

"Time I was off home," she said.

And with that, she was gone.

CHAPTER ELEVEN

Private Rimmer

It was approaching four o'clock on the afternoon of the 20th of March 1918 and Tom was exhausted. From the crest of a fortified hill, he surveyed the battle-scarred landscape beneath him. To the west: allied trenches. To the east: German lines. Beyond the German lines: the French town of St Quentin, cowering in the gathering gloom. Tom lit a cigarette; imminent as the German offensive was, nothing was going to happen at this late hour.

Tasked with breaking up the enemy advance before it reached the British lines, the men of 5th Battalion occupied three forward positions. The hill manned by Tom and B Company had been chosen as the central outpost. Extensive quarrying had sliced away its western edge, creating a sheer cliff face which rendered a successful attack from the rear impossible. Between the hill and the flanking positions to the north and south lay belts of open, unguarded ground: if the flanks were overrun, the hill would be isolated and, ultimately, lost. Gaunt and weary, his boyish good looks long since eroded by the trauma of war, Tom discarded his cigarette before once again checking the hill's defences.

Behind the curls of barbed wire that protected the forward trench, a battery of Lewis guns awaited the enemy advance. Between each machine gun placement, lines of men, bayonets fixed, stood at the ready.

"Sir!" shouted an approaching corporal.

Tom turned abruptly and returned the corporal's salute.

"Message from Colonel Carnforth, sir."

"Yes, what is it?" asked Tom quietly.

"You must stand the men down and report to the colonel immediately."

Tom made his way to the dugout from where Colonel Herbert Carnforth was coordinating the battalion's defences. A large man in his early forties, the colonel had been commissioned from the ranks shortly after the beginning of the war in 1914. Though his courage could not be questioned – he had won the Military Cross for conspicuous gallantry in the field – his excessive devotion to duty and discipline disguised a craving for personal glory that rendered him a danger to his men. Despite having risen from the ranks, he took little interest in the welfare of those he commanded and rarely consulted his junior officers, least of all Tom. Perhaps it was the fact that Tom had won the Victoria Cross that so irked the colonel: perhaps it was because he was popular with the men. Only recently back from leave, the colonel was in his usual surly mood when Tom entered the dimly lit dugout and saluted.

"Sir, you wanted to see me?"

"At ease, Captain," replied the colonel, who neither looked up nor bothered to return Tom's salute.

Seated at a table, the colonel continued to study the map spread out before him. After making Tom wait a few seconds, he finally raised his head from the map and addressed his junior officer.

"Reconnaissance has confirmed massive enemy troop movement towards the front, which means the offensive is imminent."

This much Tom already knew.

"We are pretty confident the attack will commence at dawn tomorrow, so make sure the men are prepared."

"Yes, sir," replied Tom.

Rising from his chair, the colonel looked Tom squarely in the eye.

"I am sure I need not impress upon you the vital importance of our task here. Our duty is clear: to defend our position to the last round and the last man."

Tom held the colonel's stare.

"I have no doubt, Colonel, that the men will do their duty," he said firmly.

"Yes, Captain, but to the last round and the last man. Is that clear?"

Tom did not respond. The colonel's lust for glory sickened him.

"Please convey that order to the men. That will be all."

"Thank you, sir," replied Tom, who saluted before turning to leave.

"And Captain, tell the men the padre will be available tonight to hear confessions."

"Yes, sir," replied Tom.

"And make sure I am not disturbed for the next couple of hours," added the colonel as he took to his cot in the corner of the dugout.

Once outside, Tom paused and pulled the collar of his greatcoat about his ears to deflect the cold easterly wind. Reaching into the breast pocket of his tunic, he retrieved the silver cigarette case that his father had sent him the previous Christmas. Before extracting a cigarette, he read for the thousandth time the sentiment engraved on the front of the case:

T. H.C.

Filius est pars patris

As he smoked his cigarette, Tom pushed aside thoughts of home and thought about what he would say to his men. When entering the improvised dugouts where they were resting, he did his best to soften the chilling message he carried from Colonel Carnforth.

"Looks like it's on for tomorrow, lads, so get all the rest you can," he advised.

"Hard day tomorrow, boys, but nothing we can't handle," he confidently predicted at each stop.

"The padre's looking bored and tells me he's open for business," he joked repeatedly.

"Any letters home are to be handed to Corporal Jackson no later than twenty-three hundred hours," he casually announced, his matter-of-fact tone vainly seeking to disguise the true significance of his message.

But the old hands could read between the lines and were not taken in. Despite their welcoming smiles, Tom knew that he wasn't fooling anybody. But he refused to order his men to fight to the death. Such an order could only encourage despair. If death was inevitable, Tom could see no point in announcing its approach.

Having completed his rounds, Tom retired to the dugout he shared with Lieutenants Miller and Horne, who were busy elsewhere, organising the transfer of ammunition and other supplies to the forward position. Alone in the dugout, Tom took off his greatcoat and tunic and snatched a couple of hours' sleep. Shortly before nine o'clock, he was woken by the returning Lieutenant Horne, who informed him that everything was in order and that sentries had been posted for the night. Deciding to check on the men one final time, Tom made his way along the forward trench. Shortly after entering the trench, Tom was met by Sergeant Holmes, the tall, no-nonsense former policeman who had served with him throughout the previous two years. Five years older than Tom, the two had grown to trust each other implicitly. All was quiet as the men sat about playing cards or writing letters while those assigned sentry duty peered cautiously into the night from their positions on the fire step.

"Evening, sir," said the sergeant saluting Tom.

"Evening, Bernard," replied Tom. "Are the men settled for the night?"

"Everything's fine here," assured the sergeant as they walked the trench.

"Good," said Tom, "because the German offensive is almost certainly due to commence at dawn."

"No doubt about it, sir," asserted Holmes confidently.

"How so sure?" asked Tom.

"No rats, sir, they've all jumped ship."

Tom smiled in appreciation of the sergeant's logic. Rats, some the size of cats, infested the trenches in their millions. Scampering over the faces of the men as they slept, feeding on the fallen, the hated vermin were constant companions, at least when it suited them. Relying upon some sixth sense, the rats would desert a trench shortly before a heavy artillery attack. That night, there was not a rat to be seen. Making his way through the trench, Tom repeatedly stopped to encourage the men. Roughly halfway along the trench, he stopped behind a soldier who, pitched forward on the fire step, stood motionless.

"Any sign of activity out there?" asked Tom.

There was no reply.

"Answer the officer when he speaks to you," urged Sergeant Holmes.

The soldier did not respond: he was asleep. Sergeant Holmes reached up, grabbed the soldier by the collar of his greatcoat and pulled him to the floor. Landing heavily on his back, the winded soldier stared up from the ground, his expression of surprise morphing into one of horror. Sergeant Holmes could not contain himself.

"Sleeping on duty! Get to your feet."

As he picked himself up from the floor, the blood rushed from the soldier's face. Sleeping on duty was punishable by execution.

"No, Sergeant, no … I was just … I was just …"

"Don't lie to me," interrupted Holmes. "Admit it, you were asleep."

Aware of the possible consequences, the soldier was not about to admit anything.

"No, Sergeant … I wasn't asleep, I mean … I was only …"

Recognising the abject fear in the soldier's eyes, Tom intervened.

"How old are you?" he asked quietly.

"Eighteen, sir," replied the soldier, close to tears.

"He's one of the replacements, sir," explained Holmes, his eyes fixed on the young man. "Sleeping on duty? You could be shot for this!"

The soldier flinched.

"Shall I place him under arrest?" asked Holmes.

"No, wait," said Tom. "How long has he been on watch?"

"Two hours," replied Holmes.

Tom looked up and down the trench, conscious of the expressionless stares of the onlooking men.

"Return to your post," ordered Tom, "you will be relieved in an hour."

"You heard the officer," chivvied the sergeant after a moment's pause. "Get back on that step, keep your eyes peeled and woe betide you if you fall asleep again."

Scarcely able to believe his good fortune, the young soldier leapt back on the fire step, clutched his rifle and resumed his watch.

"I would appreciate it, Sergeant, if Colonel Carnforth didn't hear about this," said Tom quietly as the pair continued along the trench.

"Mum's the word, sir," replied the sergeant.

"Who is he anyway?" asked Tom.

"Rimmer, sir, Private John Rimmer."

From his position on the fire step, Private Rimmer offered a prayer of thanks to his God. His heart was thumping. Never having seen action before, his nerves were shot. Staring into the black abyss that was no man's land, he clutched his rifle tightly and silently wept.

Upon returning to his dugout, Tom ate a light meal before writing a letter home. Confident that it would be the last letter he would ever write, he nevertheless took pains to keep that conviction to himself. That night, sleep proved impossible. Lying motionless on his bunk, Tom felt like a condemned man awaiting execution.

CHAPTER TWELVE

Engaging the Enemy

An hour before dawn, the men were roused from their dugouts. Bayonets fixed, they took up their positions on the fire step. As daylight encroached, the dense mist that cloaked the opposing lines showed no sign of lifting.

"Damn it!" muttered Tom. "This fog could kill us. If we can't see the enemy, how are we supposed to fight him?"

Sergeant Holmes did not reply.

Tom cringed as he heard the voice of Colonel Carnforth rallying the men.

"To the death! We fight to the death!" shouted the colonel as he travelled the trench.

At 6:30 am precisely, the German artillery began its deafening bombardment of the British lines, and Tom knew that the onslaught would soon commence. Serenaded by the whistling salvos of enemy shell fire, the men of B Company peered cautiously into the mist and waited. At exactly 8:30 am, the shelling gave way to the sound of rifle and machine gun fire: the flanking positions were under attack. Moments later, Tom was approached by Corporal Jackson.

"Sir, a message from Colonel Carnforth. He asks that you report to him immediately."

When Tom entered the dugout, the colonel was talking into a field telephone.

"Hold at all costs. Do I make myself clear? Do your duty."

Putting down the telephone, the colonel turned and faced Tom.

"Sir," said Tom saluting.

"Well, Captain, it would seem that the hour has come. Both A and C companies are under heavy attack and are surrounded."

"Then we are in danger of being cut off from our lines," replied Tom.

"Order the men to hold fire until the enemy is in sight."

"But sir," protested Tom, "if we were to concentrate our mortar and machine gun fire on the flanks, we might relieve the pressure on our positions."

"Are you questioning my authority, Captain?" barked the colonel. "We will not fire blind and waste ammunition. You have your orders."

Upon leaving the dugout, an exasperated Tom approached Sergeant Holmes. Visibility was a mere twenty yards.

"Pass the word, Sergeant: every man to hold their fire until the enemy is in sight."

Tom made his way to the centre of the trench, rallying the men as he went. The diminishing machine gun fire from the flanking positions told him they were close to being overrun. Moments later, enemy mortars blitzed the hill.

"Open fire!" screamed Tom as German storm-troopers, their rifle fire spitting into the trench, emerged from the fog.

Along the length of the trench, men fired at will into the advancing formation. Rank after rank of invading infantry fell before the devastating British machine gun fire, their descent to earth cushioned by the belts of barbed wire. With the bodies of the fallen providing stepping stones across the bladed entanglements, the charge briefly gained momentum before running into the bayonets of B company. Confronted with desperate resistance, the attack slowed and faltered. Somehow, for the moment at least, defeat had been postponed: the Germans were in retreat.

A breathless Tom could hear the colonel rallying the men some fifty yards to his right.

"To the death! To the death!"

Tom looked at his watch: it was not yet nine o'clock.

"Sergeant Holmes!" he bellowed, intent on evaluating the company's remaining strength.

Stumbling over the dead and wounded, Holmes approached his captain.

"Well, Sergeant?"

"I'd say we've lost half our men," reported Holmes. "Three machine gun crews are out of action, and our flanks are under increasing pressure. Orders, sir?"

"Erect bombing blocks either end of the trench. If they want to get in that way, let's give them a warm welcome."

Tom set off in search of Colonel Carnforth. After only a few yards, his progress was halted by the explosion of incoming mortar fire. Their bodies pressed into the walls of the trench, the men of B Company stoically awaited their fate. Twenty minutes later, German stormtroopers, their guttural battle cries announcing their renewed intent, surged up the hill. Those who were able mounted the fire step and fired into the mist. Sticking stubbornly to their task, their remaining Lewis guns rattling in defiance, the defenders refused to yield. With the enemy only yards from the trench, bitter hand-to-hand combat resumed. Their numbers dwindling, the British continued to hold.

Through the corner of his eye, Tom caught sight of Colonel Carnforth on the lip of the trench, beating back the invader. For all his faults, thought Tom, the man did not lack courage. Distracted by the colonel's heroics, Tom suddenly found himself on the floor, the bayonet of a burly stormtrooper slicing open his right cheek. As the German stood poised to strike the killer blow, the eyes of the two foes met. Maybe it was the look of calm resignation on Tom's face that caused his enemy to hesitate; perhaps it was the lack of a killer instinct. Tom would never know.

"Up you get, sir," encouraged Sergeant Holmes, his bayonet thrust having ended the German's war.

Back on his feet, Tom screamed at the men to keep firing. Surveying the length of the trench, he was amazed to see that it was again clear of the enemy. Unbelievably, the enemy was retreating into the mist for a second time.

"Cease fire! Cease fire!" ordered Tom, determined to save precious ammunition.

A stillness, laced with the moans of broken and dying men, fell upon the hill. Stepping over the dead and wounded, Colonel Carnforth approached his junior officer.

"Captain!" barked the colonel.

"Sir," replied Tom, his handkerchief held to his cheek in a futile attempt to stem the bleeding.

"Keep the men at the ready. I will be in my dugout. I must contact Brigade and tell them that we are still holding."

Tom had little doubt that Brigade HQ had by now been overrun. After the colonel had departed, he turned to Sergeant Holmes.

"Report, Sergeant?"

"Lieutenants Miller and Horne are dead, sir, ammunition is low, and we are down to about fifty men, including the walking wounded."

"Well, we obviously can't defend the entire trench," said Tom. "Move the men to the centre and concentrate our fire. Better make it quick, Sergeant."

"Sir!" shouted a soldier from the fire step. "Sir, you'd better get up here and listen to this."

Mounting the fire step, Tom peered into the mist and listened.

"Flag of truce. I am a German officer. Hold your fire. Flag of truce. I am unarmed."

"Pass the word to hold fire," ordered Tom.

Gaining confidence with every step, the German officer, a white rag held above his head, picked his way through the corpse-strewn barbed wire before coming to a halt some twenty yards from the trench.

"Shall I get the colonel?" asked Holmes.

"No," replied Tom, his eyes fixed on the German officer, "not yet."

"Is there an officer with whom I can parley?" shouted the German in perfect English.

Breaking open his Webley Mark VI revolver, Tom checked the chamber and saw it contained just one bullet. After pausing for a moment, he handed the weapon to Sergeant Holmes.

"Here," said Tom. "If he isn't armed, it would be an act of bad faith for me to carry this."

Tom climbed out of the trench and approached his enemy. Approximately forty years of age, angular of frame and sporting a pencil-thin moustache, the German drew himself to attention.

"Major Albrecht Hartmann," he said with a polite nod of his head.

"Captain Thomas Cole," replied Tom saluting his enemy. "What can I do for you, Major?"

Major Hartmann smiled.

"You can ease my conscience, Captain, that is what you can do for me."

"I'm sorry, sir, but I don't quite understand," replied Tom.

"Then let me get straight to the point as we do not have much time. The point is this, Captain. Your flanking positions, together with your lines to the rear, have been completely overrun. The battle is over, and, on this occasion, my side has won."

Tom had no reason to believe that the major was lying.

"Therefore, it occurs to me that there is nothing to be gained by your continued resistance," said the major. "Yes, you could fight on to the death, and no doubt you could take a few more Germans with you, but you know there can be only one possible outcome."

"Are you inviting our surrender, Major?" asked Tom.

"Yes, Captain, I am. Your men, and mine, have more than done their duty today. Don't condemn any more of them to die in this wasteland, not when the battle has been lost, not when they no longer have a cause."

"Unfortunately, Major, the decision is not mine to make," replied Tom. "But, with your permission, I will communicate your offer to my commanding officer, Colonel Carnforth, though I have little doubt that he will reject it."

"Perhaps you can persuade him otherwise," encouraged the major.

Tom looked him square in the eye and felt warmed by his decency.

"I will be happy to try, Major."

"Then be quick, Captain, as my superiors will not hold back indefinitely."

"How long have I got?" asked Tom.

"I can give you fifteen minutes at the most. If your men do not leave the trench with their hands held aloft within that time, then I do not doubt that the attack will recommence."

"Then I'd better be off," said Tom.

"Good luck, Captain," said Hartmann.

As he turned to re-join his men, Tom paused momentarily before again addressing the major.

"Major Hartmann …"

"Yes, Captain?"

"Where did you learn to speak such good English?"

"My English mother," replied the major with a smile.

"She met my father when holidaying in the United States."

Tom paused for a moment.

"Major, whatever the outcome, thank you."

With another slight nod, Major Hartmann saluted his enemy before disappearing into the mist.

"Well, sir?" asked Holmes when Tom re-entered the trench.

Tom looked around him, acutely aware of the hope invading the haunted faces of his men.

"Keep the men on stand-by, Sergeant," ordered Tom softly. "I have to see the colonel."

CHAPTER THIRTEEN

No Surrender

When Tom entered the dugout, Colonel Carnforth was hastily feeding maps and documents into a large metal box.

"Where have you been?" he asked testily.

Tom was not given time to respond.

"All lines of communication to Brigade are down," snapped the colonel as he put a match to the papers. "I must therefore assume that our lines to the rear are continuing to engage the enemy. The situation remains as before. We must continue to hold. We fight to the last. What is our remaining strength?"

"Approximately fifty men, including the wounded," replied Tom.

"Excellent. I want every man who can hold a rifle on the fire step now."

Momentarily mesmerised by the flickering flame, Tom quickly gathered his thoughts. Clearly, the colonel was determined to fight to the bitter end, however hopeless the cause.

"Colonel, I must speak with you."

"Not now, Captain, not now. Our place is on the fire step with the men. Follow me."

"Wait!" insisted Tom, blocking the exit.

"We do not have time to wait," replied the colonel sternly.

"For God's sake, hang on!" implored Tom, standing his ground. "I have to report that the enemy has invited our surrender."

"Surrender?" queried the colonel.

"Yes, surrender. Colonel, the battle is over, our lines have been overrun, and to resist further would be futile. The men have done their duty, to carry on would be tantamount to murder."

"Get out of my way," ordered Carnforth, his right hand clasping the butt of his holstered revolver.

"Colonel, think of your men," beseeched Tom.

Colonel Carnforth stepped back and drew his revolver.

"For the last time, stand aside."

"Just surrender, can't you? I won't go back out there. Please, don't make me go out there," begged a sobbing voice from the rear of the dugout.

Immediately distracted, Colonel Carnforth turned and saw Private John Rimmer, his body curled into a ball, his eyes tightly shut, cowering under the cot in the corner of the dugout. Overcome with rage, the colonel raised his revolver and pointed it at the terrified boy.

"No!" yelled Tom, too late to prevent a bullet tearing into Rimmer's right thigh.

Knocked to the floor by Tom's desperate lunge, the colonel grabbed him by the lapels of his greatcoat and took him down with him. Bigger and stronger than his junior officer, the colonel turned Tom on his back and pinned him to the floor. Sat astride his quarry, his left hand clasped tightly around his neck, Carnforth slowly brought his revolver to bear. With his strength ebbing away, Tom made one last effort to pry the colonel's fingers from the trigger. His resistance waning by the second, Tom closed his eyes in anticipation of a shot he would never hear. But hear it he did. As the crack of the shot subsided, the death grip around Tom's neck relaxed. The life knocked out of him, Colonel Carnforth slumped sideways onto the boarded earth. When Tom opened his eyes, he saw Private Rimmer, his right leg drenched in blood, his youthful features devoid of expression, sitting on the cot.

"You shot him," said Rimmer quietly. "You shot him."

Before Tom could muster a response, Sergeant Holmes rushed into the dugout.

"Are you alright, sir?"

Fighting to regain his breath, Tom raised himself to his knees.

"Is he dead?" he asked.

Bending on one knee, Holmes gently pressed two fingers into the soft hollow of flesh next to the colonel's throat. There was no pulse.

"I'm afraid so, sir."

"He left me no choice," gasped Tom.

"Look, sir ..." said Holmes.

"Never mind 'Look sir'," interrupted Tom angrily. "He left me no choice!"

"You killed him. You killed him," murmured Rimmer, his eyes fixed on the colonel's body.

Tom got to his feet.

"We have to get the men out."

"But, sir..."

"Enough, Sergeant. We haven't got time. Get the men together now. The Germans have invited our surrender. If we don't respond immediately, they will recommence their attack and that will be the end of us. Rig up a white flag, tell the men to leave their weapons and lead them out from the centre of the trench, arms held aloft. I'll bring up the rear."

"What about him?" asked Holmes with a nod towards Rimmer.

"Take him with you," replied Tom before turning to face the bewildered private. "Rimmer, pull yourself together. You were never here. This never happened. Do you understand?"

"But you killed him!" repeated Rimmer. "You killed him!"

"What about the colonel?" asked Holmes.

"Tell the men that the colonel has ordered our surrender. Tell them that he insists on staying behind to carry on the fight alone. Got it?"

"I've got it," replied Holmes without enthusiasm.

"And Sergeant?"

"Sir?"

"My revolver, if you please."

Having recovered his sidearm, Tom again turned to Rimmer.

"Go with the sergeant. Do exactly as he tells you."

Still in a state of shock, Rimmer was not listening.

"Leave him to me, sir," said Holmes, "I'll take care of him."

Within minutes of leaving the dugout, Sergeant Holmes and the surviving members of B Company stood ready at the centre of the trench.

"Take them out, Sergeant," ordered Tom, his left hand massaging his neck.

Cautiously, a white garment held high above his head, Sergeant Holmes led the men into captivity. As they filed silently out of the trench, those who were able fixed Tom with looks of gratitude. But the men were confused. They had heard shots from the dugout. Where was the colonel? Why was he not leading the surrender? For now, such questions could wait. They had been delivered, their death sentence suspended, they were re-born.

"Tell Sergeant Holmes that I won't be joining him," said Tom to the last soldier to leave the trench.

"Tell him what?" replied the confused soldier.

"Just tell him," snapped Tom before softening his tone. "Just tell him."

Some fifty yards beyond the barbed wire, the survivors of B Company were collected by their captors.

"Where is the captain?" demanded Holmes when approached by the last man out of the trench.

"He said to tell you he was staying behind," replied the soldier.

"He said what?"

"He said to tell you he was staying," repeated the soldier.

Perplexed, Holmes looked back towards the fog-bound trench.

"What's going on, Sergeant?" asked the bewildered soldier.

His eyes still fixed on the invisible hill, Holmes paused before answering.

"The captain won't be joining us."

Raising his voice, Holmes addressed the men.

"The colonel and the captain are staying behind, they won't be joining us."

A ripple of tired reaction travelled the ranks.

"Sorry, Sergeant, we don't understand," confessed a soldier on behalf of his comrades. "What were those shots we heard coming from the dugout?"

"The colonel put paid to a couple of rats, that's all," lied Holmes.

The men, he knew, were not convinced.

"Why are they staying behind?" asked another.

"It's like this," replied Holmes. "The colonel and the captain agreed to surrender on one condition: that they stay behind and carry on the fight."

"The colonel agreed to that?" asked an astonished soldier.

"He did," replied the sergeant firmly.

Murmurs of disbelief rolled through the thinning fog.

"We owe them a great debt," continued Holmes, his eyes falling on one soldier in particular. "Isn't that right, Private Rimmer?"

Pale and badly shaken, his right thigh heavily swathed in a makeshift bandage, Private Rimmer looked into the sergeant's eyes and silently nodded his head.

*

The telegram did not arrive until the beginning of April. Having cycled up the winding driveway, the postman lowered his bicycle onto the gravel before pausing for a moment to regain his breath. Ascending the steps of the grand front entrance, he pulled on the bell. When the maid opened the door, she accepted the telegram and studied it briefly before raising a hand to her mouth in dismay: telegrams from the War Office rarely contained good news. Bowing his head in silent commiseration, the postman returned to his bicycle and went on his way. The maid found Richard and Brigit Cole at the rear of the house, tending one of their impressive gardens. Busy clearing leaves and other winter debris, it was Richard who first noticed the maid's approach. When she stopped some feet away on the verge of the lawn, Richard knew. As he walked towards the maid, Brigit Cole, unaware of her presence, continued about her work. It was only when Richard began reading the telegram, his frame stooped, that some instinct caused Brigit to look over her shoulder for her husband. As she approached him, Richard drew himself to his full height before calmly reading the telegram aloud.

"We regret to inform you that Captain Thomas Howard Cole of the 5th Battalion, King's Own Border Regiment, is missing in action, presumed killed."

Crippled by the devastating news, Richard handed the telegram to Brigit, sank to his knees and stared blankly into the distance. Like a mother comforting her child, Brigit drew his head into her lap and quietly read the telegram. Having confirmed its contents, she placed the telegram into her coat pocket, drew her husband closer, and cast her eyes south toward France.

"Don't despair just yet, Richard," she advised quietly.

"But Brigit, our boy, our beautiful boy ..."

"No!" interrupted Brigit forcefully. "No. I will not have it."

"But the telegram," persisted Richard rising to his feet.

"Telegrams can be wrong," insisted Brigit fiercely. "I would have known, I tell you, I would have known."

Some months after the end of the war, Brigit and Richard Cole received official notification that their son's grave had been located in a German cemetery on the Roupy Road in the region of Picardie. They were further informed that Tom had since been moved to a British cemetery on the outskirts of Savy, some three miles west of St Quentin.

CHAPTER FOURTEEN

Making Plans

"Where shall we start?" asked Jimmy.

It was Saturday 15th October, and the boys, having been briefed by Miss Connolly and Mr Cole, were about to make their first foray into the archives in search of Michael Edwards.

"This place is huge," observed Mark.

"It must have been part of the old abbey," said Anthony, his eyes fixed on the low vaulted ceiling.

"Abbey?" queried Jimmy.

"The Cistercian abbey I told you about."

Anthony sounded irked.

"Oh yes, I remember now, the Cistercians," said Jimmy sheepishly.

"Moving on then," said Mark, desperate to avoid another history lesson.

Further into the cellar, the boys found a table and sat down.

"Well, where *do* we start?" asked Jimmy.

Placing a notebook on the table, Anthony fished inside his trouser pocket for a pen.

"Let's start by writing down what we know," he said.

"That won't take long," muttered Mark.

"Well, we know that Michael Edwards was headmaster of the school between 1937 and 1941, and we know that he was murdered," said Anthony.

"It would help if we knew what it is we are trying to find out about this Michael Edwards," said Mark with a hint of frustration. "I mean, once we find out when he began teaching here, that's it, right? We'll know when he started at Grey Stones and when he finished. What more is there to know?"

"There's much more to it than that," insisted Anthony. "Where did he come from? What did he do before he came here? How old was he when he died?"

"Which football team did he support?" quipped Jimmy.

Anthony ploughed on.

"Why was he killed?"

"Who killed him?" added Jimmy, this time seriously.

"Okay, okay," responded Mark defensively. "So, where do you think we should start?"

"We need a structure," said Anthony. "Structure, structure, structure, that's what my dad always says."

"That's because your dad's a dentist," said Mark.

"I suggest we set ourselves two preliminary tasks," enthused Anthony, his tone slightly officious. "First task: to discover when Michael Edwards began teaching at the school. Second task: to find a photograph of him. There must be a photograph somewhere."

"Well, according to Miss Connolly, there are no photographs of him in Cole Hall, and there is no portrait of him in the Great Hall," said Mark.

"You have to admit, that's pretty strange," said Jimmy.

"It's almost as if he is hiding from us," agreed Mark.

"There's only one thing for it," said Anthony. "We will have to work our way back through the yearbooks from 1941, the year of his death, and find out when he first came to the school."

"I can do that," volunteered Jimmy.

"Okay," agreed Anthony, "you take on the yearbooks while me and Mark go through the minutes of the governors' meetings and any other stuff that might reference Michael Edwards. Who knows? We might even come up with a photograph."

"Right, it's ten o'clock," said Mark looking at his watch. "Let's give it a couple of hours and see what we turn up."

And with that, the boys went to work.

*

From the window of his room on the first floor of the north dormitory, Eric Lunt, the October edition of *The Scholar* in his hand, looked down upon the deserted quad.

"*Lady of the Lake*," spat Lunt. "Who writes this garbage?"

Repeating the offending headline did nothing to improve his foul mood. Turning from the window, he threw the school magazine to one side. From the front page of the discarded magazine, Mark, Anthony and Jimmy, pictured with Margaret Arbuckle and Dominic Price, smiled at Lunt from the floor.

"Heroes. The whole school thinks they're heroes," complained Lunt.

"If it hadn't been for us, they would never have been at the lake in the first place," protested Woosey in a rather pathetic attempt to placate his leader.

"If they think I've gone away, they're wrong," snarled Lunt. "Make no mistake, they are going to suffer."

"That's easy to say, but we've got to box clever," advised Max Bradley, stooping from his chair to retrieve the magazine. "We can't just walk up to them and beat them up. They're quite popular now after saving Price."

"Not scared, are you?" joked Reilly from the couch.

"Don't be thick," replied Bradley. "I'm all for teaching them a lesson. Cole had me collecting litter for a week, thanks to Johnston. But we can't rush things, we've got to be smart."

"That scouse peasant has got it coming," said Lunt.

"All I want is a chance to get even with that fat cow, Arbuckle," said Woosey from his seat next to Reilly.

"Sure you can manage it?" scoffed Bradley. "I heard she took you out with one punch."

"She was lucky, that's all," protested Woosey, his cheeks reddening. "Next time …"

"Yeah, yeah, yeah," interrupted an unimpressed Bradley.

"Never mind the whale," barked Lunt, "it's the others I want."

"I'm with you," said Reilly, "but Brad's right. We've got to box clever, there can't be any witnesses."

"Don't you think I know that?" replied Lunt impatiently. "The thing is, I don't just want to hurt them, I want to destroy them. They may be heroes now, but by the time I've finished with them …"

"What?" asked Woosey expectantly.

"They'll be expelled from the school, that's what," replied Lunt. "But not before Cheatham has flogged them."

"And when is all this going to happen?" asked Bradley glibly.

"Before Christmas," replied Lunt, who was again staring out of the window. "We'll leave them alone for a while, let them think we've gone away, and then we'll spring the trap."

"Aren't we going to beat them up in the meantime?" asked Woosey, keen to recover some standing.

"Don't be in such a hurry," said Bradley. "Eric's right; lull them into a false sense of security. By Christmas, they won't be expecting a thing, and we can give them a Christmas present to remember. Isn't that right, Eric?"

Lunt paused before answering. He was getting rather fed up with the condescending tone that accompanied Bradley's every utterance.

"That is right as it happens," replied Lunt turning from the window. "But what I've got in mind for them amounts to something more than a simple thrashing, and it will require planning. Between now and Christmas, I want them watched. I want to know their routine. I want to know what they get up to at weekends. I want to be sure that when the time comes, nobody will be around to help them."

Bradley briefly considered a sarcastic response but thought better of it. Lunt meant business, and he knew better than to push him too far.

CHAPTER FIFTEEN

Camera Shy

Mark was getting hungry.

"It's nearly twelve o'clock," he said as he thumbed through yet another edition of *The Scholar*.

Anthony didn't respond.

"Where are you up to with the minutes?" asked Mark.

"Summer term, 1936," replied Anthony.

"Found anything yet?"

"Nothing we didn't already know," sighed Anthony. "Michael Edwards, as you would expect, attended all of the governors' meetings when he was head, but other than that, nothing to report."

"I'm hungry," said Mark. "Fancy a walk into Keswick for something to eat?"

"You're on," replied Anthony pushing the minutes to one side. "Let's get Jimmy."

When Anthony and Mark found Jimmy, he was looking through the yearbook for 1929.

"How are you getting on?" asked Anthony.

"All I can say is that he was teaching here in 1929," replied Jimmy. "Whether or not that was the year he came to the school remains to be seen. Still, it's all a bit odd. Every yearbook contains a register of all the teachers and pupils who attended the school that year."

"What of it?" asked Mark.

"See for yourselves," replied Jimmy holding out the yearbook. "Every entry on the teaching register has a photograph next to it, all except for our Mr Edwards. And it's the same in every yearbook I've looked at. Even when he was headmaster, there are no photographs next to his name."

"Are there other staff members who weren't photographed?" asked Mark.

"Not one," replied Jimmy.

"Then that proves it," said Anthony.

"Proves what?" asked Mark.

"That Michael Edwards had something to hide," replied Anthony.

"Looks like it, doesn't it?" said Jimmy. "It's all too much of a coincidence: no photographs in Cole Hall, no portrait in the Great Hall, and now this."

"But why?" asked Mark. "Why would he not want anyone to see his photograph or portrait?"

"Perhaps he didn't want to be recognised," suggested Anthony.

"Recognised by who?" asked Mark.

"By his killer, maybe," said Jimmy.

"Let's not get carried away," pleaded Mark.

"Well, it's possible, I suppose," mused Anthony.

"We can consider the possibilities later," said Mark. "I'm starving."

"Me too," said Anthony. "Come on, Jimmy, we're off to Keswick for something to eat. We can come back here this afternoon."

After leaving the library, the boys bumped into Emily Burton and Victoria Jennings.

"What are you three up to then?" asked Victoria.

"We're off to Keswick for something to eat," replied Anthony.

"We'll come with you," said Emily.

As they left Baird House, they saw Margaret Arbuckle walking towards them. Her school satchel was hanging from her shoulder, and she was pushing her bike.

"Alright, Margaret?" called Jimmy. "What are you doing in on a Saturday?"

"I left my stupid homework in the common room," replied Margaret sullenly.

"We're off to Keswick for something to eat if you fancy it," said Jimmy.

Unaccustomed to being invited anywhere by her classmates, Margaret maintained a suspicious silence.

"Oh, come on," coaxed Jimmy.

"Yes, come on, Margaret," insisted Emily.

"Hurry up, Margaret," ordered Mark, "I'm famished."

Unsure as to the sincerity of the invitation, Margaret took a chance.

"Alright," she said, "I'll come."

As they made their way through the gatehouse and onto the Borrowdale Road, Jimmy stopped.

"What about the church?" he said to nobody in particular.

"Church?" repeated Anthony.

"Yes, the church," said Jimmy. "Don't you remember? Miss Connolly and Mr Cole told us that Michael Edwards was buried at the Church of St John in Keswick."

"So?" queried Mark.

"Well, his gravestone might tell us something about him, like when he was born," said Jimmy.

"Why didn't I think of that?" reflected Anthony, who sounded slightly annoyed with himself.

"Who is Michael Edwards?" asked Emily.

"We can get to the church from Ambleside Road," said Anthony, ignoring Emily. "It's on our way."

"Great," said Jimmy, "let's do it."

"And then can we get something to eat?" pleaded Mark.

"Will somebody please tell me who Michael Edwards is?" asked Emily, who did not take kindly to being ignored.

"It's a long story," said Jimmy. "We'll fill you in on the way."

*

Situated in the heart of the bed and breakfast quarter, the pink sandstone spire of the Church of St John dominated the Keswick skyline. Renowned for its magnificent stained-glass windows, it was the beauty of the surrounding fells that persuaded parishioner and tourist alike to rest a while on the sturdy benches occupying the western terrace. Beyond the terrace, an extensive graveyard descended towards a curtain of trees behind which ran the Ambleside Road.

In the spring of 1961, intent, so he said, on supplementing his porter's earnings, Stanley Rimmer successfully applied for the part-time position of Sexton's Assistant. A regular visitor to the church, his application was well received, and his appointment unanimously confirmed. When Jimmy and his friends entered the graveyard, Rimmer was busy tending a grave further up the slope. He spotted them immediately.

"There must be hundreds of graves here," moaned Mark.

"Well, the sooner we start looking, the sooner we'll find him," said Anthony.

"Let's split up," suggested Emily.

"Good idea," agreed Anthony. "It shouldn't take long with six of us looking."

"Five of us, you mean," corrected Victoria with a nod towards Margaret.

Pushing her bike towards the benches on the terrace, Margaret was off for a rest.

"What's he doing here?" asked Jimmy after spotting Stanley Rimmer.

"He works here," replied Anthony. "I wonder if he knows where Michael Edwards is buried."

Aware that he was being approached, Rimmer stopped working on the grave he was tending, leant on his hoe and waited.

"Afternoon, Mr Rimmer," called out Jimmy brightly.

"Good afternoon," replied a baffled Rimmer. "What brings you all here today?"

"We are looking for a grave," said Victoria getting straight to the point.

"Then you've certainly come to the right place, miss," said Rimmer, who paused momentarily and smiled at his joke. "Any grave in particular?"

"Yes, the grave of Michael Edwards," answered Emily sternly. "Do you know where it is?"

"Michael Edwards?" repeated Rimmer, who was no longer smiling.

"Yes, he used to be headmaster of the school," said Jimmy.

"I know who he was," replied Rimmer cautiously.

"Did you know him?" asked Anthony.

"I knew him," admitted Rimmer, his tone slightly flustered. "What has Michael Edwards got to do with you, and why the interest in his grave?"

"I'm sorry," replied Emily, "we didn't mean to upset you."

"I'm not upset," replied Rimmer, stepping away from the grave. "I was just asking what Michael Edwards has got to do with any of you?"

"Look," said Anthony, "Miss Connolly and Mr Cole have asked us to do some research into Michael Edwards …"

"And that's why we thought we would visit his grave," interrupted Mark. "We thought we might discover when he was born."

"Well, I can't help it if the new teacher has asked you to find out about Michael Edwards," said Rimmer. "All I can say is that it's not part of my job to conduct tours of the graveyard, so, if you don't mind, it's time I was off."

As Rimmer walked towards the church, Anthony made one last effort to enlist his help.

"Mr Rimmer, please, before you go, it would save us a lot of time if you could at least tell us where his grave is."

"I'm sorry," replied Rimmer without stopping, "but I'm far too busy to be looking for graves."

"What was all that about?" asked Emily when Rimmer was out of earshot.

"I don't know," replied Anthony. "The mere mention of Michael Edwards and he goes scuttling off. Very strange."

"Stranger than you think," said Jimmy, his eyes fixed on the headstone of the grave that Rimmer had been tending.

A short silence followed while the friends read the inscription etched into the marble headstone.

Michael James Edwards

28 May 1894 – 30 August 1941

Fronti nulla fides

"How spooky," whispered Victoria.

"Look," said Mark, "somebody's left flowers on the grave."

"Is there anything to say who they are from?" asked Emily.

"There's a card," confirmed Mark, picking up the flowers. "It reads: *How I wish I could have known you. Your loving daughter, Grace.* Who's Grace?"

"Beats me," said Anthony.

Having deposited his hoe in the church basement, Rimmer returned to the western terrace just as Jimmy and his friends were making their way out of the graveyard.

"Excuse me, Mr Rimmer," shouted Emily, intent on questioning the porter further.

But Rimmer was not for talking. With a cursory glance in the direction of his would-be interrogator, he lowered himself into the driving seat of his green second-hand Morris Minor and drove away.

*

"Well, what do you make of that?" asked Anthony after the group had commandeered a table at The Blue Banana, a café close to the church.

"It's all pretty weird if you ask me," replied Mark as he concentrated on the menu.

"What do you think, Margaret?" asked Anthony.

"I think I'll have the apple pie, chocolate muffin and a lemonade," replied Margaret.

Anthony looked to heaven.

"Well, I think it is extremely weird," volunteered Emily. "We turn up looking for the grave of Michael Edwards to find it being tended by a school porter who obviously did not want us to find it."

"Perhaps he was just in a hurry," suggested Victoria touching up her nail varnish.

"And don't forget the inscription on the headstone," continued Emily ignoring her friend. "*Fronti nulla fides*, the school motto: 'don't judge a book by its cover'."

"It's like we are being asked to question what we find," said Jimmy.

Margaret and Mark left the table to order food.

"Well, at least we know when he was born," said Anthony.

"The 28th of May 1894," confirmed Emily, "which means that he was 47 when he died in 1941."

Anthony scribbled the date into his notebook.

"That's pretty old, isn't it?" said Victoria without looking up from her nails.

"Well, I agree with Mark and Emily," said Jimmy. "It's all very weird. Was it just a coincidence that Rimmer was tending the very grave that we were looking for, or what?"

"Coincidence or not," said Anthony, "he wasn't prepared to help us."

"Well, here's something else for you to think about," said Jimmy. "Michael Edwards shares a birthday with Captain Thomas Cole VC. They were both born on the 28th of May 1894."

"How do you know that?" challenged Emily.

"Because the 28th of May happens to be my birthday as well," explained Jimmy. "The captain's date of birth was the first thing I noticed when I read the plaque underneath his photograph in Cole Hall."

"What are you getting at?" asked Anthony.

"Well, what if Captain Cole and Michael Edwards are the same person?" ventured Jimmy.

"Impossible," declared Anthony. "We know the captain died in 1918."

"Do we? How?" asked Emily.

"Because it says so on the plaque under his photograph in Cole Hall," said Anthony impatiently. "Everybody knows that Captain Cole was killed in 1918 at the battle of Carnforth Hill and that Cole House was built in his memory by his father."

"The battle of Carnforth Hill?" queried Jimmy, who was clearly in the dark about the captain's war record.

"Yes, so named after Captain Cole's commanding officer, Colonel Carnforth," explained Anthony. "The colonel and his men were defending a hill near St Quentin in Northern France. When all was lost, the colonel accepted an invitation to surrender to save the lives of his men. But once his men were safe, the colonel and the captain continued to defend the hill alone until the trench was overrun: they were both killed. Colonel Carnforth was awarded a posthumous

Victoria Cross."

"So where are they buried?" asked Emily.

"Somewhere near St Quentin, I suppose," replied Anthony.

"How would we find out for sure?" asked Jimmy.

"We could always just ask Mr Cole," suggested Emily.

"I wouldn't, not yet," said Jimmy. "We might be barking up the wrong tree here. I wouldn't want to upset him for no reason."

"Why do you want to know where they are buried?" asked Anthony, uncomfortable with the thought that he might be missing something.

"Because if Captain Cole is buried in France, then he can't possibly be Michael Edwards," replied Emily.

"What about the captain's regiment?" suggested Anthony. "There must be a regimental record that would tell us where he is buried."

"Good point," agreed Emily. "Why don't I write to the regiment and ask?"

"Great idea," said Jimmy. "His regiment must have lots of information about him."

"So, are we saying Michael Edwards and Captain Cole are the same person?" asked Anthony.

"No," replied Jimmy. "But it's possible, isn't it? It's not just that they have the same date of birth, you said yourself that you thought Michael Edwards had something to hide. And remember when we saw Miss Connolly crying in front of the captain's photograph? What was all that about?"

"Miss Connolly was crying?" queried Emily. "Why?"

"Dunno," replied Anthony. "Maybe she was thinking about her father. She was telling us how he was shot down and killed in the Second World War."

"Yes, but can we be sure that was why she was crying?" asked Jimmy as Margaret and Mark returned with their food. "It's a bit odd, isn't it, that the person we found crying in front of the captain's photograph is the same person who now wants to know all about Michael Edwards, who just happens to share a birthday with the captain."

"And who is Grace, the daughter who left the flowers at the grave?" asked Emily.

"Who was crying in front of the captain's photograph?" asked Margaret taking her seat.

"Miss Connolly," replied Mark.

"Her name is Grace," said Margaret.

"How do you know that?" asked Anthony.

"Well, that's what Mr Cole called her before they took me to the hospital."

"Are you sure?" asked Jimmy.

"Very," replied Margaret, her eyes fixed on her chocolate muffin.

"This is getting stranger by the minute," said Jimmy. "If Miss Connolly is the Grace who left the flowers, she isn't asking us to research a family friend, she's asking us to research her father."

After leaving the Blue Banana, Margaret returned to her home in Keswick, and the others returned to school. By the time they arrived back at Grey Stones, it was after three o'clock.

"Right, I'm off for my run," said Mark as they approached Baird House.

"And I've got homework to do," said Victoria taking her leave.

"And then there were three," said Anthony.

Returning to the archives, Anthony, Jimmy and Emily continued to search for references to Michael Edwards. After studying the yearbooks for 1928 and 1927, they were still none the wiser as to when he had commenced teaching at the school.

"Let's call it a day," said Jimmy as he returned a yearbook to its shelf.

"Tomorrow, I'll write the letter to the captain's regiment and post it on Monday," said Emily. "By the way, what was the name of his regiment?"

"The King's Own Border Regiment, I think," replied Jimmy. "It's on the plaque in Cole Hall, we can check that now if you like."

"What's the address?" asked Emily.

"I don't know," replied Anthony. "Carlisle, I think. It will be in the phone book."

After leaving the archive, the friends headed off to Cole Hall to confirm the name of the captain's regiment. As they stood beneath his photograph, Jimmy stared at the Victoria Cross pinned to the captain's chest and again wondered for what brave deed it had been awarded.

"Do me a favour," he said to Emily. "When you write to the regiment, ask how the captain won his medal."

"Will do," said Emily.

CHAPTER SIXTEEN

Burying the Dead

In the company of the dead, Tom stared into the mist until satisfied that his men had crossed 'no man's land'. Overcome with guilt, he dismounted the fire step, retrieved his cigarette case from his pocket and gently kissed it. A few yards away, sitting against the wall of the trench, the body of Lieutenant Horne caught Tom's eye. His furrowed brow tilted slightly to one side, his eyes and mouth open, the dead Lieutenant stared at Tom in seeming disbelief. Spurred on by the prospect of imminent release, Tom drew his revolver from its holster, cocked the hammer, raised the weapon to his right temple, closed his eyes and pulled the trigger. The exquisite click of the rotating chamber lingered in Tom's ears for the few seconds it took him to regain his wits. Lowering the revolver, Tom lurched forward, doubled over and vomited. Wiping his mouth with the sleeve of his greatcoat, he slowly straightened up, approached Lieutenant Horne, and sat beside him. Having gently closed his dead comrade's eyes, Tom sat back, his eyes unblinking, deep in thought.

A few minutes later, having exited the northern end of the trench, Tom began to pick his way across the open terrain that separated the hill from the flanking position. The German advance having long passed, an eerie silence clung to the thinning fog. As he crossed the battlefield, the increasing number of German dead beneath his feet told him he was nearing his objective. Once through the barbed wire perimeter, the dead of A Company came into view, their prone bodies competing with their enemy for a place on the muddied earth. Upon entering the trench, Tom paused briefly to survey the grotesque aftermath of the battle. Some men looked like they were sleeping, others lay butchered and contorted, their faces preserving the tortured moment of their death. Knowing he might not have much time, Tom quickly walked along the trench, eyeing the bodies of dead British soldiers. He soon found what he was looking for. Sandwiched between the corpses of two German stormtroopers, the body of a British corporal invited further attention. Roughly the same height and build as Tom, the corporal's face was badly disfigured. Moving the German soldiers aside, Tom removed the corporal's wallet from his tunic, briefly checked its contents and replaced it with his own. Having swapped tunics and dog tags, Tom pulled the corporal some distance along the trench and placed him next to a fallen comrade. After placing his captain's hat on the corporal's head, Tom retrieved his cigarette case before pausing to convey a silent apology. Returning to the two German stormtroopers, he lay down between them, pulled their bodies around his own, closed his eyes and waited.

It was nearly midday when Tom heard German voices approaching the trench. Working parties had been detailed to dig pits in which to bury the fallen, and it was one such party that Tom could now hear. An hour or so later, the Germans entered the trench. One by one, the fallen of both sides were stretchered away and tipped into their respective pits. If the mass graves were properly marked, the bodies would be exhumed after the war and given proper burials. Sometimes, British officers were afforded special treatment, their bodies being buried alongside their enemy counterparts. But for those soldiers who had been blown to pieces or whose corpses had been swallowed by the battlefield, their final resting place would remain unknown.

It was nearly two o'clock when the stretcher-bearers reached Tom. As the first stormtrooper was lifted away, Tom, his eyes closed, groaned and listened to the animated conversation that followed. Unable to understand what was being said, Tom kept his eyes shut and hoped for the best. By the sound of it, an argument was taking place about what would be done with him. It was not unknown for enemy survivors to be shot immediately if it was thought that they had feigned injury. One of the stretcher-bearers stepped forward and patted Tom lightly on his left cheek to bring him around. Tom opened his eyes and affected a look of bewilderment. Convinced by the bruising to his neck and the gash to his right cheek that Tom was a genuine casualty of war, the Germans placed him on a stretcher and offered him a canteen of water. Having greedily sated his thirst, Tom lay back and checked the breast pocket of his tunic for the feel of his wallet. And with that, Michael Edwards was carried into captivity.

CHAPTER SEVENTEEN

Contradictions

"It's arrived!" exclaimed Emily as she burst into the fourth-form common room.

It was Thursday afternoon and lessons had finished for the day. Holding a large envelope, Emily's excitement was plain to see as she hurried towards her friends. It had been over a month since she had written to Captain Cole's regiment; half term had been and gone and now, at last, she had received a reply.

"I haven't opened it," said Emily. "I thought it only fair that we read it together."

"Quite right," agreed Anthony.

Hardly a week had passed without Miss Connolly or Mr Cole asking how the research into Michael Edwards was coming along. Now, perhaps, they would have something to report.

"Wait a minute," said Jimmy, aware of the attention that Emily's entrance had generated. "Why don't we take the letter to the archive and read it there?"

"Jimmy's right," said Mark, "there's no point in advertising our suspicions."

Minutes later, sitting around a dimly lit table in the archive under the library, the boys watched patiently as Emily opened the envelope.

"Okay," said Emily. "I wrote to the regiment and told them that I was co-ordinating a school project about the First World War and that I was especially interested in the battle of Carnforth Hill. I pretended that this was because a number of former pupils might have died in the battle. I specifically asked for information about Captain Cole, including how he won the Victoria Cross, how he died and where he was buried. Right, let's see what the regiment has to say."

The boys listened intently as Emily, reading aloud the regiment's reply, described how Tom had won his Victoria Cross at Thiepval Ridge. After referring to the other great engagements in which Tom and his battalion had fought, the correspondence turned to the battle of Carnforth Hill and the heroic actions of Colonel Carnforth and his young captain.

"What does it say about where they are buried?" asked Anthony after Emily had related the details of the battle.

"Here we are; listen to this," said Emily before reciting the relevant passage. *"Having ensured the survival of his remaining men by authorising their surrender, Colonel Herbert Carnforth and his loyal subordinate, Captain Thomas Cole, preserved the regiment's honour by fighting on alone. Both officers were killed. They were initially buried in a German cemetery at L'Epine-de-Dallon on the Roupy Road. Their remains were relocated to the British Cemetery at Savy in 1919."*

"Where's that?" asked Mark.

"Somewhere near St Quentin, I suppose," guessed Emily.

"Looks like I was on the wrong track," conceded Jimmy. "If the captain is buried in France, he and Michael Edwards can't be the same person."

"Well, that clears that up," said Anthony.

"Hold on, there is more," said Emily, who continued to read the correspondence aloud. *"The gallantry and perseverance displayed by B Company at the battle of Carnforth Hill have long been recognised. However, those defending the flanking positions should not be forgotten either. The scale of the loss incurred is reflected in the regimental casualty list dated 21 March 1918, an abridged version of which I have enclosed so that you might identify those former pupils of your school who died defending the forward positions all those years ago."*

Pausing momentarily, Emily reached into the envelope and recovered the casualty list, which she handed Mark.

"There must be hundreds of names on this list," he said as he scanned the pages before him.

Emily continued reading.

"*It should be noted that the German version of the defence of Carnforth Hill differs from the British account in one critical respect. The German account can be found in the memoir of Major Albrecht Hartmann entitled 'The March Offensive', the relevant passage of which I have enclosed. Major Hartmann was a highly decorated officer who survived the war, having seen action on both the Eastern and Western Fronts. His memoir, published in 1937, has largely been overlooked.*"

"What does he have to say?" asked Jimmy.

Emily retrieved the memoir from the envelope before continuing.

"Major Hartmann says as follows: *The progress made on the first day of the offensive was considerable, and many British prisoners were taken. This, I think, was due more to the dense low-lying fog that persisted late into the morning than to any element of surprise: the British knew we were coming, but they could not see us until we were pouring into their trenches. The only stubborn resistance I encountered that day was offered by the defenders of a redoubt subsequently referred to by the British as Carnforth Hill.*"

"What's a redoubt?" asked Jimmy.

"A fortified hill," replied Anthony.

Emily continued reading.

"*Having isolated the hill, we sustained heavy losses as the defenders valiantly repelled two heavy onslaughts. It was following the second assault that I suggested to my superiors that the enemy be offered the opportunity to surrender. Keen to avoid further unnecessary losses, I ventured alone to the hill under a flag of truce, where I was met by a young officer, Captain Thomas Cole. I shall never forget him. Despite what appeared to be a painful wound to his right cheek, he was very polite and respectful of my senior rank. It was clear to me that, if left to him, he would have accepted my invitation to surrender immediately. He assured me, however, that although the decision was not his to make, he would pass on my offer to his commanding officer, Colonel Carnforth. I told him that he had fifteen minutes to communicate a reply before hostilities recommenced, but he was obviously not convinced that his colonel would do anything other than fight on to the bitter end. After he had thanked me and returned to his men, I had little doubt that I would have to take the hill by force. It was a surprise, therefore, when the surviving defenders, approximately fifty men in all, eventually evacuated the hill and surrendered. Neither Colonel Carnforth nor Captain Cole appeared among the survivors. After the war, the British claimed that Colonel Carnforth and the young captain carried on defending the hill after the surrender. I can categorically state that this was not the case. After occupying the hill, I discovered Colonel Carnforth's body in a dugout. He had sustained a single shot to the head. We buried him and his fellow officers at the German Cemetery on the Roupy Road. The captain's body, despite an extensive search of the hill, which I supervised, was never found."*

It was Anthony who broke the prolonged silence that followed.

"I don't understand. If Captain Cole's body was never found, how can he have been buried with the colonel in the German cemetery?"

"And another thing," said Jimmy. "If the captain had died fighting alongside the colonel, why was his body not found by Major Hartman?"

"And how come the colonel's body was found in a dugout when he was supposed to be fighting to the death in the trench?" asked Anthony.

"So do we still think Captain Cole died at Carnforth Hill and is buried in France?" queried Emily.

"Just because Major Hartmann didn't find the captain doesn't mean that he wasn't found and buried by someone else," said Jimmy.

"Granted," replied Anthony, "but Major Hartmann's account does contradict the claim that both men fought to the death defending the hill."

"There's something else," said Jimmy. "Major Hartmann says that Captain Cole told him that it was up to Colonel Carnforth to decide whether or not to accept the surrender."

"So?" said Anthony.

"Well, that means that Colonel Carnforth was still alive during the ceasefire when the surrender was discussed," said Emily catching Jimmy's drift.

"And given," continued Jimmy, "that Major Hartman is sure that no further fighting took place after the surrender, you have to ask who *did* kill the colonel?"

"Hold on, professor," interjected Anthony. "Are you suggesting that Captain Cole killed him because if you are …"

"Well, if the Germans didn't kill him, who did?" asked Jimmy.

"Everybody, just be quiet for a minute," said Mark, who had continued to scan the casualty list. "You're not going to believe this."

"Believe what?" asked Emily. "What have you found?"

"This casualty list is dated 21st March 2018," replied Mark. "It lists Edwards 7348515 Corporal M.J. (Workington) as missing, believed killed."

"What?" queried Anthony. "Are you telling us that a person named M.J. Edwards was killed on the same day, in the same battle, as Captain Cole?"

"That's what it says here," replied Mark.

For a few moments, nobody spoke.

"That's it then," said Mark, the significance of the revelation having sunk in. "I'm convinced."

"It could be a different M.J. Edwards," suggested Jimmy.

"Might be," said Emily. "But then again, I'm thinking probably not."

"Problem is," said Jimmy, "how are we going to tell Mr Cole that we think his uncle, a war hero, quite possibly shot his commanding officer, deserted his post and stole the identity of a dead soldier before coming to teach at Grey Stones as Michael Edwards?"

"And what will we tell Miss Connolly?" asked Anthony.

"Well, I say that we don't tell anybody anything until we know more," said Emily.

"We still haven't found out when Michael Edwards began teaching here," said Mark.

"That shouldn't be a problem," said Jimmy rising to his feet. "Let me look at a few more yearbooks."

"Where are you up to?" asked Mark.

"Next stop is 1926," replied Jimmy.

After Jimmy had left the table, Mark, Anthony and Emily once again pored over the information provided by the regiment. Deep in the bowels of the archive, Jimmy studied the yearbooks for 1926, 1925 and 1924, all of which referred to Michael Edwards. After retrieving the yearbook for 1923-24, Jimmy found no such reference. Clearly, Michael Edwards had begun teaching at Grey Stones in the academic year commencing 1924. Returning to the records for that year, Jimmy recovered the minutes of the governors' meetings and went back to the table.

"Progress, I think," said Jimmy as he re-joined his friends. "The yearbooks confirm that Michael Edwards began teaching here in 1924, nearly six years after the war ended."

"Six years," repeated Anthony. "What was he doing between the end of the war and 1924?"

"What have you got there?" asked Emily.

"The minutes of the governors' meetings held in October 1924," said Jimmy. "I'm thinking that any new teaching appointment might have got a mention. Worth a look, hey?"

"Let me have them," demanded Anthony impatiently, "I've read so many of these minutes, I think I might know where to look."

Adjusting his spectacles, Anthony took the document from Jimmy.

"Well?" asked Mark after only a few seconds had elapsed.

"Give me a chance," complained Anthony. "If his appointment is mentioned anywhere, it should be under 'Staffing'."

Turning the pages, Anthony ran his finger through the minutes and soon found what he was looking for.

"Got it," he said before pausing for a few seconds. "The minutes read as follows: *The headmaster reported that the new history master, Mr Michael Edwards, had settled in well. Special thanks were extended to Richard Cole for his part in securing the new master's services.*"

Emily could hardly contain herself.

"Richard Cole! Tom Cole's father, the man who built Cole Hall in memory of his son!"

"Isn't that the bloke whose statue stands in the foyer of Cole Hall?" asked Jimmy.

"The very same," confirmed Anthony. "According to the minutes, Richard Cole was present at the meeting: he was a school governor."

"It all fits," said Mark. "Tom Cole returns home after the war having stolen the identity of a dead soldier, and his father helps to get him a job at the school."

"But why would his father help him to conceal his true identity?" asked Emily.

"It can only be because he had something very serious to hide," replied Anthony.

"Like killing his commanding officer?" suggested Jimmy.

"Well, I'm still not convinced about that," said Mark. "Granted, it looks like Captain Cole changed his name to Michael Edwards, but does that have to mean he killed Colonel Carnforth?"

"Whatever it means, we have to decide what to do next," said Emily.

"What will we tell Mr Cole and Miss Connolly?" asked Anthony.

"I say we tell them nothing," said Jimmy. "Let's think things through. I don't think I've ever told a teacher that I thought he was related to a murderer."

"Me neither," said Emily, "but we've got to tell them something."

"And don't forget Snyder," said Mark. "He won't be thrilled if we start trashing the school's reputation."

After leaving the cellar and locking the door behind them, the friends ascended the spiral staircase, turned off the lights, and headed to the refectory.

That evening in their room, the boys tried hard to put the mystery that was Michael Edwards to one side and concentrate on homework. But by ten o'clock, their academic duties fulfilled, the former headmaster once again dominated their conversation as speculation and conjecture rumbled into the night.

CHAPTER EIGHTEEN

An Inside Job

It was Monday 28th November, and the pupils of Form 4C were talking amongst themselves as they awaited the arrival of Mr Cheatham for registration.

"Silence," ordered the master as he entered the room.

After racing through the register, Mr Cheatham addressed the class.

"For reasons that will soon become apparent, this morning's first lesson has been cancelled. When you leave this room, you will report immediately to the Great Hall, where a special assembly will be held. You will make your way to the hall in absolute silence. Is that clear?"

The class exchanged quizzical looks.

"Dismissed," barked the master.

By the time 4C entered the hall, most of the school was already seated. When Mr Snyder and Mr Cheatham entered the stage, the hum of curiosity that had infiltrated the ranks subsided, and the assembly rose to its feet. Standing behind the head, Mr Cheatham flexed his rattan cane. Having approached the lectern in the middle of the stage, Mr Snyder straightened his tie and addressed his audience.

"Be seated."

The sound of pews creaking beneath the weight of six hundred pupils signalled the porters' departure from the hall. Once they had left, Mr Snyder gripped the lectern with both hands. When he spoke, his tone was solemn.

"You will undoubtedly be wondering why I have called you here this morning. Well, let me satisfy your curiosity immediately. It is my sad duty to inform you that we have thieves in our midst."

The astonished reaction that followed was short-lived.

"Silence!" ordered Mr Cheatham.

Mr Snyder hesitated for a few seconds before continuing.

"It grieves me to report that a much-valued portrait, a work of great importance, was misappropriated from my office during the night."

Sitting two rows from the front of the stage, Philip Campbell, a first-former, turned to his neighbouring classmate, Lawrence Rowlands.

"What does 'misappropriated' mean?" he whispered.

"Not sure," muttered Lawrence. "I think it means *pinched*."

"You, boy!" shouted Mr Cheatham, his eyes fixed on Lawrence. "Perhaps you would like to join me on the stage?"

All too aware of his deputy's methods, Mr Snyder stepped away from the lectern.

"Yes, you," confirmed Mr Cheatham pointing his cane at Lawrence. "The boy who thinks he can talk when the head is addressing the school."

The colour having drained from his face, Lawrence Rowlands edged out of the pew and slowly made his way onto the stage.

"Hurry up, we haven't got all day," commanded Cheatham. "What is your name?"

"Lawrence Rowlands, sir," replied the boy meekly, his arms stuck to his sides like a soldier on parade.

"Let's get on with it then," ordered Cheatham with a wave of his cane.

Trembling, Lawrence extended his right arm and presented the palm of his hand. Intent on savouring the moment, The Cheat waited a few seconds before raising the cane above his head and arching it into the boy's fingers. Shocked by the excruciating pain, Lawrence cried out.

"Up!" demanded The Cheat with a gesture of his stick.

As the boy raised his left arm, the bewildered expression on his face morphed into one of agony as Cheatham's second delivery bit more savagely than the first.

"Up!" repeated the master.

Reduced to tears by the third stroke, Lawrence looked about the stage for help. Untouched by the boy's suffering, Cheatham pressed on.

"And again!"

Having delivered the final brutal stroke, the faintest of smiles briefly played about the master's face.

"Now get back to your place and not another word."

His eyes awash, his hands pulsating with pain, and his dignity savaged, Lawrence, avoiding all eye contact, returned to his seat.

"Thank you, Mr Cheatham," said the head upon returning to the lectern. "Perhaps now I shall have everybody's attention. As I was saying, the painting in question, a rather handsome portrait, was stolen from my study. Having inspected the crime scene and given the total absence of any evidence of forced entry, it is painfully obvious that those responsible belong to the school. To embrace the criminal vernacular, this was an *inside job*."

A chorus of whispers travelled the hall.

"Quiet!" boomed Cheatham.

"Needless to say," continued the head, "when the culprits are found, their punishment will be immediate and severe. Not only will they be thrashed before the entire school, but they will also be expelled and possibly prosecuted."

His grip tightening further on the lectern, Mr Snyder struggled to control his anger.

"I must inform you that until those responsible for this reprehensible crime either give themselves up or are apprehended, every pupil in this school will be deemed a suspect."

Outraged by the headmaster's tirade and unable to hide his contempt any longer, Robert Cole rose from his seat and left the hall. Oblivious to the defection, Mr Snyder ploughed on.

"Whilst the punishment meted out for this offence shall be severe, an appropriate reward will be bestowed on those who provide information leading to the apprehension of the thieves. An especially generous reward will be afforded to those who provide information leading to the recovery of the portrait. Those with information to impart should report to Mr Cheatham immediately."

At the mention of his name, Mr Cheatham pushed out his chest and raised himself to his full height. Clutching his gown with both hands, Mr Snyder delivered his ultimatum.

"I would remind you all that the school's reputation is at stake. Today is Monday the 28th of November. If by Friday the 26th of December, the end of term, the portrait has not been returned or the culprits identified, all school privileges will be withdrawn in the New Year. The many will suffer for the actions of the few. I hope I make myself clear?"

Without bothering to bring the assembly to a close, Mr Snyder turned on his heel, dismounted the stage and left the hall. From his seat, several rows from the front of the stage, Eric Lunt pitched forward, looked to his left, made eye contact with Reilly, Woosey and Bradley, and smiled.

Following Mr Snyder's departure, it took some seconds for the assembly to find its voice. Those members of staff who had not already deserted the hall remained in their seats, unsure of what to do next. Then, as if a spell had been broken, everybody started talking at once. The older pupils, baffled as to why anybody would want to steal the head's portrait in the first place, affected a nonchalant indifference. But some of the younger pupils looked confused and troubled, especially those sitting close to Lawrence Rowlands. It was

Mr Cheatham who eventually brought the assembly to order and sent the school on its way.

By the time Mr Snyder had reached Miss Cropper's office, Robert Cole was lying in wait.

"This is really not a good time, Mr Cole," said the head brushing past him. "If you really do need to see me, I suggest you make an appointment with Miss Cropper."

But Robert Cole was not to be put off. Ignoring Mr Snyder's suggestion, he followed the head into his office and forcibly closed the door behind him.

"Just what do you think you are playing at?" asked Robert, his temper barely under control.

"How dare you!" erupted Mr Snyder. "The fact your family donated generously to the school in the past does not give you the right to barge into my office and question my authority!"

"Let's leave my family out of this, shall we? Do you realise what you have done? Some of the younger pupils were nearly in tears. And as for the poor lad who Cheatham picked on …"

"I will not tolerate any criticism of Mr Cheatham," warned the head.

"How can you possibly justify making suspects of the entire school?" asked an astonished Robert

"Mr Cole!" exploded the head.

"Encouraging pupils to spy on each other? Offering rewards? That can never be justified," persisted Robert.

"There, Mr Cole, there is my justification," quaked the head, pointing to the redundant picture hook hanging forlornly on the wall behind his desk. "We have art thieves in our midst!"

"Art thieves? It was *your* portrait that was taken, not the Mona Lisa," scoffed Robert.

"Very droll, Mr Cole, very droll," observed the head. "You are, of course, entitled to your opinion, however flawed that opinion might be, but I will not have my conduct questioned by a novice of barely two years' teaching experience."

"And I will not stand by and watch the children of this school demeaned and assaulted simply because someone has decided to play what is patently a practical joke."

"A practical joke?" repeated the head.

"What else could it be?" insisted Robert. "You don't really believe there is a market out there for portraits of bewigged headmasters intent on hiding their age, do you? If you ask me, the blasted painting is still on the school premises."

Robert realised he had gone too far.

"How dare you!" hissed the head. "It may interest you to know that this is the second time in little more than two years that a portrait has been stolen from the school."

"What are you talking about?" asked Robert.

"I am telling you that shortly before you came to teach at this school, a portrait of a former head was stolen from the Great Hall. No doubt the theft of *that* portrait was a practical joke as well."

Robert paused for a moment before responding.

"Tell me," he asked, "the portrait taken from the Great Hall, that wasn't a portrait of Michael Edwards, was it?"

"It was," replied the head. "How did you know that?"

Robert did not reply. So that was why he and Grace could not find the former head's portrait. But who, he asked himself, would want to steal a portrait of Michael Edwards?

"Well?" persisted the head.

"Oh, never mind that," replied Robert, his anger blunted by the head's revelation. "I simply wish to express my concern about how you addressed the school this morning."

Mr Snyder had heard enough.

"Your concern is noted. This meeting is over," he declared. "I think you had better leave before I forget the debt this school owes your family."

Fixing the head with a withering look, Robert bit his lip and returned to class. Alone in his office, Mr Snyder thoughtfully stroked his chin and considered his next move. Although he hated to admit it, the young history master could be right: the portrait might still be on the school premises. Of one thing Mr Snyder was sure, the culprits, whoever they were, would soon give themselves away. What was the point of carrying out such an audacious raid if not to revel in the notoriety such an exploit would inevitably generate? Sooner or later, they would brag about their deed to the wrong person and, unmasked by their own vanity, their identities would be revealed. And when that happened, Mr Cheatham, his enforcer-in-chief, would be waiting in the wings.

CHAPTER NINETEEN

A Port in a Storm

At the eleventh hour on the eleventh day of the eleventh month of 1918, the Great War ended. Although not technically a surrender, Germany's signing of the armistice signalled her complete and utter defeat. Imposed in a railway carriage at Compiegne in Northern France, the armistice, naturally, provided for the exchange of prisoners of war.

Situated on the outskirts of Berlin, conditions in the camp at Döberitz had, until the last months of the war at least, been tolerable. But food, a scarce commodity at the best of times, had become scarcer still during the autumn of 1918. By then, Germany, brought to its knees by the British naval blockade, teetered on the verge of starvation. Little priority was afforded to prisoners of war whose guards, in many places, simply abandoned their posts. Confronted with domestic turmoil, German administrators did little to facilitate repatriation. Intent on rectifying the situation, the Allies took the initiative by establishing collection centres within Germany. It was to one such centre that Tom was transported on Thursday, 23rd January 1919, before being placed on a train to France.

After reaching the Allied lines, the men were led across the devastated landscape before being driven to reception centres where they were fed, deloused, issued with new clothing and allowed a short period of rest before being sent to a transit camp in Calais. Here, the men would be debriefed and medically examined before being dispatched to Dover, where those who had volunteered for service would be sent home.

Tom now had a problem. Although his adopted identity had survived ten months of captivity, there was every chance his deception would be uncovered long before he reached Dover. Even in his present undernourished and emaciated state, he might be recognised by those with whom he had served. He was, after all, a holder of the Victoria Cross and, as such, vulnerable to the exposure his fame might trigger. A further consideration now weighed heavily on Tom's mind: the longer he maintained his deception, the more likely it was that the family of the real Michael Edwards would be informed that he had survived the war. This he could never allow. Tom had always known that he would have to desert for a second time, the question was how. On Sunday 26th January 1919, Tom was delivered to the transit camp in Calais. Informed that he was to attend a medical examination the following day, he was acutely aware that any reference to the medical records of Michael Edwards would quickly find him out. Thanks to Private John Pantling, the medical examination never took place.

By January 1919, discontent among British troops serving in France was rife. Although the war had ended, the conditions under which the men served remained harsh; discipline remained strict and was brutally maintained. Demanding better food and shorter working hours, above all else, the men simply wanted to go home. Insurgence, fuelled by ever-growing dissatisfaction, simmered below the surface. It was against this background that Private John Pantling encouraged a gathering of soldiers to protest. Deemed a rabble-rouser by his superiors, Pantling was imprisoned in the Calais Bastille, where he spent six days in irons. When word spread of Pantling's arrest, the men mutinied. On Monday 27th January, the very day Tom was to attend his medical, British soldiers went on strike, bringing the port of Calais to a standstill. That same day, some 4,000 men surrounded army headquarters, demanding Pantling's release, a demand that was met the following day when the rebellion numbered twenty thousand troops.

The strike provided Tom with the opportunity he had been looking for. The complete breakdown of the chain of command meant that his movements were no longer restricted. At eight o'clock on the morning of Tuesday the 28th of January 1919, Tom cycled out of the Calais transit camp unopposed. Concealed within the rucksack that hung from his shoulder were the civilian clothing he had obtained the previous day, the money paid in advance of the back pay he was owed, a small quantity of bread and cheese and a bottle of beer. Upon reaching the eastern outskirts of Calais, he changed into civilian clothing, discarded his uniform, except for the army greatcoat he had acquired, and set off along the coast road for Boulogne, a journey of twenty-five miles.

By the time a cold and tired Tom pedalled into Boulogne, darkness was falling. A fluent French speaker, he spent the night at an inn close to the harbour. At dawn the following morning, having stuffed his greatcoat into his rucksack, he made his way to the quayside from where local fishermen, desperate to eke out a living, ventured into the sea in search of crab, eel and shrimp. Such was their need that Tom had little difficulty in negotiating, for a modest fee, his passage across the channel. Shortly before midday, Tom waded onto a beach close to the port of Hythe on the Kent coast. The fact that he was once again on English soil failed to arouse any emotion in him. Buffeted by the biting wind, he retrieved his greatcoat from the rucksack, pulled the collar tightly around his neck and set off inland, knowing he had run out of destinations.

By the 30th of January, the striking soldiers, their demands having largely been met, returned to their duties. Surprisingly, the ringleaders of the mutiny were never disciplined. Afraid that retribution might lead to further unrest, the civil and military authorities brushed the episode under the carpet. As for Tom's saviour, Private Pantling, he never saw England again. Following his imprisonment in Calais, he contracted influenza, died and was buried in France.

Shunning society whenever possible, Tom wandered about the countryside, seeking casual employment and meaning to his existence. By mid-May, the counties of Kent and Surrey behind him, he crossed into Hampshire. With work hard to come by, surviving as a vagrant had not been easy. When he did find work, payment often amounted to nothing more than a meal and, if he was lucky, an outhouse in which to sleep. Confronted by cold and hunger at every turn, Tom kept going. If physically he was just about in one piece, mentally it was a very different story. Haunted by his experience in the trenches, tortured by flashbacks, Tom questioned his sanity.

After a night spent sleeping rough in a wood, it was a rather stiff and hungry-looking Tom who, by midday, found himself on the outskirts of Woolton Hill, a small village close to the border with Berkshire. Making his way along the winding country lane, the church of St Thomas soon came into view. Churches were always worth a visit, offering as they did the prospect of work and, consequently, a meal. Even if there were no odd jobs to perform, a church provided a place to rest for a short while, at least until asked to move on. Sauntering through the graveyard in the bright spring sunshine, Tom's spirit lifted as the feel of soft, lush grass penetrated the thin soles of his boots. Oaks, elms, yews and weeping willows, their leaves a youthful green, cast benevolent shadows on the sleeping occupants below. As he made his way toward the church, a faint smile played on his face as memories of Borrowdale and the Lake District briefly resurfaced before fading like the sound of distant guns.

Entering through the northern porch, Tom closed the heavy oak door behind him and was immediately soothed by the serene atmosphere within. Built of stone and flint, the neo-gothic arches of the church betrayed its Victorian origin. Ahead of him, a communion rail with a gate at its centre separated the absent congregation from the raised chancel and altar. Rows of pews, their padded kneelers ripped and torn, lined either side of a narrow centre aisle. In front of the altar, a pulpit to the left and a font to the right formed a symbolic trinity. Behind the altar, sunlight poured through a large stained-glass window depicting soldiers of the Great War genuflecting in prayer in the aftermath of battle.

Reaching the communion rail, Tom looked behind him to make sure he was alone. It had been a long time since he had prayed, and the thought of doing so now made him self-conscious. Satisfied that the church was empty, he dropped to his knees, rested his clasped hands on the rail and bowed his head. But prayer proved difficult and he began to have second thoughts. What good could prayer do? Did he even believe in God anymore? How could a caring God have tolerated the slaughter of war? Tom opened his eyes and looked up at the crucifix that stared down at him from the middle of the altar. The silence that had earlier offered serenity now accentuated his isolation and amplified the doubts of his tormented soul as he struggled to initiate a conversation with the Almighty. With his eyes trained on the stained-glass battlefield, silence gave way to the terrifying sound of exploding shells, the repetitive rat-a-tat-tat of machine gun fire, the cries of advancing troops and the screams of wounded and dying men as he was transported back to the trenches. Black storm clouds chased away the spring sunshine and battered the stained-glass window with rods of rain as sheet lightning interspersed with loud claps of thunder danced above the church. His head in his hands, Tom could do nothing but wait for the recurring nightmare to pass.

"Can I help you?" asked a male voice.

Tom did not respond. He was still in France.

"Excuse me, are you alright?" persisted the male.

Tom opened his eyes and grasped the communion rail with both hands. The rain had stopped, the storm had moved on, and bright sunshine again flooded through the window. Tom, his face bathed in sweat, slowly stood up. Composing himself, he turned to face his inquisitor, a dark-suited man in his mid-thirties. Slightly built with thinning hair and a ready smile illuminated by striking blue eyes, the man wore a dog collar.

"I'm sorry," said Tom. "I was just sheltering from the storm. I'll be leaving now."

"Storm? What Storm?" asked the cleric. "It's a glorious day."

"The storm," repeated Tom, "the storm …"

"There hasn't been a storm today," insisted the cleric. "Are you sure you've not been dreaming?"

Tom looked down at the floor and, once again, silently questioned his sanity.

"Look, I'm sorry. I'll be on my way."

"Oh, you don't have to apologise," assured the cleric. "The house of God welcomes visitors."

"Well, my visit is just about over," said Tom quietly.

"No need to go yet," said the cleric, extending his right hand. "My name is Vincent Worrall, I'm the new vicar of St Thomas's."

Conscious of his bedraggled state, Tom wiped the palm of his right hand on his greatcoat before accepting the handshake in silence.

"I could not help but notice you admiring our stained-glass window," said the vicar as he passed Tom and approached the altar.

"It's very fine," said Tom, more out of politeness than conviction.

"Yes, it is," agreed the vicar with enthusiasm. "It was donated to the church last year, I believe, by the father of Captain George Gates of the 6th Royal Berkshires. The captain was killed on the Somme in 1916."

Tom turned and walked towards the church door, somewhat put out by the vicar's matter-of-fact tone. But the vicar had not finished with him.

"Can I take it from your greatcoat that you also served in the conflict?"

Tom stopped and paused before turning to confront the smiling cleric. There was something about his smile that irked him. Only those who had not served in the war, he thought, could talk about it and smile at the same time.

"Yes, I did," replied Tom with uncharacteristic impatience. "Did you?"

The question dripped with challenge.

"Oh yes," replied the vicar, his ready smile dissolving and his blue eyes hardening. "From start to finish. Left my dog collar at home, though."

The two men stared at each other for a few seconds in silence.

"*Fronti nulla fides*," said Tom quietly before averting his stare.

"Ah, a scholar," exclaimed the vicar as he advanced on Tom, his smile returning. "'Never judge a book by its cover'. I always thought that would make a damn fine school motto. Tell me, when did you last eat?"

The question immediately placed Tom on the defensive.

"Look, I couldn't possibly accept your hospitality, I really should be leaving."

"Wait," ordered the vicar, placing a friendly hand on Tom's shoulder. "Come on, you look like you could do with a meal. Don't let pride starve you to death."

"You are very kind, but I could not possibly accept charity," said Tom, his discomfort growing by the second.

"Well," cajoled the vicar, "if charity is out of the question, how about working for your dinner? Look around you; this place needs work and a good spring clean. What say you give me a hand in return for your rations?"

Although Tom hesitated before replying, no further persuasion was required.

"You win. What would you like me to do?" he asked, mustering a faint smile.

"It's almost lunchtime," said the vicar leading Tom out of the church. "The vicarage is just on the other side of the lane. First, we eat, then we work."

"Right," said Tom, his compliance encouraged by the fact that he had not eaten for two days.

"Wait," commanded the vicar. "If we are going to be working together, then I insist you call me Vincent. What do I call you?"

Hesitation again preceded Tom's reply.

"Michael, Michael Edwards, but my friends call me Tom."

"Tom it is then," beamed Vincent. "Follow me."

CHAPTER TWENTY

Restoration

Standing in splendid rustic isolation, the vicarage was less than five minutes' walk from the church. Surrounded by well-kept gardens and hidden from the lane by a wall of thick privet hedges, the large Victorian house did not lack appeal. But its charm was lost on Tom as he silently followed Vincent through the rear garden and into the kitchen.

"Evelyn, we have a guest for lunch," shouted Vincent.

Tom remained on the threshold: he had not expected to be introduced to members of Vincent's family and was suddenly conscious of his appearance. Gaunt, dirty, and in need of a haircut, his tangled beard struggling to camouflage his scarred face and hollow cheeks, Tom was embarrassed.

"Evelyn! Mrs Duke!" shouted Vincent as he reached into a cupboard and retrieved a large frying pan.

"We're coming," responded Evelyn as she and Mrs Duke hurriedly entered the kitchen. "What is the matter?"

"Ah, Evelyn," said Vincent, "meet Tom; he's going to help out in the church this afternoon after he has eaten. Tom, meet Evelyn and Mrs Duke, our housekeeper."

Fair-haired with blue eyes, Evelyn's handsome features momentarily froze when she saw Tom standing in the doorway. Blessed with natural kindness and wisdom that surpassed her twenty-six years, she quickly recovered her poise, crossed the kitchen, took Tom's hand and gently shook it.

"Tom, how nice to meet you," she said warmly.

Her initial reaction not having gone unnoticed, Tom looked Evelyn squarely in the eye, but she matched his stare, and he could discern no obvious insincerity. It was with some difficulty that he finally managed to avert his gaze.

"Come in from the doorway and sit yourself down," said Evelyn as she ushered Tom to the kitchen table.

"Mrs Duke will look after you, Tom," said Vincent as he opened the larder door and checked its contents. "Evelyn and I have to pop out for an hour or two. We can get cracking on the church when I get back."

Standing behind Tom, Evelyn shot Vincent a quizzical look which he ignored.

"May I ask a question?" said Mrs Duke, a stout and formidable-looking lady in her mid-fifties.

"Certainly, Mrs Duke, ask away," encouraged Vincent cheerfully.

"Will the gentleman be washing before lunch?" she asked.

Peering down at Tom from the other side of the table, her nostrils flaring, it was apparent that Mrs Duke had detected a bad smell. Cut to the quick and determined to escape further humiliation, Tom was about to get to his feet when he felt the gentle touch of Evelyn Worrall's restraining hands infiltrate the worn shoulders of his greatcoat and radiate through his being. It was the first intimate contact he had experienced in years, and it rendered him helpless.

"You mustn't take too much notice of our Mrs Duke," said Evelyn softly. "Her bark is much worse than her bite."

"That said," chirped Vincent, "you don't want to get on her wrong side."

"I'll try not to," said Tom quietly.

"Right, you come with me, Evelyn. Let's leave Tom and Mrs Duke to it. Mrs Duke, a word with you before we go," said Vincent as he and Evelyn left the room.

Five minutes later, Mrs Duke returned to the kitchen.

"Right then," she said firmly with a look that bordered on fierce. "You follow me."

Tom eyed the housekeeper suspiciously and did not move.

Mrs Duke rolled her eyes and looked to heaven.

"Look, my dear," she said, her tone softening and her fierce look disintegrating into a sympathetic smile, "you're as dirty as a sweep, and you smells like a pig. Now, if you are going to eat at my table, then we have to do something about that, so will you please follow me?"

Tom stood up. For the first time in a very long time, he wanted to laugh.

"Better lead the way then," he said, keeping a straight face.

Taking Tom through the house and up the stairs, Mrs Duke escorted him to a large, sunlit bathroom.

"Right, here we are then," she said as she put the plug in the bath and turned on the taps. "There are towels in that cupboard behind you, and soap, a razor, scissors and a toothbrush on the window ledge. Your food will be ready when you are."

As she was leaving the bathroom, Mrs Duke fired one last shot.

"And make sure you clean the bath when you've finished."

Alone in the bathroom, Tom stood for a few moments and looked about him as the gushing water filled the bath. Placing his hand into his rear trouser pocket, he retrieved his silver cigarette case and wallet and put them on the shelf above the wash basin. Having taken off his greatcoat and boots, he stepped towards the mirror and took a long look at himself before reaching for the scissors, clipping his beard and applying the razor. Within fifteen minutes, he was lowering himself into the bath, his tattered clothes abandoned in a heap in the middle of the floor. As the hot water enveloped his body, he laid back his head, closed his eyes and allowed himself to drift. Moments later, the door burst open.

"Don't mind me, dear," said Mrs Duke causing Tom to sit up immediately.

The invasion of his privacy rendered him speechless.

"Oh, take that startled look off your face," scolded the housekeeper. "I had four sons of my own, you know. Now, these are for you."

Tom watched helplessly as Mrs Duke placed a set of clean clothes and a pair of shoes on the bathroom chair before sweeping up the boots and garments that he had only minutes before discarded.

"A gift from the vicar," said Mrs Duke. "He's always receiving donations of clothes for the poor. Now hurry up, your food will be ready soon."

And with that, she was gone.

It was a barely recognisable Tom who sheepishly entered the kitchen some thirty minutes later.

"There you are," exclaimed Mrs Duke turning from the sizzling contents of the frying pan. "Let me have a look at you."

Tom felt like he was on parade.

"Trousers look a bit loose, but they will do. Shoes fit?"

"Yes, they're fine, thank you," replied Tom.

"Right then, I've set you a place at the table, so sit yourself down."

Tom did as he was told and watched Mrs Duke as she prepared his meal.

"What did you mean when you said you had four sons?" he asked.

Mrs Duke did not answer immediately, and when she did, she did not turn to face Tom.

"I think you can guess what I meant," she said.

Tom bowed his head, ashamed that he had asked the question in such an indifferent and direct fashion.

"I'm sorry, that was very thoughtless of me. Please forgive me."

Mrs Duke did not reply. A couple of minutes later, she silently approached Tom and placed a tray of food before him. A basket of bread and butter, a steaming mug of tea and a plate heaped with bacon, sausage, mushrooms and two fried eggs occupied the tray. Tom stared briefly at his food before looking up at Mrs Duke, who could not disguise the deep-seated grief his question had exposed. For the first time in a long time, Tom thought about his parents.

"I am so sorry," he repeated, appalled by his insensitivity.

Mrs Duke's expression softened.

"Get that down you, lad. I must get on with my work. Call me if you need anything."

Left alone in the kitchen, Tom attacked his food with gusto.

It was nearly two o'clock when he returned to the church. His sleeves rolled up, Vincent was busy sweeping the floor when Tom walked through the door.

"Ah, there you are, Tom. If you don't mind my saying, you look like a new man. Good meal?"

"Very good and very much appreciated," replied Tom.

"Clothes fit?"

"Very well, thank you, though I don't know how I am going to repay your kindness in the space of one afternoon's work."

"I'm sure you will be of great assistance," sang Vincent.

"Then please, tell me what it is you would like me to do," said Tom, anxious to settle his debt.

"Well, for a start, you can take over the sweeping as I have to nip into Newbury for an hour. When you have finished, you could perhaps make a start on the church door."

"The church door?" queried Tom.

"The church door," repeated Vincent. "As with most of the woodwork around here, the door needs rubbing down and a new coat of varnish applied. You will find sandpaper and a smock on the table inside the porch."

"Well, I'll certainly make a start on it, but I don't think the job can be done in one afternoon."

"Then just make a start and see how far you get," said Vincent with his customary smile. "Now, I must be off. I'll see you later."

After he had swept the church and adjoining chapel floor, Tom put on the smock and set about sanding the weathered exterior of the large oak door. Standing on a chair, his sandpaper wrapped around a wooden block, Tom systematically worked his way across the surface. But progress was slow, and when Vincent returned shortly after six o'clock, Tom was far from completing his task.

"Sorry I took so long," said Vincent. "How are we doing?"

"A long way to go, I'm afraid," said Tom apologetically. "This stuff is proving difficult to shift."

"You're doing a fine job," enthused Vincent as he ran his fingers across the sanded surface. "Tell you what, you can finish it tomorrow."

Tom stopped sanding.

"Look, you have been very kind to me, but I really couldn't …"

"Nonsense!" interrupted Vincent. "Come with me, there's something I want to show you."

Before Tom could respond, Vincent had walked into the church. After hesitating for a few seconds, Tom followed.

"This way," beckoned Vincent from the corner of the chapel before disappearing down a flight of steps.

"Welcome to the church basement," said Vincent as Tom descended the steps. "What do you think? Evelyn and I fixed the place up when you were eating."

Tom looked bemused. The basement had been converted into rudimentary living quarters. A bed dressed in clean sheets and blankets occupied the right-hand corner of the room. A table, covered with a thick cloth and boasting a vase of freshly picked flowers, occupied the middle of the floor. To the left, above a large square sink, a mirror captured the reflection of a large boiler, its pipes lagged with rags, radiating heat from the opposite corner of the basement.

"You can thank Evelyn for the flowers," smiled Vincent. "Now, I know it looks a little rough and ready, but it's warm, dry and comfortable."

Tom felt exposed.

"I don't understand," he said quietly.

"Let me explain," said Vincent, the smile having deserted his face and his eyes steadfastly fixed on Tom. "I fought in that war for four years, not as a man of the cloth but as a soldier. The horror I encountered, the friends I lost, the numbness I felt and the guilt that followed, I thought would stay with me forever. But I suspect you know all about that."

Tom shifted uncomfortably on his feet, unable to hold Vincent's stare.

"You know very little about me," he said.

"After watching you in church this morning, I know enough," countered Vincent.

"So where do you hide your demons, Vincent?" asked Tom aggressively as he again looked the vicar in the eye. "How did you get off so lightly?"

"What makes you so sure I did?" replied Vincent calmly. "I have my nightmares. I have questioned my God."

"God?" mocked Tom, his voice rising. "Don't you think your god bears some responsibility for the untold suffering, the carnage, the millions of deaths? How can you talk of God? God was the first casualty of the war."

"You don't really believe that," said Vincent firmly. "Why were you kneeling at the altar this morning? Look, I don't pretend to have all the answers, but it wasn't God who started that war, it was men."

"Men created in God's image," retorted Tom.

"Men blessed with free will," countered Vincent.

Tom closed his eyes, threw back his head in anguish and tried to make sense of it all. Was he using God as a scapegoat? Regaining his composure, Tom once again looked Vincent in the eye.

"You are a very kind and generous man," he said, the quiet having returned to his voice, "but I think I should be moving on."

"Well, before you do, listen to what I have to say and think carefully. Like you, my church is in a state of disrepair, it needs restoring, it needs help. In return for your help, my church can offer you a bed, three meals a day, a small weekly wage and weekends off. This is not an offer of charity. What is on offer here is the chance to mend, heal, and regain the strength you need to face the world. I am offering you the chance to take control of your demons."

A short silence followed as Tom considered his reply.

"Tell me, Vincent, why would you and your wife do this for me?"

"Because he suspects that if your roles were reversed, you would do the same for him," replied Evelyn Worrall.

Surprised by her sudden appearance, Tom turned sharply and watched her descend the basement steps.

"Mrs Duke was right," said Evelyn smiling. "I would never have recognised you. Well, how about it? Tell me you will accept our offer after all our hard work down here."

"Yes, tell us you accept," encouraged Vincent.

For the second time that day, Tom looked Evelyn Worrall directly in the eye. For the second time that day, she held his stare. Tom's mind was made up when Evelyn next spoke.

"And by the way," she said, still holding his gaze. "I must apologise for not introducing myself properly this morning. Vincent is not my husband, he's my brother."

CHAPTER TWENTY-ONE

A Letter Home

Sitting at the table in the morning room, the late spring sunshine pouring through the window, Brigit and Richard Cole finished their breakfast in silence. Although two months had passed since their journey to the war cemetery at Savy, the visit had not brought closure. Richard, his hair now completely white, had lost weight and was ageing quickly. Brigit, who had yet to begin to grieve, had hardly aged at all. Despite having seen her son's grave, she stubbornly refused to accept that he was dead. "I would have known," she repeatedly told Richard. "I would have known." But Brigit's unflagging optimism hung heavily around Richard's neck; how could he ever let go of his boy while his wife looked forward daily to news of his deliverance?

A maid entered the room and approached the breakfast table.

"Excuse me, madam, this letter has just arrived."

As Brigit opened the letter, Richard, oblivious to the maid's presence, stared out of the window into the distance. When he eventually looked at his wife, he saw that she was smiling. She was smiling the way she used to smile before Tom had enlisted.

"What is it?" he asked.

"Read it," she commanded quietly. "Read it to me."

Taking the letter from his wife, Richard placed it on the table and donned his spectacles.

"*Dear Ma and Pa ...*"

Richard hesitated.

"Read it," repeated Brigit softly.

"*Dear Ma and Pa, please forgive me for not having had the courage to write to you sooner. I am alive …*"

Confused, Richard paused again before continuing.

"*I am alive and living in Hampshire. I can't say where, but I will confide all soon.*"

Richard, his voice faltering, his eyes filling with tears, once again looked at Brigit and clasped her extended hand.

"*On no account must the news of my survival be announced to anybody other than Edward. I will write again soon and explain everything. Forgive me. Your loving son, Tom.*"

Still clasping his wife's hand, Richard slowly shook his head.

"It cannot be," he protested gently. "We have been to his grave."

"No, not his grave," insisted Brigit.

"But anybody could have written this letter."

"Don't you recognise your own son's handwriting?" countered Brigit.

"It looks like Tom's, but …"

"Read the postscript," interrupted Brigit, smiling. "Read the Latin postscript."

"*Filius est pars patris*," recited Richard. "A son is part of the father … the inscription on the cigarette case …"

"The cigarette case that you sent him in 1917," declared Brigit in the manner of an advocate triumphantly proving her case. "Now, do you believe?"

Richard did not answer. Still holding his wife's hand, he bowed his head and wept.

CHAPTER TWENTY-TWO

Decision Time

Curled on a sofa at Derwent Cottage, Grace Connelly stared into the open fire and unconsciously toyed with the cigarette case. It was the end of another week. Appalled by Mr Snyder's address to the assembly two weeks before, she was no longer sure that she wanted to teach at Grey Stones. The Christmas break was only a week away, and she knew she had a lot of thinking to do. When her mind turned to Robert Cole, her heart sank yet further. Dear Robert. How difficult it was not to love him, even from a distance. And they had become distant. In the weeks since their hospital visit, they had hardly spoken, their mutual embarrassment encouraging mutual avoidance.

Grace did not doubt that she had mishandled the situation. She had hoped that the boys' research into Michael Edwards would prove her wrong, but that hope had proved forlorn. It was now the 9th of December and they had yet to report back to her, probably, she suspected, because they had lost interest in their assignment. But it didn't matter. Even if they had managed to profile Michael Edwards, she was confident that she now knew everything she needed to know about the former head. That being the case, she had to accept that the time had come to sit Robert down and tell him everything. It simply wasn't fair that he should be left guessing as to why, without so much as a word, she had abandoned him. The only sensible thing to do, she now realised, was square things with Robert and move on, probably back to London. Her mind made up, and determined to act positively, Grace resolved to meet with Robert before the Christmas break. Staring into the fire, she sipped her wine and allowed the flames to draw her in. Stirred by the ringing telephone, she placed the cigarette case on the table and entered the dimly lit hall.

"Hello?"

"Hello. Is that you, Grace?"

Grace recognised the caller's voice instantly.

"Robert!" she exclaimed, delighted that he had called. "Don't ask me how but I just knew it was you."

"You're not too disappointed then?"

"Of course not, don't be silly."

"How are you?"

"I'm fine," replied Grace, sitting on the chair beside the phone. "I'm just so glad you called."

"Why, there's nothing wrong, is there?"

Grace paused before answering.

"Well, actually, there is. Robert. We should meet somewhere away from Grey Stones ... we need to talk."

"My sentiments exactly; that's why I called."

Grace again hesitated for a moment before taking the bull by the horns.

"The fact is, Robert, I've been thinking about my future and have decided that it would probably be for the best if I moved back to London in the New Year."

"What?"

Grace pressed on.

"Look, I know that I haven't treated you very well in recent weeks, the fact is I have treated you most unfairly, but, believe me, I had my reasons."

"Slow down ... what reasons? What are you talking about?"

"I can't tell you now," replied Grace, "not over the phone."

"At least give me a clue …"

"Meet me somewhere away from school, and I'll tell you everything, I promise."

"Okay, if that's what you want."

"Thanks, Robert," said Grace quietly.

"Tell me something," he said, "has this got anything to do with that character Michael Edwards you were so interested in?"

"How did you know that?"

"I don't know, intuition, I suppose."

Robert's intuition tempted Grace to tell him everything there and then, but she resisted.

"Listen, why don't you come to the house tomorrow afternoon?" suggested Robert. "The Keswick Choral Singers are coming over."

"The Keswick *who*?"

"The Keswick Choral Singers," repeated Robert. "My mother was one of their leading lights. She used to invite them over every Christmas for cheese and wine, and since her passing, it's fallen on me to keep the tradition going."

"Robert, how sweet of you," declared Grace playfully.

"Yes, well … Look, don't think you'll be expected to sing or anything, though they do tend to let rip when they've had a few. It's just that I think you might feel more comfortable if there were people around, safety in numbers and all that."

"Oh, Robert, I don't need people around me to feel safe with you," protested Grace gently.

"Well … I'm glad to hear it," replied Robert, a touch bashfully. "So, you'll come then?"

"Of course, I'll come. What time do you want me there?

"I'll have a taxi pick you up between two-thirty and three."

CHAPTER TWENTY-THREE

Moving On

It was Saturday 6th August 1924, and the Church of St Thomas basked in glorious sunshine. Wearing a black cassock, white surplice and violet stole, Vincent Worrall addressed the private congregation from a central position in front of the altar. There was genuine joy in his voice as he brought the service to an end.

"In the presence of God, and before this congregation, Michael James Edwards and Evelyn Virginia Worrall have declared their marriage by the joining of hands. I therefore proclaim that they are husband and wife. Those whom God has joined together let no man put asunder. Tom, you may kiss your bride."

Turning to Evelyn, Tom looked at her for a few seconds, his expression one of quiet contentment.

"Well?" smiled Evelyn.

Drawing her towards him, Tom lifted the simple white veil from Evelyn's face and tenderly kissed her.

"Till death do us part," whispered Tom.

"And beyond," replied Evelyn.

As the ageing organist struck up the *Wedding March*, Tom and Evelyn led the small congregation down the aisle and out of the church. Pausing briefly at the entrance, Tom brushed his fingers along the smooth exterior of the oak door and remembered the task he had been set five years before.

"Somebody did a fine job there," smiled Evelyn.

Once outside the church, unable to contain herself any longer, a tearful Brigit Cole abandoned her husband and advanced towards the happy couple.

"My dear, let me wish you all the happiness in the world," she said with feeling as she clasped both of Evelyn's hands.

"Thank you, thank you so much," smiled Evelyn drawing Brigit close.

"No, thank *you*, Evelyn," whispered Brigit into her ear. "Thank you for mending our son."

Turning to Tom, Brigit stared at him intently, embraced him tightly and said nothing. Shaking hands with Vincent, Richard Cole's cheerful demeanour was clear for all to see. But when it came to congratulating Tom, different emotions threatened to overwhelm him.

"Well done, my boy, well done," said Richard extending his right hand while trying to maintain a smile.

Foregoing the handshake, Tom pulled his father towards him and gently hugged him.

"*Fillius est pars patris*," said Tom softly.

Knowing he could do nothing about the tears welling in his eyes, Richard patted his son's shoulder fondly and moved off to congratulate Evelyn. Spotting his chance, Edward stepped in.

"I still can't believe that my brother is actually married," he said, shaking Tom's hand and grinning from ear to ear. "What's it like?"

"You'll know yourself soon enough," laughed Tom.

"Don't know about that," replied Edward, his tone self-effacing, "I don't think anyone would have me."

"Nonsense," chided a smiling Evelyn. "I'll wager the young ladies of Borrowdale are queuing up as we speak. And anyway, as best man, shouldn't you be looking after the bridesmaid?"

"I can look after myself, thank you very much," declared Mrs Duke as she bustled towards Tom. "Where is he? Let me at him."

Tom stooped forward, allowing Mrs Duke to throw her arms around his neck and press a lingering kiss on his cheek.

"When I think of the half-starved tramp that turned up here after the war and see the handsome chap standing before me now. And as for you," she said gruffly, turning her attention to Evelyn, "who's going to look after you and keep house for you in a boy's school?"

This time, Mrs Duke's eyes welled up with tears.

"None of that now," said Evelyn, embracing the housekeeper. "There will be many opportunities for us to come and see you during the school holidays, isn't that right, Tom?"

"Of course it is," confirmed Tom, "and you can always come and visit us in Keswick."

"What, and leave the vicar? I don't know about that," replied Mrs Duke, recovering her poise.

As the party moved towards the vicarage for the wedding tea, Tom held back to walk with Vincent.

"How are the demons?" asked the vicar.

"Under control," replied Tom. "I can say no more than that. Anyway, I don't think it would be fair if they completely disappeared. They are my punishment, my penance, the price I must pay for letting the side down."

The two men stopped for a moment and looked back at the church.

"You say you let the side down; others might say you saved lives."

"At the end of the day, Vincent, the fact remains that I disobeyed orders, caused the death of my commanding officer and embarked upon a massive deception to hide the fact."

Vincent let the matter drop. They had discussed it many times over the years, and today, the day of Tom's leaving, was not the occasion to re-open old wounds.

"My God, we did some work on that church, though, didn't we?" said Vincent.

"We certainly did," agreed Tom wistfully.

Vincent smiled.

"I owe you so much, Vincent. I will never be able to repay you."

Vincent placed his hand on the younger man's shoulder.

"I've told you before, I think God saved us from the carnage for a reason. Perhaps he saved me to help you. Perhaps he saved you to help someone else. Time will tell. But be assured that you owe me absolutely nothing. If anybody saved you, it was Evelyn. All I ask is that you take good care of her."

"You can depend on it," replied Tom.

"And can I take it that the salary of a history master at Grey Stones will afford myself and Mrs Duke the prospect of regular visits from you both?" asked Vincent.

"You can depend on that as well," promised Tom.

That afternoon, as the wedding party celebrated in the garden of the vicarage, Tom kept an eye on Mrs Duke. The two had grown very close, and he could see that, despite her typically brusque attempts to hide the fact, she was subdued. Maybe it was because he and Evelyn were leaving later that afternoon for Keswick. Perhaps it was because she was remembering her four sons and thinking about the weddings they never had. When the opportunity arose, Tom followed her to a corner of the garden and thanked her for the kindness she had shown him.

"You don't have to thank me for anything, my dear," protested Mrs Duke. "Anyway, it was thanks enough when you engraved the names of my four boys into the church wall. It's good to know they'll be remembered long after I'm gone."

"You are a remarkable lady, Mrs Duke," said Tom. "I will never forget you."

Mrs Duke stared into Tom's eyes, an apologetic look on her face. Eventually, she spoke.

"I'm sorry if I've been out of sorts, this being your wedding day and all. It's just that, well, I look at your family and see how happy they are that you have been returned to them, and I can't help but think … I can't help but think that God could have let me have kept just one of my boys … I'm sorry, I hope that doesn't sound …"

Mrs Duke never finished her sentence. Frustrated by his inability to shield her from her grief, Tom enveloped her in his arms, drew her face into his chest and peered over her head into the distance. Watching from the other side of the garden, Evelyn and Brigit Cole exchanged glances.

"Time to cut the cake, I think. Edward, be a dear and fetch your brother and Mrs Duke," directed Brigit.

Obeying his mother's instruction, Edward set off across the garden.

"We were just reminiscing," said Tom as his brother approached.

"Well, ma says you and Mrs Duke must come and have some cake," advised Edward.

"How about it, Mrs Duke? Are we ready to face the world?" asked Tom.

"Of course we are," replied Mrs Duke, dabbing her handkerchief to the corners of her eyes. "And may God help those who think we're not."

After Vincent had recharged everybody's glass with champagne, Tom and Evelyn clasped the knife and cut the cake.

"Speech!" demanded Edward.

"How about a toast instead? To family and friends, past and present," said Tom raising his glass.

"To family and friends," repeated one and all.

"I think this would be a good time to give the happy couple their wedding present, don't you?" said Brigit to Richard.

"I do," replied Richard, retrieving a set of keys from his pocket.

Evelyn and Tom looked slightly puzzled as Richard cleared his throat and shuffled uncomfortably on his feet.

"For reasons that I know will never be betrayed by those here, it is clear that Tom and Evelyn cannot live at our family home in Keswick. That would be too dangerous. As far as the world is concerned, Tom Cole died in France in 1918. When securing Tom a post at Grey Stones, the school agreed to my request that Mr and Mrs Edwards be provided with married accommodation, a request it could hardly refuse given our gift of Cole House. Well, having viewed the accommodation in question, we thought we could do better, and we think we have. So, without further ado, please accept our gift: the keys to Derwent Cottage, a charming residence situated on the banks of Derwentwater … that's how the agent described it, anyway."

"Mr Cole," protested Evelyn. "This is too much. We couldn't possibly …"

"Hush now, my dear," interrupted Brigit. "Your reluctance does you credit, but we will not take no for an answer."

"We are sure you will like it," said Richard handing the keys to Tom. "It boasts something of an isolated location, overlooking the lake."

"Which means that we can visit whenever we like, free from prying eyes," added Brigit.

"Thank you, thank you both," said Tom. "I'm not sure I deserve such generosity."

"Let us be the judge of that," replied Richard.

"I have a present as well," declared Edward, stepping forward.

"Edward. How kind of you," responded Evelyn.

"Well, it's not really a present, it's more like a …"

Edward paused as he searched for the appropriate word.

"It's more like what?" asked Tom.

"Oh, here," said Edward giving up. "I looked after it for you just like I said I would."

The distant sound of machine gun fire, exploding shells and the cries of charging men steadily became louder as Tom fixed his eyes on the Victoria Cross resting in the palm of Edward's outstretched hand. Tom picked up the medal and caressed it between his thumb and forefinger, oblivious to all around him. To his right, he could see Captain Percival charging towards the German trench. Tom knew he couldn't let him go alone. Where was his revolver? He needed a Mills bomb. He needed to get going.

"You never told me that you won the Victoria Cross," said Vincent taking the medal from Tom's hand.

"I'm sorry?" queried Tom as he left the battlefield.

"The Victoria Cross," repeated Vincent. "You never told me."

"Are you alright, Tom?" asked Evelyn taking his hand.

"I'm fine," replied Tom re-engaging with the present. "Seeing the medal again took me back for a moment. I'm fine."

"Do you want to tell me how you won this?" asked Vincent.

"He took a German trench single-handed, that's how," said Edward proudly.

"That must have taken a lot of courage," said Vincent.

"Not really," replied Tom. "As you well know, Vincent, you don't need that much courage when your back is to the wall, you just fight. Carrying on when you have lost everything in the world you hold dear, that requires real courage."

Squeezing her husband's hand, Evelyn reached up and kissed him on his cheek. Having returned her smile, Tom next turned to Mrs Duke.

"This is for you," he said brightly as he stepped towards her and pressed the medal into her hand.

"I can't take your medal," said Mrs Duke.

"Why not?" asked Tom. "You are a far braver person than I could ever be."

"You are a lovely boy, but I can't take it," repeated Mrs Duke. "It just wouldn't be right."

"Then keep it for me," said Tom. "Look after it. Will you do that for me, Mrs Duke? Look after it for a friend?"

Any doubts harboured by the housekeeper evaporated completely.

"That, my dear, I would be proud to do."

CHAPTER TWENTY-FOUR

Pressing On

"Well, let's go over what we know," said Anthony after they had settled at a table in the busy refectory.

It was late Friday afternoon, and weeks had passed since Emily had received the letter from the regiment. With the end of term only a week away, the time had come to decide precisely what they would tell Mr Cole and Miss Connolly.

"In a nutshell," said Emily, "we now know that Captain Thomas Cole and Michael Edwards were the same person."

"Which means that Captain Cole was not killed in the war as everyone believes," said Jimmy.

"Which also means that he must have had a pretty good reason for deserting the army and changing his identity," added Mark.

"Which gives rise to the possibility that he killed Colonel Carnforth," concluded Anthony.

"So, what shall we tell Miss Connolly and Robert Cole?" asked Emily. "If Miss Connolly thinks that Michael Edwards was her father, she isn't going to take kindly to us telling her that we think he killed his commanding officer and changed his name."

"The same goes for Robert Cole," said Anthony. "After all, 'Michael Edwards' was his uncle."

"We can only tell them what we know," said Jimmy.

"You mean what we *think* we know," corrected Mark.

"Well, whatever we tell them, I don't think we are going to be very popular," moaned Anthony.

Margaret Arbuckle appeared at the table.

"Is it okay if I join you?" she asked.

"You don't have to ask, Margaret, just take a seat," said Jimmy.

Margaret sat down between Jimmy and Anthony.

"I hope I haven't interrupted anything," said Margaret, conscious of the silence that greeted her arrival.

"Sorry, Margaret," said Mark, "we were just talking about something."

"Well, don't let me stop you," encouraged Margaret. "I can keep a secret. It wasn't you lot who pinched Snyder's portrait, was it?"

"Certainly not," protested Emily.

"We were talking about Michael Edwards," whispered Anthony.

"You know, the bloke who used to be headmaster here." said Jimmy. "You came with us when we went to look for his grave."

"Oh, him," replied Margaret, her tone betraying her disinterest.

"The thing is," said Jimmy, "we don't want everybody to know what we have found out …"

"Not a problem," interrupted Margaret. "I told you, I can keep a secret."

"Well, if you ask me," said Mark, "there's still a lot we don't know about Michael Edwards. Who killed him for a start?"

"And why?" asked Emily.

"I don't think we'll find the answers to those questions in the school archives," said Jimmy.

"Looks like we've hit a dead end, then," said Anthony with a smirk.

Mark cringed.

"That was a joke," said Anthony, slightly annoyed that he had to announce the fact.

"When did this bloke snuff it then?" asked Margaret.

"1941," replied Emily.

"You could always try the press," suggested Margaret.

"We didn't think of that," said Mark.

"Well then, if I were you, I should pop down to *The Keswickian* and ask for Harry," advised Margaret.

"The what?" queried Jimmy.

"*The Keswickian,* the local paper," explained Margaret. "Ask for Harry, he's the owner. One of his reporters might have covered the murder."

"But it was twenty-five years ago! There might not be anybody there who remembers anything about it," said Jimmy.

"But there might be records," enthused Emily.

"I think it's a great idea," said Anthony. "Where is the paper based?"

"On Main Street in the middle of Keswick," replied Margaret.

"Well, if we do go and see this Harry bloke, we can't let him or anyone else know that we think Captain Cole and Michael Edwards were the same person," said Mark. "We could get into a lot of trouble, even if we are right."

"Agreed," said Jimmy.

"How do you know this Harry character?" asked Emily.

"Harry? Harry Morgan?" replied Margaret. "He's my uncle."

The occupants of the table stared at Margaret in bemused silence.

"If you like, I'll take you to see him tomorrow," said Margaret.

"Great," said Jimmy. "Where shall we meet you?"

"Meet me under the clock on Main Street at twelve."

The following morning, Mark, Anthony and Jimmy met Emily at the bike shed and set off for Keswick. It was an exceptionally dark and wet morning, and by the time they arrived on Main Street, the rain was seeping through their anoraks. After meeting Margaret as arranged, she took them to the premises of *The Keswickian*.

"This is the place," announced Margaret, bringing her bike to a halt.

Pushing on along a dark passageway, she stopped outside a weather-beaten door and rested her bicycle against the wall. The others followed suit. A brass plate on the door read:

The Keswickian

Established 1882

Proprietor: Harold Morgan

"Are you sure your uncle won't mind us just turning up?" asked Mark.

"Of course not," replied Margaret as she retrieved her bicycle lamp and placed it in her pocket. "He's always pleased to see me."

Once inside the premises, Margaret led the visitors up a dimly lit stairwell, the bare boards of which amplified every step of their ascent. At the top of the stairs in an office that doubled as a reception area, Jean Fury, Harry Morgan's secretary, was typing at her desk. Aged in her early sixties, her hair tied up in a bun, the horn-rimmed spectacles that had slipped to the tip of her nose did nothing to soften her angular features or pinched expression.

"And what can I do for you?" she asked sternly as the group entered her office.

Then she recognised Margaret.

"Margaret? Is that you, dear?" she asked, her tone softening considerably.

"Hello, Mrs Fury. Are you okay? We're here to see my uncle Harry."

"I'm very well, dear, thank you, come in. All of you come in, take off your coats, you're all drenched."

A door opened behind Mrs Fury and Harry Morgan stepped into the reception area.

"Margaret? What the devil are you doing here?" asked a smiling Harry.

"Hello, Uncle," said Margaret returning his smile. "We've come to see you if you're not too busy."

"Too busy? Never too busy to see you, Margaret," replied Harry warmly. "And who are these young people with you?"

Margaret paused before responding.

"They're my … they're my friends," she said before quickly moving on. "There's a chance you may be able to help them."

"Right then," said Harry cheerfully. "Everyone into my office and you can tell me what this is all about."

"Make sure they put their anoraks on the radiators," ordered Mrs Fury. "They'll catch their deaths if they're not careful."

A small, middle-aged man of wiry build and a receding hairline, Harry clearly welcomed the intrusion. Sitting behind his desk, he invited his guests to pull up an assortment of chairs.

"And how is your Miss Connolly getting along?" he asked.

"How do you know her?" asked Jimmy.

"Grace Connolly? I've known her since she was a girl. She used to make her pocket money delivering our paper on her bike. Didn't you see that lovely photo of her on our front page after she joined Grey Stones? A nice little story that was. You know, local girl makes good sort of thing. Give her my regards when you see her. Well now, what is it I can do for you lot?"

By the time Mrs Fury entered the office with a tray laden with tea and biscuits, Harry had been told all he needed to know about Michael Edwards.

"Thanks, Jean. Just put everything down on the table here," encouraged Harry.

Having done as she was asked, Mrs Fury took a biscuit from the tray, made her way to the door, turned and smiled at Margaret.

"It really is good to see you again, dear."

"Right, help yourselves," ordered Harry after Mrs Fury had left the room.

"What do you think, Mr Morgan? Can you help us?" asked Anthony before taking a careful bite out of a chocolate bourbon.

"First things first: less of the 'Mr Morgan' if you don't mind. Everybody around here calls me Harry, and I wouldn't have it any other way."

Sitting back in his chair, Harry paused for a moment before answering Anthony's question.

"The truth is I can't help you because I didn't take the paper over until 1946, after I left the army. I'm afraid I know nothing about your Michael Edwards."

"Well, it was very kind of you to see us," said Emily, her tone laced with disappointment.

"Now, just hold your horses," chided Harry. "Just because *I* can't help you doesn't mean to say I don't know somebody who *can*. Wait here a minute."

Leaving his office by a side door, Harry crossed a large room full of desks and typewriters and disappeared.

"That's the press room where the reporters work," advised Margaret.

"There doesn't seem to be many of them about," observed Anthony.

"Maybe they're all out covering stories," suggested Mark.

A few minutes later, Harry returned accompanied by a tall, craggy, grey-haired man carrying a rather battered folder.

"This is one of my star reporters," announced Harry with a smile. "Meet Frank Hardy. This is the man you need to talk to."

"Margaret? Long time, no see. How are you doing?"

"Hello, Scoop," replied Margaret. "I'm okay, thanks."

"Scoop?" queried Emily.

"Don't tell me you've never heard of Scoop Hardy!" declared Harry. "The man's a legend of the free press. Courageous, bold, always first with the story ... they don't make 'em like Scoop any more, I can tell you. He mainly covers flower shows these days. Sit yourself down, Scoop."

"Do you mind if I take notes?" asked Anthony with typical enthusiasm.

"Feel free," replied Harry. "Well, Scoop, tell them what you know about the Michael Edwards case."

"Well, it was a long time ago ..."

"August 1941, to be exact," interrupted Anthony.

"August 1941," repeated Scoop thoughtfully. "I remember covering the story, alright. It's not often we get a murder to report around these parts. What is it exactly that you want to know?"

"Anything you can tell us, really," replied Jimmy. "All we know is that Michael Edwards was the headmaster of Grey Stones and that he is buried at St John's. We don't know who killed him, why he was killed or even if the killer was ever caught."

"Seems to me that we need to start at the beginning," said Scoop.

Opening the tattered folder that rested on his lap, Scoop Hardy retrieved his glasses from the breast pocket of his shirt and proceeded to flick through its contents.

"These are the notes I made at the time," he explained.

By this time, even Margaret seemed curious about what Scoop might say.

"Right then," said Scoop as he continued to peruse his notes. "I can tell you that on the evening of 30th August 1941, someone at the school called the Fire Brigade to report that the school boathouse was on fire. By the time the fire brigade arrived, it was too late to save the building and the fire was allowed to burn itself out. Efforts to contact Michael Edwards, the headmaster, proved unsuccessful. The following day a body was found in what was left of the boathouse. By this time, Michael Edwards had still not turned up, and the police began to suspect he might be the victim. Their suspicions were confirmed on the afternoon of 31st August when Evelyn Edwards, Michael's wife, identified the body."

"How could she be sure it was him?" asked Emily. "I mean, surely if his body had been burned …"

"You're quite right, miss," said Scoop. "The body was burned beyond recognition."

Emily shuddered. Scoop again referred to the contents of the battered folder before continuing.

"According to my notes, Inspector Holmes, the investigating officer, confirmed that Mrs Edwards had identified her husband by the wedding ring he was wearing."

"Inspector who?" asked Jimmy taken aback.

"Inspector Bernard Holmes," replied Scoop.

"We didn't know Michael Edwards was married," said Mark, moving the conversation on.

"Oh yes," confirmed Scoop. "Mr and Mrs Edwards lived at the Old Mill on the school grounds."

"That's where Mr Snyder and his wife live," said Mark.

"But what made the police think that Michael Edwards had been murdered?" asked Jimmy.

"Well, once his body had been identified, the police searched his office and found a note," explained Scoop, who again referred to his folder. "The note read: Meet me in the boathouse at 8:00 pm. Bring the money. No tricks or else."

"You mean he was being blackmailed?" asked a shocked Anthony.

"That's what Inspector Holmes thought," said Scoop.

"What a pity the blackmailer didn't sign the note," said Emily flippantly.

"Oh, but he did," replied Scoop.

"That was rather stupid, wasn't it?" said Mark.

"Never mind that," said Emily impatiently. "Who signed the note?"

"A person by the name of John Rimmer," replied Scoop.

"J-John *who?*" stuttered Jimmy.

"You okay?" asked Margaret. "Have you heard of this John Rimmer before then?"

"No," said Jimmy rather too quickly before turning to Scoop. "I just got a bit mixed up because one of the porters at school is called Rimmer."

"Oh, that will be Stanley Rimmer, John Rimmer's son," explained Scoop, rummaging through his folder in search of another old note.

"Here we are, John and Stanley Rimmer. They became porters at the school in the summer of 1941 when Stanley was only fifteen. You won't be surprised to hear that John Rimmer disappeared off the face of the earth after the murder and was never seen again. The son was questioned about his father's whereabouts, but the lad couldn't assist and the police concluded that he was innocent of any wrongdoing. The school took a charitable view and, given the boy's age and the fact that he had nowhere else to go, Stanley kept his job."

"And what about Mrs Edwards?" asked Mark. "What happened to her?"

"Couldn't rightly tell you," replied Scoop. "Following her husband's funeral, she stayed at the school for a short time before moving on."

"Is she still alive?" asked Anthony.

"She might be," said Emily. "She certainly isn't buried with her husband."

"Is there anything else you can tell them?" asked Harry.

"That's about it, I'm afraid," replied Scoop.

"Just one more question," said Jimmy. "What was it that Michael Edwards was being blackmailed about?"

The veteran reporter shook his head slowly.

"Sorry," he replied, "that remains a mystery to this day."

*

"Okay, what was all that about?" demanded Emily as they spilled onto Main Street. "You nearly fell off your chair when that Scoop person mentioned John Rimmer."

"It wasn't just John Rimmer," replied Jimmy. "When we get back to school, I'll show you something."

"Show us what?" asked Anthony.

"Wait and see," replied Jimmy. "Come on, we need to pay a visit to Cole Hall."

The rain was still falling heavily, and by the time they reached Cole Hall, the friends were soaked to the skin.

"Well then?" asked a shivering Anthony as they stood before the captain's photograph. "What is it you want to show us?"

"This," said Jimmy pointing into the glass cabinet that displayed the captain's last letter home.

"The letter? What about it?" asked Emily.

"I think the captain should tell you himself," said Jimmy. "Listen."

After looking around him to make sure that there was nobody else in earshot, Jimmy read the letter aloud.

"*20th March 1918. Dear Ma and Pa, just a short letter to let you know that the cigarettes and socks you sent arrived last week.*

The socks were particularly welcome: if you don't look after your feet over here, you're simply asking for trouble. It's been pretty quiet over the last few weeks though nobody expects the lull to continue. With the Americans having entered the war, the Hun knows he will have to take the initiative quickly before the balance shifts decisively in our favour."

"Where is this leading?" asked Mark.

"It's here somewhere, just listen," replied Jimmy before returning to the letter. "*Oh, how I miss home. Surely this war cannot continue for much longer. It seems to me that both sides have fought each other to a standstill. If only the politicians could be put in the trenches for just a week, hostilities would soon give way to negotiation. But then, what do I know? I'm only a soldier. I am just grabbing some rest, having done the rounds with Bernard Holmes, my sergeant. What a fine fellow he is. I hope that one day you will get to meet him, though not, I hope, in his official capacity. In civilian life, he is a policeman."*

Jimmy stopped reading and looked at his friends.

"Didn't Scoop mention somebody called Holmes?" asked Emily.

"Yes, Inspector Bernard Holmes," confirmed Anthony, referring to his notebook. "He was in charge of the Michael Edwards murder case."

"Are you saying Inspector Holmes and Sergeant Holmes are the same person?" asked Mark.

"Well, it looks like, doesn't it?" replied Jimmy. "We know from this letter that Sergeant Holmes was a policeman before the war. He most likely returned to the police after it was over."

"It could be just a coincidence," said Emily.

Ignoring her, Jimmy took up from where he had left off.

"Colonel Carnforth has recently returned from leave and is ensuring everybody gives of their best. The men appear to be in good spirits and seem ready for anything. On the other hand, our replacements seem to be getting younger and younger. I've just met one of them: Private John Rimmer. He looks no more than a boy—"

"Private *who*?" interrupted Mark.

"Private John Rimmer," repeated Jimmy, "the man who was to blackmail Michael Edwards twenty-three years later."

"But why wait twenty-three years to blackmail someone?" asked Anthony.

"Because John Rimmer thought he was dead," explained Jimmy. "He turns up here in 1941 as a porter, sees Michael Edwards, recognises him as Captain Cole and tries to blackmail him."

"Well, if that's right," concluded Anthony, "whatever Michael Edwards was being blackmailed about must have had something to do with the war."

"Which brings us back to the captain's desertion and the possibility that he killed Colonel Carnforth," said Mark.

"But wouldn't Inspector Holmes have known they were linked?" queried Emily. "If he had been in the trenches with them, why didn't he mention any of this in his investigation?"

"He might not have known," replied Jimmy. "Don't forget what Scoop said about Michael Edwards only being identified by his wedding ring. If his body was unrecognisable, it would have been impossible for the inspector to have made the connection."

"Well," said Mark, "as far as I'm concerned, it has to be at least possible that the blackmail had something to do with the colonel's death."

"What about him?" asked Margaret, her hand pointing to the board that commemorated the dead of the Second World War.

"Who?" asked Emily.

"Him, Tristan Herbert Carnforth," replied Margaret, "the one who died in 1940. Is he related to the Colonel Carnforth mentioned in the letter?"

All eyes followed Margaret's outstretched hand to the inscription carved into the mahogany panel above them:

Pilot Officer Tristan Herbert Carnforth

Royal Air Force

3rd June 1940, aged 21

"Hold on! Why does the name *Tristan* sound familiar?" asked Anthony.

"Miss Connolly. Don't you remember?" said Jimmy.

"Remember what?" asked Mark.

"The day we saw her looking at the captain's photograph," replied Jimmy. "The day she was crying. She told us about her father, Tristan Connolly. She told us he had won a Victoria Cross flying for the RAF. She told us he died in 1940."

"That's right," confirmed Anthony. "June 1940."

"So what?" asked Mark. "The question is whether or not Tristan Carnforth is related to Colonel Carnforth."

"When was he a pupil here?" asked Anthony.

"Who knows?" replied Emily. "Must have been during the 1930s."

"We need to follow this up," said Jimmy. "We need to go back to the archives and see if we can trace him there."

"Let's do it," said Emily enthusiastically.

"Not me," said Mark. "I've done enough sleuthing for one day. I'm off for my run."

"In this weather?" questioned Jimmy.

"In any weather," replied Mark. "In case you've forgotten, the Christmas Chase is next Wednesday. I'll meet you in the refectory later and you can fill me in then."

As the classmates reached the foyer, Jimmy turned around to see that Margaret, her eyes fixed on the photograph of Captain Cole, had not moved.

"Margaret," hissed Jimmy loudly. "Come on."

Released from the captain's hypnotic gaze by Jimmy's intervention, Margaret followed him out of the hall.

CHAPTER TWENTY-FIVE

An Inspector Calls

By early 1919, Bernard Holmes had returned to Carlisle where he did his best to put the past behind him. Determined to make his survival count for something, he returned to the police force and was immediately promoted to sergeant. Before the year was out, he had married his sweetheart, who, in due course, produced four children. As the war retreated into the distance, life moved on for the better. But Bernard Holmes would never forget the comrades he had fought with or the debt he owed the young captain whose leadership and courage had saved so many lives.

In April 1919, Holmes visited Tom's parents at Blackberry Hill. Mrs Cole, he soon realised, refused to accept her son's passing on the basis that nobody had witnessed his death. On the other hand, the world-weary demeanour of Mr Cole convinced Holmes that he had long accepted that he would never see his son again. Of one thing Holmes was sure: there was nothing to be gained by exploding the myth that their son and Colonel Carnforth had died at their posts after authorising the surrender of their men.

Having paid his respects to the Cole family, Holmes next visited Catherine Carnforth, the colonel's wife. Although he had never formed any particular bond with the colonel, Holmes felt duty-bound to offer his condolences. A single parent living in a poor neighbourhood of Carlisle, Catherine's financial plight was hardly surprising. That the colonel had been promoted from the ranks meant that his career as an officer, whilst meteoric in terms of promotion, had been relatively short: following his death, the family's modest savings soon dwindled. In the years that followed, Holmes continued to visit Catherine to see how she and her young son, Tristan, were coping. Although Catherine would never ask Holmes for financial help, she came to accept him as a trusted advisor.

In June 1929, Bernard Holmes, now an inspector, was on his way to visit the Carnforth family. Turning the corner into Percy Street, his pace slowed when, from a distance, he saw a man leave the Carnforth address, cross the road and get into a car. Attaching little significance to this sighting, Holmes quickened his step and continued towards his destination. As the car drove past him, his curiosity got the better of him and he succeeded in getting a good look at the driver. One look was enough. After noting the driver's scarred right cheek, Inspector Holmes stood rooted to the spot.

"Mr Holmes, what a pleasure to see you," said a smiling Catherine Carnforth upon opening her front door. "Your visit could not be better timed."

"Hello, Mrs Carnforth," responded a still-dazed Holmes.

Crossing the threshold into the living room, he saw Tristan sitting at a table near the window.

"Hello, Tristan, how are you doing?" asked Holmes warmly.

"Very well, thank you, sir," replied the eleven-year-old.

Dark-haired with angelic good looks, the boy, thought Holmes, was a credit to his mother.

"Sit down, Mr Holmes," insisted Catherine as she took his hat and ushered him towards the table. "Sit down and let me get tea. I have news."

A small woman, her hair turned prematurely grey by the strain of single parenthood and life on the poverty line, Catherine Carnforth looked significantly older than her forty-five years. But the news that she wished to impart had, for the moment at least, animated her demeanour to a degree that Holmes had never before witnessed.

"News?" queried Holmes as he looked at Tristan and smiled.

"Yes," replied Catherine, "possibly very good news. But I need your advice."

"Has this got anything to do with the man who has just left?" asked Holmes.

"Everything," confirmed Catherine. "Do you know him?"

"I don't think so," lied the inspector.

"Well, his name is Michael Edwards, and he is a history master at Grey Stones School for Boys in Keswick," explained Catherine. "It would appear that the school has connections with the family of Captain Cole, the officer who died at my husband's side. Of course, you remember him."

"I do indeed," confirmed Holmes.

"Before I go any further," said Catherine, "I must have your word that our conversation remains strictly confidential. You must not repeat a word of it to anybody. Do I have your word?"

Bernard Holmes paused before answering.

"You have it."

"Thank you," said Catherine before turning to Tristan. "Tristan, dearest, I need to discuss something with Mr Holmes alone."

"That's alright, Mother," replied Tristan, his tone rendering any further explanation unnecessary. "Shall I see you before you leave, Mr Holmes?"

"Of course," smiled the inspector.

Once Tristan had left the room, the thought of tea having escaped her mind completely, Catherine Carnforth got to the point.

"According to Mr Edwards, a new wing of Grey Stones was built some years ago in memory of Captain Cole. Well, it would appear that the school has decided to commemorate the connection between the captain and my husband by offering Tristan a scholarship."

"Mr Edwards told you this?"

"Yes," replied Catherine.

"Did he mention anything about the cost of sending Tristan to Grey Stones?"

"There is no cost, hence my concern and my need of your advice. Mr Edwards says that everything is to be paid for by the school and that I am to receive a grant of two hundred pounds a month to pay for any unforeseen expense and enable me to move closer to Keswick."

"Two hundred pounds a month?" repeated Holmes.

"I know, it's a ludicrous amount of money, a small fortune which would obviously transform our lives."

"Well, it's an exceptionally generous offer," said Holmes. "Did Mr Edwards seek to impose any conditions?"

"Only one. Mr Edwards informed me that if I accept, I must not disclose the school's offer to anybody. There must be no publicity, and Tristan must know nothing of the arrangement. Does that not seem strange to you? Surely the school would wish to exploit the favourable publicity such a generous offer would generate."

Inspector Holmes looked out of the window and grimaced.

"Mr Holmes? What would you advise?"

"I'm sorry, I was miles away."

"Should I accept the offer, or should I be cautious? What if, somewhere along the line, the offer is amended or rescinded? What then? Mr Holmes, please advise me. Should I trust Mr Edwards?"

Looking Catherine Carnforth in the eye, Holmes placed his hands gently on her burdened shoulders.

"I have known you for a long time and have always tried to advise you honestly."

"I know that," responded Catherine quietly. "You have been a dear and honourable friend to Tristan and myself."

"Then listen to me now and accept my advice without reservation. Trust Michael Edwards. Trust him implicitly. Accept his offer."

As he returned to the centre of Carlisle, Bernard Holmes wondered what he should do next. It did not take him long to reach a decision. Although tempted to approach the captain, he would not do so. The captain's deception had, he assumed, been successful in its purpose: reputations, including his own, had been spared damaging scrutiny. The war was behind them, and millions had paid a price. Better to let sleeping dogs lie. Better to let people get on with their lives.

CHAPTER TWENTY-SIX

Finding Tristan

As they hurried through the deserted library towards the cellar, Jimmy already had a good idea about where to look for information about Tristan Carnforth. At the top of the spiral staircase, Anthony switched on the cellar lights.

"Just what is it exactly that we are hoping to find out?" he asked as they descended the steps.

"Whether or not Tristan Carnforth was related to Colonel Carnforth," replied Emily.

"Spooky or what?" said Margaret after Anthony had unlocked the cellar door.

"Spooky and cold," replied Emily.

"Right, follow me," said Jimmy. "If he was twenty-one when he died in June 1940, then I'm guessing he joined the school in 1929 or 1930."

Leading the way into the belly of the cellar, Jimmy stopped in front of the shelving marked '1929'. Retrieving the yearbook for that year, he briefly flicked through the pages before looking up in triumph.

"Got him. He's listed under 'First Form Intake' as Tristan Herbert Carnforth."

"Is there a photograph?" asked Anthony.

"No," replied Jimmy. "It was only members of staff who were photographed for the yearbook."

Within minutes, every yearbook covering Tristan's time at Grey Stones had been recovered. Each yearbook confirmed the attendance of T.H. Carnforth at the school but nothing more. By 1936, his name had fallen away from the pupil register forever.

"Well, that didn't tell us much, did it?" said a slightly fed-up Anthony.

"There must be something down here we are missing," insisted Emily.

"We could look at the school reports," suggested Anthony without much enthusiasm.

"They're not likely to tell us much about him, nothing about his family anyway," said Jimmy.

"We could always go back to Uncle Harry," suggested Margaret. "You never know, there may be a report in *The Keswickian* about his plane being shot down."

"I doubt it," replied Jimmy. "I mean, *The Keswickian* is a small local paper which reports on local stories."

"Hold on a minute," said Anthony. "There is a readership that would have been interested."

"Enlighten us," invited Emily dryly.

"The readership of *The Scholar*," replied Anthony.

"The school magazine?" queried Jimmy.

"Why not?" said Emily, warming to the idea. "Why wouldn't the school magazine report the passing of former pupils killed during the war?"

Needing no further encouragement, Anthony returned to the shelving marked '1940'. On the bottom shelf sat a cardboard box containing copies of *The Scholar*, which Mark, only a few weeks before, had looked through when researching Michael Edwards. Retrieving the box, Anthony returned to his friends and placed it on a table.

"I suppose if Tristan Carnforth is going to be mentioned anywhere, it will be in the June or July edition," said Anthony.

The others sat silently as Anthony, his eyes straining in the dim light, sifted through the box.

"Here, use this," said Margaret, producing her bicycle lamp from her anorak pocket.

"Thanks," said Anthony without looking up.

Having recovered the June edition, Anthony placed it on the table and, bicycle lamp to the fore, turned its pages.

"There's no mention of him here," confirmed Anthony before reaching for the July edition and repeating the exercise.

With the turning of each page, Anthony's expression did not change. Only when he reached the last page did a smile appear on his face.

"I've got it," he said quietly. "An obituary entitled, 'In Memory of Tristan Carnforth'."

"Read what it says," instructed Emily softly.

Adjusting his glasses slightly, Anthony read the obituary aloud.

"It is with huge regret and deep sorrow that I must inform the school of the tragic passing of Pilot Officer Tristan Carnforth, who was shot down over the English Channel during an engagement with enemy aircraft on 3rd June, 1940. Tristan attended Grey Stones between 1929 and 1935 before going up to Cambridge, where he learned to fly with the University Air Squadron. He was posted to his RAF squadron in the spring of 1939. Like his father before him, Colonel Herbert Carnforth V.C., Tristan died defending his country."

"So, they *were* related," said Margaret.

Anthony read on.

"His classmates and those who taught him will remember a polite and conscientious boy who was always willing to help others. Many will remember the seemingly carefree young man who only last April, during what transpired to be his last leave, visited the school with his young lady, Miss Jane Connolly."

Anthony looked up and paused for a few seconds before continuing.

"Persuaded against his better judgment to address the school, he confessed to those present that he looked upon Grey Stones as his home and those who passed

through its halls as his family. When he fought, he said, he fought for us. Though not a warrior by nature, Tristan never shirked the fight. We needed the protection he could offer, and he freely gave it. The nation has lost a loyal and true defender, one who put others before himself. We at Grey Stones have lost one of our own. We have lost a son and a brother. Jane has lost her soul mate. Rest in peace, Tristan, and may your sacrifice not be in vain."

A respectful hush fell upon the table.

"He was very well-liked, loved even," said Emily.

"Where to from here then?" asked Anthony, switching off the bicycle lamp.

"Well, isn't it rather obvious?" volunteered Margaret quietly.

The others looked at her expectantly, their silence inviting her to continue.

"Well, you think that Michael Edwards, formerly known as Captain Cole, killed Colonel Carnforth, don't you?"

"Well, we think that's a possibility," replied Anthony.

"More than a possibility," said Jimmy.

"Then surely the first question you should be asking is whether it was just coincidence that Tristan Carnforth ended up at the school where his father's suspected killer was teaching?" said Margaret.

"And your second question?" asked a cautiously impressed Anthony.

"My second question," replied an increasingly confident Margaret, "my second question is more of a hunch than a question."

"What's that, then?" asked Jimmy.

Margaret hesitated before taking the plunge.

"Well, it seems highly probable that Tristan Carnforth was Miss Connolly's father."

"Okay, Sherlock, how did you work that out?" asked an exasperated Anthony.

"Easy," replied Margaret. "First, Miss Connolly tells you about her father, Tristan Connolly, who was shot down in June 1940. Next, we discover that Tristan Carnforth was also shot down in June 1940."

"So what?" challenged Anthony.

"And now," continued Margaret, "we know that Tristan Carnforth was seeing a lady called Jane Connolly. It's all a bit obvious, isn't it?

"Margaret's right." conceded Emily. "If it turns out that Miss Connolly's mother's name was Jane, Tristan Carnforth must have been her father."

"Then who is Tristan Connolly?" asked a confused Anthony. "And if Tristan Carnforth is Miss Connolly's father, why isn't Miss Connolly called Miss Carnforth?"

"Well, if you ask me," said Margaret, her chin now resting in the palms of her upturned hands, "I'd say that Miss Connolly isn't called Miss Carnforth because …"

"They never married," interrupted Jimmy, the penny having dropped. "Tristan Carnforth and Jane Connolly never married."

"You've got it," said Margaret.

"But if it was Miss Connolly who left the flowers at the grave, she thinks that Michael Edwards was her father," said Emily.

Before anybody could respond, the lights went out, plunging the cellar into total darkness.

"What's happening?" demanded Emily as she instinctively grabbed Jimmy's arm.

For a few seconds, everybody sat motionless, hoping the lights would flicker back to life.

"And what was that?" hissed Anthony into the blackness.

Jimmy recognised the sound immediately. It was the sound of a turning key.

"Is somebody having a laugh?" he asked, rising to his feet.

"What do you mean?" asked Emily.

"He means," replied Margaret, "that we've just been locked in."

CHAPTER TWENTY-SEVEN

An Invitation

It was late August 1941, and the start of the new school year was just two weeks away. Situated behind Baird House within throwing distance of the cricket pavilion, the Old Mill had been the home of every serving headmaster since 1875. Sitting with her husband at a table in the walled garden, Evelyn smiled and took his hand.

"So, what are you up to this morning?" she asked.

"Nothing exciting," replied Tom. "I told Martin Giles I would review the new timetable with him. Will you be visiting Derwent Cottage today?"

"Of course," replied Evelyn. "I thought I would take Jane into Keswick for lunch."

"Give her my love. How are mother and child coping?"

"Grace is fine, she's a very healthy baby. It's her mother I worry about."

"Jane? Is she ill?"

"Not physically, no, but I'm not sure she's coping. She just appears so vacant at times."

"That's to be expected, surely," said Tom. "To lose Tristan, her entire family, and to have a child out of …" Tom hesitated. "Has there been talk?"

"No," assured Evelyn. "Jane's secret is safe. And anyway, people have more important things to worry about these days. The world has moved on."

"Well, nobody should bother her now she's living in the cottage," said Tom. "She's lucky to have you."

"No, Tom, we are lucky to have them," replied Evelyn.

Tom reached across the table, kissed his wife and took his leave.

Upon entering the quad on his way to Baird House, Tom saw Mr Grimes, the school caretaker, and four porters approaching from the opposite direction. A delivery of refurbished tables and chairs had arrived, and Mr Grimes and his crew were taking them to the refectory.

"Morning, sir," chimed Grimes.

"Morning, Mr Grimes," replied Tom returning the caretaker's smile. "Everything in hand?"

"We're getting there, sir," replied Grimes without stopping, "we're getting there."

"Well, let me know if you need anything," called Tom, who stopped momentarily to acknowledge the passing porters, one of whom was just a boy.

"You must be new," said Tom as the boy was passing. "How old are you?"

"Fifteen, sir," replied the boy.

"Is Mr Grimes looking after you alright?"

"Yes, sir," confirmed the boy with a sheepish smile.

"Glad to hear it," said Tom. "Let me know if you have any problems."

Behind the boy, an older man, his face void of expression, stared at Tom in silence. Acknowledging the porter with a smile and a nod, Tom continued on his way, but only after observing the porter's pronounced limp. After Tom had moved on, the porter stopped and turned to follow the head's progress.

"Come on then, Mr Rimmer," shouted Grimes. "We haven't got all day."

"Sorry, Mr Grimes," responded Rimmer apologetically, his face now as white as a sheet.

"What's the matter with you, man?" asked Grimes as he approached Rimmer. "You look like you've seen a ghost."

"Not at all, Mr Grimes," said Rimmer, "it was just that I thought I recognised that gentleman, that's all."

"Who? Mr Edwards, the head? You know him, do you?" asked Grimes.

"No, sir," lied Rimmer, "I was mistaken. I've never seen him before in my life."

Sitting at his desk in his office, Tom stared blankly out of the window. He was back in France. He had recognised Private John Rimmer the moment he set eyes on him.

*

When John Rimmer returned home to Carlisle in March 1919, he did so as a young war hero. For the first time in his life, he had attracted admiration and respect, and he liked it. It was with an untroubled conscience that Rimmer accepted the numerous pints of ale thrust into his hand by those eager to hear first-hand his account of the Battle of Carnforth Hill. It was with the insight of a battle-hardened warrior that he paid tribute to the gallantry and leadership displayed by his commanding officers, Colonel Carnforth and Captain Cole, in whose glory he bathed. And it was with affected modesty that he described how he had finished off numerous German stormtroopers despite being shot in the leg. But as interest in returning war heroes waned, the flow of free drinks reduced to a trickle.

When attending his first regimental reunion, Rimmer found that the praise heaped upon him in the pubs of Carlisle was not echoed by his former comrades who, he thought, eyed him with suspicion. Had Sergeant Holmes, the only other man who knew what had happened in the dugout, told them his secret? The sergeant had been friendly enough, but Rimmer detected a certain reserve, a reluctance to engage: he felt as though he was being tolerated, and he feared exposure. Having attended one reunion, Rimmer would never attend another. When the back-slapping ceased and the free drinks dried up completely, he found himself out of a job, his lack of prospects reflecting his lack of ambition.

Two years after returning from France, John Rimmer married Peggy Gilks, a mild-mannered textile worker who, in 1926, bore him a son, Stanley. For Rimmer, the marriage was one of complete convenience. Peggy had a job: she paid for their rented accommodation and put food on the table. She negotiated life on the poverty line and never complained. By the beginning of the 1930s, trapped in a loveless marriage and tired of being exploited, Peggy Rimmer was sliding into deepening depression. In 1935, her resilience spent, she tied a rope to the landing banister, placed the noose around her neck and hurled herself into oblivion.

By 1941, out of work, in debt and about to be evicted from the slum he called home, John Rimmer was desperate. With an eye on the circling loan sharks, he concluded that the time had come to leave Carlisle for good, even if it meant seeking employment. Thanks to the outbreak of war in 1939, Rimmer, despite his bad leg, was confident that even he could find a job somewhere. When told about the vacancies at Grey Stones, he was immediately interested, especially when discovering that the job came with accommodation. When interviewed by Mr Grimes, Rimmer, attempting to impress, played heavily on his time in the trenches. That Mr Grimes was won over was not because of any gullibility on his part but because he realised that in recruiting John Rimmer, he was getting the fifteen-year-old Stanley for next to nothing. Shaking the hands of his two new recruits, Mr Grimes informed them that they were to report for work at 8:30 am on Monday the 25th of August, two weeks before the start of the academic year.

Having left Carlisle behind them, their mutual belongings stashed into a worn canvas bag, John and Stanley Rimmer duly arrived at Grey Stones on the appointed day at the appointed hour. After being shown to their simple living quarters in the old stables and allowed a short time to unpack, they were each given a blue work coat and directed to Baird House, where they were to help convey a delivery of furniture to the refectory. As he made his way across the quad, John Rimmer gave little thought to the person approaching from the opposite direction. Even after he had stopped to engage with the porters, Rimmer was none the wiser as to the man's identity. But that all changed as soon as he heard him address his son.

"How old are you?"

The question sent Rimmer spiralling back in time to the lull before the storm that was the Battle of Carnforth Hill.

"How old are you?"

The question pierced his sub-conscious and invaded the place where his most terrifying memories slept.

"How old are you?"

"Eighteen, sir."

"He's one of the new replacements, sir."

"Sleeping on duty? You could be shot for this!"

The words echoed through time with terrifying effect. And then Rimmer saw the scar on the man's right cheek, and he was sure, as sure as he had been of anything in his entire life. Captain Cole, the man who shot Colonel Carnforth, was alive and well.

The day passed quickly for Rimmer as shock and distraction gave way to calculation. A golden opportunity had presented itself, and Rimmer was not about to waste it. A few innocuous questions asked of his new colleagues soon confirmed the Cole family to be a family of substance. Had the Coles not built Cole House? Was Richard Cole not a governor of the school? Rimmer did not doubt that Captain Cole, or Michael Edwards as he now called himself, was a man of wealth.

When he took to his cot that evening, Rimmer applied his mind to three options. The first option, to do nothing and keep quiet, he rejected on the ground that silence and inaction would not profit him at all. The second option, to go to the police, was rendered no more attractive than the first because there could be no guarantee that he would receive anything by way of a reward. Furthermore, reporting the matter to the police might expose the act of cowardice which had enabled him to witness the shooting of Colonel Carnforth in the first place. No, the more Rimmer thought about it, the more he was convinced that his best option, the third option, was to confront the captain, threaten him with exposure and sell his silence. He could think of no reason why the captain would not be prepared to negotiate.

*

The following morning, Tom took his leave of Evelyn and made his way to his office. Sleep had proved impossible. He was sure Rimmer had recognised him within seconds of their encounter the previous day. Tom entered his secretary's office shortly after ten o'clock and checked her desk for messages; none were found. Most of the administrative staff were still on their summer break, and the office was empty. Upon entering his own office, Tom immediately spotted the crumpled brown envelope that had been pushed under the door. His heart sank. Opening the envelope, he read the enclosed note.

Meet me today at the boathouse at six. Come alone.

The note was not signed: it didn't need to be.

*

A large wooden structure built on the bank of an inlet, the boathouse was largely protected from public view. Two wide sliding doors opened onto a concrete ramp which sloped gently to the water's edge. To the rear, a single door offered an alternative means of entry. Inside, to the left, a flight of wooden steps led to a small office. Within the office, an open hatch provided an unobstructed view of the boathouse floor below. Having arrived at the stipulated time, Tom pushed open one of the sliding doors just enough to allow him access. Once inside, he paused and looked about him. Stretching into the dim interior, units of wooden racking accommodated a variety of crafts. As his eyes adjusted to the gloom, Tom tried to read the time on his watch. Then, Rimmer stepped forward from behind one of the wooden units at the forefront of the boathouse.

"Evenin', Captain, I see you got my note then," said Rimmer gruffly.

"I received it," said Tom, who moved towards the porter to get a better view of him.

"No further, if you please, Captain, that's quite close enough," said Rimmer firmly. "I wouldn't want you gettin' too close now, would I, especially if you're going to lose your temper. I've seen how you act when you lose your temper."

"Alright, Rimmer, get to the point. What is it you want from me?"

"Let's just say that I have a proposition for you."

Rimmer paused in anticipation of a response, but none was forthcoming.

"Don't you want to know what my proposition is?" he asked playfully.

Tom remained silent.

"Well, I'll tell you. Do you remember when we were in that dugout all those years ago? Of course you do. Well, I saw things that day that I've done my best to forget, things that came floodin' back to me when we bumped into each other yesterday. I think you know what I'm talkin' about."

"Just exactly what did you see, Rimmer?" asked Tom quietly.

Rimmer, annoyed by Tom's unruffled response, spat out his reply.

"I'll tell you what I saw. I saw you fightin' with the colonel. I saw you fightin' with the colonel because you wanted to surrender to the Bosch, and I saw you shoot him dead."

Seconds passed before Tom replied.

"That wasn't why I was fighting with him …"

"Maybe it wasn't," interrupted Rimmer, "but the fact is you shot him dead."

"There was a struggle," recalled Tom quietly. "I was trying to disarm him …"

"You killed him," insisted Rimmer.

Tom did not respond.

"Now, I reckon that a lot of people, especially the police and the people who pay you to run this school, would be really interested in what I might tell them."

Tom played his only card, but he knew it was a weak one.

"Won't the police want to know why you haven't revealed all this before? What will they do when they discover that the colonel shot you for cowardice?"

"Well, I've been givin' that some thought," replied Rimmer. "You see, I've never mentioned it before because, thinkin' you were dead, I just didn't see the point in causin' the Carnforth family any more grief than was necessary. Very decent of me, don't you think? And as far as me bein' a coward is concerned, who do you think they are going to believe? Me, the brave soldier who fought on after bein' wounded in the leg, or you, the coward who shot his commandin' officer, deserted the army and changed his name?"

"You know how you got your wound," said Tom softly.

"What I know and what I will tell are two very different things," said Rimmer smiling.

"How much is it you want?" asked Tom.

"You're an educated man, guess."

"How much?" repeated Tom.

"Two thousand," replied Rimmer testing the waters. "Cash, of course."

"And how much after that?" asked Tom, a half-smile appearing on his face.

Rimmer smiled back at him.

"I'll bet you're wishin' you'd let old Carnforth finish me off."

"I need time to think," said Tom.

"Well, they all say that, don't they," replied Rimmer. "But fair enough, I'll give you 'til Saturday. That'll give you time to get the money."

"You seem pretty sure that I'm going to pay up."

"Like I say, you're an educated man. What choice do you have? You either pay me or lose everythin' and end up swingin' from a rope. You'll pay. Meet me back here at eight o'clock on Saturday evenin' with the money."

Tom held Rimmer's stare for a few seconds before turning to leave the boathouse.

"And Captain," said Rimmer. "No tricks. My boy Stanley knows everything. If anything happens to me, he knows exactly what to do."

CHAPTER TWENTY-EIGHT

The Eavesdropper

Sitting in a rowing boat in the middle of Derwentwater, Bernard Holmes expertly reeled in another fish. Calmed by the gentle motion of the lake and soothed by the sound of lapping water, he dedicated his catch, a silvery blue roach, to his wife, Jenny. It was Jenny who had insisted that he take the weekend off to indulge in his favourite pastime. In truth, he had needed little persuading. With many of his younger colleagues called up, his workload had doubled, and he needed a break. Jenny had been right: he was of no use to anybody if he couldn't function properly. Having booked him a room at The Pheasant Inn on the outskirts of Keswick, she had waved him off with a kiss and a smile. Dear Jenny, his wife, friend, and confidante, she knew him better than anyone alive. But even she did not know about Tom Cole. That secret he would take to the grave.

Since recognising Tom in 1929, Holmes had done his best to keep an eye on him, albeit from a distance. For a while this had been relatively easy: Catherine Carnforth, through Tristan, had proved an unwitting source of information whenever he called to see her. When, in 1936, Catherine told him that Tristan was to go up to Cambridge, Holmes, who was genuinely delighted for the boy, did not doubt that Michael Edwards would again be footing the bill. By this time, Catherine's strength was clearly failing. Worry and a sense of foreboding caused her health to deteriorate yet further when, with the approach of another war with Germany, Tristan joined the University Air Squadron. In 1938, Catherine Carnforth died following a short illness. Michael Edwards, afraid that he might be recognised by former comrades-in-arms, did not attend her funeral. But Holmes did, and at the small reception that followed, he skilfully quizzed Tristan as to the wellbeing of the person he still thought of as his captain.

The news of Tristan's death in June 1940 affected Bernard Holmes deeply. Having considered approaching Tom Cole, he quickly abandoned the idea: why threaten to expose a fiction that had prevailed over two decades to the advantage of all? Better, thought Holmes, to carry on as before and let the past alone.

Pulling on the boat's oars, his fishing tackle strewn about his feet, Bernard Holmes looked across the lake toward Grey Stones and wondered how his former captain was getting on. He had no idea that within a few short hours, their paths would not so much cross as collide. It was approaching 5:30 pm on the 30th of August 1941, and Bernard Holmes was rowing back to the shore.

It had been a successful afternoon, even if he had thrown his entire catch back into the lake. As he drove to The Pheasant, Holmes, tired and thirsty, licked his lips in anticipation of the pint of ale he had promised himself. After registering his arrival, he ordered his pint and looked for a quiet place to sit. Opting for a high-backed 'monk's bench' near the window, he took his seat, knowing he would be hidden from the majority of those occupying the bar. His privacy intact, he drew from his pint, sat back and relived the victories of the day. After fifteen minutes or so, just as he was about to return to the bar for a refill, he picked up on a conversation taking place behind him. Something about the speaker's tone of voice aroused his professional curiosity. Thanks to the 'monk's bench', Holmes could eavesdrop with impunity.

"Well, anyway, it's done," confirmed a gruff male voice. "I saw him on Tuesday and had it out with him."

"What did he say, Dad?" asked a younger voice.

"Well, he didn't deny anythin', how could he? I told him it was goin' to cost him two thousand, which I'm already thinkin' isn't enough. He said he needed time to think, but I've got him over a barrel, and he knows it. I'm seein' him again tonight in the boathouse at eight o'clock."

"Will he pay?"

"He'll pay. We've got him, don't you see?" replied the gruff voice with confidence. "I knew who he was as soon as I laid eyes on him. All these years me thinkin' he was dead. All these years, then suddenly, there he is standin' right in front of me, noddin' and smilin', the famous Captain Cole, hero of Carnforth Hill."

Bernard Holmes momentarily stopped breathing.

"I told him, I said to him, 'I was there, I saw you shoot Colonel Carnforth.' All these years people thinkin' him and Carnforth defended the trench alone after saving their men. All these years people thinkin' they were heroes."

"Well, he *did* save you, didn't he?" observed the younger man. "He saved all the others as well."

"He saved himself, you mean," hissed Rimmer. "We've got him, Stanley, don't you see? And now he's goin' to pay."

"Are you sure about this, Dad?" asked Stanley nervously. "I mean, people will ask why you didn't tell anyone about this before. They'll want to know what you was doin' in the dugout in the first place."

"I was wounded, wasn't I?" replied Rimmer with feeling. "I was wounded in the fightin', and the only reason I kept quiet was out of compassion for the colonel's family. And anyway, I thought Cole was dead. No use me goin' around upsettin' people when I thought he was dead."

"What if he denies it?" asked Stanley.

"How can he?" replied Rimmer impatiently. "He changed his name and deserted the army. You don't go to all that trouble if you're not guilty of somethin' pretty serious."

"Are you sure you know what you're doin', Dad?"

"Course I am. He'll pay, alright. It'll be the hangman's rope for him if he doesn't. Right, come on, it's time we were I' off. I'm goin' to need you to be there with me tonight."

"Me? Why do you need me?" asked an alarmed Stanley.

"I'll tell you when we get there. Now, come on."

Rising from his seat, Bernard Holmes watched John Rimmer limp from the inn. Uncertainty prevailed as he pondered his next move. But of one thing Holmes was sure: when Rimmer arrived at the boathouse, he would be waiting for him.

CHAPTER TWENTY-NINE

Trailblazers

"What do you mean, we've been locked in?" whispered an anxious Emily.

Realising she was still gripping Jimmy's arm, she quickly withdrew her hand.

"Why do people always whisper when the lights go out?" pondered Margaret.

"Never mind about that, turn your bicycle lamp on," ordered Anthony.

Margaret turned on the lamp and pointed it towards the door.

"Come on," said Jimmy leading the way.

Reaching the door, they found that it was indeed locked.

"This is stupid," moaned Anthony.

"Hello! Is anybody there? Is anybody there?" shouted Emily, her face inches from the door.

There was no reply.

"Hello!" yelled Jimmy. "Can anybody hear me?"

Again, there was no reply.

"This is hopeless," lamented Anthony.

"The library doesn't shut 'til four on a Saturday," said Margaret. "Why would anybody want to lock the door now?"

"That's a good question," said Jimmy turning to Anthony. "You don't think our friend Lunt has anything to do with this, do you?"

"I wouldn't put anything past him," replied Anthony sullenly.

"Well, one thing's for sure," said Emily, "we're going to have to find another way out of here. It's cold, we're already soaked, and it could be days before we are discovered."

"Perhaps Mark will come looking for us," said Anthony.

"If he does, it won't be for hours," said Jimmy, "and by that time, the batteries in Margaret's lamp will have run out."

"Great," groaned Emily.

"Margaret, best turn the lamp off until we decide what to do," advised Anthony.

"If you say so," replied Margaret.

Standing in the darkness, it was Emily who impatiently broke the silence.

"Well, someone think of something. Just standing here isn't working!"

"Okay," said Jimmy, "I think we should keep calm and …"

"What are those glowing things on the floor?" interrupted Margaret.

"Glowing?" asked Anthony.

"There, on the floor," said Margaret. "Little glowing diamond shapes stretching all the way down the cellar."

"I see them," said Jimmy, his curiosity aroused. "What are they?"

"Let me have the lamp, Margaret," said Emily.

Taking the lamp, Emily fell to her hands and knees and studied the floor. Anthony did likewise.

"Floor tiles," confirmed Emily. "The entire floor is made up of small square tiles. They've been laid diagonally, that's why they look diamond-shaped."

"They're ceramic, and some of them are illustrated with rosettes," confirmed an excited Anthony.

"Surely not," muttered an underwhelmed Margaret.

"I wonder if the Cistercian monks laid these," pondered Anthony.

"Never mind the Cistercians for now," said Jimmy. "Why are some of them glowing?"

"They must have been treated with something ... phosphorous maybe," guessed Emily.

"But why?" asked Jimmy.

"Maybe they lead somewhere," suggested Margaret.

"I think you might be right," said Emily getting to her feet and peering back into the cellar. "They light up the floor like lights on a runway. Perhaps they do lead somewhere."

"Well, there's only one way to find out," said Anthony. "Let's follow them."

"Beats standing here freezing to death," said Jimmy.

"Here," said Emily giving Jimmy the bicycle lamp, "you go first."

Moving away from the door, they cautiously followed the glowing trail deep into the cellar. When the cellar door was some distance behind them, Jimmy stopped and pointed the lamp into one of the alcoves.

"Why have you stopped?" asked Emily.

"Just getting our bearings," replied Jimmy. "The date on the shelving is 1912; we've never been this far into the archive before."

"Keep going," ordered Anthony impatiently.

Pointing the lamp ahead, Jimmy led the way further into the cellar until only two glowing tiles could be seen.

"The trail seems to have ended," said Emily, close to despair.

"There, to the left," directed Margaret. "The trail continues left."

"There must be a way out somewhere," insisted Emily.

Passing under a low arch and leaving the main cellar behind them, they entered a small antechamber. Before them, a solitary luminous floor tile lay embedded in the floor while another clung to a thick oak wall panel.

"A wall?" queried Anthony. "The trail leads to a wall?"

"Marvellous. Now what are we supposed to do?" groaned Emily.

"Turn off this lamp for a start," said Anthony. "No use wasting the batteries."

Jimmy switched the lamp off.

"I am so cold," said Emily sounding really fed up.

"I suppose we had better head back to the door," said Anthony. "Perhaps someone will have unlocked it."

"Pull the other," muttered Margaret.

"This is so frustrating," complained Emily. "Just what is the point of these glowing tiles?"

"Maybe they're just decorations," suggested Jimmy thinking out loud.

"Then why does the trail finish in here rather than continuing the full length of the cellar?" asked Emily. "It doesn't make sense."

"The tile on the wall is a different shape to the one on the floor," observed Jimmy.

"You're right," said Anthony who approached the wall to take a closer look. "It's not a diamond shape at all; it's a stone rosette like the rosettes on the floor tiles."

Fascinated, Anthony raised his right hand and lightly applied his fingers to the circumference of the rosette. Like a child playing with a torch, he sought to conceal the emanating glow by covering it with his pressing palm. Succumbing to this pressure, the rosette, accompanied by a sound like that of a snapping pencil, retreated into the panel causing it to open slightly.

"What was that noise?" asked Emily nervously.

"Turn on the lamp," ordered Anthony.

Jimmy switched the lamp back on and instinctively pointed it at the wall.

"Wow," said Margaret robotically.

"What's happening?" asked Emily. "What is it?"

"It's a sort of door," answered Jimmy. "A concealed door."

Easing the panel open, Anthony stepped across the threshold onto a flight of stone steps that descended into a narrow passageway. Pausing at the top of the steps, he took the torch from Jimmy and examined the door.

"Look," he explained. "When I pushed the rosette, it activated this spring mechanism which caused the panel to open. So, Compton Hobbs was right."

"Compton who?" queried Emily.

"Compton Hobbs. One of Anthony's heroes," explained Jimmy.

"He said all along that the Cistercians had built secret escape routes out of the abbey," continued Anthony. "I wonder how many more there are."

"Where do you think it leads to?" whispered Emily.

"There's only one way to find out," replied Anthony, gleefully leading the way.

"Wait for us," demanded Emily, none too keen to be left behind in the dark.

Standing back, Jimmy allowed Margaret and Emily to descend the steps before closing the panel behind him.

"Now what?" asked Jimmy.

"Now, we follow our noses," said Anthony.

CHAPTER THIRTY

Four Against One

Having collected his running kit from his room, Mark went to the gym and changed. The Christmas Chase was only days away, and as much as he had wanted to return to the archive, his addictive need to run was just too great. As he travelled the lakeside path through the heavy rain, Mark settled into a rhythm and regulated his breathing. By the time he had climbed the slope towards Walla Crag and entered the Great Wood, his thoughts had turned to his rivals. Having pondered their strengths and weaknesses, of one thing he was sure; whoever he was up against, whatever their pedigree, he could only do his best.

After re-joining the lakeside path and with the boathouse behind him, Mark quickened his pace as the school loomed into sight. Veering from the path onto the shale running track, he pumped his arms and sprinted the final quarter of a mile before slowing to a jog. Coming to a halt, he pitched forward, his hands resting on his thighs, and sucked in draughts of rejuvenating air. Regaining his breath and soaked to the skin, Mark returned to the gym through the gathering gloom. Once showered, he would search out his friends and find out what, if anything, they had discovered about Tristan Carnforth.

As he approached the changing rooms, Mark noticed that the gym lights were on. Looking inside, he saw that the gym was empty. Thinking nothing of it, he entered the deserted changing room and reached into his locker for a towel. Pulling off his rain-soaked shirt, he heard the changing room door close behind him. Turning around, he saw Lunt, Woosey, Reilly and Bradley staring at him.

"Well, look who it is," said Lunt with a smile. "Long time no see, Pecky."

"What do you want, Lunt?" asked Mark quietly.

"We want you, Pecky," mocked Woosey, eager as ever to get in on the act.

"Been training for the race on Wednesday, have you?" asked Reilly.

"Of course he has," said Bradley. "Haven't you heard? Pecky here actually thinks he can win the thing."

"I don't know," sighed Riley, shaking his head. "How disrespectful is that? The only black kid in the school, and he thinks he can beat his betters."

"Needs to be put in his place if you ask me," said Woosey.

Mark looked about the changing room in the forlorn hope that help might suddenly appear.

"It's no good looking for help," said a smiling Riley, "we're quite alone."

"And if you're wondering where your four-eyed friend and that peasant from Liverpool are," said Woosey, "well, we heard that someone locked them in the cellar under the library. They could be stuck there for days."

"I'm getting bored now; can't we get on with it?" asked Bradley.

"Get him into the gym," ordered Lunt, the smile having disappeared from his face.

Bradley and Reilly stepped forward, grabbed Mark by the arms and led him out of the changing room.

"Get off me!" protested Mark. "Why are you taking me to the gym?"

"You'll find out," snarled Bradley.

His resistance easily overcome, Mark was quickly bundled out of the changing room.

"Get him into the ring and get the gloves on him," commanded Lunt when inside the gym.

A struggling Mark was dragged to the boxing ring at the far end of the gym.

"I'd save my energy if I were you," advised Bradley, "you're going to need it."

Once inside the ring, Reilly and Woosey held out Mark's arms allowing Bradley to force on the gloves and lace them up. Watching from the opposite corner of the ring, Lunt was putting on boxing gloves of his own.

"You see, the fact is, Pecky, we are here to help you," taunted Lunt. "Everybody knows how keen you are to run in the Christmas Chase, and everybody knows how hard you have been training."

Resigned to his fate, Mark eyed Lunt defiantly.

"And my friends here," continued Lunt, "will tell anyone who's interested how you asked me to help you with your stamina training by sparring with you in the ring. I mean, who better to ask than the Fifth-Form boxing champion? Of course, I was only too delighted to help, but once inside the ring, you went completely berserk, forcing me to defend myself. That's what my friends will say ... but only if anybody asks."

After receiving a nod from Lunt, Reilly retreated to the entrance of the gym to act as lookout. When Lunt next spoke, his manner was matter-of-fact.

"Of course, it's highly unlikely that anybody will ask. Who cares what happens to a misfit whose parents work abroad because they can't stand the sight of him?"

The spirit fuelling Mark's defiance suddenly evaporated. The terrible secret he had long been hiding had been exposed. Vulnerable and alone, he adopted the only defence left to him; he told himself that he no longer cared.

"Hold him," shouted Lunt.

The first punch caught Mark in the middle of his forehead, causing his head to snap backwards. The second landed squarely on his face causing blood to seep from his nose.

"Well, come on then," encouraged Lunt. "You were happy to take me on in the refectory with your friends. Or did you think I had forgotten about that?"

Releasing their victim, Bradley and Woosey pushed Mark into the centre of the ring. His technique momentarily flawed by rage and impatience, Lunt launched a haymaker that glanced off Mark's chin. Recovering his poise, Lunt's third and fourth punches, a right-left combination, crashed into either side of Mark's face.

"Give it to him, Eric!" encouraged Woosey. "Put him down!"

His arms raised to his face in an attempt to deflect Lunt's blows, Mark made no effort to fight back. But neither would he go to the floor. Changing his angle of attack, Lunt drove his fists into Mark's midriff, forcing him to double over before unleashing a torrent of uppercuts into the boy's face.

"Not so cocky now, are we, Pecky?" shouted a breathless Lunt.

Pushing Mark into a corner of the ring, Lunt held him up against the ropes and pummelled him with a flurry of indiscriminate punches.

"Get to the deck!" he yelled.

Placing Mark in a head-lock, Lunt pulled him from the ropes, kicked his legs from beneath him and threw him to the floor. His eyes closing, his lips and nose swollen and bleeding, Mark looked up at his attacker but said nothing. Not satisfied that he had forced his victim to the floor, Lunt hesitated momentarily before aiming two heavy kicks into Mark's side.

"That's enough!" shouted Bradley from the ringside.

"I'll decide when he's had enough!" insisted an enraged Lunt.

"Have it your way," replied Bradley calmly, "but don't expect me to back you up if this gets out of hand. You didn't want him running in the race, and now he won't be. Let's leave it at that, shall we?"

Lunt glared at Bradley long enough to confirm his authority was not being challenged. He then turned his gaze on the motionless form at his feet before pulling off his gloves and bending down on one knee.

"Tell anybody about this, and you can be sure your friends will be next. Good luck in the race."

Rising to his feet, Lunt threw his gloves to the canvas and stepped out of the ring.

"Let's get out of here," he said. "I'm hungry."

It took a few minutes for Mark to attempt to get to his feet: his head was aching, his battered face bleeding and throbbing, and his side was sore to the touch. In the end, he gave up trying. Wanting to hide, he curled into a ball and closed his eyes. Now that his tormentors had gone, it was safe to cry.

*

Shortly after half-past-three, Dominic Price and his squash partner, Peter Scott, came off court and made their way to the boys' changing room. The pair had pushed each other hard and were both in need of a shower.

"Someone's in a hurry," said Peter when he saw the discarded shirt and towel on the changing room floor.

Above the towel, a locker, its door hanging open, displayed its contents of clothes.

"Whoever it is, he won't get far without his clothes," replied Dominic.

Having showered, changed and packed up their kit, the boys headed to the refectory for something to eat.

"I wonder if Dudley is about," said Dominic as they passed the gym on their way out. "The Third Form has a rugby match tomorrow morning, and I think he wants me to run the line."

Pulling open one of the double doors, Dominic entered the gym, followed by Peter.

"Well, he's not here," said Peter looking around him. "Let's try his office. If he's not there, I'll catch up with him tomorrow."

Turning to leave, Dominic flicked off the row of light switches next to the door, plunging the gym into darkness.

"What was that?" asked Peter, looking back into the gym.

"What was what?" replied Dominic.

"I thought I heard something."

"I didn't hear anything," said Dominic looking around.

Just as they were crossing the threshold to leave, both boys stopped in their tracks.

"I heard it that time," said Dominic, turning back and switching the lights back on.

"It sounded like sobbing," said Peter.

As they walked deeper into the gym, the sobbing became more persistent.

"There's someone in the ring," said Dominic quickening his stride.

"What's happened here?" asked Peter as they climbed through the ropes.

Mark did not look up.

"I've no idea, but it looks like he's taken a right beating," said Dominic as he knelt to help the boy sit up.

Recognition dawned.

"This is Mark Peck, one of the fourth-formers who saved me at the lake. Come on, Mark, you remember me, don't you? It's Dominic, Dominic Price."

Mark turned his face toward the head boy and, through stuttering breath, tried to stop crying.

"Someone's certainly gone to town on him," said Peter. "His face is a mess."

"It's okay now, Mark, we'll look after you," said Dominic placing a protective arm around the boy. "If it hadn't been for this lad, I wouldn't be here. He sprinted nearly half a mile to get help. It was thanks to him that Robert Cole got to me in time."

"I've heard he's a good runner," said Peter. "Some thought he was in with a chance of winning the Christmas Chase on Wednesday."

"Well, there's no way he'll be taking part now," said Dominic. "Come on, let's get him to the infirmary and see if we can find Robert Cole."

CHAPTER THIRTY-ONE

Visiting Time

"Here we are, miss," said the driver as the taxi turned off the main road. "Blackberry Hill."

As arranged the previous evening, Grace was on her way to see Robert Cole. As the taxi approached its destination, she suddenly felt uneasy. How would Robert react to the news she was about to deliver? What would she do if he chose to disbelieve her? Perhaps it would have been wiser to have told him everything over the phone.

As the taxi negotiated the winding drive, its headlights illuminating the surrounding woodland, apprehension gave way to curiosity. She had never been to Robert's home before, and the fact that it boasted grounds surprised her. Surprise turned to delight when the rambling country house eventually loomed into view. Surrounded on three sides by rolling lawns, its face set towards Derwentwater, the house appeared perfectly at one with the landscape. A beacon of warmth in the enveloping gloom, the soft glow emanating from its interior, attracted Grace like a moth to a light.

As she stepped out of the taxi, Robert was already descending the steps from the front door to greet her.

"You made it then?" he said, smiling.

"Well, I wasn't going to miss a gathering of the Keswick Choral Singers for the world," replied Grace flippantly.

"You'll love 'em," said Robert leading Grace up the steps towards the veranda. "They've been coming here for years. Just hope you enjoy a sing-song."

"I can't wait," said Grace.

Upon reaching the top of the steps, Robert guided Grace through the vestibule and into a large reception hall full of people. As they entered the hall, he paused for a moment and looked her in the eye.

"Are you okay?" he asked quietly.

"I'm fine, Robert," replied Grace softly.

"Here, let me take your coat and bag."

"I'll keep the bag if you don't mind; I've brought some things I need to show you."

"Let me get you a drink first," said Robert, who, for the moment at least, was in no hurry to hear why Grace wanted to leave Grey Stones.

Having put her coat in the cloakroom, Robert took Grace into the drawing room and poured her a glass of red wine.

"Good health," he said, passing her the glass.

"Cheers," responded Grace.

Looking about the room, Grace noticed an elderly lady in a black dress offering refreshments to guests from a tray. The lady seemed vaguely familiar. A large bay window on the other side of the floor accommodated a door that opened onto a lawn. Drawn to the window, Grace turned to Robert.

"Shall we?" she asked.

"Lead the way," said Robert.

Having crossed the floor, Grace sipped her wine before addressing her host.

"You're a dark horse, aren't you?"

"What do you mean?" asked Robert.

"What do I mean? I mean all this. This house … it's a mansion. And the grounds! I had no idea."

"Well, yes, I suppose Blackberry Hill is something of a step-up from my digs at school," replied Robert airily.

"It's stunning, even in the gloom," said Grace, looking out the window.

"I'm a fortunate fellow," admitted Robert.

Turning from the window, Grace once again scanned the room.

"Who is that elderly lady serving drinks; one of your servants?" she asked mischievously.

"Old Ginny? She's been in the family for years," explained Robert, doing his best to sound pompous and indifferent.

Grace poked him in the ribs.

"Don't joke," she scolded with a smile. "It's nearly 1967! You can't have servants running around after you."

"Why not?" protested Robert. "We give her a place to sleep and feed her our leftovers. She's happy enough."

Grace poked him in the ribs again.

"Be serious," she hissed.

"Aunt Ginny is not a servant; she and her husband are friends of the family, very dear friends as it happens," explained Robert. "I've known them since I was about ten. Ginny knew my parents before the war. She and her husband, Compton, live on Lord's Island."

"Well, the more I look at her, the more I'm convinced I've met her before," said Grace. "How old were you when you lost your father? I never knew mine."

"I was only five when he died; I really didn't know him at all."

"You are obviously very fond of her," observed Grace, who was again looking at Ginny.

"I'm very fond of both of them," confessed Robert.

"So, tell me then, where did all of this magnificent wealth come from?" asked Grace, changing the subject.

"Do you really want to know? I wouldn't want to bore you with the sordid detail."

"You won't bore me, I promise," replied Grace dryly.

"Well, if it's a history lesson you want, you've come to the right man. It all began with an ancestor of mine named Abraham Cole, a linen draper from Leeds. When Abraham died in the 1780s, his son William took over the business."

"Lucky William," said Grace.

"William was not one to rest on his father's laurels," continued Robert. "He invested heavily in the development of flax spinning machines which he used to manufacture linen thread on an industrial scale."

"Quite the innovator then, this William," said Grace.

"I'll say. By 1790, he'd built his own mill near Leeds, which he packed with his new machines. Other mills followed, and William soon became very wealthy, as did his descendants, I'm glad to say."

"But Keswick is a long way from Leeds; how did the Cole family end up here?"

"The story goes that when William married in 1802, he and his bride honeymooned in the Lake District and spent some time in Keswick. They must have liked the place because when William's health declined in the 1830s, he and his wife purchased Blackberry Hill and retired here."

"Well, this place must have cost him a pretty penny," said Grace looking about the room.

"Oh, William was not short of a bob or two. When he died in 1847, his estate was estimated to be worth over two million pounds, that's approximately one hundred and fifty million pounds in today's money."

Grace nearly dropped her glass.

"Don't tell me, you suddenly find me irresistible," said Robert.

Grace could not laugh at the joke.

"Oh, Robert, can we go somewhere and talk? There is something I must tell you."

Before Robert could respond, he was distracted by a woman's voice.

"Now, Robert, shouldn't you be circulating among all of your guests rather than concentrating on just one of them?"

"Aunt Ginny," replied a smiling Robert. "Let me introduce you to Grace Connolly. Grace is a colleague of mine from school."

Her blue eyes fixed on Grace, Aunt Ginny took her hand and gently squeezed it.

"My dear Grace, what a pleasure this is. Robert has spoken of you often."

The quizzical look on Grace's face suddenly turned to one of recognition as Aunt Ginny continued to press her hand.

"Mum's funeral. I have met you before. You approached me at the graveside and offered your condolences. You squeezed my hand and left, I remember."

The suddenness of her recollection rendered Grace quite excitable.

"You were with a man. He was standing behind you, wearing a heavy overcoat. He didn't say anything. You both left before I could ask you how you knew my mother. That was you, wasn't it?"

"Is Grace right? Did you know her mother?" asked Robert.

Aunt Ginny looked at Robert and considered her reply. Just as she was about to speak, Robert felt a hand grip his arm. Turning to his left, he saw the familiar figure of Reverend Grundy.

"Hello, Vicar," smiled Robert. "Glad you could make it."

"Hello, everybody," replied the vicar, his tone rather downbeat. "Robert, I've just taken a telephone call from Dominic Price, the head boy."

"Dominic?" replied Robert. "What on earth can he want on a Saturday afternoon? Nothing wrong, I hope?"

"He asked me to tell you that one of your pupils, Mark Peck, has been badly beaten and is in the infirmary."

"Not again," said Robert. "Somebody's got it in for this lad, and I suspect I know who. Did Dominic say if he was badly hurt?"

"All he said was that the boy had taken quite a beating and he thought you should know," replied the vicar.

"Right, I'd better get over there. Aunt Ginny, can I leave you to hold the fort while I'm gone?"

"Of course, you can; get yourself off to that boy."

"Wait for me," said Grace. "I'll come with you."

*

Shortly after four o'clock, Robert and Grace reached the school infirmary. Entering the building, they went straight to Sister Lucas's office where they found Dominic Price and Peter Scott.

"Hello, Dominic, Peter," said Robert, nodding to each boy in turn. "We got here as quickly as we could."

"Hope you didn't mind me ringing you, sir, what with it being the weekend and all," said Dominic, "but I wasn't sure who else to call."

"Of course I don't mind; you did exactly the right thing," replied Robert.

"Where is Sister Lucas?" asked Grace.

"She's with Mark, miss," replied Dominic.

"We had better wait here then," advised Robert. "Sister Lucas doesn't take kindly to people wandering around the infirmary unannounced."

At that moment, Sister Lucas entered the office. A stout lady in her late forties, she was not one to stand on ceremony.

"Sister, I hope you don't mind the intrusion," said Robert, "but the boys here contacted us and told us about Mark Peck."

"I know, I've been expecting you," she said as she brushed past Robert on the way to her desk.

"How is he?" asked Grace. "What happened to him?"

"I'll tell you what's happened to him," replied an unhappy Sister Lucas. "Somebody has given him a good hiding, that's what's happened to him."

"He's been in a fight?" asked Robert.

"The boys say they found him in the boxing ring in the gym," replied the sister, "but take my word for it, the lad I've got upstairs has not been in a fight. I have been at this school for twenty-five years and have treated plenty of boys who have been in fights. The odd cut or bruise, a thick lip or a black eye are the injuries I get to treat when boys have been fighting. This boy has been beaten up. He's been repeatedly punched to the face and body and, if I'm not mistaken, kicked for good measure. This wasn't a fight; it was a vicious assault."

"How badly is he hurt?" asked Robert.

"Badly enough for me to have sent for Mr Snyder," replied Sister Lucas. "Luckily, his injuries appear superficial, but his face is a mess, and his body is sore to the touch."

"Has he told you who did it?" asked Robert.

"Of course I asked him, but you know what the boys in this school are like," said the sister, glancing at Dominic and Peter. "They think that reporting bullying is something to be ashamed of."

"Can we see him?" asked Grace.

"Perhaps now is not the best time," replied the sister. "He's had a nasty experience and needs to rest."

"Look," said Robert. "I know this boy. His parents work abroad and he will be feeling pretty abandoned right now. Just give us five minutes to let him know that somebody is taking an interest."

Sister Lucas pondered Robert's request for a few moments before replying.

"Very well, Robert, just a few minutes. He's upstairs, first room on the right."

When they entered the room, Mark was lying motionless in bed, staring at the ceiling.

"Hello Mark," said Grace from the door. "Its Miss Connolly and Mr Cole. Is it alright if we come in?"

Diverting his gaze from the ceiling, Mark turned his head towards his visitors.

"We got here as soon as we could," said Robert as he and Grace approached the bed.

"Oh, Mark, who did this to you?" asked Grace taking hold of the boy's hand.

Mark did not reply. Looking at the boy's bruised and swollen face, Robert struggled to contain his anger.

"It's okay, Mark, we don't have to talk about this now," he said.

The silence became awkward as Robert and Grace wondered what to say next.

"We've spoken to Dominic and Peter. They're still here. They waited for us to arrive so you wouldn't be left alone," said Grace.

"You are going to be alright, Mark," assured Robert. "Sister Lucas says so."

"Is there anything we can bring you, Mark? Is there anything we can do?" asked Grace, still holding his hand.

Directing his stare back to the ceiling, Mark remained silent.

"Well, if you think of anything," said Robert, "be sure to …"

"Did you say Dominic Price was still here?" asked Mark quietly.

"Yes," replied Robert.

"Can I see him, please? Just for a minute."

"We will have to ask Sister Lucas," said Grace, "but if it's only for a minute, I'm sure she won't mind."

Mark again fell silent.

"Well, we had better go. Try and get some rest," said Robert.

When Grace and Robert returned downstairs, Dominic Price and

Peter Scott were still with Sister Lucas.

"I've one last favour to ask," said Robert. "Mark wants to see Dominic, just for a minute."

"Make it quick then," said Sister Lucas, nodding towards the stairs.

As Dominic and Peter disappeared up the stairs, Mr Snyder and Mr Cheatham entered the infirmary. Ignoring Robert and Grace completely, Mr Snyder, his frustration all too evident, addressed Sister Lucas directly.

"Sister Lucas, can you please tell me why I have been called away from my home on a Saturday afternoon?"

"I asked you to come here because one of our boys has been assaulted," explained Sister Lucas frostily.

"To which of our boys do you refer?" asked the head with a sigh of disinterest.

"Mark Peck," replied Sister Lucas.

"Mark Peck?" queried the head, offering his ear to Mr Cheatham.

"Mark Peck, a fourth form pupil. A fish from the shallow end of the pool," murmured The Cheat knowingly.

"I see," said the head. "And you say he has been assaulted?"

"I do," replied Sister Lucas. "He was found in the boxing ring by …"

"In the boxing ring? Are you telling me the boy had been boxing?" asked the head.

"I am telling you he has been assaulted," insisted Sister Lucas. "I am telling you that the matter needs investigating. I am telling you that you may wish to involve the police."

"The police?" queried Mr Snyder.

"Tell me, Sister, has the boy made a complaint?" asked Mr Cheatham.

"No, but…"

"I didn't think so," interrupted the head. "The boys of this school never complain when they come off second best in a fight; it's simply bad form."

Sister Lucas looked horrified.

"No complaint means no assault means no need for the police," quipped Mr Snyder.

"Quite right," agreed Mr Cheatham. "I am afraid the good sister is overreacting."

"I beg your pardon!" said an offended Sister Lucas.

"Perhaps you could take the trouble to look at the boy's injuries before accusing Sister Lucas of overreacting," suggested Robert firmly.

"Ah, Mr Cole," said Mr Snyder acknowledging Robert for the first time. "I wondered how long I would have to wait for your contribution. The fact is that all boys get into fights now and again; it's a natural part of school life."

"Character building, I say," said Mr Cheatham. "As is an occasional beating with a cane, I might add."

Grace could remain silent no longer.

"Mr Snyder, the boy has been badly beaten; he needs your protection. He is lying injured upstairs because we, the school, have let him down."

Grace was ignored.

"Sister Lucas, can I take it that you are not recommending that the boy be hospitalised?" asked Mr Snyder.

"I see no need for that," replied Sister Lucas. "His injuries, though painful, are superficial. I have given him painkillers and intend to keep him in the infirmary for a day or two, but other than that …"

"Then there is no need for me to pay the boy a personal visit," declared the head looking at Grace.

"Of course, there isn't," confirmed Mr Cheatham. "If you were to visit the boy, people might consider the incident more serious than it is."

"Exactly," agreed the head. "Next thing you know, the school's reputation is undermined and our numbers begin to fall."

"But Mr Snyder ..."

"Enough, Miss Connolly. I shall not hear another word on the subject," warned the head firmly. "My mind is made up. Come, Cheatham, let us be on our way."

"I give up," said Robert when the head and his deputy had left the office.

"Don't do that," said Grace placing her hand on his arm.

"But what can we do?" asked Robert. "That man is more concerned about his stupid portrait than he is about the welfare of his pupils."

"Well, if you ask me, somebody should contact that boy's parents and tell them what has happened," said Sister Lucas.

"You're quite right, Sister," replied Robert. "I'll dig out their contact details from the school office and deal with it."

"Won't that get you into trouble with the head?" asked Grace.

"Probably," replied Robert, "but to do nothing would be unthinkable. Look, about that chat that you wanted to have, can we put it off until next week?"

"Of course we can," replied Grace.

Peter Scott and Dominic Price re-entered the office.

"How is he?" asked Grace.

"He's pretty quiet, miss," replied Peter. "He didn't have very much to say at all."

"He must have said something ... or did he speak to you in confidence?" asked Robert.

Peter and Dominic looked at each other, their reluctance to reply all too evident.

"Well, I can see that your conversation was clearly confidential, so I won't press you," said Robert.

It was Dominic who took the plunge.

"Sir, do you remember when you and Miss Connolly brought Mark and his friends to see me in hospital?"

"Of course we do," replied Grace.

"And do you remember me saying that if there was anything I could ever do for them, all they had to do was ask?"

"I remember," replied Robert.

"Well, so does Mark," said Dominic.

"Has he asked you to do something for him?" asked Grace.

"Yes," replied Dominic. "He wants me to teach him how to box."

CHAPTER THIRTY-TWO

The Room

"This passageway must be hundreds of years old," enthused Anthony as he held the bicycle lamp aloft.

"Well, hooray for that," said Emily sarcastically. "Just keep the lamp pointed straight ahead and find us a way out of here."

"Has anybody any idea what direction we're heading?" asked Jimmy.

"I'd say we are somewhere under the Great Hall heading west," replied Anthony.

"What's that smell?" asked Margaret.

"What smell? I can't smell anything," replied Anthony.

"Well, I can," said Jimmy, "and it's getting stronger."

"Paraffin," said Emily. "It smells like paraffin."

"Look, on the right. There's a door," said Margaret.

"Salvation," muttered Emily, quickening her step.

"Hold your horses," warned Jimmy. "We have no idea who or what might be on the other side of that door."

Reaching the door, her enthusiasm curbed by Jimmy's words of caution, Emily stopped and turned to Anthony.

"Jimmy's right; you go first."

Slightly put out, Anthony lifted the wooden latch, cautiously pushed open the door, raised the bicycle lamp into the air and pointed it into the room.

"Well?" whispered Emily.

"Sorry to disappoint you all," said Anthony looking over his shoulder, "but it doesn't appear to lead anywhere. It just seems to be full of photographs and all sorts of junk."

"Are you sure?" asked Emily, her disappointment all too apparent.

"That smell of paraffin is stronger than ever," said Margaret.

"What's that over there?" asked Jimmy, taking the bicycle lamp off Anthony and advancing slowly into the room.

"What is it? What have you found?" asked Anthony.

"Come and have a look," replied Jimmy after a few seconds.

In the middle of the room, two paraffin lamps and a box of Swan Vesta matches occupied the middle of a table. After shaking the box to his ear, Jimmy held it up to his friends.

"Matches," he said.

"Cistercian matches?" enquired Margaret.

"Very funny," said Anthony.

"Try and light the lamps," instructed Emily.

"Here, hold this," said Jimmy, passing the bicycle lamp to Margaret.

Carefully removing the glass chimneys from their base, Jimmy struck a match, ignited the wicks, replaced the chimneys and looked about him as a pale yellow glow lit up the room.

"The place is full of photographs," observed Anthony. "On the walls, in boxes ... everywhere."

"And not just photographs," added Jimmy as he stared at a desk and bookcase in the corner of the room. "What are all these books and papers doing down here?"

"Never mind books and papers, look at this," said Emily.

Resting against the far wall, a life-sized portrait of a man in his mid-forties, his pale blue eyes illuminating the faintest of smiles, his right cheek accommodating a fading scar, looked across the room.

"It's him," said Margaret softly, her eyes glued to the portrait. "It's the captain."

Emily approached the portrait, bent down on one knee, and read aloud the words inscribed upon the small brass plate attached to the lower frame.

Michael Edwards

Headmaster of Grey Stones 1937–1941

"The missing portrait from the Great Hall," said Anthony.

"But how did it get here?" asked Jimmy.

"I bet Michael Edwards brought it here himself because he was afraid he might be recognised as Thomas Cole," said Anthony.

"That's impossible," replied Emily. "The inscription confirms he was headmaster from 1937 to 1941."

"So?" said Anthony.

"So, whoever brought the portrait here must have done so after Michael Edwards was killed," explained Jimmy.

Anthony cringed.

"Look, he's in the photographs on the wall," said Margaret.

"And just look who he is standing next to in this one," said Emily picking up a photograph of a cricket team. "T. H. Carnforth."

"It's the same on this one," said Anthony looking at a different photograph. "Coincidence or what?"

"If you want to know what I think, coincidence doesn't come into it," said Margaret.

The room fell silent.

"Go on then," encouraged Anthony, his patience tested by the frequency of Margaret's logical deductions.

"Well," said Margaret, "it's all rather obvious, isn't it? The whole school must have known that Tristan Carnforth was the son of the famous Colonel Carnforth, we know that from the obituary in *The Scholar*. If the whole school knew who Tristan was, then Michael Edwards knew too. So why does he end up being photographed next to the son of the person he killed? If anything, I would have expected him to avoid Tristan like the plague. Why risk drawing attention to himself?"

"Why?" asked Jimmy.

"I dunno," replied Margaret. "All I'm saying is that Michael Edwards *chose* to be photographed with Tristan, coincidence doesn't come into it."

"She has a point ... again," conceded Anthony.

"But why hide all of these photographs and not the one that hangs in Cole Hall, the one of him wearing his Victoria Cross?" asked Jimmy.

"It hasn't been there long," said Anthony. "Robert Cole donated it to the school a couple of years ago."

"Why would anybody want to hide the portrait and photographs of a dead person?" asked Emily. "What would be the point? It wouldn't matter if he were recognised after he was dead."

"Who knows," sighed Anthony. "Whoever brought the portrait down here is probably long dead. We are probably the first people to set foot inside this room for donkey's years."

"Wrong again," sang Margaret as she browsed through the contents of the bookcase.

"Well, who else would come here?" challenged Anthony.

"I dunno," replied Margaret, "but someone has."

"How do you know?" asked Jimmy, who was not one to underestimate Margaret.

"Because of this," she said, holding up a book.

"What about it?" asked Jimmy.

"Well, if I had been lying on this shelf untouched for years, I'd be covered in dust, but look at it: it's as clean as a whistle, as is everything else in this bookcase."

"Wait a minute, let me see that," demanded Anthony.

Margaret passed Anthony the book.

"I thought I recognised it: *The Borrowdale Valley* by Compton Hobbs. Margaret's right," said Anthony.

"No need to sound so surprised," muttered Margaret.

"What are you on about? What's so special about the book?" asked Emily.

"That book was published in 1955," explained Anthony, "which means that whoever left it down here did so long after Michael Edwards left the scene."

"And that's not all," said Margaret holding up a newspaper she had retrieved from the bookshelf. "Take a look at this."

"What is it?" asked Emily.

"A copy of *The Keswickian* dated the 20th of August 1966," replied Margaret, holding up the paper for all to see. "Look whose photograph is on the front page."

"That's Miss Connolly. What does it say?" asked Emily.

"Not much," replied Margaret, casting her eye over the page. "The article is headed, *Local girl comes home to teach at Grey Stones*."

"That's the article your Uncle Harry told us about," said Jimmy.

"Well," said Anthony, "if someone was down here as recently as the 20th of August, who's to say that this place hasn't been visited since then?"

"Right, that's it," said Emily firmly. "Not only am I cold and wet, I'm getting a bit scared. Whoever is using this place could make an appearance any minute. I think it's about time we concentrated on getting out of here, don't you?"

"Emily's right," said Jimmy. "We'd better get moving. Come on, we'll take these lamps."

"If we take the lamps, won't we be giving the game away?" asked

Anthony. "Won't it be obvious that somebody's been here?"

"Well, that can't be helped," said Emily grabbing a lamp. "The light from Margaret's bicycle lamp is becoming dimmer than you are, and if you think I'm going to stumble about in the dark looking for a way out, think again."

"Steady on," protested a wounded Anthony.

"Sorry," said Emily sincerely, "but I'm getting really frightened now."

"Then let's go," said Jimmy.

"Which way then?" asked Anthony when they had re-entered the passageway.

"We'll have to go right," said Jimmy. "There's no point heading back toward the archive; we could be locked in there for days."

"Right it is then," said Anthony. "Follow me."

After walking approximately sixty yards, the passageway forked, causing them to stop.

"What do you think?" asked Jimmy. "Left or right?"

"I say we go right," said Anthony licking his forefinger and holding it in the air. "My inner compass tells me we are under the Great Hall."

Margaret and Emily looked at each other and shook their heads.

"I agree with Christopher Columbus here," said Jimmy, almost apologetically.

"Yes, well, Christopher Columbus didn't know where he was either," said Emily before branching right after Anthony.

After another twenty yards or so, they came to another flight of steps which led to another hinged panel. Having activated the spring mechanism, Anthony held the panel open.

"What's that on the wall?" asked Margaret.

Protruding from the wall, a bulbous light switch invited activation. Jimmy reached up and flicked the switch into the 'on' position.

"Wow," said Anthony as an orange glow enveloped the passageway. "Electricity."

"Then why the lamps?" asked Jimmy.

"I don't know," replied Anthony. "Maybe there are passageways that have no lighting."

"Never mind that for now," said Emily. "Just turn the light off, put the lamps down and let's get out of here."

"Where are we?" asked Margaret.

"We're in the Great Hall," said Anthony peering through the displaced panel. "We've come out behind the organ."

Closing the panel behind them, they edged themselves from behind the organ casing into the hall.

"Thank God for that," said a much-relieved Emily. "We could have been lost for days."

"What now?" asked Margaret.

"I say we go and get changed into some dry clothes and meet up in the refectory," said Jimmy. "Then we can decide what we're going to do next."

"Good idea," said Anthony. "Mark should be back from his run by now."

"In the meantime," said Jimmy, "let's keep quiet about the secret passageways. Agreed?"

"Agreed," replied Emily.

"Agreed," repeated Anthony.

"My lips are sealed," said Margaret.

"Right," said Emily. "Margaret, you come with me to my room and get dry."

Half an hour later, Anthony and Jimmy arrived at the refectory to find Margaret and Emily sitting at a table eating a packet of crisps.

"I've no idea where Mark is," said Anthony taking a seat. "He should have finished his run by now."

"He's not going to believe what we have to tell him," said Emily.

"I'm not sure I believe it myself," said Jimmy. "I mean, secret doors and passageways?"

"And where do they lead?" mused Anthony. "We could be sitting on a labyrinth of tunnels which …"

"Watch it," whispered Margaret.

Turning his head, Anthony saw Dominic Price and Peter Scott approaching the table.

"Hi there," said Dominic. "We've been looking for you. Mind if we join you for a minute?"

"Of course we don't. You're not in trouble again, are you?" asked Margaret.

"Not this time," said Dominic forcing a smile.

Emily sensed immediately that something was wrong.

"What's up?" she asked.

"Look, I'll get straight to the point," said Dominic. "Peter and I found Mark in the gym a little while ago. He'd been beaten up, so we took him to the infirmary. Sister Lucas is keeping him in for a day or two."

"Lunt!" spat Anthony, his face contorted with anger.

Dominic and Peter exchanged glances.

"Who?" asked Dominic. "Did you say, Lunt?"

"Sorry," said Anthony, rising to his feet. "I have to go."

Jimmy and Emily followed him from the table.

"Hey, there's no need to panic or anything," assured Peter. "We've been to see him, and Sister Lucas says his injuries aren't serious."

"Thanks for coming to tell us," said Jimmy over his shoulder. "Margaret, are you coming?"

"In a minute," replied Margaret.

Once her friends had left the refectory, Margaret turned to Dominic.

"Right, Dominic Price, there is something you need to know."

CHAPTER THIRTY-THREE

Snow Fights

"It's still snowing," reported Jimmy, looking into the night sky.

"Is it sticking?" asked Anthony, joining Jimmy at the window.

"It's chucking it down," replied Jimmy with a smile.

"Mark, come and look," encouraged Anthony.

Mark looked up from the table where he was working.

"It's okay, I can see it from here," he replied, his tone betraying his lack of interest.

Anthony and Jimmy glanced at each other, their excitement tempered by concern for their friend. Since returning from the infirmary the previous day, Mark had been very quiet, detached almost. When quizzed about his run-in with Lunt, he seemed disinterested, his account lacking any trace of anger or bitterness. In fact, it was proving difficult to arouse Mark's interest in anything. The news about Tristan Carnforth, the discovery of the passageways and the portrait, nothing appeared to fire his curiosity. Unsure of how to react, Anthony and Jimmy kept their distance; the last thing they wanted was to irritate their friend with constant questions or awkward attempts to cheer him up.

"Come on," said Anthony putting on his school blazer. "It's time we were off."

Every year on the last Tuesday of term, the staff and pupils of Grey Stones were called upon to join the school choir in the Great Hall for the singing of Christmas carols.

"Not me," said Mark. "I've been excused."

The injuries to Mark's face were far from healed; his cheeks remained bruised, his eyes partially closed, and his nose swollen. In addition, his right side remained tender.

"Oh, come on, Mark, it's Christmas and it's snowing. We can't go without you," said Jimmy.

"Yes, you can. I want you to. The truth is, I would actually like to spend some time alone."

Mark's reply left little room for negotiation. Before Anthony could speak, there was a knock on the door. It was Mr Haynes, the House Parent.

"Let's be having you then," he said, popping his head across the threshold. "Proceedings begin in ten minutes."

"Are you sure you won't come?" asked Anthony after Mr Haynes had moved down the corridor.

"Positive," replied Mark.

As they made their way across the quad, Anthony and Jimmy stopped and looked back toward the dormitory, hoping their friend had changed his mind. But Mark was nowhere to be seen. With the snow getting heavier by the minute, the boys re-joined the throng heading for the hall. A huge Christmas tree, its branches decorated with gold-coloured baubles and illuminated by miniature silver lanterns, welcomed all who passed through the great oak doors. Having collected their carol sheets and taken their seats, those assembled fell silent as the school choir, led by the head of the Music Department, Miss Swan, entered the stage.

Tall, in her late thirties, her dark hair draping the shoulders of her slim figure, Gloria Swan smiled generously at her audience before speaking brightly into the microphone.

"Good evening, everyone and welcome to this year's carol concert."

The cheers that followed served to confirm Miss Swan's popularity.

"Now, before we begin," beamed Miss Swan, "I have been asked to make the following announcements. Firstly, may I remind you that the final assembly of term will be held on Thursday morning at eleven o'clock. As usual, no lessons will take place on Thursday afternoon, and boarders will be free to depart for the Christmas break on Friday morning."

More cheers rang around the hall.

"Secondly," continued Miss Swan when the cheering had subsided, "secondly, the Christmas Chase will take place tomorrow morning at eleven o'clock. Mr Snyder will start the race and present the winner's trophy outside the gym as soon as it's over. The head has asked me to remind you that all pupils and staff are expected to attend this, the school's oldest competitive event."

At the mention of the race, Jimmy and Anthony looked at each other and grimaced.

"And finally," said Miss Swan, "I am asked to remind you that immediately following this concert, mince pies and refreshments will be served in the refectory."

Her announcements made, Miss Swan cast a nod in the direction of the organist before addressing the assembly once more.

"And now, will you please lift your voices and join the Grey Stones Choir in singing the first carol on your song sheet, *Come All Ye Faithful*."

Lying on his bed, Mark stared impassively at the ceiling as the singing rang out from the hall and carried across the quad.

It was nearly half-past eight when the concert came to an end. Having basked in the generous applause of its audience, the choir left the stage to Miss Swan, who wished everyone a happy Christmas before heading off to the refectory. When the great oak doors were thrown open to the night, the majority of those departing had but one question in mind: was it still snowing?

As Jimmy made his way out of the hall, the sound of laughter told its own story. The snow was falling faster and heavier than before and was lying three to four inches deep on the ground. All over the quad, pupils and teachers were hurling snowballs at each other on their way to the refectory. As the confines of the quad were left behind, pitch battles raged all over the school grounds. Unable to resist the temptation any longer, Jimmy stooped to the floor, armed himself with a suitably sized missile and searched for a target. Hardly believing his luck, he saw Victoria Jennings and Chloe Saunders trying to pick their way through the mayhem some twenty yards to his left. Thinking he couldn't miss, he was just about to pull the trigger when Anthony beat him to it, hitting Victoria right between the shoulder blades. Stung into action, their piercing screams a complete overreaction, the girls made a dash for the refectory. Confronted with two moving targets, Jimmy took hurried aim, hurled his snowball through the night air … and missed. Before he could re-load, Emily Burton crept up behind him and scored a direct hit to the back of his neck from point-blank range.

"That's for aiming at my friends," she laughed.

With snow lodged in his collar and dripping down his back, Jimmy sought immediate revenge.

"Get her!" he shouted to Anthony as Emily scuttled off.

Before he could obey his friend's command, Anthony was hauled to the ground, landing flat on his back. Towering over him, a snowball in one hand and a mince pie in the other, stood a smiling Margaret Arbuckle.

"Get her!" yelled Anthony.

"*You* get her!" laughed Jimmy.

"Nobody gets me," muttered Margaret before devouring the pie.

Out of the corner of his eye, Jimmy spotted Emily, Victoria and Chloe attempting a sneak attack. As he prepared another snowball, he felt Anthony's hand clutch his arm.

"What's the matter?" asked Jimmy turning around.

"Look," warned Anthony.

Turning to his left, Jimmy saw Lunt, Bradley, Reilly and Woosey striding towards them.

"Did you just throw snowballs at me?"

Lunt's tone was accusatory. Jimmy and Anthony stood their ground.

"It was these two, wasn't it?" asked Lunt of his cronies.

"It was them alright, Eric," attested Woosey. "I saw them."

"Well, you know what that means, don't you?" said Bradley conversationally. "It means that as they attacked you, you're entitled to attack them back. It's called self-defence."

Jimmy looked at Anthony before responding.

"What are you going to do, Lunt? Get your mates to hold us for you? We all know how you defend yourself."

From her position behind Jimmy, Margaret calmly weighed up the situation. If Lunt moved any closer, he was going to get a snowball right between the eyes.

"I think he just called you a coward," said Bradley, egging Lunt on as snowballs continued to fill the night sky.

But Lunt did not need any encouragement. Enraged by Jimmy's remark, his fists clenched, he was about to step forward when somebody barged into him from the side, nearly knocking him over.

"What the …?"

Regaining his balance, Lunt fell silent after identifying the person responsible. It was Dominic Price.

"Oh, I'm terribly sorry, Eric, I really should look where I'm going," said Dominic, feigning concern.

Standing a few feet behind the head boy, Peter Scott provided conspicuous support for his friend.

"That's okay, no harm done," said Lunt avoiding eye contact.

"Well, I'm so glad to hear that, Eric. I see you know my friends here, Jimmy, Margaret and Anthony," said Dominic, his tone altogether too friendly.

Bradley, Woosey and Reilly backed away as they realised that Dominic's collision with Lunt had been no accident.

"I know them," conceded Lunt cautiously.

"And I see that you are all having a snowball fight. Can we join in the fun?" asked Dominic taking the snowball from Margaret's hand.

"Actually, we were just going," said Lunt.

"Well, I'll tell you what," said Dominic, "why don't you take this with you?"

Before Lunt could move, Dominic rammed the snowball into his face rocking his head backwards. Wiping the snow from his stinging lips, Lunt glared at Dominic but did not retaliate.

"What was that for, Price?" he hissed.

"That's for beating up a friend of mine," replied Dominic coldly.

"Friend? What friend?" asked an infuriated Lunt.

"I think you know what friend," replied Dominic.

"Fighting other people's battles now, are we?" asked Lunt bitterly.

"If I was, Lunt, you wouldn't be standing, let alone talking," replied Dominic. "No, my friend is quite capable of fighting his own battles."

Jimmy and Anthony looked at each other. Was there something Mark hadn't told them?

"Oh yeah?" scoffed Lunt. "And when will he do that, then?"

Dominic stooped to the floor and scooped up two handfuls of snow.

"You'll find out," he said, compacting the snow into a ball. "Now disappear before I give you another one of these, and take your spineless crew with you."

Lunt stared at Dominic for a few seconds before turning to Jimmy.

"He won't always be around to protect you," he sneered.

Dominic raised his arm as if to throw the snowball, causing Lunt to flinch.

"Get lost," ordered Dominic.

Recovering his composure, Lunt cast a vicious look at Jimmy and Anthony before storming off towards his friends. As soon as they had travelled a safe distance, Woosey sought to reassure his leader.

"You could have Price any time, Eric, especially with us backing you up."

"Definitely," agreed Reilly.

Humiliated and angry, Lunt turned on both stooges.

"Just shut up! Not another word."

"Take it easy," advised Bradley. "Don't let Price get to you. By the end of the week, you'll have that scouse peasant and his friends exactly where you want them."

Looking back toward the refectory, Lunt watched as Jimmy and Anthony talked to Dominic Price. Placated by Bradley's calming words, he allowed himself a smile.

"You're right," said Lunt. "Tomorrow, they won't know what hit them."

*

When the boys returned to their room, they found Mark standing at the window, looking out onto the quad.

"We brought you some mince pies back," said Jimmy.

"You'll never believe what happened outside the refectory," said Anthony, eager to relate Lunt's humiliation.

Mark turned from the window and smiled. It was not a huge smile, but it was a smile, and it was the first he had imparted since returning from the infirmary.

"You should have been there," continued Anthony. "Dominic Price shoved a snowball straight down Lunt's throat."

"What's all this?" asked Jimmy, looking at the neat pile on Mark's bed.

At the bottom of the bed, a pair of running shoes sat on top of a neatly folded running vest, a pair of shorts and a tracksuit top.

"My running kit," replied Mark. "I've decided to run in the race tomorrow."

"Don't be ridiculous," said Anthony forgetting all about Lunt. "You can hardly walk, never mind run."

"Anthony's right," said Jimmy. "You wouldn't stand a chance."

"I know that," replied Mark. "The point is that Lunt set out to stop me running in the race. If I don't run, he wins. Well, he's not going to win. I'm running."

"But Mark …" protested Anthony.

"No buts; I'm running, and if you don't like it, you don't have to watch," said Mark impatiently.

Put out by Mark's curt manner, Anthony was about to object but thought better of it. If Lunt had beaten him up, perhaps he, too, would have wanted to prove a point.

"Have it your way then," said Anthony calmly, "but don't expect me to stand and watch. I'm running with you."

"And that goes for me, too," said Jimmy.

CHAPTER THIRTY-FOUR

The Christmas Chase

Standing outside the gym, hundreds of pupils and staff patiently awaited the appearance of those who were to contest the Christmas Chase. It was a quarter to eleven, and the start of the race was just fifteen minutes away. Having glanced at his watch, Mr Dudley mounted the steps of the gym and addressed the spectators through a loudhailer.

"Okay, everybody, your attention, please."

Although it had stopped snowing, the bitter cold encouraged Mr Dudley to be brief.

"Mr Snyder will send the runners off at eleven o'clock on the dot. As you know, the race usually finishes with a lap of the running track. Well, thanks to the snow and the fact that we can no longer see the track, the race will now finish outside the gym. Taking into account the conditions, I expect the winning time to be around the fifty-five-minute mark. Following the start of the race, non-runners may wish to take shelter from the cold in the refectory and return here at about a quarter to twelve. Thank you."

Turning off his loudhailer, Mr Dudley scuttled off to his warm office to await the arrival of Mr Snyder. Inside the changing room, the competitors made their final preparations in silence. Of the thirty-four runners present, all were fifth and sixth-formers. Five minutes before the start of the race, Mr Dudley entered the changing room.

"Okay, everybody, the head has arrived, so could you make your way outside, please?"

Spontaneous applause greeted the runners as they approached the start and formed a rough line in accordance with Mr Snyder's instructions. It was three minutes before eleven o'clock when Mr Dudley, loudhailer in hand, again took up position on the steps of the gym.

"Will the spectators stand back and give the runners some space, please?"

Those standing directly behind the runners duly shuffled a few steps backwards. With less than two minutes to go before the start, the runners were going through their final stretching exercises when Mr Dudley again resorted to his loudhailer.

"Is everybody in position? Are all the runners in place?"

"Hold on," shouted a spectator. "There's three more here."

Their concentration interrupted, the runners turned to see Mark, Anthony and Jimmy emerging from the crowd.

"Come on then, you three," shouted Mr Dudley. "You were nearly left behind."

"Aren't they the lads who helped you at the lake?" asked Adam Pawsey from his starting position next to Dominic Price.

"Helped me? They saved my life. See that one with the battered face? He ran for help while his friends helped get me back to the shore. What I didn't know until last Saturday was that Eric Lunt tried to stop him by knocking him to the ground and splitting his lip. If that lad hadn't got up, I wouldn't be here today."

"He's no quitter then," observed Adam.

"No, he's not," replied Dominic staring at Mark.

"Well, he doesn't look in any fit condition to run," said Adam.

Looking along the line, Mark caught Dominic's gaze and returned his nod of recognition. Seconds later, the crack of the starting pistol sent the runners on their way.

With the crowd's cheers ringing in their ears, the runners set off at pace across the playing field towards the boathouse, each determined not to be caught out by a fast start. By the time they had reached the path and disappeared into the trees, the pack began to stretch as the front runners sought to press home their early advantage. Already some distance behind, Mark, Anthony and Jimmy brought up the rear.

"Who were those three latecomers?" asked Mr Snyder as the runners disappeared from view.

"I'm not sure, Head," replied Mr Dudley. "My view was partially obstructed by the crowd."

"Well, whoever they are, they're well behind already."

As everybody moved toward the refectory, Daniel Peters, the physics master, caught up with Robert Cole.

"Wasn't that young Peck and his friends arriving late?" he asked.

"It certainly was," said Robert.

"I'm surprised he was allowed to run in his condition," said Daniel.

"That's probably why he arrived late, to make sure nobody stopped him," replied Robert.

Jogging along the lakeside, Jimmy watched the runners ahead move farther away.

"How are you doing?" he asked, looking at Mark.

"I'm alright," grimaced Mark, holding his side.

"Just remember," said Anthony, "you can always stop if it gets too much."

"No stopping," insisted Mark. "Not until we cross the finishing line."

*

Sitting in her small study in Baird House, Grace Connolly read over the finalised letter and added her signature to the last page. Sitting back in her chair, she closed her eyes briefly, relieved to have completed her task. Taking an envelope from her desk drawer, she marked it 'Letter of Resignation', placed the letter inside and sealed it. Intent on handing the letter to Mr Snyder the following day, she placed the envelope in her bag. Glancing at her watch, she saw it was nearly half-past eleven. Putting on her coat, she left the study and headed for the gym and the finish of the Christmas Chase.

*

"Who's your money on, then?" asked Daniel Peters as he and Robert Cole left the refectory.

"Oh, I don't know. One of the Cooke boys perhaps or Richard Caldwell. I wouldn't rule him out," replied Robert.

As the crowd outside the gym grew, Mr Dudley provided two first-year pupils with a tape and instructed them to take up their positions at the finishing line.

"Well? Where are they, Dudley?" asked Mr Snyder impatiently. "It's gone twelve o'clock. Have they stopped for dinner?"

"I hope not, Head. They should be approaching the finish any minute now," replied Mr Dudley optimistically.

"Well, they had better hurry up, I can't feel my feet."

On a rickety table next to Mr Snyder, the Christmas Chase Cup, its tarnished pewter betraying its age, tried to look presentable as all around stamped their feet or blew into their hands in an attempt to keep warm. Next to the cup, three cheap medals awaited presentation. From her position in the crowd, Margaret Arbuckle peered toward the lake.

"Do you think they've got lost?" she asked.

"The snow's slowed them up more like," replied a shivering Victoria Jennings.

"Well, I wish they would hurry up, my blood is turning to ice," moaned Emily.

As the minutes passed, a sense of anti-climax filled the cold air.

"Hello, fancy meeting you here," said Grace sardonically.

"I didn't see you arrive," replied Robert.

"I've been here for ages," said Grace. "I thought the race would have finished by now."

"Well, I'm beginning to think something is wrong," said Daniel looking at his watch. "It's nearly half-past twelve. Surely the snow wouldn't have slowed them up this much. I think I'll go and have a word with Dudley."

"Wait a minute," said Robert. "Look."

To the sound of ironic cheers, three runners emerged from the tree line, jogging alongside each other. They were moving at little more than walking pace. Robert recognised them immediately.

"I don't believe it," he whispered.

As the boys drew nearer, the cheering increased as the crowd realised its ordeal was nearly over.

"Isn't that Mark, Anthony and Jimmy?" asked Grace.

"Too right it is," confirmed Robert, holding his hands above his head and applauding with the rest of the crowd.

"Well, good on them," said Daniel, joining in the applause. "But this must be the slowest Christmas Chase in the school's history."

"And perhaps the finest," said Robert. "Look over there."

Approximately two hundred and fifty yards away, thirty-four runners emerged from the tree line and stopped.

"What are they doing?" asked Grace.

"They're waiting," replied Robert.

"For what?" asked Daniel.

Robert smiled before answering.

"They're waiting for Mark Peck to cross the finishing line."

*

With fifty yards to go, Mark was on his last legs.

"Keep going, you're nearly there," encouraged Anthony, "though why all these people are hanging about is beyond me."

"And what's Snyder still doing here?" asked Jimmy.

"Who cares," replied Mark, still holding his side. "We're going to finish, that's the important thing."

"You're right," said Jimmy as the cheers got louder. "That *is* the important thing."

"We must have finished well behind," observed Anthony. "I can't see any of the other runners."

"Never mind that," said Jimmy. "Lead us in then, Mark."

"Let's finish together," said Mark.

"No chance," insisted Anthony. "We haven't gone through all this so that Lunt can say you finished joint last."

Just yards from the line, Jimmy and Anthony slowed down and allowed Mark to break the tape before them.

"They're having a laugh, aren't they?" said Jimmy, referring to the cheering crowd.

"Let them. Winning isn't everything," said Anthony who, arms held aloft, put on a quick spurt to finish ahead of Jimmy.

Having finished his race, Mark turned to welcome his friends over the line.

"What's the matter?" asked Anthony when confronted by the blank look on Mark's face.

"Look behind you," said Mark quietly.

Charging from the tree line, the rest of the field was bearing down on the finish. As they crossed the line, each carried a smile, and each offered Mark their congratulations. Finishing last, Dominic Price was the last to approach him and shake his hand.

"Well done, you three," said Dominic.

"You didn't have to do that," said Mark sheepishly.

"And you didn't have to get up and get help for me after Lunt had knocked you to the ground," replied Dominic.

"I don't know what to say. I feel a bit of a fraud, to be honest," said Mark.

"I don't!" said a euphoric Anthony. "I can't believe I finished second!"

Jimmy shook his head, unsure as to whether or not Anthony was joking.

"Let's just say it's one in the eye for Lunt," said Dominic smiling.

As Dominic moved away, he was buttonholed by Robert Cole.

"Was that your idea?" asked Robert.

"I might have suggested it," replied Dominic, "but not one boy objected."

"You have no idea how proud that makes me feel, Dominic."

"Actually, sir, I think I do."

"May I have your attention, please?"

An agitated Mr Dudley, his loudhailer to the fore, was back on the steps of the gym.

"Quiet ... will you please quieten down!" shouted Mr Dudley. "Mr Snyder will now make the presentations."

After passing the loudhailer to Mr Snyder, Mr Dudley ushered the three boys towards the rickety table. Totally bemused by what he had just witnessed and frozen to the marrow, The Snide was in no mood to stand on ceremony. As he was about to speak, a familiar voice caused him to pause.

"Mr Snyder! Mr Snyder! Stop the presentation," called Mr Cheatham.

Turning around, Mr Snyder waited as his trusted deputy pushed through the crowd.

"Headmaster, I must have a word with you," insisted The Cheat, whose face, on seeing Mark, Anthony and Jimmy, contorted into a scowl.

"What is it, Cheatham? Can't it wait? I am feeling distinctly hypothermic."

Ushering the headmaster to one side, The Cheat cupped his hand

and whispered into the head's ear.

"What!" erupted the head. "Are you sure?"

The Cheat stood back, a look of triumph stamped upon his face, and nodded.

"Mr Dudley!" boomed The Snide. "This presentation is cancelled."

"Cancelled? May I ask why, Head?" asked a confused Mr Dudley.

"I have just been informed that my ... that the stolen portrait has been found. It has been found in the room occupied by these three boys."

Gasps of astonishment accompanied Mr Snyder's revelation.

"Cups and medals? I don't think so," continued the head. "Rather a flogging at the hands of Mr Cheatham at tomorrow's assembly. Confine them to their room."

Turning on his heels, Mr Snyder departed at speed. He had a portrait to inspect.

"What's going on?" asked Anthony. "What is he talking about?"

"Can't you guess?" asked Jimmy. "Pardon the pun, but we've been framed, and I'll give you one guess who by."

"You three, follow me. Now!" commanded Mr Cheatham.

Utterly deflated, Mark retreated into his shell, unsure he could take another beating so soon after his last.

CHAPTER THIRTY-FIVE

Stage Fright

It had been a long night. Confined to their room, sleep had proved fitful as each boy contemplated the beating to come and the disgrace of expulsion. Breakfast was a silent affair, and their food went mostly untouched. It was an exasperated Anthony who eventually vented his frustration.

"Is anybody going to ask us for our side of the story?" he asked.

"Probably not," replied Jimmy. "Anyway, what would we say? 'It wasn't us, sir'. I'll bet Snyder's never heard that one before."

"But what about all that stuff about being innocent until proven guilty?" protested Anthony.

"What more proof does he need?" asked Jimmy. "His stupid portrait was found in our room. How do we prove that it was Lunt who brought it here?"

"But it had to be him," said Anthony.

"You don't need to convince *me*. Think about how you are going to convince The Snide," replied Jimmy.

"My dad will go mad if I'm expelled from here," moaned Anthony.

"My mum will kill me," said Jimmy.

"Well, my parents probably have other things to worry about," said Mark from the window. "Some Christmas this is going to be."

"Look, I know we're in trouble but try not to show it," said Jimmy. "Remember, Lunt and his mates will be sitting in the hall just waiting for us to fall apart. Don't give them the satisfaction."

"Does it hurt, the cane?" asked Anthony.

"Of course, it hurts," replied Jimmy. "What sort of question is that?"

"Well, I just thought that coming from Liverpool, you must have been caned lots of times," said Anthony.

"Thanks very much," replied Jimmy, a touch put out.

"Sorry," said Anthony, "it's just that I've never really been in trouble before."

"Look, best not to think about it," advised Jimmy.

"Don't think about it?" repeated Anthony. "That's easier said than done."

"I know it is," said Jimmy, "but don't you see? The Snide wants us to think about it; he wants to make us as scared as he can before setting Cheatham on us."

"He wants more than that," added Mark from the window. "He wants to humiliate us before the entire school."

"Then let's make sure he doesn't," said Jimmy, his tone resolute. "Whatever gets thrown at us, don't cry out. Agreed?"

A few seconds passed before Anthony replied.

"I'll try not to," he said unconvincingly.

Not wanting to make a promise he might not be able to keep, Mark stared out of the window in silence.

*

It was half-past ten, and Mr Snyder could no longer avoid his visitor.

"You can send him in now, Miss Cropper," he said into the intercom on his desk.

Seconds later, Robert Cole entered the office.

"Good morning, Mr Cole, and what can I do for you as if I didn't know?"

Robert looked up at the portrait hanging on the wall behind Mr

Snyder.

"I see it's back in its rightful place," he said.

"Oh yes," confirmed the head as he turned to admire the painting. "It would appear that you were right all along, Mr Cole. The portrait never left the school premises."

"And the boys? What is going to happen to them?" asked Robert.

"You mean the thieves?" corrected Mr Snyder. "Well, as promised, they will be punished before the entire school this morning."

"You mean beaten," asserted Robert.

"Yes, Mr Cole, I mean beaten."

"Tell me, have you spoken to the boys? Have they admitted to taking the painting?"

"Come now, Mr Cole, what is there to admit? The portrait was found in their room, for heaven's sake."

"Yes, but how can you be sure the boys put it there?"

"Because they confessed."

"Confessed? To whom?"

"To their friends, of course," replied Mr Snyder.

"I don't understand," said Robert.

"It is quite simple," explained the head smiling. "Having stolen my portrait and eager to attract the notoriety they so craved, they could not resist bragging about their exploit to anybody who would listen."

"Who did they tell?"

"Oh, it doesn't matter who they told. What matters is that they were heard telling their friends how they had taken the portrait and hidden it in their room."

"And who was it who overheard this conversation?" asked Robert.

"Eric Lunt and Maxwell Bradley, if you must know," replied the head. "I do not doubt that both are fine upstanding fifth-formers whose word can be trusted. They overheard the conversation and immediately reported the matter to Mr Cheatham."

"What do you mean by 'immediately'?"

"I mean immediately, Mr Cole, as in straight away."

"When exactly did they report the matter to Mr Cheatham?"

"Mr Cole, I will not be cross-examined in this fashion," protested the head.

"Please, bear with me. You say they reported the conversation to Mr Cheatham immediately after they heard it. When exactly was that?"

"Shortly before midday yesterday," replied the head testily.

"Then they are lying."

"And how, Mr Cole, do you arrive at that conclusion?"

"Because between eleven o'clock and half past twelve yesterday, your so-called thieves were running in the Christmas Chase. They could not possibly have been overheard talking to anybody."

Mr Snyder grimaced.

"Then Lunt and Bradley must have got their times mixed up. The fact is they overheard the conversation and reported it. The fact is that the portrait was found in the boys' room."

"I have to tell you that I strongly suspect that Lunt and his friends have been bullying Mark Peck for some time," said Robert. "If you ask me, they were responsible for the beating he took last Saturday."

"Did Mark Peck tell you that?" asked the head, his impatience growing.

"No ..."

"Has *anybody* told you that?"

"No, but ..."

"Then you have no evidence whatsoever to support your outrageous allegation. You are clutching at straws in an attempt, dare I say, to curry favour with your pupils. But don't be embarrassed, Mr

Cole, it's a trap many inexperienced teachers fall into. May I point out that Eric Lunt is one of our most prominent students and a strong candidate to be the next head boy? You should also know that his father, a man of great influence, donates generously to the school."

"What has that got to do with anything?" snapped Robert.

"Really, Mr Cole, your naivety is almost touching. Take my advice; if you ever have to take sides, always side with influence."

"Look," said Robert, "all I ask is that you call off the flogging you have planned and investigate the matter properly. It beggars belief that you could contemplate meting out punishment to a boy who was only released from the infirmary on Monday."

"The same boy who beat the entire school in a cross-country race. Surely, in the light of that triumph, you are not suggesting that he is unfit to be punished?"

Realising that he was getting nowhere, Robert played his final card.

"If you insist on punishing these boys, I will have no option other than to raise the matter with the school governors."

"Then this meeting is over," declared the head looking at his watch. "I refuse to sit here and be threatened. It is nearly eleven o'clock, and I have an assembly to attend. If you wish to see justice done, I suggest you accompany me to the Great Hall."

*

By the time Robert reached the Great Hall, most of the school had already taken their seats. Standing at the rear of the hall, Grace beckoned him to her.

"Well?" she asked.

"It's hopeless," said Robert. "He wouldn't budge an inch."

"So much for the spirit of Christmas," said Grace. "I feel like I'm attending an execution."

Sitting in the middle of the stage, Mark, Anthony and Jimmy quietly awaited their fate. Behind them, flexing his rattan cane, Mr Cheatham looked to the rear of the hall in anticipation of Mr

Snyder's arrival. At the stroke of eleven o'clock, The Snide made his entrance. Pursued by a rolling hush, he made his way along the central aisle and ascended the steps of the stage.

"All stand!" boomed Mr Cheatham.

Acknowledging his deputy, Mr Snyder approached the lectern and, as was his habit, paused for effect.

"Be seated," he ordered.

As those assembled took their seats, the porters left the hall, closing all doors behind them. Raising both hands, Mr Snyder clutched his gown in the manner of a barrister addressing a jury.

"Tomorrow, you will leave school for the Christmas break," he announced, his tone bereft of festive cheer. "On behalf of the staff of Grey Stones, let me take this opportunity to wish each of you a happy Christmas and a safe return to school in the New Year."

Underwhelmed by the solemnity of Mr Snyder's delivery, the assembly sat in silence.

"Unfortunately, the three boys behind me will not be returning to the school. It pains me to say these boys have dishonoured themselves and betrayed the school in the most despicable way. I refer, of course, to the theft of a portrait from my office. You may recall my promise that those responsible would be punished before the entire school and expelled. Well, the day of reckoning has arrived, but before asking Mr Cheatham to carry out the punishment, I have a far happier duty to perform."

Mr Snyder's disposition suddenly brightened.

"For their part in bringing the thieves to book and ensuring the recovery of the portrait in question, I would like to present a small reward to Eric Lunt and Maxwell Bradley. I would be grateful if both boys would approach the stage."

Robert Cole could not believe what he was hearing. As the two fifth-formers made their way forward, Mr Snyder reached into his jacket pocket and retrieved two envelopes, each containing a five-pound note. Ascending the steps of the stage, the informers cast a quick smile in the direction of the condemned boys before approaching the head.

"Boys," proclaimed The Snide, "you have set a fine example to your fellow pupils. Please accept this small reward in recognition of the high regard in which I have no doubt you are universally held."

Clutching their envelopes, Lunt and Bradley left the stage. As they returned to their seats, Mr Snyder again addressed the assembly.

"Perhaps a round of applause would be in order?"

Responding immediately to The Snide's invitation, the unaccompanied ovations of Reilly and Woosey quickly petered out. Unperturbed, Mr Snyder again spoke into the microphone, his tone now brisk and business-like.

"Very well, let us proceed. The punishment to be administered is eight strokes."

A startled murmur rippled through the hall.

"However," continued The Snide, "I shall consider reducing the punishment by two strokes for any boy prepared to voice an apology before this assembly."

"Well?" asked Cheatham staring at the boys.

Mark, Anthony and Jimmy silently remained in their seats.

"Mr Cheatham, proceed with the punishment," ordered the head.

Like a master of ceremonies, The Snide stepped to one side, leaving centre stage to his deputy.

"You boy, you're first," ordered Cheatham, beckoning Mark forward with his cane.

Mark lifted his bruised and swollen face and looked the master squarely in the eye. As he was about to leave his seat, Anthony stood up.

"No, I'll go first."

"Have it your way," said Cheatham.

Anthony stepped forward.

"Raise your right hand."

Afraid and feeling very alone, Anthony did as he was told and waited for the first strike to land. When it did, excruciating pain seared through his fingers and into his arm, the force of the strike causing his facial muscles to quiver. But Anthony remained silent.

"Left hand," barked Cheatham.

Clamping his jaw firmly shut, Anthony raised his hand and stared directly ahead as the cane bit into his flesh for a second time. But he did not murmur.

"Right hand," demanded Cheatham, determined to provoke a response.

Afraid he might be losing his touch, Cheatham extended his backswing further before angling his third strike hard into the boy's hand. Anthony's mouth flew open as the pain hit him like an electric shock. But still, he did not cry out.

At the back of the hall, Grace Connolly gripped Robert's arm.

"This is barbaric," she whispered.

"And we are the barbarians," replied Robert.

From their pew in the centre of the hall, Lunt, Bradley, Reilly and Woosey giggled and nudged each other as Anthony, his face contorted with pain, repeatedly refused to cry out. From their pews in front of Lunt, the pupils of Form 4C looked on in horror as the vicious attack on their classmate continued. But not a sound escaped Anthony's lips.

"Left hand," growled Cheatham, who had one strike left with which to extract a verbal admission of pain.

Anthony raised his hand, but this time he looked his tormentor straight in the eye. Fear had abandoned him; nothing would make him cry out now. As the final stroke found its target, the cruel intent etched on Cheatham's face was witnessed by the entire assembly.

"Sit down!" ordered The Cheat, his exasperation all too clear.

His hands immobile with pain, Anthony returned to his seat, his face drained of colour and his eyes swimming.

"Well taken, Anthony," whispered Jimmy.

"Thanks," hissed Anthony through gritted teeth. "Don't cry out. Agreed?"

"Agreed," whispered Jimmy.

"You boy, you're next," growled Cheatham, again pointing his cane at Mark.

But before Mark could respond, Jimmy was on his feet.

"No, it's my turn," he said.

"Very well, it's all the same to me. Step forward."

Moving away from his chair, Jimmy looked into the hall, made eye contact with Lunt and silently vowed that he would get even. Behind him, Mark again bowed his head and stared at the floor.

"Right hand!" snapped Cheatham.

As he raised his hand, Jimmy fixed Cheatham with a look of defiance that dared him to do his worst. Outraged, The Cheat delivered his most ferocious stroke yet. Jimmy did not make a sound. Anticipating the next command, he stuck out his left hand before Cheatham could utter a word. Losing self-control, Cheatham, intent on generating maximum momentum, took a step backwards before whipping the cane through the air and across the boy's hand. His resolve fuelled by his pain, Jimmy took the blow in silence and thrust out his right hand.

"Mark will never be able to take this," said Grace, unable to look upon the stage any longer.

"Don't worry," said Robert, his mind made up. "He won't have to."

"What are you going to do?" asked Grace.

"What I should have done in the first place," replied Robert. "I'm going to stop it."

As Robert got to his feet, a restraining hand grasped his shoulder.

On stage, his hands on fire, Anthony sat ashen-faced. A stranger to such savagery, he thought the world a very unfair place. After another whistling stroke had ripped into Jimmy's hand, Anthony noticed a man and a woman enter the hall and approach Robert Cole. The man was wearing a dog collar and was pressing a restraining hand on Mr Cole's shoulder. Within seconds the man was striding purposely down the centre aisle, the woman running to keep up with him.

With his mouth firmly clamped shut, Jimmy continued to seek eye contact with Cheatham. After administering the eighth stroke, the master stood back and glared at his victim, who had not made a sound.

"Back to your seat!" snarled The Cheat.

Jimmy stood his ground and continued to look the master in the eye. Unable to return the boy's stare, Cheatham turned his attention to Mark.

"You boy, you're next. On your feet. Now!"

Jimmy placed himself between Cheatham and Mark.

"Leave him alone," he ordered. "I'll take his."

"That's fine by me!" shouted Cheatham drawing back his cane.

But Mr Cheatham had delivered his last stroke. With two bounds, the man in the dog collar had cleared the steps of the stage. Grabbing The Cheat by the shoulder, he spun him around and sent him sprawling across the platform with a right cross to the jaw. As if released from a spell, the entire assembly, except for Lunt and his cronies, rose to its feet and delivered a massive roar of approval.

"Dad!" shouted Mark rising to his feet.

"Sorry, son," said George Peck embracing his lad. "We left as soon as we got Mr Cole's telegram."

"What telegram?" asked Anthony, the colour slowly returning to his cheeks.

"Mark!" called Mrs Peck above the uproar.

"Mum?"

Pulling her son toward her, Elizabeth Peck embraced him tightly before holding him at arm's length and looking into his eyes.

"We're home, we're home for good. We've decided ... but who did this to your face?"

Confronted by her son's silence, Elizabeth Peck looked across the stage and saw Mr Snyder helping a dazed Mr Cheatham to his feet.

"Wait here," she said before crossing the stage to challenge the head.

"Madam, how dare you ..."

But before he could utter another word, Elizabeth Peck slapped him fiercely across the face, provoking a further roar from the assembly. Tottering backwards, The Snide was only saved from further punishment by the intervention of Robert Cole.

"I think he's had enough, don't you?" said Robert guiding a determined Elizabeth Peck away from her quarry.

With the stage now full of staff, Mr Snyder and a still groggy Mr Cheatham made their escape. It was Miss Swan who eventually approached the lectern in an attempt to restore order.

"Please be quiet and sit down," she pleaded into the microphone.

But the pupils of Grey Stones were too excited to take notice.

"Sit down and be quiet!" shouted Miss Swan angrily.

Unaccustomed to Miss Swan losing her temper, the assembly immediately fell silent.

"Thank you," she said, the calm having returned to her voice. "This assembly is now at an end. On behalf of the staff, let me wish you all a very happy and safe Christmas."

As the pupils left the hall, a bewildered-looking Mark, Anthony and Jimmy remained on stage.

"I don't believe it," muttered Jimmy, blowing into his burning hands. "A fighting vicar?"

"Meet my mum and dad," beamed Mark.

As the parties introduced themselves, Emily Burton and Margaret

Arbuckle approached the stage.

"Are you three alright?" asked Emily.

"Mark is," winced Anthony, flexing his fingers to alleviate the pain.

"Here, I got this for you, Mark," said Margaret, advancing onto the stage. "I pinched it when no one was looking."

"It's the Christmas Chase Cup," explained Jimmy for the benefit of Mark's parents.

"Mark won it yesterday," said Margaret.

"And I came second," added Anthony.

"Thanks, Margaret," said Mark. "I don't suppose they let you keep it if you get expelled."

"Who is getting expelled?" asked Elizabeth Peck, pulling her son toward her.

"Why were you three being punished in the first place, and what's all this I've been hearing about bullying?" asked George Peck.

"Where has Mr Cole gone?" asked Elizabeth.

"I'm here," said Robert stepping forward with Grace. "Please, allow me to introduce my colleague, Miss Connolly."

Elizabeth Peck got straight to the point.

"Can either of you explain what was happening when we entered the hall? That man Cheatham was assaulting this boy and was clearly intent on assaulting Mark next."

"What did they do to deserve a public beating?" asked George Peck.

Before Robert could respond, Stanley Rimmer entered the stage.

"Excuse me, sir," said the porter. "I have a message from Mr Snyder. He wants to see you in his office at two o'clock this afternoon."

"I'll bet he does," said Robert.

"Look," said Grace addressing the Pecks, "can I suggest that Mr Cole and I meet up with you later this afternoon? You must have a lot to ask Mark, and I need to sort out some ice packs for Jimmy and Anthony."

"That's a good idea," said Robert. "We could get together after I've met with Mr Snyder."

"Very well. Where?" asked George Peck.

"It's probably best if we meet somewhere off the school premises," said Grace.

"Very wise," agreed Elizabeth. "If I see Mr Snyder again, I might not be responsible for my actions."

"Well, if you're agreeable, we can meet at Blackberry Hill, my home," suggested Robert. "It's not far from here."

George and Elizabeth Peck looked at each other and nodded.

"That's settled then," said Robert. "I'll write down the directions for you. Shall we say three o'clock?"

"Three o'clock it is," confirmed Elizabeth Peck.

"Good," said Grace. "It will be nice to see Blackberry Hill again before I leave."

"Leave, miss?" queried Jimmy.

"Yes," replied Grace. "I'm afraid I'll be resigning from Grey Stones tomorrow."

"But why, miss?" asked Emily.

"Oh, lots of reasons," replied Grace, glancing at Robert.

"Does that mean we won't see you again, miss?" asked Margaret.

"Probably," replied Grace.

"Never mind, miss," said Anthony gloomily. "It doesn't look like me, Jimmy or Mark are coming back, either."

"Well, let's wait and see about that," said Robert.

Catching Emily's eye, Jimmy appeared to be encouraging her to say something when Robert spotted him.

"Are you alright, Jimmy?" he asked.

Reluctant to respond, Margaret came to his rescue.

"Well, the thing is, sir, you know that assignment you and Miss Connolly set the boys, the one about researching Michael Edwards? Well, me and Emily have been helping them."

"Really?" said Grace. "I thought that particular project had long been forgotten."

"Oh no, miss," replied Emily. "We've spent hours doing the research and were waiting for the right time to report back with our findings."

"You have findings?" asked Robert.

"Quite a few, sir," replied Mark, looking nervously at Anthony.

"The point is, sir," said Jimmy, "if Miss Connolly is leaving …"

"And if we're about to be expelled …" added Anthony.

"Then that only leaves today for us to tell you what we've found out," said Margaret.

"I'm very grateful," said Grace, "but I have to tell you that I think I've found out all I need to know about Michael Edwards."

"Nevertheless," said Robert, "If you have done the research, it's only right that you present your findings. If it's alright with Mark's parents, why don't we all meet at Blackberry Hill this afternoon?"

"I'm sure we don't mind," replied George Peck."

"Good," said Robert.

"Right, then," said Margaret, turning to her friends. "I'll see you later."

"Where are you going?" asked Jimmy.

"To make a phone call," replied Margaret.

CHAPTER THIRTY-SIX

Second Thoughts

"Mr Cole is here to see you," announced Miss Cropper.

"Good, send him in and make sure we are not interrupted," ordered Mr Snyder.

Sitting behind his desk, the head cast a final glance into the hand mirror he was holding and gently caressed the red mark below his right eye socket. As the door to his office opened, he deftly placed the mirror into a drawer.

"You wanted to see me?" asked Robert entering the office.

"Mr Cole, be seated," ordered Mr Snyder coldly.

Pursued by a frosty stare, Robert did as he was told.

"Never, I repeat, never have I witnessed such appalling behaviour as that exhibited this morning by the parents of Mark Peck," said the head solemnly.

"Mr Snyder …"

"Do not interrupt me!" exploded the head. "Believe it or not, being attacked during school assembly is a new experience for me."

"Well, it's a pity the same can't be said of our pupils," retorted Robert defiantly.

A fragile silence accompanied the head's vain attempt to control his temper.

"I have but one question for you, Mr Cole, and it is this," he hissed. "Can you explain how Mr and Mrs Peck came to be present at this morning's assembly?"

Robert took a deep breath before replying.

"They came because of the telegram I sent them."

"What telegram was that?" thundered the head.

"The one informing them that their son had been beaten up and was in the infirmary," replied Robert, his voice rising. "The one telling them that their son was being bullied. The one telling them …"

"Enough!" barked Snyder. "I have heard enough. It is clear to me that this morning's outrage would never have occurred without your encouragement. In addition to the three expulsions I have already announced, it is my regrettable duty to inform you that …"

The buzzing intervention of the intercom on Mr Snyder's desk caused him to pick up his telephone.

"Miss Cropper, I thought I told you we were not to be disturbed."

Robert watched as the angry expression on Snyder's face gave way to one of shock.

"The press? *The Keswickian*?" echoed the head, who momentarily placed his hand over the receiver and looked at Robert.

"Is this your doing?" he asked.

"I haven't a clue what you're talking about."

Unconvinced, Mr Snyder again addressed Miss Cropper.

"Very well then, put him on."

After a few seconds, Mr Snyder again spoke into the telephone.

"Hello, yes, my name is Snyder; who am I speaking to?"

A short silence followed.

"Harry Morgan? The proprietor of *The Keswickian* …" repeated the head whose eyes were now raised to the heavens.

Unable to hear the caller, Robert gleaned what information he could from Mr Snyder's replies.

"And what source might that be, Mr Morgan?" enquired the head.

The ensuing silence lasted seconds.

"A whistle-blower, you say?"

The head's frustration was palpable.

"You have a photograph of the deputy head being punched by a man of the cloth and another of me being assaulted by ..."

Mr Snyder placed his free hand on his bald pate and listened for some seconds before responding.

"Front page story, you say? National headlines?"

Mr Snyder looked bewildered.

"Scoop who?" he asked. "Scoop Hardy? Never heard of him! No, no, I wouldn't dream of challenging his credentials."

The furrows on Mr Snyder's forehead faded slightly as the conversation took another turn.

"Yes, I am an extremely reasonable man ...What? No expulsions? No complaints against the parents?"

Mr Snyder looked a beaten man as he again turned his gaze on Robert Cole.

"Wonderful teachers ... yes indeed, yes ... I can assure you that everybody at Grey Stones rates Mr Cole and Miss Connolly very highly."

Still listening into the phone and unable to look at Robert any longer, Mr Snyder stood up and faced the window

"Agreement? What sort of agreement?" he asked cautiously.

When he next spoke, Mr Snyder almost sounded relieved.

"Yes, of course ... the reputation of the school must come first ... yes, yes, my sentiments exactly ... thank you, yes, of course, we have an agreement. Thank you for your time, Mr Morgan. The pleasure has been entirely mine."

Mr Snyder put down the phone and walked to the window. With

his hands clasped behind his back, he looked into the distance and gathered his thoughts before turning to address Robert.

"Perhaps, on reflection, Mr Cheatham and I may have overreacted slightly to the situation. Please inform all parties that the expulsions have been rescinded and pass on my sincere apologies to those who may feel aggrieved by recent events. Thank you, Mr Cole, this meeting is over."

CHAPTER THIRTY-SEVEN

First Impressions

It was shortly before three o'clock and the light was fading when Robert arrived at Blackberry Hill. As he ascended the steps of the veranda, Grace opened the door to greet him.

"How did it go?" she asked.

"Far better than I could ever have hoped," beamed Robert. "Is everybody here?"

"Yes, including your aunt Ginny," replied Grace. "She's looking after everybody in the drawing room."

When Robert and Grace entered the drawing room, everyone was sitting around a table, drinking tea and eating biscuits. A roaring fire, ably assisted by the fairy lights on an impressive-looking Christmas tree, radiated a cosy glow. To the left of the tree, darkening skies peered into the room through the large bay window.

"Robert, there you are," said Aunt Ginny rising from her chair. "How did your meeting go? I've been told everything. Do we have a verdict?"

"Indeed we have," replied Robert. "Has anybody here heard of a man called Harry Morgan?"

"The owner of *The Keswickian*?" queried Grace.

The classmates looked at Margaret but said nothing.

As Robert gave his account of the meeting, Aunt Ginny crossed the floor to the bay window and drew the curtains, cutting off the bay from the rest of the room. After placing a couple of logs on the fire, she returned to her seat.

"Well, to be honest, the fact that Mark's expulsion has been withdrawn is neither here or there," said George Peck when Robert had finished talking. "I see no good reason why Elizabeth and I should not withdraw him from the school. Look at him. Look at his face. He has been bullied, beaten and was about to be thrashed for an offence he assures me he did not commit."

"No, Dad, I can't leave. I want to stay. It would be like running away," protested Mark. "And anyway, my friends are here."

Elizabeth Peck looked around the table and smiled.

"We can see you have friends here," she conceded.

"And anyway," said Mark looking to his mother, "now that you and Dad are back in Lancaster for good, things are bound to get better."

"What do you say, Mr Cole?" asked Elizabeth.

Not wishing to cause undue embarrassment, Robert paused before replying.

"I think the school should be proud to have pupils like this bunch. I hope they will stay."

"That goes for me, too," said Grace.

"You will forgive me, Miss Connolly," said George Peck, "but that's easy for you to say. You are resigning from your post tomorrow. Why should we be swayed by your opinion?"

"You are quite right," admitted Grace.

Reaching to the floor, Grace retrieved an envelope from her handbag, walked across the room to the fire and tossed it into the flames.

"What are you doing?" asked Robert.

"My letter of resignation," replied Grace. "If Mark won't run away, then neither shall I."

"That was very well said, my dear," observed Aunt Ginny with feeling, "and so very like of a young man I once knew."

George Peck exchanged glances with his wife before holding up his hands in a gesture of surrender.

"That's good enough for us. Mark, if you want to stay, we won't object."

Mark released a quiet sigh of relief.

"Well, now that's sorted out, let me order some more tea," said Aunt Ginny.

"Not for us, thank you, we must be on our way," said Elizabeth Peck.

"Yes, we have to book into our accommodation in Keswick," explained George. "We will pick Mark up from school in the morning."

Amid farewells and mutual best wishes, Robert, Grace and Aunt Ginny escorted George and Elizabeth Peck to the front door leaving the pupils of Form 4C alone in the drawing room.

"Right," said Emily, "this is where the real fun starts."

*

"Well then," said Robert when everyone had returned to the drawing-room table. "Who's going to tell us about Michael Edwards?"

There was no response.

"Come on," encouraged Robert. "Who wants to start?"

Galvanised by the ensuing silence, Grace took the lead.

"Well, seeing as I was the one who got everybody involved, perhaps I should go first."

In the absence of any objection, Grace pressed on.

"Before I start, I have a request to make. I want you to promise me that you will not repeat a word of what I am about to tell you to anyone. Everything I tell you must remain within these four walls. Do I have your promise?"

"You can trust us, miss," said Emily.

"What is it you want to tell us?" asked Robert.

"Let me start by telling everybody a little bit about myself. I was born on Christmas Day, 1940, which makes me nearly twenty-six. I was born in Keswick, where my mum, Jane, raised me. After she died last May, I returned home from London and decided to stay here for good. My mum, who was from Liverpool, came to Keswick in 1939, shortly after war was declared. Not long after her arrival, she met my father, Tristan Connolly, a fighter pilot in the RAF. They married in early 1940. Sadly, two terrible tragedies then befell my mother in quick succession. In June 1940, before I was born, my father was shot down over the English Channel and killed. Not long after that, my mum's family was wiped out during an air raid on Liverpool."

The stunned look on the faces of her pupils caused Grace to pause for a moment.

"I know. It's not a nice story, and neither is it entirely accurate. You see, I now know that Tristan Connolly never existed."

Moving forward in her chair slightly, Aunt Ginny glanced briefly at the curtains drawn across the bay window.

"When did you make that discovery?" asked Robert.

"At the beginning of term," replied Grace. "I should have told you earlier. Sorry."

"How did you find out?" asked Robert.

"The evidence was all around me. Following Mum's funeral, I found various items of family memorabilia in Derwent Cottage."

Reaching into her handbag, Grace took out a folded newspaper cutting, a small velvet-clad box and a silver cigarette case.

"This newspaper cutting is taken from the *Liverpool Echo* dated 22nd December 1940," explained Grace, who unfolded it and placed it on the table. "Do you remember coming to see me on the Sunday before the first day of term?"

"I remember," said Robert. "The vicar was with you."

"That's right, I showed him this cutting. It tells how a makeshift air raid shelter in Liverpool took a direct hit, causing great loss of life. After you left, I sat down and read the cutting again. It was only then that it hit me."

"What did?" asked Robert.

"The cutting refers to the names of the families who suffered the worst casualties in the raid. It makes specific reference to the Connolly family. Listen."

Grace proceeded to read from the cutting.

"*Mrs Ann Kenny, a resident of Bentinck Street, was staying with her mother on the night of the raid. She returned home to find that her husband Reginald Kenny had been killed, as had her neighbours Mr and Mrs Connolly and their two daughters. A third daughter survives them.*"

Grace paused briefly before looking up from the cutting.

"If my mother's parents were called Connolly, then Connolly must have been her maiden name. This cutting proves that my mother never married."

"I am sorry, that must have come as a shock," said Robert.

Anxious to conceal any trace of self-pity, Grace put on a brave face, smiled and moved on.

"Then there is the medal and the cigarette case."

Opening the small velvet box, Grace took out a medal and manoeuvred it across the table towards the boys.

"What do you make of that then?" she asked.

"It's a Victoria Cross!" gasped Anthony.

"Quite right," replied Grace. "Though, I have to admit, I didn't know that until Reverend Grundy told me."

"Whose is it, miss?" asked Mark.

"I assumed that it had been won by my father, Tristan Connolly, but the newspaper cutting put paid to that particular theory. My final piece of evidence is this cigarette case," said Grace, placing it in the middle of the table. "As you can see, it bears an inscription: *T.H.C:*

Filius est pars patris."

"A son is part of the father," said Jimmy, remembering the translation.

"What do the initials T.H.C. stand for?" asked Robert.

"At first, I thought the initials stood for Tristan Herbert Connolly, but, again, that assumption was shattered by the newspaper cutting."

Leaning across the table, Grace opened the case to reveal the photographs inside.

"My father and mother," she announced.

As the case was passed between the classmates, their eyes widened with surprise.

"It's Captain …"

The impact of Emily's elbow into her side prevented Margaret from completing her identification.

"What was that, Margaret?" asked Grace.

"Nothing, miss," replied Margaret, forcing a smile.

"I have to say, he looks rather familiar," said Robert when the case was passed to him.

Aunt Ginny looked at the photographs but said nothing.

"So, what's the significance of the case?" asked Robert.

"The Latin inscription, *Filius est pars patris*. I was sure I had come across the phrase somewhere before," explained Grace. "After I had read the cutting again, I remembered where. Shortly after being appointed, I was taken on a tour of the school by Mr Snyder. The phrase is etched into the plinth of a statue in the foyer of Cole House."

"The statue of my grandfather, Richard Cole," confirmed Robert.

"Wondering whether I had stumbled across nothing more than a coincidence, I went to have another look at the statue the next day after school. I then decided to look around Cole Hall. It was then that I saw the photograph, and everything became clear."

"We saw you there, miss," said Jimmy.

"Yes, I remember," replied Grace. "You must have thought my behaviour very strange."

"What photograph?" asked Robert.

"The photograph of your uncle, Captain Thomas Howard Cole V.C.," replied Grace. "You donated it to the school not so long ago, I believe."

"The summer before I started teaching here," confirmed Robert. "That photograph was taken in this very room. It shows my uncle in uniform, wearing his Victoria Cross."

"This Victoria Cross," said Grace pointing to the medal on the table. "I recognised him immediately. Don't you see? The photograph in the cigarette case, it's the same person. It's a photograph of your uncle."

"You might be right," said Robert studying the photograph closely.

"What are you saying, dear?" asked Aunt Ginny.

"I am saying that the initials T.H.C. on the cigarette case do not stand for Tristan Herbert Connolly at all; they stand for Thomas Howard Cole. The Latin phrasing, the initials and the photograph inside prove the case was his. The fact that his photograph sits next to a photograph of my mother proves that they were in a relationship. Why else would the cigarette case and the captain's medal be in my mother's possession? What am I saying? I'm saying that Captain Thomas Cole was my father."

Aunt Ginny sat back in her chair and glanced again at the curtains concealing the bay window.

"But that's impossible," argued Robert. "My uncle died in 1918."

"Then how do you explain the photograph in the cigarette case?" countered Grace.

"I don't know. They can't be the same person, it's just not possible," said Robert, retreating from his previous position.

"Oh, Robert," declared Grace, tears forming in her eyes. "The photographs speak for themselves: Thomas Cole was my father."

Confused, Robert continued to stare at the photograph inside the cigarette case.

"The fact is, Robert, you are my cousin, we are related, which means I could never ... we could never ... Oh, Robert, do I have to spell it out?"

"So that's why you ..." remembering that his pupils were present, Robert went no further.

"That's right, Robert," replied Grace softly. "That's why I was going to leave Grey Stones."

"But tell me, my dear, what has any of this to do with Michael Edwards?" asked Aunt Ginny.

"After visiting Cole Hall, I returned home and tried to make sense of it all. I had another look at the cigarette case, but this time I removed the veneer that kept his photograph in place and took it out of the case. You will find an inscription on the back of the photograph."

Peeling back the veneer, Robert retrieved the photograph and read the inscription aloud.

"*Michael Edwards, Headmaster of Grey Stones, October 1937*. So that was why you asked me about him?"

"I wanted to know why Thomas Cole had changed his name to Michael Edwards," confessed Grace. "Of course, from the moment I saw his name on the back of the photograph, the mystery deepened. Not only were there no photographs of Michael Edwards in Cole Hall, but we also discovered that his portrait had gone missing from the Great Hall."

"Funnily enough," said Robert, "I found out from the head that the portrait went missing a couple of years ago, shortly before I started teaching here."

"Well, anyway," continued Grace, "once you told me that Michael Edwards had been killed in 1941, I visited his grave and left some flowers; what more could I do? I didn't want to sully my mother's good name by highlighting the fact that she was not married when she had me, and I certainly didn't want to embarrass you. But there is a person sitting at this table who I believe might shed some light on the matter."

Ignoring the puzzled look on Robert's face, Grace addressed Aunt Ginny.

"The last time we met, I asked you if you were the person who attended my mother's funeral. You were about to answer when we were interrupted. I know it was you. Can you tell me anything about my father? And what did you mean earlier when you said I reminded you of a young man you once knew?"

Aunt Ginny looked across the table at Grace and met her stare with a sympathetic smile.

"Excuse me, miss," said Jimmy, who could contain himself no longer. "There is something we need to tell you: Captain Cole was not your father."

Saved by Jimmy's intervention, Aunt Ginny cast another glance toward the bay window, sat back in her chair, and listened.

CHAPTER THIRTY-EIGHT

Resurrection

It took a few seconds for Grace Connolly to respond. When she did, her tone was almost defiant.

"Jimmy, how can you say that after all I've told you?"

"But he's right, miss," said Margaret.

Grace looked to Robert for support, but none was forthcoming.

"Well, I, for one, would like to hear what these youngsters have to say," said Aunt Ginny.

"Me too," said Robert. "That, after all, is why they are here. Come on then, you lot, what have you got to tell us?"

Hesitation loomed.

"Well?" challenged Grace.

"Well, before we start," said Mark, "we just want you to know that we don't want to upset anyone … erm … what I mean is …"

"What Mark is trying to say," said Emily, "is that our findings might cause offence."

"Don't worry about that; I'm sure you haven't set out to offend anybody," said Robert. "What is it you think you have discovered?"

Opening his notebook, Anthony went first.

"Well, sir, when we began researching Michael Edwards, we had little to go on. You told us he was headmaster of the school between 1937 and 1941 and was buried in the Church of St John. You also told us that there were no photographs of him in Cole Hall and that his portrait was missing from the Great Hall."

"And that he had been murdered," added Mark.

Anthony moved on.

"When we got to the archive, we decided to work backwards from 1941. We were hoping to find a photograph of him and discover when he started teaching at the school. But we came across something very strange."

"When he was going through the yearbooks," continued Mark, "Jimmy found that they contained a photograph of every master who taught at the school, every master except for Michael Edwards."

"No photographs in Cole Hall, no portrait in the Great Hall and no photographs in the yearbooks; it was like Michael Edwards was hiding from us," said Jimmy.

"When we left the archive, we decided to walk into Keswick for lunch," continued Anthony. "Margaret and Emily came with us. Then Jimmy remembered what you had said about Michael Edwards being buried at the Church of St John, so we decided to visit his grave."

"We thought that if we could find the gravestone, we would at least find out when Michael Edwards was born," explained Mark.

Emily took up the baton.

"But when we arrived at the church, we saw something really weird. One of the school porters, Mr Rimmer, was tending a grave in the churchyard. We asked him if he knew where Michael Edwards was buried, but he refused to help us even though it turned out that the grave he was tending was the one we were looking for."

"A coincidence?" suggested Robert.

"I don't think so, sir," replied Anthony. "It turned out that Mr Rimmer knew exactly who Michael Edwards was, but that comes later. According to the inscription on the gravestone, Michael Edwards was born on the 28th of May 1894."

"That's the same date of birth as Captain Cole," said Jimmy.

"I missed that," admitted Grace.

"I only noticed it because it happens to be my birthday as well, miss," explained Jimmy. "But once we knew that they shared the same date of birth, well, then we wondered whether Michael Edwards and Captain Cole might not be the same person."

"Just because they shared the same date of birth?" queried Robert.

"Not just that, sir," replied Jimmy. "We already suspected that Michael Edwards was covering his tracks and, well, we had seen Miss Connolly crying in front of the captain's photograph in Cole Hall."

"Yes, I was crying," confirmed Grace.

"That was something else that made us think they might be linked, miss," continued Jimmy. "It seemed strange that the person crying in front of the captain's photograph was the same person who had asked us to research Michael Edwards."

"So where did you go from there?" asked Robert.

"I wasn't convinced Captain Cole and Michael Edwards could have been the same person," admitted Anthony. "I remembered what you had told us about the Battle of Carnforth Hill and how Colonel Carnforth and Captain Cole had fought on to the death after allowing their men to surrender."

"Then Emily had the idea of writing to the captain's regiment to find out where he was buried," said Mark. "If it turned out that the captain was buried in France, then that would mean that he and Michael Edwards could not be the same person."

Reaching to the floor, Emily took a large envelope from her bag and pushed it across the table towards Robert.

"As you can see, sir, the letter from the regiment was very helpful. It confirmed that the captain was originally buried in a German cemetery before his body was relocated to a British cemetery at a place called Savy near St Quentin in Northern France."

"Well, there you go then," said Robert, casting his eyes over the letter. "My uncle and Michael Edwards could not have been the same person."

"That's what we thought, at least until we read what Major Hartmann had to say," replied Emily.

"Major who?" asked Grace.

"Major Albrecht Hartmann," replied Mark. "He was the German officer who offered Captain Cole the chance to surrender."

"He wrote about the battle in his memoirs," said Anthony before allowing Emily to continue.

"Major Hartmann confirmed that he had met with Captain Cole, who told him that only Colonel Carnforth could agree to a surrender. The captain went to find the colonel, and soon after, the men surrendered. But Major Hartmann is certain there was no further fighting after the surrender. He says that when he entered the British trench, he found Colonel Carnforth dead in a dugout. He then looked for the captain but never found him."

"That raised two questions," continued Jimmy. "Why wasn't the captain in the trench if he was supposed to have fought on to the death?"

Jimmy paused, uncertain as to whether he should continue.

"And the second question?" asked Robert.

"The second question is this," said Anthony. "If the Germans didn't kill Colonel Carnforth, who did?"

The inference underpinning Anthony's question hung in the air like a lingering cloud of cigar smoke. Robert Cole sat back in his chair and stared at the ceiling.

"Would it be right to say that you think my uncle killed him?" asked Robert.

Nobody replied.

"Don't worry," assured Robert looking at Anthony. "I'm not angry with you. Did you discover anything else?"

"Tell them, Emily," encouraged Jimmy.

"When I wrote to the captain's regiment, I justified my enquiry by pretending that a number of former pupils from Grey Stones might have been killed in the battle. To help me check whether or not that was the case, the regiment sent me a casualty list."

"And?" encouraged Grace.

Emily paused a moment before answering.

"The casualty list confirmed that Corporal M.J. Edwards was killed on the same day as Captain Cole."

It took Robert a few seconds to respond.

"So, you think that my uncle killed Colonel Carnforth, left the trench and adopted the identity of a dead soldier?"

"Yes, sir," replied Anthony as firmly as he could. "By working his way back through the yearbooks, Jimmy discovered that Michael Edwards first came to teach at Grey Stones in 1924."

"We then looked through the minutes of the governors' meetings for that year, hoping they might tell us where Michael Edwards had come from," said Jimmy.

"And did they?" asked Robert.

"No, sir," replied Jimmy, "but they did tell us who brought him to the school."

"Who?" asked Robert.

Jimmy paused before replying.

"Your grandfather, sir, Richard Cole."

Momentarily lost for words, Robert again turned to Aunt Ginny before responding.

"And on top of all that, we have the photograph of my uncle in the cigarette case, which was taken in 1937. It would appear that I have to accept that Michael Edwards and my uncle were the same person. But does that mean he killed Colonel Carnforth?"

It was Jimmy who responded first.

"I think he did … I'm sorry, but the evidence …" Jimmy looked to his classmates for help.

"Jimmy, there's no need to apologise," assured Robert. "What makes you think that Captain Cole killed Colonel Carnforth?"

"Well, sir," said Emily, "he must have done something wrong to make him desert the battlefield and change his name."

"Perhaps he just lost his nerve," suggested Robert. "He had been in the thick of the fighting for years."

"There's something else," said Mark. "We know that he was later blackmailed by one of the soldiers who served under him at Carnforth Hill."

"And how do you know that?" asked Robert, taken aback.

"We needed to find out more about the murder of Michael Edwards, and Margaret suggested we visit her uncle, Harry Morgan," said Anthony.

"As you know, miss, Harry Morgan owns *The Keswickian*," said Mark.

Grace allowed herself a smile before responding.

"I used to do a paper round for him."

"Harry Morgan?" queried Robert. "Would this, by any chance, be the same Harry Morgan who contacted Mr Snyder this afternoon?"

"It could have been, sir," said Margaret before moving quickly on. "Uncle Harry let us chat to his top reporter, Scoop Hardy, who covered the murder for the paper in 1941."

"That's how we learned about the blackmail," continued Anthony. "The body of Michael Edwards was found burnt beyond recognition in the school boathouse."

Shocked by this revelation, Grace raised both hands to her mouth.

"Sorry, miss," said Anthony, regretting his insensitivity.

"How was he identified?" asked Robert.

"His wife identified him by his wedding ring," replied Emily.

Aunt Ginny stared into the fire as if in a trance.

"The police then found a blackmail note signed by a man called

John Rimmer," said Anthony. "John Rimmer came to work at the school in 1941 with his son, Stanley Rimmer."

"The same Stanley Rimmer who is a porter here today?" asked Robert.

"Yes, sir," replied Mark. "After the murder, John Rimmer disappeared and was never heard of again."

"Did you find out what he was blackmailing my uncle about?" asked Robert.

"No, sir," replied Anthony.

"But how is any of this connected to Captain Cole's time in the trenches?" asked Grace.

Jimmy turned to Robert Cole.

"Do you remember Captain Cole's last letter home, the one displayed under his photograph in Cole Hall?"

"I remember it," replied Robert, "but I haven't read it for years."

"In the letter, the captain talks about a new recruit to the regiment, Private John Rimmer," explained Jimmy. "He also writes about Sergeant Bernard Holmes, who was a policeman before the war."

"And you think he is the John Rimmer who was blackmailing him over twenty years later?" asked Robert.

"We think it has to be," said Anthony.

"What about Sergeant Holmes? Where does he come in?" asked Grace.

"The inspector in charge of the murder investigation was called Bernard Holmes," replied Jimmy. "We think he was the same Bernard Holmes who was in the trenches with the captain."

"You told me that Captain Cole was not my father. Do you have any evidence for that?" asked Grace.

"After our meeting with Scoop Hardy, we returned to Cole Hall because Jimmy wanted to read the captain's letter," explained Anthony.

"As I was reading the letter out loud, I read out the name of

Colonel Carnforth," said Jimmy.

"Then Margaret noticed the name of Tristan Herbert Carnforth on the board commemorating those who died in the Second World War," said Mark.

Anthony again referred to his notebook before addressing Miss Connolly.

"The inscription on the board read: *Pilot Officer Tristan Herbert Carnforth, Royal Air Force, 3rd June 1940, aged 21.*"

Grace Connolly closed her eyes as the significance of what she had been told sank in.

"Tristan Herbert Carnforth," she whispered. "T.H.C."

"We remembered what you had told us in Cole Hall about your father being a fighter pilot and how he was shot down in June 1940," said Mark.

"We needed to know whether Tristan Carnforth was related to the colonel, so we went back to the archives," said Emily.

"We eventually found an obituary in *The Scholar*," continued Anthony. "It confirmed that Tristan Carnforth was the colonel's son. It also confirmed that Tristan visited the school with his girlfriend during his last home leave in April 1940."

Anthony paused for a moment before continuing.

"You tell her, Margaret. It was thanks to you that we found out."

"Tristan's girlfriend, miss," said Margaret. "Well, her name was Jane Connolly. We think that Tristan Carnforth was your father."

Speechless, Grace sat back in her chair and looked around the table. When her eyes settled on Aunt Ginny, she saw a solitary tear rolling down the older woman's cheek.

"You knew?" asked Grace, her tone almost accusatory. "You knew?"

Aunt Ginny took a few seconds to compose herself.

"Yes, my dear, I knew."

"But the cigarette case, the initials, the photograph," protested Grace. "I don't understand."

"Then perhaps I should explain."

The voice came from the other end of the room. Next to the Christmas tree, a slim man in his seventies had appeared as if from nowhere. Robert recognised him immediately.

"Compton! Where did you spring from?" he asked.

"Oh, I hope you don't mind. I let myself in through the bay window, and I've been sitting behind the curtains listening with great interest to your young friends here."

"Well, do come and join us," encouraged Robert.

The man approached the table in silence. Silver-haired with pale blue eyes, his presence filled the room. When greeted by Aunt Ginny, he reacted to her warm embrace with an enigmatic smile. It was then that Jimmy knew. He knew even before he saw the fading scar that traversed the right side of the man's face.

"Hello everybody, my name is …"

"Captain Thomas Cole," interrupted Margaret. "Your name is Captain Thomas Cole."

CHAPTER THIRTY-NINE

Recollections

Tom stared at Margaret for a few moments.

"Forgive me," he said, "it has been many years since I have been called by my real name. You must be Miss Arbuckle."

"How did you know that?" asked Margaret.

"Oh, I have my sources," replied Tom.

Robert looked on, slightly aggrieved by what he had just heard.

"Compton, I have to say that's not very funny."

Tom looked Robert squarely in the eye. When he spoke, his tone was sincere and deliberate.

"Robert, please listen to what I have to say. My name is Thomas Howard Cole, formerly of the King's Own Border Regiment, eldest son of Richard and Brigit Cole and elder brother of Edward Cole, your father."

Robert stood up from his chair.

"No, you are not," he insisted with a laugh. "Your name is Compton Hobbs, writer, local historian and school benefactor. Aunt Ginny, please put a stop to this nonsense."

Aunt Ginny's reply left Robert reeling.

"It isn't nonsense, Robert. This is my husband, Thomas Howard Cole. My name is Evelyn Virginia Cole. I am his wife. He is your uncle. He is telling you the truth."

"His name is Compton Hobbs," persisted Robert. "I've known

him since I was a boy."

"Do you think I would lie to you, Robert?" asked Evelyn quietly.

Robert knew she would not. Bewildered and unsure of himself, he sat down.

"All will become clear, Robert, I promise you," said Tom. "As for you, Grace, please believe me when I tell you that Tristan Carnforth was your father."

"But I have your medal and your cigarette case," said Grace, who harboured no doubt as to Tom's identity.

Tom delved into his pocket and produced a medal which he placed next to the one on the table.

"That's not possible," said Tom. "You see, *this* is my Victoria Cross."

"Where did you get that?" asked Grace.

"It was returned to me many years ago after a very dear friend passed away. The medal in your possession belonged to your grandfather, Colonel Herbert Carnforth. It was awarded to him posthumously and presented to his wife, your grandmother, Catherine Carnforth. When she died, the medal was left to your father, Tristan, who left it to your mother Jane. That is how it came into your possession."

"And the cigarette case?" asked Grace quietly.

"That was mine," conceded Tom. "It was given to me by my father during the Great War. My father had the case inscribed and sent out to me in 1917. It was very dear to me."

"THC: Thomas Howard Cole," said Robert to nobody in particular.

"Then you must have it back," insisted Grace.

"No," said Tom, "the case is yours. I gave it to your father when he went to war. I believed the case had brought me luck, and I hoped it would do the same for Tristan. Well, obviously, it didn't. Before he died, he left everything to your mother, including his personal belongings. So, you see, the case is rightfully yours."

"I'll treasure it," said Grace fighting back the tears.

"But tell me," asked Robert, "how did your photograph come to be inside the cigarette case?"

"Tristan must have taken that photograph on one of our walks. I had no idea it existed. We were very close. As for Jane's photograph, the explanation is obvious."

"But why the secrecy? Why has it taken you so long to tell me who my father was?"

"Necessity?" suggested Tom, as though trying to convince himself. "There is so much to tell you, though I have to say, your young friends here have made an excellent job of their investigation."

"Are they right?" asked Robert. "Were you being blackmailed for killing Colonel Carnforth?"

Before answering, Tom sat at the table and looked at the youngsters for a few seconds.

"Yes, they are right about that."

"Tell them, Tom," encouraged Evelyn gently, "tell them everything."

"Yes, please tell us," urged Grace.

"Very well," said Tom, "but most of it you already know."

Reaching across the table, he retrieved the cigarette case, caressed it gently with his fingers and listened to the noise of the battlefield grow steadily louder.

"I take it you know all about the Battle of Carnforth Hill," said Tom, concentrating his mind and silencing the guns.

"We thought we did," said Anthony.

"Well, yes, I see what you mean," said Tom. "My presence here today rather contradicts the official version of events, doesn't it?"

"What version was that?" asked Grace.

"The version that tells how Captain Cole and Colonel Carnforth fought on to the death after ordering their men to surrender," explained Robert.

"Please, won't you tell us what happened?" asked Grace.

Tom placed the cigarette case back on the table and paused briefly to gather his thoughts.

"It was March 1918, and my company was defending a hill outside St Quentin in Northern France. Although greatly outnumbered, our orders were to fight to the death. After we had repelled two heavy attacks, a German officer stepped forward and offered us the chance to surrender."

"Major Albrecht Hartmann," declared Emily. "He wrote about the battle in his memoirs."

"Yes, I know," smiled Tom. "I've read them. Including the wounded, about fifty of us were left when the major invited our surrender. I told him I would take his offer to the colonel, and we parted. The colonel, of course, would have nothing to do with the idea. He insisted that we join the surviving men and fight on to the end. We argued. I couldn't see the point of sacrificing further lives when the battle had already been lost. As we argued, a young private in his first action, John Rimmer, made himself known. He was hiding under the colonel's cot, trying to escape the fighting. The colonel lost all self-control when he saw Rimmer and shot him in the thigh. Before he could finish the boy off, I intervened, we struggled, and the colonel turned his revolver on me. Moments later, there was a second shot, and the colonel slumped to the floor, dead. Rimmer witnessed everything … or so I thought. When Sergeant Holmes entered the dugout, I told him to organise the surrender quickly, as a further German assault was imminent. After the men had surrendered, I left the trench, swapped identities with a dead corporal, Michael Edwards, and allowed myself to be captured."

"Were we right about Sergeant Holmes?" asked Mark. "Was he the person who investigated the 'murder' of Michael Edwards?"

"Yes, you were right about that," confirmed Tom.

Leaving the table, Evelyn placed another log on the fire. When she returned, she stood behind her husband and placed her hands gently on his shoulders. Before continuing, Tom looked up at her and smiled.

"I was repatriated from Germany in January 1919. I knew I had to act quickly if my true identity was not to be discovered. I eventually found myself in Calais, awaiting a medical and a boat home. It was only a matter of time before I was exposed as an imposter."

"What did you do?" asked Emily.

"I literally cycled out of Calais and made for Boulogne. From there, I paid local fishermen to take me across the channel."

"Then what did you do?" asked Anthony. "According to our research, you didn't come to Grey Stones until 1924, more than five years after your return from France."

"After months of roaming the countryside looking for work and sleeping rough, I got lucky," replied Tom, reaching for Evelyn's hand. "I was just about spent when I wandered into a village in Hampshire. A very kind man took me in and offered me work. Not long after that, I contacted my parents and swore them to secrecy."

"What happened to the man who helped you?" asked Margaret.

"The Reverend Vincent Worrall? He died several years ago," replied Tom. "I'm afraid I've reached an age when losing friends happens all too frequently. Still, I have his sister here to remind me of him."

Tom squeezed Evelyn's hand lightly.

"By the time Evelyn and I married, my father had arranged for me to take up a teaching position at Grey Stones under the name of Michael Edwards. We moved into Derwent Cottage in the summer of 1924."

"Derwent Cottage? The Derwent Cottage where *I* live?" asked Grace.

"Yes," confirmed Evelyn.

"But how …? I don't understand. How did my mother come to live there?"

"After returning to Keswick," explained Tom, "I needed to see how the colonel's family was coping. I made some enquiries and discovered that his widow, Catherine Carnforth, was bringing up their only child in Carlisle. The child's name was Tristan. It became apparent that Catherine was struggling to get by. Her husband had been promoted from the ranks; he was never a wealthy man. I decided that I wanted to help Catherine and her son. Whatever my feelings towards her husband, he was a former comrade and a very brave man. I had played a part in his death: I needed to help them. In 1929, when Tristan was eleven, I visited Catherine and told her there was a place for her son at Grey Stones. As far as Catherine knew, the offer had come from the school in recognition of the role played by her husband at the Battle of Carnforth Hill and his connection with the late Captain Cole. Catherine accepted my offer, and Tristan was enrolled."

"What was he like, my father? What was he like as a boy? Describe him for me," implored Grace.

"He was a fine-looking boy," replied Evelyn. "Dark wavy hair, blue eyes, tall for his age with a wicked sense of humour and bright, very bright."

"And game, game for anything," added Tom. "He got into a few scrapes when he first arrived at the school, but nothing seemed to get him down. Tristan soon made friends, especially among those who lacked confidence or were unsure of themselves. He attracted underdogs; only once he befriended them they stopped being underdogs and flourished. It was impossible not to like Tristan, and I did my best to take him under my wing, not just because of his father's death but because he brought the best out of those he met, including me."

"Suffice to say that by the time he went up to Cambridge, we felt we were losing a son," said Evelyn, "though, of course, he remained fiercely loyal to Catherine, whom he adored."

"When Catherine died in 1938, he was devastated," continued Tom. "He asked us to attend the funeral with him, but we had to say no. The chances of my being recognised by mourners who had served with the colonel were too great. After Catherine's death, he struggled with his loss."

"But that all changed when he met your mother," said Evelyn.

"So, you did know my mother?" said Grace.

"Know her? We were there when she first met your father," replied Evelyn.

"It was during the late summer of 1939," recalled Tom. "Tristan had joined the RAF and was home on leave."

"Since Catherine's death, 'home' had pretty much become Derwent Cottage," explained Evelyn. "We had moved into the headmaster's accommodation at the Old Mill, so Tristan had the run of the place."

"The school was holding a garden party in aid of some fundraiser or another, and having Tristan there in his RAF uniform lent real dash to the proceedings," recalled Tom. "Everybody was there, including the girls of the W.L.A."

"The W.L.A?" queried Emily.

"The Woman's Land Army, dear," replied Evelyn. "The girls who worked on the farms and in the forests while the men were away at war."

"Jane and your father hit it off immediately," said Tom.

"From the moment they met," agreed Evelyn. "They simply could not take their eyes off each other. Romance blossomed, and within days, they became inseparable."

Grace looked at Robert, held his stare and smiled.

"Of course, the war got in the way," continued Tom. "Tristan would return to Keswick whenever he could to be with your mother, but such opportunities were few and far between. After six months or so, there was talk of marriage, but the war was warming up; Britain was virtually isolated, and Tristan knew that if he married your mother, there was every chance he would soon make her a widow. He was right."

"But when your mother wrote to Tristan telling him she was with child, of course, he wanted to marry her straight away," said Evelyn. "The marriage was to take place on his next home leave."

"But, by this time, Tristan's squadron was busy providing air cover for the troops stranded at Dunkirk," continued Tom. "Leave was out of the question. He had, however, made a will leaving everything he owned to your mother. That shows you how committed he was to you both. Within days of being told by Jane that he was going to be a father, he was shot down over the channel."

"But none of this explains how my mother came to live in Derwent Cottage," said Grace.

"Following Tristan's death, Jane went to pieces," explained Evelyn.

"So, we moved her into the cottage and did our best to look after her," said Tom. "As you know, shortly before you were born, she returned home to her family only to find they had been killed during a bombing raid. Thankfully, she returned to us and went back to the cottage where she gave birth to you on Christmas Day, 1940."

"So, the cottage is really yours?" asked Grace.

"No, my dear," replied Evelyn. "Given the circumstances, we signed the cottage over to your mother as a gift. The property is legally yours."

"And my mother's income? Was that also provided by you?"

"With Tristan gone, we took it upon ourselves to help in any way we could," explained Tom.

"And believe me, Grace," said Evelyn, "if fate had not intervened, we would not have become the strangers we are."

"Are you talking about the blackmail?" asked Jimmy.

"Yes," replied Tom candidly. "As the years passed, I was not looking over my shoulder as much as I used to. I had a new identity, a loving wife, a job I loved and access to great wealth. But a year or so after Tristan's death, the past came back to haunt me with a vengeance."

"What can you tell us about the blackmail?" asked Robert.

Tom settled back in his chair before responding.

"Shortly before the start of the autumn term in 1941, the school took on several new porters as replacements for those who had been conscripted. One of the recruits had a limp, and I recognised him immediately. It was John Rimmer. His son, Stanley, who was only fifteen, had also been taken on. I knew that John Rimmer had recognised me, and I waited to see what he would do. The next day, I found a note pushed under my office door asking me to meet him in the boathouse. When we met, he told me that he remembered everything that had occurred in the dugout. As far as he was concerned, I had fought with the colonel because I didn't want to fight, and had shot him to save myself. He told me he would forget what he had seen if I paid him £2,000. We agreed to meet again at the boathouse the following Saturday. There was never the remotest possibility that I would pay him; I simply needed time to think."

"Did you meet with him as arranged?" asked Robert.

"Oh yes," replied Tom. "But the meeting went extremely badly. When I returned to the boathouse on the Saturday, Rimmer and his son were waiting for me, and both were armed."

"Armed?" repeated Anthony.

"Yes, armed," confirmed Tom. "But, luckily for me, I was not alone …"

CHAPTER FORTY

A Logical Deduction

It was twenty to eight in the evening. Shunning the path from the school, John and Stanley Rimmer skirted the playing fields and approached the boathouse through thick woodland. Shortly before reaching the lake, John Rimmer stopped in front of an ageing tree, the base of which was hollow. Leaning inside the cavity, he retrieved an object wrapped in newspaper.

"You can use this to cover me," said Rimmer tearing away the wrapping.

"Cover you? What do you mean?" asked Stanley.

"Well, you don't think I trust this fella, do you?" replied Rimmer as he thrust an ancient looking twelve-bore double-barrelled shotgun into his son's hands.

"You never said nothin' about guns," complained Stanley.

"Look, all I want you to do is hide in the boathouse. He won't even know you're there. But if he starts any trouble, you step out and point the shotgun at him. That ought to make him think twice about tryin' anythin' clever."

"Where did you get it from, anyway?" asked Stanley, eyeing the relic with suspicion.

"Bought it in Keswick. Be careful, it's loaded."

As Stanley examined the shotgun, Rimmer placed his right hand into the pocket of his work coat. Reassured by the feel of his Webley Mk VI revolver, he ordered Stanley to follow him.

Emerging from the woodland, the pair crossed the Borrowdale Road, descended a gentle rise and approached the boathouse.

"Right," said Rimmer, "I reckon we've got another fifteen minutes before he gets here. Let's go in the back way and find you a place to hide."

Stanley said nothing. He was beginning to wish he had never left Carlisle. Once inside the boathouse, he ascended the wooden steps into the unlit office on the landing, positioned himself at the open hatch and waited.

It was shortly before eight o'clock when Bernard Holmes reached the lake. Giving the boathouse a wide berth, he made his way to the water's edge, concealed himself in an accommodating hollow and waited. Unsure as to whether or not Rimmer had arrived, he berated himself for not having left The Pheasant earlier. Aware that he was reacting to events, Holmes felt vulnerable. A few minutes later, he caught sight of Tom Cole striding along the path from the school. As far as Holmes could tell, there seemed nothing hesitant in the manner of his approach; quite the opposite. If his body language conveyed any message at all, it was one of composed determination.

Having reached the front of the boathouse, Tom hesitated before slipping through the door.

"Hello," he called.

Almost immediately, Rimmer stepped into view.

"I'm here; I made sure I got here early."

"Then I'll try not to detain you any longer than is necessary," replied Tom politely.

"You've got the money then?" asked Rimmer eagerly.

"I'm afraid not."

"What do you mean *I'm afraid not*?' Do you need more time? Is that it?"

"No, I do not need more time."

"What is this? What are you playin' at?"

"That's just it, Rimmer, I'm not playing, and I'm not paying."

From his vantage point in the office, Stanley Rimmer looked down on the two men and wished he was somewhere else.

"Am I hearin' you right?" sneered Rimmer. "Are you tellin' me that you're goin' to let me go to the police? You'll be hung for murder. And what about your wife? She must know what you did. What do you think will happen to her?"

"Leave my wife out of this," commanded Tom.

"I can't believe my ears. I've got you over a barrel, and you don't seem to realise it."

"Do you not think you owe me something, Rimmer?"

"What do you mean *owe you?*" retorted Rimmer, all too aware that his son could hear every word of the exchange.

"Do I really have to explain?" asked Tom.

"You officers are all the same, always makin' out that you were lookin' after your men. You only ever looked after yourselves. I don't owe you anythin'. I'd bet you would never even have remembered me if I hadn't sent you my note."

"There's nothing wrong with my memory, Rimmer," countered Tom. "I remember the young soldier who fell asleep on duty the night before the German offensive. Do you?"

"No, I don't," snapped Rimmer.

"The same young soldier who hid in the colonel's dugout to escape the fighting? Surely you remember him?" challenged Tom.

"No," replied Rimmer firmly.

"The same young soldier who the colonel shot in the leg."

"What are you talkin' about?" challenged Rimmer. "It never happened like that."

"And what about the captain who intervened just as the colonel was going to finish the young soldier off? The captain who fought with the colonel and saved the soldier's life? Don't you remember him?"

"I never asked you to help me. I never asked you to..." Rimmer stopped mid-sentence.

"No, you didn't, you didn't have to," replied Tom.

His forefinger hovering over the trigger of the shotgun, his eyes fixed on his father, Stanley was confused. Why wasn't his father telling the captain about the Germans he had killed and how he had fought on after he was wounded? Why hadn't he told the captain that it was him who was the coward, that it was him who had refused to fight?

"Alright," conceded Rimmer, "what if you did save me from Carnforth? What if you saved the others as well? So what? The fact is, you deserted and changed your name. It doesn't matter what you say. Even if everybody knew the truth, you'd still be hung as a traitor."

"Then go to the police," replied Tom. "I can't stop you. Go to the police and claim any reward they might think I'm worth. But be sure of this: whatever happens to me, I will expose you for the blackmailing coward you are."

"I don't think so," snarled Rimmer, pulling the revolver from his pocket.

Watching from the shadows at the rear of the boathouse, Bernard Holmes grimaced at the sight of the gun. Slowly, silently, he edged towards Rimmer.

"A souvenir from the war," explained Rimmer. "Always knew it would come in handy one day."

"Listen to me. Stop this lunacy before it's too late," ordered Tom. "Go back to the school, go back to your son and carry on as if you had never recognised me. Forget about the past. Give me the gun."

Tom moved towards Rimmer.

"Give me the gun," he repeated quietly.

Rimmer was close to panic.

"Stay back. Don't come any closer," he snarled. "You don't know it, but there's a shotgun pointin' at you as we speak. If I don't get you, my son Stanley will."

Upon hearing the word 'shotgun', Holmes froze.

"One word from me, and you're gone, and then it will be easy," explained Rimmer. "I'll tell the police that after I started working here, you recognised me and arranged this meetin'. You were afraid I might give you away, and you threatened me with a shotgun."

On the move again, Holmes hugged the rear of the boathouse, peering intently down every darkened aisle in search of Rimmer's accomplice.

"We struggled, and the gun went off. History repeatin' itself, you could say," continued Rimmer. "And when they check up and find out you are the famous Captain Cole and that you deserted the army and changed your name, I'll be in the clear. Alright, any reward I get will be less than I wanted from you, but it will be better than nothin'."

"Shoot me? You haven't got the guts!" said Tom with loathing.

The taunt made Holmes wince. The ensuing silence convinced him that the dialogue was nearing its end: he was running out of time.

"Stanley! Shoot him!" yelled Rimmer. "Shoot him, Stanley, do it now!"

Stunned by his father's command, his vision compromised by the sweat trickling down his forehead, Stanley caressed the trigger of the shotgun with his forefinger.

"Stanley!" yelled Rimmer. "Do it! Shoot him now!"

Holding his breath, Stanley focused on his target.

"Well, if he won't, I will," said Rimmer, his voice suddenly calm and his finger tightening around the trigger of the Webley.

As the discharge of the shotgun reverberated across the lake, Stanley Rimmer dropped his weapon to the office floor. Almost immediately, Holmes appeared in the office doorway. Rushing forward, he pinned the boy against the wall with his right hand. Turning his head to peer through the hatch, the inspector could see Tom Cole kneeling beside the body of John Rimmer. It was a totally bemused Holmes who gradually released his grip on the boy.

"Stanley?" he asked, looking intently into his eyes.

"I'm sorry, really sorry," said the boy before rushing past Holmes and out of the building. Holmes did not attempt to follow him. Retrieving the shotgun, he removed the remaining cartridge before descending the wooden steps. Still kneeling beside the motionless body, Tom searched in vain for a pulse. When Holmes emerged from the shadows, Tom looked up. Neither man spoke. Leaving the boathouse through the sliding doors, Tom sat on a bench and looked across the lake. After checking the body for himself, Holmes followed him.

"Hello, Inspector," said Tom.

His voice devoid of emotion, he continued to look across the lake.

"Have you just saved my life again?"

"No, not this time," replied Holmes.

Tom spun around.

"Then who …?"

"Young Stanley," interjected Holmes. "He shot his father."

Tom leant forward, his face in his hands.

"Where is he?" he asked.

"He's run off, probably back to the school. I don't think he'll be going anywhere."

Holmes joined Tom on the bench.

"How did you know I was still in the force?"

"I keep myself informed," replied Tom, "especially when it comes to my former sergeants."

Holmes allowed himself a brief smile.

"How long have you known?" asked Tom.

"Ever since your visit to Catherine Carnforth in 1929. I saw you leave her house the day you offered Tristan a place at Grey Stones."

"I suppose I should thank you for not exposing me," said Tom.

"There was never any danger of that," replied Holmes.

"And today, Bernard? How on earth could you have known that I was meeting Rimmer today?"

"Do you believe in divine intervention?" asked Holmes.

"More than you might think," replied Tom.

"Well, *I'm* certainly beginning to. I was sitting in a pub after a day spent fishing on the lake when I overheard Rimmer talking to Stanley. After all these years … incredible, isn't it?"

Holmes leant back into the bench, tilted his head towards the sky, and laughed half-heartedly.

"I actually went to visit your grave in France. Obviously, I knew you hadn't died during the fighting and could only assume that you had wandered out of the trench and got yourself killed in the aftermath."

"Joining the surrender was out of the question," explained Tom. "The story that Carnforth wanted to carry on the fight alone was never going to stand up. The men knew he was still alive after the ceasefire and had heard the shots fired in the dugout. Given that the Germans knew that no fighting had taken place following the surrender, it was inevitable that the colonel's death would arouse suspicion. It was equally inevitable that, sooner or later, Rimmer's assertion that I had shot my commanding officer would find its way onto the record. The thought of being court-martialled, the prospect of the hangman's rope, and the shame to be endured by my family … it was all too much. Better, I thought, to take matters into my own hands, to finish things there and then, to take the easy way out."

"What stopped you?" asked Holmes.

"You did," replied Tom.

Holmes looked bewildered. "*I* did? How did I do that?"

Tom paused briefly before responding.

"Once the last man had left the trench, I drew my revolver, held it to my head and pulled the trigger. The chamber was empty.

Confronted by my unexpected survival, I immediately threw up. Realising that I didn't have the stomach to repeat the attempt, I sat on the ground and tried to think things through. I remembered that before meeting with the German officer in 'no man's land', I had checked my revolver and found one bullet in the chamber. At that moment, the German officer called out that he was unarmed. I then passed my revolver to you and left the trench. Later, you returned the gun to me as you were leaving the dugout. Only two shots had been fired between the ceasefire and the surrender. The first was at Private Rimmer, hitting him in the leg, and the second was the shot that killed Colonel Carnforth. If that second shot had been fired from Carnforth's revolver, my revolver would still have had one bullet in its chamber. It was you who emptied my revolver … you did so when you shot Colonel Carnforth. That's what happened, isn't it?"

Holmes did not hesitate.

"That's exactly what happened …"

CHAPTER FORTY-ONE

Re-wind

"What's going on, Sergeant?" asked a wounded soldier from the floor of the trench. "Are we surrendering? Are we going to get out of here or what?"

"Don't you be getting your hopes up, Barnes," cautioned Holmes as he stared into 'no man's land' from the fire step. "And that goes for the rest of you. We'll know soon enough what's going on."

"For God's sake," pleaded another voice. "They can't possibly expect us to carry on, can they? We've done our bit, haven't we?"

The chorus of agreement that followed could not be left unchallenged.

"That's enough of that," rebuked the sergeant firmly. "Until I tell you otherwise, we remain on readiness to defend this hill. Is that clear?"

"Sergeant," warned another voice, "the captain … he's on his way back."

Turning away from the men, Holmes watched Tom pick his way through the dead and wounded and re-enter the trench.

"Well, sir?" asked Holmes.

Distracted by the piercing stares of the men, Tom hesitated before responding.

"Keep the men at the ready, I have to see the colonel."

"You heard the officer," barked Holmes. "Keep your eyes peeled."

Those that were able manned the fire step and peered into the mist. The tension generated by the hope of deliverance far exceeded that generated by the fear of death, and when raised voices were heard coming from the dugout, the men became restless.

"What's happening, Sergeant?" asked a soldier from the fire-step. "I mean, what is there to argue about? We either surrender, or we're dead."

"Let's try and stay calm, shall we?" replied Holmes.

A shot rang out from the dugout.

"I don't believe this," exclaimed the exasperated soldier. "What's going on?"

"Stay here," ordered Holmes. "All of you, stay here and shoot anything that comes out of the fog."

Hurrying through the communication trench, Holmes descended into the dugout but stopped a few yards from the entrance. Ahead of him, pinned to the floor, he saw the captain struggling to keep the colonel's revolver at bay. With his left hand clasped tightly around the captain's neck, the colonel slowly brought the revolver to bear. Before the struggle could reach its inevitable conclusion, Holmes drew the captain's revolver from his belt, took careful aim and shot the colonel dead …

*

Holmes stood up from the bench.

"Yes, I shot the colonel, and I'd do it again," he said. "My conscience is clear, at least it was until I discovered that you were alive. After that, I assumed you had changed your identity because you thought you had killed the colonel. As much as I wanted to put the record straight, pragmatism and, yes, self-interest dictated otherwise. I desperately wanted to believe that my silence could be vindicated. You had a wife, a career and a future, and I knew you were looking after Tristan. I had my own family to think about. In the end, I believed it best just to leave things alone, even if that meant you living with a guilt that was not your own."

Tom got up from the bench and took a few steps towards the lake.

"How strange that after all these years, the colonel's death should lead to another," he said.

Holmes moved towards Tom before responding.

"Tell me, if you knew before leaving the trench that it was me who shot the colonel, why the deception? Why change your identity?"

"Because I couldn't trust you," replied Tom.

"What do you mean?"

"If the matter had been investigated and Rimmer's evidence believed, I couldn't trust you not to come forward and confess everything to get me off the hook. With me out of the picture, that possibility vanished. My debt to you, Bernard, can never be repaid. God knows how many times you came to my rescue, not only in the field but when I thought I was losing my mind. You shot the colonel to save me. I was not going to put you at risk by hanging around."

Holmes looked stunned.

"You changed your identity for my sake? I'm so sorry."

"No need to apologise," assured Tom, mustering a smile.

"You may have fired the shot, but I aimed the gun. If I had not disobeyed the colonel's orders, then …"

"We wouldn't be standing here having this conversation," interrupted Holmes.

Holmes reached into his jacket pocket for his wallet.

"Can I show you something?"

Tom nodded.

"Take a look at this," said Holmes handing over a photograph. "That's Jenny, my wife, with our four children. That's Tom, our eldest, aged twenty-one: he's named after a bloke I used to serve with in the army. That's his brother Oscar, aged nineteen, and these are my two daughters, Rachael, seventeen, and Bryony, fifteen."

Tom studied the photograph politely.

"You have a beautiful family," he said without looking up.

"I have," replied Holmes with conviction. "I am so proud of them and love them all dearly. But for you, my children would never have been born. And what about the other lads who got out of that trench? Some of them are still about; we all meet up once a year. You should see the photographs they carry about with them. How do you think they remember their captain? As the finest officer they ever served under, that's how. I know, and they know, who got us out of that trench. There was no honour in fighting to the death, not when all was lost on a foreign battlefield hundreds of miles from home. You didn't just save the lives of fifty-four men that day, you saved the lives of hundreds."

"I'm afraid history won't remember me so kindly," said Tom as he returned the photograph.

"I wouldn't be too concerned about that," said Holmes. "History isn't going to know."

CHAPTER FORTY-TWO

Grave Mistakes

It was Emily who broke the prolonged silence.

"What did he mean when he said 'history isn't going to know'?"

His gaze fixed on the fire, it took Tom a few seconds to return to the present.

"After sending me back to school to find Stanley, Inspector Holmes found some petrol, placed Rimmer in one of the rowing boats and set the place alight. He then came to my office and wrote a blackmail note which he signed in Rimmer's name. After pulling a few strings, he made sure that he would be the officer leading the investigation. Once that was confirmed, he let it be known that a ring had been recovered from the dead man's hand, which Evelyn had identified as mine. From that moment on, Michael Edwards ceased to exist."

"What happened to John Rimmer?" asked Anthony.

"Can't you guess?" replied Tom.

Jimmy was the first to respond.

"So that's why Mr Rimmer was tending the grave of Michael Edwards: he was tending the grave of his father."

"But how did he cope?" asked Mark. "With killing his father, I mean?"

"He was haunted by what he had done and probably still is," replied Tom. "To this day, I don't know whether he was aiming the shotgun at me or his father, and I will never ask him. Of course, I told him everything. I told him why I had changed my name and how I had come to teach at the school. I told him about Jane and Grace and explained why Evelyn and I had to look after them. Whatever his intentions were that day, the truth is that Stanley was very much a victim in all of this, a boy ambushed by circumstance. I have tried to do right by him, and he has rewarded me with his loyalty."

"Did he have anything to do with the 'Michael Edwards' portrait disappearing from the Great Hall a couple of years ago?" asked Robert.

"He did," confirmed Tom with a wry smile. "Your gift to the school of my photograph created something of a problem. The possibility that someone might notice the resemblance between my portrait and the photograph in Cole Hall was too great to ignore. In fact, not only did Stanley remove my portrait from the Great Hall, he removed every photograph of me he could find."

"What about the yearbooks? How did you keep your photograph out of them?" asked Emily.

"Oh, that wasn't difficult," replied Tom. "I simply made out that I was terribly self-conscious about the scar on my face."

"What did you do after John Rimmer was buried?" asked Mark.

"Staying in Keswick was out of the question," replied Tom. "Evelyn and I returned to Woolton Hill and stayed with Vincent Worral. Stanley stayed on at the school, and Bernard Holmes did his best to keep a friendly eye on him."

Tom paused for a moment before looking at Robert.

"But with the death of your father in 1945, everything changed. Your mother was distraught, and in the years that followed, it became increasingly obvious that she was struggling to cope. The loss of Edward touched everyone who knew him. It was agreed that Evelyn should move back ahead of me and stay with your mother at Blackberry Hill. I followed later, once the house on Lord's Island had been bought."

"Compton Hobbs of Lord's Island? That was overplaying the

cricketing theme a touch, wasn't it?" remarked Robert.

"Perhaps," replied Tom, "but the name did lend itself to the idea of an ageing recluse keeping himself to himself on his island."

"Of course, the one person we could not re-acquaint ourselves with was your mother, Jane," said Evelyn to Grace. "If Tom was not to be exposed, she had to continue to believe that Michael Edwards had perished in 1941."

"But why now?" asked Robert, who was still struggling to come to terms with everything he had been told. "Why choose this particular moment to admit your deception?"

"Various reasons," replied Tom with a wearied sigh. "I was always going to tell you at some point. When I found out that Grace was coming to Grey Stones, I asked Stanley Rimmer to keep an eye on her. He was in Cole Hall when she started crying in front of my photograph, and, thanks to his meeting with our young friends at the graveyard, he knew that she was looking into the history of Michael Edwards. When he told me about the card left at the graveside, it became obvious that Grace had jumped to the wrong conclusion."

"And when we learned that Grace was planning to resign her post at the school," added Evelyn, "we knew that time had come to put the record straight."

"How did you know I was planning to resign?" asked Grace.

"Stanley Rimmer," replied Tom. "He was present on the stage this afternoon when you announced the fact."

"Well, you can trust us to keep our mouths shut, honest; we won't tell anybody who you really are," promised Margaret.

Tom looked across the table at Margaret and held her stare for a moment before replying.

"Thank you, Margaret. I have no doubt whatsoever that Evelyn and I could rely on the silence of every person sitting around this table. But the need for secrecy has passed."

"What do you mean?" asked Robert.

"A letter telling everything was posted to the Ministry of Defence this afternoon," replied Evelyn.

"Well, not entirely everything," corrected Tom. "I wrote the letter last year. It does not refer to the presence of Sergeant Holmes in the dugout. But by 'confessing' to having shot the colonel in self-defence, I have at least ensured that Bernard's reputation, and that of his family, will remain intact."

"Why did you write it last year?" asked Anthony.

"Because last year, Bernard Holmes, my guardian angel, passed away. From that moment on, I was free to tell my story, knowing that no harm could befall my friend."

Sadness infiltrated the room.

"Of course," continued Tom, "my letter to the authorities serves another very important purpose: it has enabled me, in part at least, to repay the huge debt I owe to the person whose identity I stole, Michael Edwards. His family have been deceived long enough. They deserve to know where he rests, and he deserves to lie in a grave which at least bears his name."

"What will you do now?" asked Robert.

"Wait for the authorities to turn up at Lord's Island, I suppose," replied Tom. "But, before that happens, Evelyn and I would like to spend the time we have left with you and Grace."

"There is so much we want to tell you," said Evelyn.

"Not just about Tristan, but about your father too," said Tom to Robert. "But for now, I think you should congratulate these youngsters on the thoroughness of their investigation. Bernard Holmes would have been proud."

CHAPTER FORTY-THREE

Farewells

Mr Snyder stood at the window of his study and watched the steady procession of motor vehicles navigate the snow-covered drive. It was Friday, the last day of term, and the pupils of Grey Stones were heading home for Christmas. Spotting George and Elizabeth Peck getting out of their car, Mr Snyder immediately stepped back from the window for fear of being seen. The risk of another confrontation with the redoubtable Mrs Peck was just too much to contemplate.

"Are we ready then?" bellowed George Peck from a distance.

"I'm coming," shouted Mark before turning to his friends.

"Right, I'm off. See you all next term."

"Have a really good Christmas, Mark," said Emily, "and try to stay out of trouble."

"I will," replied Mark.

"See you when we get back," said Jimmy.

"Here, this is for you," said Margaret, thrusting a bar of chocolate into Mark's hand.

"Thanks, Margaret," replied Mark, his expression brightening.

"Have I got one?" asked Anthony.

"No," said Margaret.

"Fair enough," said Anthony before turning to Mark. "See you after Christmas, then."

"You bet," grinned Mark as he placed the chocolate bar into the breast pocket of Anthony's blazer.

Picking up his case, Mark made his way to his parents' car and placed it in the boot.

"Hey, Mark!" shouted Dominic Price from across the drive.

Mark looked up and watched a snowball pass harmlessly over his head. With a final wave and a smile, he got into the car and headed home.

Further along the drive, Eric Lunt stood in conversation with his father, Morris, a taller version of his son. Neither was smiling. Having followed Mark's progress to his parents' car, both were now looking at Jimmy and his friends. As Lunt continued to talk, his father's head continued to nod in silent acknowledgement. Before departing in a chauffeur-driven Bentley, Lunt senior aimed a brief wave at Mr Snyder, who, his courage restored, was again standing at the window of his study.

And so the cars came and went, each departure thinning the throng.

"This is me," said Anthony as a tall, elegant lady, her teeth a luminous white, approached from the direction of Cole House.

"Anthony, there you are. We're over here, darling," advised Mrs Letts-Hyde, who stopped for a minute to make everybody's acquaintance.

With goodbyes filling the air, Anthony lifted his case and followed his glamorous mum.

"And then there were three," said Jimmy after Anthony had departed.

"Two, actually," corrected Emily upon seeing her father striding towards her.

"Daddy! Daddy!"

The glee in Emily's voice betrayed her adoration.

"*Daddy?*" queried Jimmy.

"Yes, *Daddy*," retorted Emily defiantly. "Have you got a problem with that?"

"Not at all," said Jimmy quickly.

"Good," replied Emily before turning her attention to Margaret.

"Have a great Christmas, Margaret, and remember, Kendal isn't a million miles away if you fancy a sleep-over. Just give me a ring."

"That would be great … See you when we get back," replied Margaret, ambushed by her floundering self-esteem.

Dragging her case towards her fast-approaching father, Emily suddenly stopped and turned around.

"Hey, Jimmy," she shouted, a huge grin lighting her face. "See you after Christmas."

Before Jimmy could respond, Emily threw herself into her father's arms and another world.

"Have a safe journey home, Jimmy," said Robert Cole as he walked Grace Connolly to her car.

"And have a great Christmas, the pair of you," added Grace.

Upon reaching her car, Grace quickly looked around before reaching up to Robert to steal a kiss.

"Well, you don't have to be Albert Einstein to see what's going on there," said Margaret with a sigh.

Jimmy looked at Margaret and smiled.

"Got any more chocolate?" he asked.

EPILOGUE

The fact that Tom's letter had landed on the Permanent Secretary's desk was informative in itself: the senior civil servant at the Ministry of Defence was not a man to be bothered with anything but the most important of matters. Having pored over the letter's content and after studying the file on his desk, he sat back in his chair and stared for a moment at the photograph on the mantelpiece to his right. The photograph captured the Permanent Secretary as a young officer, standing with his fellow officers shortly before the Somme Offensive of 1916. Taking off his glasses, he unconsciously polished the lenses with his handkerchief and considered his options.

"You have to admit that he did his bit," he said.

"Excuse me?" replied the young subordinate standing at his desk.

"He did his bit. I mean, look at his file, look at his record, look at the number of lives he saved during his time in the trenches. The man was a hero."

"That may well be, but he disobeyed orders, fought with his commanding officer and was responsible for his death," replied the subordinate.

"Was he? I thought he was trying to prevent the colonel from killing a young, panic-stricken soldier. And surely, if he was responsible, he was entitled to act in self-defence when the colonel turned his gun on him."

"But he was guilty of failing to carry out his orders," countered the subordinate. "You have to accept that."

"Yes," replied the older man, "but are you saying that every order must be obeyed whatever the circumstance? That way lies tyranny.

Have you ever fought in a war?"

The subordinate shifted uneasily on his feet.

"No, sir."

"Well, I have."

"I sympathise, I do," continued the subordinate, "but if you were to sit on your hands and do nothing, what sort of precedent would that set?"

"All I know is that I am not prepared to rewrite history."

"Rewrite history? What do you mean?" asked the subordinate.

"Well, if I decide to open this can of worms after all these years, what do you think that will do for the reputation of Colonel Carnforth, the man who saved the lives of his men, the man who insisted on fighting on alone, the man who was awarded a posthumous Victoria Cross? No, sometimes it's best to let sleeping dogs lie."

Sitting back in his chair, the Permanent Secretary stared at the file on his desk and made his decision. Having returned his handkerchief to his pocket, he put on his glasses, placed the letter on the file and pressed the button on his desk. Within seconds, a secretary entered the room.

"Here," said the Permanent Secretary, "put this on ice. Mark the letter 'secret to lie on the file'."

"Am I to send a reply?" asked the secretary.

"Certainly. Thank him for his correspondence. Tell him that as per his request, the headstone identifying Captain Cole at the British cemetery at Savy will be replaced by one in the name of Corporal Michael Edwards. Assure him that the corporal's family will be informed. Tell him that no further action is contemplated. Tell him that we do not consider it in the public interest to pursue the matters raised after all these years. Tell him … tell him he can have his name back."

Would you like to review this novel on Amazon?

Dear Reader

If you are reading this, it hopefully means that you stayed with the novel. If that is the case, might I ask you to leave a review on Amazon? Authors, especially new authors, depend greatly on the reviewing process to develop and maintain momentum. Honest reviews, including the negative ones, will always be welcome.

I hope you enjoyed the book.

Gideon Jones